THE WEAPON

Previous Books by David Poyer

Tales of the Modern Navy

Korea Strait
The Threat
The Command
Black Storm
China Sea
Tomahawk
The Passage
The Circle
The Gulf
The Med

Tiller Galloway

Down to a Sunless Sea
Louisiana Blue
Bahamas Blue
Hatteras Blue

The Civil War at Sea

That Anvil of Our Souls
A Country of Our Own
Fire on the Waters

Hemlock County

Thunder on the Mountain
As the Wolf Loves Winter
Winter in the Heart
The Dead of Winter

Other Novels

The Only Thing to Fear
Stepfather Bank
The Return of Philo T. McGiffin
Star Seed
The Shiloh Project
White Continent

THE WEAPON

DAVID POYER

ST. MARTIN'S PRESS
New York

This is a work of fiction. Characters, companies, and organizations in this novel are either the product of the author's imagination or, if real, are used fictitiously, without intent to describe their actual conduct.

THE WEAPON. Copyright © 2008 by David Poyer. All rights reserved. Printed in the United States of America. For information, address St. Martin's Press, 175 Fifth Avenue, New York, N.Y. 10010.

www.stmartins.com

Library of Congress Cataloging-in-Publication Data

Poyer, David.
　The weapon / David Poyer.—1st ed.
　　p.　cm.
　ISBN-13: 978-0-312-37493-8
　ISBN-10: 0-312-37493-3
　1. Lenson, Dan (Fictitious character)—Fiction. 2. United States. Navy—Officers—Fiction. 3. Terrorism—Prevention—Fiction. 4. Submarines (Ships)—Fiction. 5. Persian Gulf Region—Fiction. I. Title.
　PS3566.O978W43　2008
　813'.54—dc22

2008025779

First Edition: December 2008

10　9　8　7　6　5　4　3　2　1

Acknowledgments

*E*X *nihilo nihil fit.* For this book I owe thanks to Bob Albee, Harry Black, John Castano, Richard H. Enderly, Dave Faught, Jim Franciskovic, John T. Fusselman, Catherine "Queekie" Gladden, Carlos Godoy, Frank Green, Rick Hedman, Donna Hopkins, Bill Hunteman, Ken Johnson, David Luckett, Leslie Lykins, Warren L. Potts, David Sander, Tommy Schultz, Bill Sheridan, J. Michael Zias, and many others who preferred anonymity. Thanks also to Charle Ricci of the Eastern Shore Public Library, who was unendingly patient with my loan requests; Commander, Naval Surface Forces Atlantic; Office of the Chief of Naval Information; the USS Saratoga Museum and the staff and "crew" of Juliett 484/K-77 at the Russian Sub Museum in Providence; the Maritime Museum of San Diego; and the Nimitz Library at the U.S. Naval Academy. My most grateful thanks to George Witte, editor of long standing; to Sally Richardson and Matt Shear; and to Lenore Hart, best friend, first reader, and reality check.

The specifics of personalities, locations, and procedures in various locales, and the units and theaters of operations described are employed as the settings and materials of *fiction*, not as reportage. Some details have been altered to protect classified information.

As always, all errors and deficiencies are my own.

Moral judgements are singularly out of place in espionage.

—Graham Greene

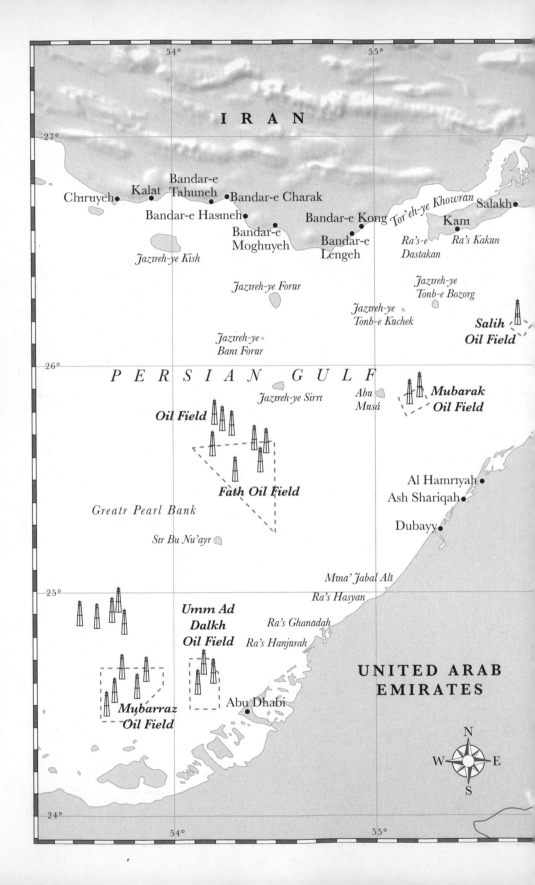

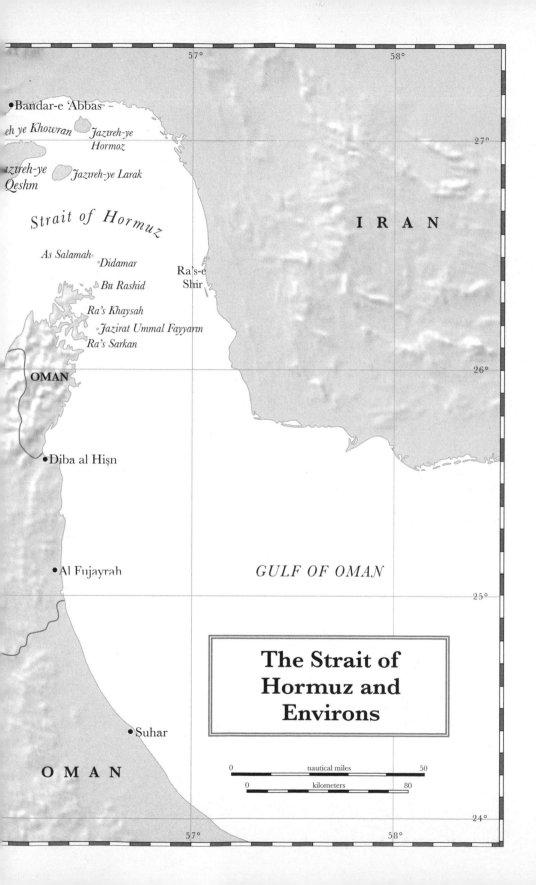

•Bandar-e 'Abbas

eh ye Khowran   *Jazıreh-ye*
                   Hormoz

izıreh-ye   *Jazıreh-ye Larak*
Qeshm

Strait of Hormuz

As Salamah   *Didamar*

         Bu Rashid   Ra's-e
                        Shir
Ra's Khaysah
    Jazirat Ummal Fayyarın
Ra's Sarkan

OMAN

•Diba al Hişn

•Al Fujayrah   *GULF OF OMAN*

IRAN

27°

26°

25°

24°

The Strait of Hormuz and Environs

•Suhar

O M A N

| 0 | nautical miles | 50 |
| 0 | kilometers | 80 |

57°   58°

I

TAG

1

Camp Bandit, Western Virginia

TILTED mountains surrounded the valley like massive firing berms. Gravel slides had wiped out whole glades of the second-growth forests that clung to their rocky slopes. Clouds drifted ghost-white against shadowed hollows. Each time Team Charlie had gone out on the range, their gunfire had echoed in those hills as if lost divisions were still locked in battle, the Blue against the Gray.

As they took a knee in front of the instructor this morning, the team's drab digital-pattern battle dress was hard for the eye to focus on. They wore black nylon knee and elbow pads, black tactical vests, ballistic eye protection, belts of fat red twelve-gauge shells, and nine-millimeter SIGs in thigh holsters. They held pump shotguns with black nylon stocks muzzle down. Their shoulders were aching, chests heaving after two hours of running, climbing, and thinking around corners against their trainers.

One of whom barked, "Next problem. Lenson, you got six guys. Task: assault and clear that green building. What's your plan?"

Commander Dan Lenson, USN, tried to think. But concepts only oozed through his brain, like used motor oil. They hadn't gotten much sleep the past few nights. And it felt bizarre, blasphemous in some deep way, six men genuflecting around one who stood. He noted another instructor headed for the control booth. "Uh, my plan . . . I need to dominate the path with two shooters at, uh, that sandbag pile and behind the black tank. . . ."

"And?" The harsh voice goaded him. The GrayWolf instructor was in black BDUs and peaked cap. The name tape on his blouse read WHALEN. The night before, Dan's team had discussed how much more they'd take before they shot him themselves. "Think fast, Team Leader! You're not gonna have time to *cog*-itate out in booger-eating country."

"Flash-bang through the window. Push in a four-man stack? Redeploy my fire team to the back to catch any skedaddlers?"

"Don't *ask* me, tell me. If you don't know, for Christ's sake, don't advertise the fact! Positions! Fifteen rounds sabot slug, fifteen rounds of buck, lock and load. Keep in mind your tactical reload drills. A dry weapon is no weapon. And remember, the problem goes from whistle to whistle; you're not done till the signal goes."

Lenson dragged a sleeve across his face. Tactical Analysis Group, Team Charlie had been running and shooting since before dawn. But his guys were looking at him. He cleared his throat. "I'll go in first and take position on the sandbags. Covering fire on my signal. Donny, break right, suppression position behind the tank. Teddy, you take point on the stack, with Yeong-Min, and Monty, and Rit. Live rounds, guys! Take your time and make sure the line of fire's clear before you shoot."

Waiting for the whistle, he mopped his face again. He still wasn't sure why a U.S. Navy tactics development team needed two weeks of pistol and shotgun training, house clearing, CQC and CQM—mil-speak for close-quarters combat and close-quarters marksmanship—including low-light and target identification drills. They weren't exactly Marine Recon material. Some of his guys weren't even on active duty anymore. But Captain Todd Mullaly had insisted. "Team Charlie's new for us, Dan," he'd said. "You did all right in Korea, but there at the end—it wouldn't have hurt to have more tactical training, would it?"

And he'd had to agree. Taking out an AK-armed North Korean political officer, on the surge-swept deck of a surfaced sub, with a pistol he hadn't even been sure how to fire—yeah. He'd been lucky to come out alive.

"You'll have a great time," Mullaly had said, closing the discussion. "Great country out there. Just like a paid vacation."

Right. Two weeks of sixteen-hour days more like Marine boot camp than any Navy school he'd ever been to. Range training and quick reaction drills, dry firing, and tactics and procedures in the Glass House. Classroom hours on dominating the environment, cover, travel, clearing rooms and hallways, and his personal least favorite, stairwells. In the evenings they played a video game "Obie" Oberg had brought, pursuing faceless enemies through mazes of abandoned, smoking ruins till the world itself seemed less real than digital, and the game more real than reality.

He'd gotten stuck, forced to replay one scenario over and over. His teammate, behind him, had shouted, "On your six, on your six!" And Dan had wheeled, trying to fire past him at a figure that suddenly appeared out of a side corridor. But his buddy had moved, and Dan's bullet had blown apart his head. The screen had frozen to the accompaniment of a scream, and MISSION FAILED pulsated in red letters. He'd failed over and over, until the blank face of his computer-generated teammate had begun to haunt his dreams—

He realized they were all looking at him, still waiting. His *real* team members. The whistle went, a blast that pierced ear protectors like a high-velocity bullet. He shook off the unease that lingered from the dream, twisting his voice into something approximating their instructor's gravelly snarl. "All right, goddamn it. Taggers, *move!*"

TWO yards ahead of Lenson, leaning against a timber barrier so chewed by bullets it sagged as he put his weight on it, Teddy "Obie" Oberg racked the big twelve-gauge slug shells one after the other through the Mossberg. You didn't need to precycle your ammo with a pump action, but habit was hard to break. And he'd built up a lot of habits in eight years with SEAL Team Eight, on floats in the Med, antiterror missions out of Stuttgart, trying to snatch PIs—persons of interest—in the Balkans.

Obie had studied the commander—that was what they called Lenson, "the commander"—through the two weeks at Bandit. He'd met Medal of Honor winners before, SEALs from Vietnam. But this guy wasn't like them.

For one thing, officers hardly ever got the Medal. For another, Lenson didn't talk about it, or about where the rest of his ribbons had come from. The Silver Star. The Bronze Star. Teddy'd heard rumors about foreign decorations, too: Israeli, Saudi, Korean. The guy moved like he'd been hurt more than once. He looked like a thinker, but didn't act like he had all the answers, like too many fucking officers.

What made him uneasy was, Lenson didn't seem comfortable maneuvering a squad. Maybe you couldn't expect that from a surface line type, what SEALs called "blackshoes," usually with a sneer. It could mean trouble, if they got in a situation.

But sometimes he caught a glimpse of something else behind those flat gray seaman's eyes, the irises like stamped lead discs in crimped copper. A detached coldness Teddy had only seen once or twice before in his life.

Who knew? Maybe the guy was a killer, after all.

THE whistle. At the same moment a tracer-burst swivelled just over their heads. GrayWolf trained with live ammo. Dan thought, *They must get it cheap.* He racked the first round into the chamber and lurched forward. He hoped the employee on the other end of that machine gun didn't decide to fire low.

He squinted through a sudden stinging in his eyes as his senses ratcheted into danger gear, as the world stuttered into the tunnel-visioned slow-time of combat. The Killing House lay fifty yards ahead, surrounded by wrecked cars, piles of old tires, concertina, a rusting T-76 spray-painted black. The instructors had torched the tire-pile and the black smoke blew toward them, alternately revealing and concealing what lay ahead. Just the smell of burning diesel, rubber, and old powder would have brought back memories, if he'd had time for them. Syria. Iraq. The China Sea. Places he'd had to do things he didn't like to remember. Most of those places, though, he'd had Navy deck gray under his feet. Where was Mullaly sending Team Charlie? It wasn't how the Tactical Analysis Group had been explained to him, when he'd been assigned. Which was another whole story, why "Nick" Niles had decided he had to hide him after the debacle in the White House.

He got to the sandbags, rolled, and came up aiming not over them, where a sniper would expect you, but at the corner. Black steel popper targets jumped up by the house. He dropped them one after the other, the heavy Federal slugs slamming out of the eighteen-inch barrel with a blast that nailgunned his sinuses and slammed his already sore shoulder. He twisted to cover Wenck as Donnie broke into a run. A popper jumped up on the water tower, overlooking the house. He took careful aim and held over, guessing seventy yards, and blasted it down.

Wenck got to the tank and oriented to cover the stack. When Dan looked up from reloading, a small figure in too-large BDUs was shooting and advancing. A popper went down with each crack, but the little Korean wasn't using cover and concealment. He was charging in the way they must have taught them to attack in the North Korean Army. "Im! Watch your cover, goddamn it!"

AS Im got to the corner he picked up the hidden shooter, the one behind the tank, just before it sprang up. He took it out as Oberg sprinted past. Hesitated, then tore after him.

His name wasn't really Yeong-Min Im. That had been his captain's name, on the submarine the destroyers had cornered in the Eastern Sea. But his captain was dead now, shot by the political officer when Captain Im had decided to save his crew. And he couldn't use his real name, ever again.

That was the price of living, when so many others, who'd started the voyage with him, were dead.

He was beginning to understand this strange game. The hidden angles. The all-too-obvious targets. The way everyone emphasized crouching, and hiding, and not leaving cover unless the rest of the team was firing. The Americans—except maybe Obie—were afraid of getting shot. The People's Army trained to a different mind-set.

But he wasn't part of the great collective anymore. This was an odd land, a curious culture. But for some reason, they valued him at TAG. Even asked his advice. They'd brought him to America, and put him in charge of "enemy" submarines in their war games. Maybe they even trusted him.

He was still trying to decide if they were right to do so.

DONNIE Wenck got to the tank and skidded into it, slamming his head on the flaking steel so hard he almost blacked out. "Damn it," he howled.

Donnie was sweating hard and feeling like crap. It was too fucking hot, for one thing. There wasn't even air-conditioning in the bunkrooms. And no e-mail! For two weeks! He wasn't like Oberg, buffed and toned in black T-shirts. That asshole loved this shit, out running before dawn, shooting all day long, evasive driving, learning how to fire RPGs. Obie knew motors, cars, give him that. But hand him a circuit board to fix, or a program to debug, see how he'd do.

Still blinking through the stars, Donnie realized somebody was yelling at him. Lenson. Oberg, running past in a crouch, was shouting, too. "Wenck! Quit daydreaming. Cover the stack. Cover the fucking *stack!*"

He leaned out, keeping his finger outside the trigger guard, and swept the yard. Two targets, one to Lenson's left, the other above the moving stack of guys. Fuck fuck . . . buckshot or slugs? . . . he pulled the trigger and nothing happened. The fucking safety . . . he pushed it off and fired five times and hit nothing. He pulled back and fed in buckshot rounds. That worked better but he aimed high, not wanting to endanger the guys in the open, and the targets still didn't go all the way down. Not until Oberg drew his pistol and double-tapped them one after the other, on the run, not even stopping to aim. Donnie squeezed his eyes shut. He'd fucked up again. Fuck!

It was enough to make you want to go back to sea.

MONTY Henrickson had stuck close behind Oberg crossing the open yard, but his back prickled every time he heard Wenck fire. The kid was dangerous to everything but the targets. Monty was almost forty, neither as big nor as fast as the others, but to his surprise he liked this camp. It was stressful, but different from what he usually did, which was mainly mathematics, probability, and statistical analysis.

Still, was this where a doctorate got you? He should have stayed at the Massachusetts Institute of Technology. He'd have had tenure by now. Or gone with that offer from PRC, back when they were gearing up to go public. He'd have been a partner, counting his money in the tens of millions.

He caught a flash of Oberg's backturned face, eyes bright blue as ammoniated copper, the strange radiating scars on his cheeks standing out like a Maori warrior's. Then they were freight-training into the side of the house, Oberg cushioning him from the front as Carpenter's bulk slammed into him from behind. Monty took high position.

"Flash," Im yelled, the accent making it more like "Frash," and they ducked as the pyrotechnic sailed in through the window.

DAN didn't see any more outside targets. Hoping they'd gotten them all, he jammed five more rounds of buck into his magazine, then jumped to his feet. *Don't shoot till you're sure of your target.* The instructor had hammered that into them. The team was its own gravest enemy; in low light and the confusion of combat, it was all too easy to target your own. He flashed Wenck the follow-me signal.

They hit the house together as Im's flash bang went off, a hollow crack and a bolt of lightning so bright even not looking at it seared his eyes. Oberg, the breacher, kicked the door in and the stack went in after him, high-low-high, just as the instructors had kicked it into them; number one in sweeping center to right, two sweeping the left corner to center, three sweeping right corner to center, then the breacher buttonhooking in behind. The hours in the Glass House and the Corral were paying off.

"Break right, around back," Monty yelled to Wenck, and shuffled forward in the combat crouch, taking the lead again.

RIT Carpenter went in last in the stack. Seeing Im roll right, Henrickson left, he hustled through and swept the interior with the muzzle of his shotgun. Why did Lenson always put him last? The bastard was still pissed at him about that mama-san in Pusan. What the fuck, who could fault a fucking white hat for knocking off a little young pussy? How was he to know the fucking Koreans had MPs patrolling the ceremonial grounds? So maybe sometimes he had to stop to catch his breath on the runs. At least he paid attention to what he was doing, unlike Wenck. Now there was a space cadet. Good enough at card-swapping when a piece of gear went down, but you could never count on him.

Rit had retired, but still thought of himself as Navy all the way. He'd qualified in *Tiru*, last of the wartime "smokeboats," as their proud crews called them; had his "diesel boats forever" pin at home; he'd stood on her deck when they hauled down her commissioning pennant in Charleston. Went to *Bonefish* after that, then served the rest of his time in nukes, retiring off *Batfish*.

All those years at sea didn't do much for your marriage. No kids, thank God. His last active duty had been at the Sub School in New London, training the latest and greatest. Then he'd picked up this job at TAG. At first it had been routine, riding the boats during exercises, grading them. Then they'd asked if he'd be interested in something more exciting. Something he wouldn't be able to talk about. But hey, things had happened on patrol he couldn't talk about, either.

He trailed Henrickson, keeping an eye over his shoulder the way they trained the Tail-End Charlie, and was rewarded with a popper that jerked up from behind a stack of barrels. He blasted it down first shot. "Try that on, Lenson," he muttered. "Not too bad for an old bubblehead pussy hound, huh?"

DONNIE got to the alley and almost shot before the shape moved and he saw it wasn't a popper. Jeez, he'd almost blasted one of his own guys. He swept and was on it when a target jumped up. He slammed it down first shot and yelled "Take that, you sonofabitch!—I got it! I got it! Didja see that, Commander?"

"Good shot, Donnie. Real good shot. Now get in the house."

OBERG inched up the stairwell one riser at a time, a foot off the wall, to keep a close round from richocheting into him, keeping his right hand free. The staff here liked to place their targets deep in the room, but from the oil rigs he'd cleared in the Gulf, once they knew you were on your way up the bad guys put somebody at the top of the stairs with a grenade. The only chance you had in a stairwell—no place to run, and no fragment cover—was to throw it back up.

If he ever had to take these overweight, overage techies and blackshoes into combat, he'd have to carry 80 percent of the load. He didn't look forward to it, but it was pretty clear that was why they'd TAD'd Teddy Oberg to TAG Charlie.

Just as he'd figured, there they were, deep in the room. Only he guessed they'd guess he'd guess, and instead of taking the ones at the window first he swung and there it was, in the corner behind him. He blasted it down and ducked, swung, and took out the ones at the window. Then in one fluid motion he drew his pistol and scissored up and over the banister—if they had IEDs they set them at the top of the stairs—and dropped to a knee and took out two more poppers in a side room.

Behind him came rapid blasts as Im pumped extra rounds into the targets he'd already dropped. The little Korean didn't mind shooting a bad guy again, just to make sure. Which Oberg thoroughly approved of. Once on the beach in Kuwait, when he'd gone in with the swimmer scouts to set up the diversion, a Republican Guard had stood up from a pile of bodies and tried to gut him with a bayonet.

"Clear!" he yelled down the stairwell. He heard them repeating it, passing it on till it reached the instructor outside.

He found the camera in the corner and gave it the finger, holding his black leather shooting glove up in a contemptuous salute.

WHALEN was standing easy when they filed out, hands clamped behind him. Maybe he even looked pleased. Dan wasn't sure, since he'd never seemed satisfied before. But they'd moved fast, done well. And it was the last day. Maybe the guy would let them go on a positive note. "So, seemed to go all right," Dan said. "Didn't it?"

"Team was pretty hot today," Whalen said, nodding back. He stepped forward, hand outstretched. Surprised—he'd never offered to shake before—Dan lowered his shotgun and reached out.

From the sandbags behind Whalen, two black-coveralled instructors stood up with AKs. "Bap, bap, bap," they shouted, imitating the high-pitched bark of 7.62×39s.

"You're fucking dead, all of you," Whalen smirked. "Remember? Whistle to whistle. And I didn't whistle. So your grade . . . let's just say you crapheads aren't as outstanding as you think you are. Always be ready. Never let down your guard. That's when they'll hit you. Believe me."

Dan felt the guys tense around him. "Get fucking real," Oberg muttered. "Fucking snakes," hissed Wenck.

"Hang on to that combat mind-set," Whalen went on. "Keep asking yourself 'what if.' You're gonna fuck up, when the shit goes down. You just gotta keep going. Stay tactical. As long as you're alive, you can fight. Maybe not save yourself, but if you put another bullet in a bad guy, maybe you save your teammate."

Carpenter took a step forward. Dan grabbed his arm. "Just take it easy, guys. We're done here; we'll be back at TAG tomorrow, and do some real work." To Whalen's taunting grin he said, "Thanks for the warning, Instructor. I'm sure we'll remember it long after your other lessons have faded."

THEIR instructor disappeared; maybe he sensed his last prank hadn't made the impact he'd hoped for. Or maybe it had. The rest of the staff slapped them on the back, congratulated them on finishing. "Wolf's Den for beers all around," one said.

"Gee, really? We weren't allowed in there before," said Wenck, grinning like a third-grader just allowed up into the treehouse club.

"Well, you are now."

His guys looked to him. Dan shrugged; they'd earned it, but he'd leave after a token appearance. He didn't drink anymore. A GrayWolf pickup braked in a murk of yellow dust. He was unslinging his gear, tossing it into the bed with that of the others, when a voice called, "Commander Lenson?"

"Yeah?"

"Got a helo coming in for you."

A high-pitched drone, a fat black speck drawn swiftly against the sky. A small Hughes. He frowned. "I'd rather stay with my team—"

"Special invitation. Don't think you want to turn it down." The instructor waited until he gave a reluctant nod, then wheeled and hand-signaled the aircraft.

DOUBLE-TIMING along its roads before dawn, or being trucked between fields of tall corn, he hadn't grasped how huge Camp Bandit was. Or rather, that Bandit itself was only a puzzle-piece of a far larger entity. The Hughes hurtled over ranges and cornfields, bunkers and barracks. A sports complex with a baseball diamond, and football and soccer fields. More cornfields, then another entire compound with the same green steel-roofed shooting houses as Bandit. Gray and green smoke roiled up, tracers sparkled as troops in unfamiliar uniforms maneuvered through what looked like an entire village.

He leaned to tap the copilot's shoulder. "Is this all GrayWolf?" Dan yelled.

"Oh, yeah. And a lot more." They climbed, and as the man swept his arm from one corner of the horizon to the other, Dan realized it was all one whole, green expanses of corn and soybeans isolating dozens of camps, compounds, ranges, and what looked like housing developments but probably weren't. Aircraft were practicing touch-and-gos on a grass strip. Graders and 'dozers were cutting roads through the fields, raising dust as they cleared land for new construction. The Hughes swept over acres of concrete prefabs surrounded by sparkling new concertina, cornered by guard towers: a prison.

His skin crawled. GrayWolf wasn't a camp. It was an empire.

Twenty minutes later they squatted in a roiling cloud. He scrambled off to be greeted by a gray-haired Hispanic in the black coveralls and black cap with the wolf's head. The man said nothing, just checked his name tag and motioned for him to follow.

The low building was no different in its bland anonymous no-style from the lounge-and-office back at Bandit. Green prefab walls. Russet steel roofing. You saw buildings like it at U.S. bases overseas, or in industrial parks in small towns. Contractor-built cubic, furnished with heating, ventilation, and air-conditioning in hundred-thousand-square-foot buys. The wolf's head by the door was discreet. Three gray Expeditions were parked to the side. But the name on one of the parking signs focused his attention.

The air inside was cold and dry, as if they were in the Montana mountains instead of the muggy South. They went down a corridor floored with gray industrial-grade carpet. To either side, men worked at computers in spartan offices. Dan didn't see any women.

"Lenson. Come on in. Coke? Ice-cold Heineken?"

Since Torgild Schrade had been two classes ahead of him, they hadn't had much to do with each other at Annapolis. Dan had read about him now and then over the years, but they'd never met again. After a brief stint in uniform, Schrade had gone into cell phones, where he'd made a lot of money; then into politics, where he hadn't done nearly as well. In person, he wasn't quite as tall as Dan. He wore the same black battle dress as his employees, but the wolves' heads on his shoulders were silver. His thin lips were curved in a mocking smile. His black hair was buzzed short, with a widow's peak. He looked more like a hawk than a wolf, with deep-set eyes, an almost Arabic nose, shining white capped teeth, and a double-handed handshake whose warmth belied the penetrating gaze of those dark eyes. His bare steel desk was not just clean, but waxed to a shine. But the walls of his office were painted concrete block. Without waiting for an answer Schrade rooted two diet Dr Peppers from a fridge, tossed Dan one, waved at a sofa. "I didn't know you were with us until yesterday. Was looking over the pre-grad reports and saw your name."

Dan cleared his throat. "Uh, Mr. Schrade—"

"Tor, Dan. Just Tor. We played lacrosse together, remember? You're at TAG now, huh?" He didn't wait for answers. "What do you think of the tactical course? Instructors okay? Facilities? Training?"

"It was demanding. Right now I can't think of a thing to change, uh, Tor. It's not really my area of expertise. The instructors seem on top of things."

"Why's TAG sending us people for tactical training, Dan? I always thought of it as more like the Navy's think tank. Not what we think of as operators."

"I don't know the answer to that, Tor." He thought of adding, *and if I did, it'd be classified,* but this seemed petty—Schrade had deep roots in the spec ops community—so he didn't.

"I've been hearing about you now and then. Sounds like a rocky career."

Dan sat forward on the sofa. "It's had its ups and downs. Like yours, I guess."

Schrade chuckled. They studied each other. "Ever heard of Skip Froelinghausen? General Froelinghausen?"

Dan tensed. He'd heard the name, from his boss in the West Wing, associated with the shadowy group of advisers who'd turned around the war in Bosnia. "Heard of him. He with GrayWolf now?"

"No, no, but we move in the same circles . . . we're doing well out here. As you probably picked up, flying over. It's a growth industry, private military contracting. The way the administration's been downsizing our regular military. With your wife's help, I might add."

Schrade paused for his reaction, but Dan didn't rise to it. He just took another slug of fizzy black chemicals and waited.

"The Navy's most highly decorated officer. People I know, know what you've done. A warfighter, but a thinker, too. Titanium balls, when the warning lights all go red. But it seems like the 'sea lords' are not that impressed with you.

"You get the Medal, but only because the Army put you in for it. You get the rank, but you're not fast-tracked for promotion. It's like, you're the go-to when there's some high-stakes off-the-net issue nobody else wants to own up to. But then you get stashed when it's over, and all the knife scars get makeup smeared over them."

"I'm not sure I'd agree with that," Dan said. "Several flag officers have shown some confidence."

"Maybe on a personal level you get a compliment, but how's that translate into your career? Is it going to get you to flag level? Correct me if I'm wrong, but that's your goal, isn't it?"

"Not really, Tor."

"Stars are not your goal?"

"No."

"Well, I think that's good. Because to the ones who're wearing them, you come across as the kind of guy they need in wartime but would just as soon not have making them look incompetent, otherwise. So why should they ask you into the tent?"

Schrade gave him a chance, went on when he didn't speak. "I'm asking 'cause that's the model we like very much here in the PMC world. You know? The kind of lad who can bring things off even when they don't look particularly promising. One who can handle situations out there at the toasty edge of deniability, the ones the brass hats can't deal with by throwing money at General Dynamics. What makes you happiest about your Navy time, Dan? The people, right?"

"Sure, the people . . . and the sea."

"What's been your best assignment? What you enjoyed most?"

"Destroyer command."

"Well, we can't offer that. Though we can get you to sea now and then, with the riverine folks. Might be opportunities there. You've got your twenty years in? So you're effectively working for half pay now, right? Since you'll get the retirement the day you take off the uniform. We can offer you the chance to make some money. No, a *lot* of money. You'd like some of the things we're doing. Programs that'll use your talents."

One thing you learned in the military was that courtesy paid; the man your boss set you against today might be your boss himself tomorrow. "Well, I appreciate the offer, Tor. But you might want somebody more like one of my men. Teddy Oberg, maybe. Not that he's looking, but—"

"I know Teddy and respect him. He's a real operator. But management skills, that's where we're short-handed. And contacts—we always find those useful."

Suddenly Dan understood. "My wife."

Schrade cocked his head; the half-smile sharpened. "Actually I didn't mean Blair, but it's intriguing you bring her up. She's definitely a player. Not a major one right now as far as we're concerned, not where she's at. But she's got the possibility of becoming one. Not in this administration—for obvious reasons. But I could see Blair filling a big job one day." He shrugged. "But that's down the road. Right now I'm interested in the people *you* know. And not just in the United States. We're doing a lot of work training foreign militaries. Foreign contractors, too."

"I'm not really interested in private contracting," Dan told him. "Don't get me wrong, Tor. But if I want to serve my country, I'll do it in uniform. I'm not comfortable with the idea of doing it for the money."

"You cash your Navy paycheck?"

"I see your point, but there's more involved. Accountability. Tradition. Just . . . hiring out to the highest bidder, that doesn't feel right to me."

"Even if the bidder's the same government that pays you now? Every contract we take's approved by State or Defense. When they're not the customer, themselves. You're not making sense, guy."

He hung fire, trying to figure it out himself. The obvious rejoinder was: But what if the highest bidder wasn't the U.S. government? When did profit trump loyalty? And not only that. He'd seen, inside the Beltway, how cash bought policy. Once it could buy an army, too, what would America look like then?

Schrade spoke into his silence. "The Navy's most decorated officer, but over the years you've stepped on a lot of toes. Your combat record and command experience, the Congressional, your expertise in advanced weapons systems, that's earned you—what? TAG Charlie? Here's your chance to live well doing exactly what you're doing, only without the brass and the politicians second-guessing you."

"They don't second-guess you?"

"They don't even want to look." Schrade barked a short laugh. "They really don't. What they don't know, they can't be held responsible for. You know I ran for the Senate."

"I was at sea, but I read about it. Yeah."

"Well, I lost, but guess what: I'm glad I did. You know, when I was a boy, my dad took me into a doughnut shop. I was a chubby kid, loved the doughnuts. He told me I had three choices in life: Be the guy who makes the doughnuts. Be the guy who buys the doughnuts. Or be the guy who owns the store."

The thin lips recurved and Schrade sat back. "I have a major contract coming up in Africa. Put in your letter now and get in on the ground floor. This is going to be even bigger than cell phones."

Dan looked for a trash can. He two-pointed the empty Dr P and stood. "Tor, nice seeing you again. But screwed up as the Navy is, I'm going to stay with it."

Schrade paused a beat, maybe waiting for him to change his mind. When Dan didn't, he got up and shook his hand, thanking him again for coming in. "Stay in touch. And the bird'll be ready when you are, take you back to your troops. We'll meet again. Guarantee you that."

Dan nodded, tried to smile back. But he doubted it looked all that convincing.

2

Little Creek, Virginia

THE main drag at Little Creek Naval Amphibious Base led from the gray behemoths at their piers east to what Dan remembered had once been the main exchange. It and the commissary had relocated to a new complex, but Headquarters, U.S. Navy Tactical Assessment Group, was near neither. It was down a side road that headed off into what years before had been scrub pines, dunes, sea oats, and sand fleas, a wind-whipped waste with verdigrised cartridges still littering the damp sand where draftees had trained before shipping out for Africa in 1942.

Now those bayfront dunes housed commands whose tenancy went un-advertised. TAG was housed in a low tan brick building that reminded him of a half-buried bunker. A Mark 48 torpedo and a Tomahawk missile pointed skyward on steel pylons before the entrance, and discreet bronze letters announced TACTICAL ASSESSMENT GROUP.

He and Henrickson showed their IDs at the front desk. The rest of the team had taken the weekend, and would be in on Monday. They clipped on their badges and headed to the back, down a hallway past the Game Room and the mainframe. The big IBM didn't get used much anymore; the crunchers used workstations that were faster and friendlier, but it was still there. It was Saturday but the offices were still full; a reserve unit came in on weekends. Dan punched numbers into the door lock and let himself into his office.

Home, or as close to it as shore duty Navy got. His office was window-less and not much more luxurious than Schrade's, but it did have central air. He skated his duffel next to the plywood cruise box that held what uniforms he hadn't left at the house in Arlington. There was a bunk bed down the hall, but usually he stayed at the BOQ. He ought to get an apart-ment. But it didn't feel right, to set up housekeeping when he hoped to get back to Blair. The complexes he'd looked at in Ocean View and along Shore Drive had been too depressing to consider.

He slotted his cap into the rack and flipped on the coffeemaker. Unlocked his desk and checked that the Beretta Nine Mullaly had issued him when he reported aboard was still there. He booted up the terminal and went to the LAN.

Forty-six messages. Some were from the Surface Navy and the Alumni associations, others from friends, others relating to the operation they'd just finished off Korea, one from a former West Wing subordinate asking for a reference. He was working through them when the IM popped up with a request for him and Henrickson to report to Captain Mullaly.

NORMAN Todd Mullaly, TAG's CO, was heavyset and balding. When Dan closed the door the commanding officer flicked his fingers at the chair and swivelled away the screen. He did it every time anyone came in. Monty was already there; the little analyst nodded to Dan.

"Dan. Siddown. How'd it go? GrayWolf trains rough, I hear."

"Yessir, I dropped a few pounds. I think they usually get younger people, trigger-pullers. Cops, Marines, the spec ops folks. They seemed a little uncertain what to do with us."

"Well, you can't tell everybody everything." Mullaly looked back at the computer. "By the way, word is, Dick O'Quinn? He's going to recover. Maybe not to a duty status, but he'll walk again. Figured you'd want to hear."

Dan nodded. In the operation in the Korea Strait in which Im's submarine had been sunk, O'Quinn—a retired captain—had nearly died trying to rescue a Korean sailor from a flooding compartment. It had been touch and go whether he'd regain consciousness. "That's good. I'll go by and see him, if he's still at Portsmouth."

Mullaly nodded. He cleared his throat, then carouseled the screen to face them.

Dan blinked. For a moment he couldn't guess what he was looking at. An oblately pointed cylinder rested base down on what looked like a black felt drop-cloth. The upper portion was cut away to show interior details. A pop-out fin stuck out from either side. A projectile of some sort? But at the bottom was a bell-shape that suggested a rocket engine.

"Some kind of terminal-guided munition?"

"Looks like it, doesn't it. But it's not. You fire this underwater."

"Underwater?" Dan leaned closer, trying to make out the lettering, but his eyes were giving him trouble. The call-outs wouldn't resolve into words. Then he realized why. They were in Cyrillic. "This is Russian?"

"You're looking at the VA-111 'Shkval' supercavitating projectile. It's not really a torpedo. Not really a rocket, either. But you could call it a rocket torpedo, and get the idea across." Mullaly keyed another window and brought up a document of which the image was apparently a part. "We don't have anything like it, which is maybe why the terminology difficulty. Thing's completely new to us."

"Well, Norm," Henrickson put in, folding his arms. Dan started before he remembered that a civilian analyst was perfectly correct calling their commanding officer by his first name. "Not *completely* new. I remember some work on cavitation envelopment back in the eighties. From NRL, I think."

"Monty, what we're hearing is pretty appalling," Mullaly said complacently, as if however appalling it was, it couldn't be that bad. "It uses a shaped noseplate to create cavitation—a bubble of water vapor—that's then fed with more gas to surround the body. Then the rocket motor kicks in, and it really accelerates. The Russians claim a top speed of two hundred knots."

No one spoke, as all three contemplated the tactical advantages of a weapon that ran four times as fast as the U.S. Navy's fastest torpedo, and five times faster than its speediest submarine. Dan rubbed his face. He'd had torpedoes fired at him, and the ordinary versions had been terrifying enough. "Wait a minute. You said they're *claiming* this speed? You mean, like . . . *advertising* it?"

"Advertising it, exactly. For government-to-government sale." Mullaly tapped more keys and hit Enter. "I'm sending you the package on the secure LAN. A flyer from the 'Komponent' Scientific and Production Enterprise, Moscow. A Defense Intelligence Agency notice. Some open-source stuff from a Ukrainian scientific journal. And a classified evaluation from the Joint Chiefs of what a weapon like this means strategically."

"I thought the Russians were our buddies," Henrickson said.

"They're buddies to anyone with cash. And they're coming back as a problem set. They might see their national interest as to help out any of our regional challengers. North Korea, China, Iran, Syria—the usual suspects."

Henrickson said, "This is starting to sound familiar. The 53-65K. The wake-homer. They sold those to the Chinese."

Mullaly said, "That's right. And we sent Team Charlie after them. That was back when Christine was the CO, right?"

"We got three of them," Henrickson told Dan. "Gave one to DARPA, one to DIS, and kept the one with the fewest bullet holes. Did fifteen instrument runs down at Tongue of the Ocean."

Dan said, through dawning apprehension, "Are you saying, Captain—are you saying you want us to steal one of these? Is that the sense here?"

"Well, steal's a harsh word," Mullaly said. "But we have a tasking to get specs and if possible a working model or best of all, one of the issue rounds and associated equipment—software and so forth. Because this is causing some stir up at J-3, and over at Sublant. The Russians have actually been carrying these around for some time. At least, an early model."

He explained that the sub community suspected Soviet strategic ballistic missile submarines, like the Typhoons, had carried Shkvals as engagement breakers. As soon as they heard an incoming torpedo, they could fire into the noise spoke. If they could force the launching platform to turn away, that would break the guidance wire, after which both subs would be on equal ground, since the American would have lost the advantage of surprise.

"Uh, wait a minute, sir. This thing's surrounded by supercavitation, and going two hundred plus? That's got to be way past the self-noise threshold for passive transducers."

"It is."

"So how's it guided?"

"You're right, it can't sonar-guide like a conventional homer. And it goes too fast and the turbulence trail's too violent to wire-guide or wake-home, either. The consensus is that up to now it's been a straight-run weapon. Like the old steam torpedoes, only a lot faster."

Henrickson said, "They just pick up a target bearing, and shoot down it? That's not going to give them much probability of hit."

"With a nuke, you don't need a hit."

"A nuke?" Dan tried to keep his face from showing anything, though just the word brought back images of charred flesh, smashed metal, the ripping snarl of radiation meters. USS *Horn* was now a deserted, radioactive shell behind barbed wire at Norfolk Naval Shipyard. "What's the range, on this thing?"

"A couple thousand yards."

"With a *nuclear* warhead? That'd destroy both subs."

"Maybe they thought their double hulls would take it. Or didn't care, as long as they took down a *Los Angeles* class, too. But you're right—being unguided made it less dangerous. But now there's a twist. A kicker." He glanced at the screen, which was turned away from them again. "I'll summarize. Since this is beyond TS/SCI. There's a source—a spy—in the Russian Admiralty. According to this source, one of their designers has figured out a way around the homing problem."

TS/SCI stood for Top-Secret/Sensitive Compartmented Information. Which Dan had been cleared for in the past, on the White House staff. But either Mullaly didn't know this, or his clearance had been revoked. He rubbed his chin, feeling as if he was being shadowed by something evil, like the Hound of the Baskervilles, or Hannibal Lector.

"What way?" Henrickson muttered.

"Our source doesn't know. Either that, or he's holding out for more money."

"Guided, that could be nasty," Dan said.

"It gets worse. This guided version—they call it the 'Shkval-K,' with the K for 'Komponent,' I guess—that's the name of the design bureau—the Iranians are looking at buying it. And that has *really* got some knickers kinked."

Dan said, "Because of the carriers?"

"Exactly," Mullaly told him. "Something this fast, and terminally guided, the Iranians could close the Gulf, cut off our oil. If the Chinese get it they can take out our stalkers, use the Sea of Japan as a strategic haven—that would screw us up big time in Asia. We have to find out whether this thing works, and if so, how. That's the Chief of Naval Operation's tasking to us. Get our hands on a sample, so we can build countermeasures.

"Read up on it and we'll talk tomorrow about how you're going to go about it."

HENRICKSON nodded. He got up and left. But Dan stayed. When the door was closed he cleared his throat. "Sir, we've got a slight problem."

"With Monty? Yeah, he can be kind of a know-it-all—"

"No, no. Monty and I get along fine. It's GrayWolf. I think the Army knows where I am."

"Well . . . it's not exactly a secret," Mullaly said cautiously. Dan frowned inside; he'd never really known how much his commanding officer knew about what had happened in the East Wing, and how convenient it might be for certain circles to be sure Dan Lenson would never give an interview or write a tell-all. "My understanding from Admiral Niles was, keep you outside the Beltway, and out of the country as much as possible. He even said to make sure you had a sidearm, which didn't make me popular with the base commander—his security people don't like firearms they don't control inside the gate. There more to it than that?"

Dan wondered if he, or maybe Niles, was being paranoid. Surely it was fantasy to think he might be in danger. This wasn't Byzantium or Florence. No matter how senior, military men weren't in service just for their own aggrandizement. He had to believe that, or he was in the wrong business and always had been. But he decided to push. "Has anyone asked? Any inquiries as to my whereabouts?"

Mullaly shook his head and looked back at the screen. Vertical lines appeared between his eyes. "No. But if Niles wants you out of the country, this tasking will require some travel. Like I said, look over the package, think about it, and we'll get together tomorrow. Let's say, zero-nine."

HE read through the material, then searched the classified Internet, using key words like "high-speed," and "choke point," and "strategic threat." He found information on the State Scientific and Production Enterprise "Komponent" and on somebody named Yevgeny Dvorov, but very little detail. Which meant either this was all still below the radar, or else was classified tighter than Secret. He returned a call from Idaho, from the grandmother of a little girl whose mother had died helping to save *Horn* when Dan had been in command. The grandmother said the indemnity compensation checks had stopped. He made some calls to the VA. By the time he found the glitch and got a promise the checks would start again, it was time to knock off for the day.

Before he left, though, he punched in a Washington area code. Clarice, his wife's secretary, said she was on the phone, but if he'd hold she'd see if she could free up. He listened to Pentagon elevator music.

"Dan. They let you out?"

"Hi, hon. Yeah. Back in the Navy, and glad to be here."

He was tempted to tell her about Schrade. She could give him chapter and verse about his backers, his contracts, but he didn't. The trouble with being married to an undersecretary of defense was that your wife was better plugged in than you were. Sometimes, even about things you thought you already knew. So much so that he found himself keeping things to himself. It wasn't that great for intimacy. But they'd managed to build a relationship, then a marriage, around not being together for long periods of time.

She sounded rushed, as usual. He checked his watch; she'd be there for two or three more hours. "You getting home anytime?" she asked.

"Uh, not really sure at this point. Just had a sit down with Mullaly. They might have something overseas for me."

"Can you make it this weekend?"

"I'll see. He didn't say when departure date would be. Or where we were going."

Her voice sharpened; he sensed the intense beam of her actual interest swinging his way for the first time in the conversation. "Something important?"

"Might be. I'll tell you about it if I can get back. How's everything going?"

"The bathroom's still a mess. The floor's gone, but I can't get a commitment from the tiling guys. You really think you might have to leave before this weekend?"

Her voice was softer now, as if it took a few minutes to melt her official persona. He knew the feeling, and suddenly missed her, and the quiet house in Arlington, and the new shelves he'd promised he'd build but hadn't gotten to yet. "Like I said, can't tell yet. But I miss you."

"I miss you, too."

"If I can get up even for a day, I'll be there."

"I'm looking at travel, too, but maybe we could get away. Go up to the Blue Ridge."

He jotted a note to himself to get the brakes checked on the Escort. Though if they went to the mountains they'd probably take her Lexus. She thought his car was too small to be safe. "That'd be nice. Oh, and Homecoming's coming up. Interested in that?"

"If I can go as your wife."

She meant, so she didn't have to talk to generals and admirals. "Absolutely. In a veil."

"That's more like it."

After some sappy endearments he hung up. He thought about calling his daughter, and at last he did. But the phone rang and rang in Nan's room and she didn't answer. She had a cell, too, but he didn't know its number. He left a message.

HE changed in the locker room at the back of the building, broke out new shoes and fresh socks, a USNA tee laundered so many times the blue lettering was a shadow against the gray, and headed out for a run. The stored sun-energy blazed up off the pavement. A breeze tossed the treetops behind Rodriguez Range. Marines doubletimed past, chanting in

unison. God, had he ever been that fresh-faced, that unreflectingly confident? Yeah, maybe he had. Back when he was an ensign, aboard *Reynolds
Ryan* . . .

He jogged on, caught in memories that only after a time did he manage
to wall off. He shook out his arms and shoulders, and picked up the pace.

When he slowed again, sweating in the heat, he was almost to the piers
on the west bank of the inlet. He turned north, thinking to at least get a
look—you couldn't jog down the piers anymore, a security fence cut them
off from the rest of the base, but at least he could *look* at the ships—when
a note caught his ear.

It was the slow tolling of braided wire clanging wind-driven against
hollow aluminum. Masts loomed. He turned off the road and jogged past
trailered powerboats waiting for the ramp. Then slowed to a walk as he
reached the base marina. He hesitated, then headed past the OWNERS AND
AUTHORIZED VISITORS ONLY sign, out onto the salt-weathered planks.

He was admiring a green-and-white sloop when a gray head popped out
of the companionway. "Looking for me?"

"Uh, not really, sir. Just taking a break." He turned away.

"Just looking, eh? Come on aboard, then."

The owner's name was Adridge. He was retired, to judge by a paunch
that wouldn't have passed the current fat standards. A captain or master
chief, retired on thirty, Dan guessed. But he put on no airs. He showed
Dan around, through main cabin to forward cabin, quarter berth, galley,
head.

It wasn't new, but there was no scent of mold or rot, which was the
smell of a badly kept boat. The bilges were dry and sweet. When Adridge
unshipped the housing, the engine looked new. Even the fire extinguish-
ers had inked tags with current inspection dates.

"Put a lot of elbow grease into her over the years," the owner mused,
showing him the ball valves on the through-hulls. "All the electronics are
up to date. But it's time to let somebody else enjoy her."

"Putting her on the market?"

"Yup. Just tinkering today, getting her ready for the broker to take pictures. Have to admit, though, I like the idea of another Navy guy sailing
her."

Dan looked around the cabin again. He could change after work and
jog to the marina. It wasn't an apartment, so he wouldn't be setting up
separate housekeeping. And living on base meant that much added security, if Nick Niles was right and there really were people who'd just as
soon keep him quiet.

"So . . . what're you asking?"

Adridge named a price. It was affordable; his car was paid off, his daughter's tuition was pretty much taken care of and she was even interning at a company in Springfield; he could do 10 percent down from his checking account, and USAA would be happy to loan him the rest. He asked about slip rental. Adridge said the slips went with the boat, not the owner, and the monthly fee sounded doable even with power and water included. Dan said he'd need a survey. Adridge said he wouldn't buy a boat without a survey, either. "Do you live around here, Dan?"

"Staying at the Q, right now. Share a suite with a guy from ATGLANT."

"Where you stationed? Aboard ship?"

"No, shore duty. Stationed over at—over at one of the tenant commands."

Adridge looked at the sky, then the channel. The basin was choppy with the wind coming over the dunes. "Well, what do you say we fire her up, see whether she likes you?"

THE diesel stroked on the first press of the button, kicking out a gossamer blue smoke that vanished as it warmed up. Adridge backed out with one hand on the wheel—not a negligible performance, with one screw and an adverse wind—and headed out past the massive gray cliffs of the landing ships. Sailors shaded their eyes from the decks. Once past the jetty and in the Chesapeake, Adridge turned over the wheel. Moving about the deck stiffly but with perfect balance, reaching from shroud to shroud like a seagoing chimpanzee, the older man hoisted the main and set a roller-furled jib, then came aft to kill the engine as they accelerated, tilting on a starboard tack.

They sailed to Lynnhaven Roads and back, tacking through a stiff northeast breeze. She came about in her own length and cut through three-foot swells fast and clean as a sharp chisel through poplar. By the time they picked up the lines again Dan was sold, having remembered he'd promised to teach Nan to sail when she came East for college. He made an offer, conditional on the survey. Adridge held out his hand. "There were a couple of things I was going to do. Have the injectors checked. Replace the fore and aft stays—they've been up there a time. But if you wanted to take care of those, I could make your price."

"Injectors. Stays. Anything else I should keep an eye on?"

"There's a maintenance log in the navigator's desk. Oil change schedule and all the repair records and guarantees and so forth." Adridge looked up at the masthead. "We've had a lot of good times. Hope you have as much fun with her as we had, my wife and me." His eyes went far and Dan knew she wasn't with them anymore, that he was saying good-bye to a lot of memories with her in them. He blinked and lowered his gaze. " 'Course, it's your call. But I've heard it said, it's bad luck to change a boat's name."

"*Naiad?* It's a fine name," Dan said. "I'll keep it."

Adridge's weathered lips creased. "Grab that line then. Cross the stern lines—yeah. Like that. That way, she'll ride out anything that comes her way."

3

Naval Undersea Warfare Center, Newport, Rhode Island

D AN had been homeported in Newport when he'd first joined the Navy. So he knew these dark forested hills, the twisting narrow roads and quaint villages turning more expensive-looking each time he'd been back. But he'd never been to NUWC, the Naval Undersea Warfare Center, though every surface line officer knew of it. From the hilltop above the old pier complex its brick buildings looked like the campus of a technical college. They stared out over the gray bay that looked cold even in summertime, or maybe he just remembered the Narragansett that way from what had seemed like eternal winter when he'd been stationed here. A carrier lay alongside Pier Two, ghostly with the queer lifelessness of a mothballed and crewless ship. The bay was flat and leaden, and cloud-shadows hunted over it in the early morning light.

Dr. Chandra Chone had asked them to come in early. He said he got his best work done late in the evening, which showed where a deputation from TAG came in his priority list. Their rather long wait in the lobby, before a young staffer came out to get them, was another clue.

Building 106 was a late-1940s structure. Chone's office had a very high ceiling, strange liquid shapes of machined metal on top of gray file cabinets, Renoir's self-portrait, a whiteboard, and a safe in one corner just big enough to contain Harry Houdini. The staffer sat Dan and Monty Henrickson at a four-person table with three chairs.

When Chone rolled in at last he extended his hand from a sleek graphite wheelchair. He was dark-complected, with a cottony-white goatee. The staffer took the third seat, introducing himself as Dr. Charles Pirrell. Both scientists were in slacks and short-sleeve shirts with ties.

As soon as the door was closed the lights dimmed. A screen glowed. The PowerPoint slide showed the NUWC logo and the motto *We are undersea warfare.* The second slide read, *The Naval Undersea Warfare Center is the Navy's full-spectrum research, development, test and evaluation, engineering and fleet support center for submarines, autonomous underwater systems, and offensive and defensive weapons systems associated with undersea warfare.*

Dan twisted and cleared his throat. In the dim three pairs of eyes met his. "Uh, Doctor—this isn't the command brief, is it?"

"Yes, Commander, it is."

"Could we skip it? We're familiar with NUWC's mission."

Chone and Pirrell exchanged glances. The presentation froze, then flickered with incredible swiftness until it came to a blue screen and went out. Chone brought the room lights back up and set the remote aside. "You wanted to know about the VA-111. The so-called 'Shkval.'"

"Yessir." Dan wondered why "so-called"—he'd been under the impression that was its Russian designation. "We'd like to understand the scientific basis—"

"You don't need to sir me, I don't hold military rank. I don't do much research, either. Most of what I do is sit in meetings."

"Lot of that going around where we work, too," Henrickson said.

"Uh-huh. Well. I hope you won't leave feeling you've wasted your time. You got the Patchell report?" They nodded. "Read it?"

"We read it," Dan said, irritated. "We even understood it. We've both worked in program development."

"How nice for you. Well, we're required to provide you support. Your CO's letter—Mullahy?"

"Mullaly."

"OPNAV info'd me on the request. You wanted everything we've got on supercavitating vehicle technologies?"

Dan said that was right. Chone drummed his fingertips on the armrest and squinted at the Renoir. "That's a broad request. So I have to ask: Why do you want to know? To what level of detail should we tailor our briefing? Help me out, Commander."

"Well, first, we'd like to hear about its propulsion. Then guidance. Then warhead. Then tactical employment. Then strategic effect."

"Most of that's outside our purview," Chone said. "But we'll do what we can. Charles? Why don't you address the propulsion angle."

Pirrell pulled over a note pad. He drew a long torpedo shape, but with a rod extending from the blunt stern. He etched in rings of small dots around its circumference, and carefully pencilled something small at the nose that Dan couldn't clearly see from the far side of the table.

Then leaned back and sighed. "Uh . . . I'd better start with the phenomenon of supercavitation."

Dan was already familiar with cavitation, which occurred when something was dragged through a fluid at very high speed—for example, the rotating blade of a fast-moving prop, which was where the phenomenon had first been observed. The water pressure dropped behind the moving blade, and the water vaporized—boiled instantaneously—forming steam. He'd listened on sonar to submarine screws cavitating; as the vapor bubbles imploded they made a distinctive racket. They could erode or even crack metal blades.

*Super*cavitation, Pirrell said, was deliberate sustained cavitation along the length of a moving vehicle, harnessing a phenomenon that up to now had been a nuisance. A supercavitating nose was designed to "wedge" the water apart. When the vehicle got going fast enough, and the bubble was pumped up by injecting additional gas through bleed holes, this wedged-open area sheathed the entire projectile in a skin of vapor and hot gas, reducing hydrodynamic drag to near zero. It would never touch the water, but tear through it enveloped in a slippery bubble.

Pirrell occupied the next forty minutes plodding through papers, trials, and projects dating back to 1940, when a Nazi scientist had proposed a supercavitating air-to-sea missile. He went on to an Aerojet General study on hydroreactive gas generation from 1962 and ventilated-cavity studies and enveloping-vapor-flow simulations someone had done around 1969. Henrickson asked a couple of detail questions; Dan and Chone were silent.

The younger scientist went on to more recent ONR and DARPA studies. Dan sat forward when he got to a program that had actually built a ten-inch-diameter supercavitating vehicle with an eye to testing it as an antitorpedo torpedo. The CAV-X had been dynamically simulated and then "in-water test-bedded," as Pirrell said, there in Newport. In two years they'd fired it three times. Twice the vehicle had self-destructed. The third time it had run, but in an erratic corkscrew that ended by burying itself in the mucky bottom of Newport Harbor. The development team thought lengthening the body would stabilize it, but the program had been run in parallel with a high-power fuel/oxidizer combination being developed for a prospective Air Force antisatellite missile. When Congress terminated the Air Force program, funding for the Navy research had been insufficient to continue. Meanwhile, the undersea warfare community had focused on reducing signatures and using advanced digital signal processing to detect enemy subs early, so torpedo countermeasures were less urgent. Like so many other projects, it had been boxed up and shelved.

"Okay," Dan said. "What I'm hearing is, the Russians have put together various pieces of technology, some of which we might've developed, to build a two-hundred-knot supercavitating torpedo. But we don't have anything like it, or any program to develop one. Correct?"

Neither scientist seemed to relish his summary. "It's not exactly our choice, Commander. We can propose areas of research, but our funding points us down certain avenues and away from others. The Shkval has come up at interagency meetings. We have a foreign technology tracking program. But when the director proposed test-bedding something of our own, as recently as four years ago, PMS-415 downplayed it. And you may disagree, but they have sound reasoning behind that decision."

"How so?" Henrickson said.

Pirrell went to the whiteboard. "This is no wonder weapon. It sounds scary, but when you look closely, it's less intimidating. It's fast, but it goes deaf and blind inside that bubble as soon as they fire it. Finally, power density's a critical limiter. As it always has been with torpedoes. Even with low drag, pushing metal through the water that fast takes an incredible amount of thrust. Even with hydroreactive metal gas generation—that's what we think the Russians are using—that means, short range."

"How short?" Henrickson asked.

"We estimate Shkval at less than three thousand yards."

"And we know this, how?" Dan asked.

The door cracked an inch or two; they all went silent.

It opened the rest of the way, and a captain in dress blues came in. He looked as if he'd just come from having his official picture taken. Dan started to get up, then noticed none of the others rose and sank back. "Gene Boscow," said Chone. "ONR. He asked to sit in, that all right? He chairs Antimine Weaponry now, but he dates back to the CAV-X project Charlie mentioned."

ONR was the Officer of Naval Research, which funded and administered the various labs, centers, and universities that developed technologies for the Navy. "I don't remember, I wasn't there, and I lost the T-shirt," Boscow said, shaking hands around the table. "We digging that up again? What's the occasion?"

Dan said, "Dan Lenson, sir. From TAG, Little Creek. We're trying to get smart on supercavitating vehicles."

"Lenson? You said Lenson?"

"Yes, sir."

"*Horn?*"

"Her CO."

Boscow nodded, lips pushed out. "Heard of you. Sounds like you managed to—well. I guess that's beside the point, here. Supercavitating vehicles? I'd try Yurly Savchenko, in Kiev."

"Well, he doesn't work for us, sir." When they were seated again he asked Boscow, "So you were on the CAV-X project? Why didn't that work, Captain?"

"It *did* work." Boscow sounded surprised. "Though we had vehicle control issues—how to stabilize the bubble cavity, how to vector the flow for low drag. We didn't have vectorable nozzles then. Not small enough to go on a torpedo. So we were limited to fins, and whenever the fin pierces the bubble, there's an area we couldn't dynamically model—we didn't have the computational capacity then to model turbulent flow.

"We finally figured out the corkscrewing was due to the tail hammering back and forth from one side of the cavity to the other. We had plenty of power with the TM-382—a neat little dual-thrust engine we could siphon gas off of to feed the cavity—but we sized everything for that thrust regime, and when motor development got zeroed out we couldn't go to a lower-power unit with that diameter body of rotation. The project rolled up its eyes and died."

Henrickson pressed, "But you could have made it work?"

Boscow shrugged. "The Russians did."

Dan asked why ONR and NUSC hadn't thought a superfast weapon worth pursuing. Boscow said, "Well, a rocket-propelled supercavitator, take away the glamor, it's really nothing but the old Mark 45 Astor—fast, straight-run, nuke warhead—except louder and shorter-range. Today, the main use we see for something like the Shkval is in antisubmarine scenarios."

They discussed how the weapon could be employed. Boscow said the main effect would be in a radical compression of the time available for the decisionmaker's detect-to-engage sequence—or as he called it, DLAK, for detect, localize, attack, and kill. "The loop execute time goes down to maybe a minute and a half total, instead of seven to eight minutes. The major advantage for the guy who has it, if he's being attacked, he can turn the tables, especially if your round is wire-guided, which most all of our weapons now are."

Dan understood that; Mullaly had said much the same back at TAG. "Okay, but that's all sub on sub. What about surface ships?"

Pirrell said, "The original Henschel design, the HS 294, was an antiship weapon."

Chone said, "As far as I can see, the only time a superfast straight-runner gives you an advantage is when you have the drop on the surface platform. Either that, or against a technologically sophisticated enemy that can jam or decoy homers."

Dan rubbed his face, remembering the Korea Strait, the wake-homing torpedoes no one had thought the enemy had until ships had started exploding. He didn't want to face a homer that ran at two hundred knots and couldn't be decoyed. "Okay . . . thanks for backgrounding us. But we're getting to the tough part. And, like they say in the movies, this can't go outside this room."

He waited until they nodded. "I can't address sources. But we have intel the Russians have solved the homing issue."

Pirrell sat up straighter; Chone, who'd been polishing his glasses, stopped. Boscow narrowed his eyes and whistled. "How?"

"That's what we don't know."

"What we thought you could tell us," Henrickson put in. "At least, if it's possible. Because if it is, our tactical assumptions change radically."

The scientists looked at each other. "I guess they would," Chone said.

"It would be fearsome then," Boscow said. He was patting his pockets as if looking for a cigarette.

The discussion went technical. Dan was fascinated at how they all seemed to drop their personalities and, moving up to the table, before long were so deep in impedance of supercavitating flows, sensor topology, wavelet theory, and parameter extraction that even Henrickson looked nonplussed. They seized paper and begin scribbling equations, or drawing rough supercavities with variously shaped bodies within them. At one point Boscow seemed convinced that a partially supercavitated body that trailed a flexible stinger might be able to register enough of a return sonar pulse that acoustic homing was possible, but Chone showed him he was wrong.

Pirrell was arguing for what he called "heterodox" solutions. "The high vehicle speed and bubble noise rules out any kind of acoustic guidance. Even water-based guidance: V sub I in a dense medium's too slow to keep up with the update rate. Thus, we're forced to conclude it has to be guided by a non-water-based system."

"Wire guidance? I don't think so."

"Maybe electromagnetic?"

"Translation?" Dan said.

"Radio-controlled," Henrickson said.

"I got that, damn it. But what about the sensors? Are you saying the sensors are offboard?"

"Possibly," the younger scientist said, but his tone was cautious. "Can't you give us anything more to work with?"

He hadn't mentioned the Admiralty, but he didn't think that had any bearing on the technical aspect. Chone and Boscow were raising their voices now, pushing equations back and forth. He raised his, too. "Uh, Chandra . . . Doctor Chone?"

"I told you—no, you'll still have to pierce the interface. And anytime you do that, there's instability in the reentrant jet intensity—yeah?"

"Uh, the impression I'm getting here—"

"Is that we'll need some time to study the question."

"Is that you don't know?"

Chone smiled condescendingly. "It's not that we 'don't know.' In most technical matters, Commander, once you know something can be done, you're halfway to doing it yourself. My opinion is, your most likely possibility is some kind of simplistic acoustic guidance."

"How would that work?"

The older scientist turned a sketch for him to see. "Two fold-out vanes near the base of the vehicle. Passive transducers on the tips. A rocket jet puts out mainly high frequency sound. If the transducers are carefully tuned, enough low-frequency signal might come through that they could pick up a carrier's screws. The vehicle travels at a constant depth, so all it needs is left-right homing, bang-bang, down the middle to the target."

"They wouldn't be at the base," Boscow put in. "Tail fins would be right in the flow. They'd have to be on canards, up front. Unless you want a tail boom—"

"It won't have a *tail boom.* Supercavity closure means a reentrant jet—"

"Captain, we've heard from Dr. Chone and Dr. Pirrell. How would you guide this thing?" Dan interrupted. "Any other possibilities?"

Boscow squinted. "We've played around on paper. Penn State, the Applied Research Lab, I mean. Wire guidance, or fiber optic, but there's that fucking jet back there. Or, have the weapon sense the magnetic field of the target, like a magnetic mine. But that's effective only at very short ranges—fifty to sixty yards. The local fields of the weapon itself, its own steel and electrical currents, are much more powerful than the external field you're trying to pick up."

Chone stretched in his wheelchair, so thoroughly Dan heard his spine pop. "To really answer your question, Commander? We can argue over how it could be done, but bottom line, we're just speculating. If we actually knew how it was guided, OPNAV could set money aside to evaluate it. NAVSEA would task us, 415 or 404 would manage us, and we'd emulate it in the Weapons Analysis Facility. Reverse engineer from that, then breadboard a countermeasure. But we need details. Plans, circuit diagrams, programming, sensor specifications. Best of all—"

"A complete round."

Chone smiled. "Exactly. Best of all."

THERE didn't seem to be much to add to that. Pirrell offered to take him through the Weapons Analysis Facility, where he watched a disconcertingly intelligent Block III ADCAP Mark 48 warhead track a virtual Chinese Xia-class sub under twenty feet of ice. They "saw" everything the warhead saw, watched every decision it made; as far as its computer knew, it was two hundred feet down in the deep Arctic. It made him wonder how much of what he himself thought was authentic, unquestionable, might be only illusion. That took an hour, then they had tomato soup and sandwiches in Building 990. "Let's head on out of here," Dan muttered when the scientist went back for a refill on his Coke. Henrickson hesitated, but finally nodded.

They stopped on the way to the gate to look at the bay and the great spidery bridge that vaulted across it. The Narragansett glittered in the noon light, a gray-green expanse that made Dan wish he was sailing now.

THE grass on Warden Field was greener than he remembered it; the sky, the hill-walled Severn even lovelier. The steady bass thud of the Naval Academy Band echoed from the walls of the alumni auditorium as the first glittering of the oncoming parade swung into view.

He hadn't come back to Annapolis that often over the years. Walking through the Yard with Blair on his arm, memories surfaced. When he'd walked these bricks as a mid, women had been a mystery, a yearning, seen only on weekends or when you went home on leave. Now on the carefully tended walks young women marched in dark blue, their faces as serious as those of the men.

"Did you ever think, when you were here, there'd be women?" his wife asked.

"Never crossed my mind. And if it had, I'd have hated the idea."

She grinned. "Changed your opinion?"

"Worked with too many of 'em to think they're not just as good as the guys."

In her heels Blair was taller than he was. Her hair was shining blond and she slouched, even standing. He'd met her in the Persian Gulf, when she'd been the chief adviser to the Senate Armed Services Committee. Now she was undersecretary of defense for personnel and readiness in an administration as unpopular with the military as any had ever been. Which puzzled Dan, as she seemed to spend most of her time fighting for better pay, better housing, increased readiness . . . though she didn't automatically believe the latest and greatest missile or radar was worth any price. When she got angry, people got out of her way. He'd seen her intimidate four-star generals. She'd turned that emotionless logic on him a couple of times, and he didn't relish it happening again. But she didn't hold a grudge, and when they argued, making up made it worth staying.

Now they stood in the VIP stand with the generals and admirals Blair outranked, the Commandant and the reviewing officer holding the salute as the guns boomed, making babies scream in the stands, dogs bark, and dozens of car alarms go off at once. Amid their discordant wailing the steady thud . . . thud . . . thud of the battery was like the heavy dull strokes of a sledge.

Then young voices echoed high in the cool air. "Pass . . . in. . . . review." And a leatherfaced Marine next to Dan muttered the irreverent parody passed from generation to generation: "Piss . . . in . . . your . . . shoes."

With a renewed blare of brass and crash of drums the march-past began. Dan stood at attention as the Brigade went by. From here he couldn't smell dust and crushed grass, gun oil and sweat-soaked wool, but he remembered them. And how simple Duty had been, when he'd been one of the marching thousands. How clear and clean everything had seemed.

"What are you thinking?"

"Just that I thought it'd all be different."

"The Navy? Life?"

"Everything." He blinked at the bright faces trooping by. They put the women at the end of each company, or maybe it was just that they tended to be shorter, so they ended up in the rear rank. There were a lot of female stripers, though; the Brigade Commander was a stocky brunette the PA system announced was from Montana. "It makes you think, coming back."

"Would you like to, really? To teach, or on the staff? That could be a nice assignment."

He told her maybe, but to *please* not try to help him in any way. "I'll take what I'm assigned."

"Dan, believe me, if you don't ask for what you want, you will not go far."

"At this point, I don't think it makes a difference in my promotability."

"Are you kidding? With a Congressional?"

"My record's not held in my favor in most quarters," he told her. "There are a lot of people on those boards who don't think I ought to get another command."

"By which you mean, another ship. But there are better opportunities than another ship, Dan."

"Maybe. But that's what I want."

He heard the stubbornness in his voice. She looked unhappy or angry, too, and to break the mood he put his arm around her. Leaned to brush her cheek with his lips. Then remembered he was on the Academy grounds, and she was a four-star equivalent, and a marine general was watching them; he let the arm drop. She didn't seem to notice. She was looking at the Homecoming schedule he'd printed out for her. "Feels funny not having an aide to tell me where to go next . . . okay, so six P.M.'s the dinner, with the guys from your old company. Then the dance, and tomorrow's the game."

He smiled. Her tone said she'd accepted what he'd said. Maybe not agreed, but accepted it. "Yeah," he said. "Tomorrow's the game."

IT was a close one, against Rice. Navy trailed from the first quarter, rallied after the half, then scored two touchdowns in quick succession to win. The stadium had been quiet during the first half, but wound up till by the end they were all on their feet and screaming, even Blair. When they finished singing "Navy Blue and Gold" and were filing out he grinned. "Never saw you this excited over a game."

"It was a good one."

They went to the class dinner in King Hall and for once no one near them was obnoxiously drunk, or wanted to start a food fight. She looked lovely and he wanted her. By the time they got back to the hotel he couldn't keep his hands off her, and she had her hand in his trouser pocket. As soon as the door was closed they were tearing each other's clothes off.

The main event was over and they were lying tangled together when the phone rang. She grimaced. "How do they always know?"

"Well, they were a little late this time." He untangled himself and got it, then hesitated, unsure how to identify himself in an unofficial environment. Jeez, maybe he'd been in the Navy too long. Said at last, "Uh— Lenson here."

"Dan? This is Captain Calvin Carroll Hines. SURFLANT N2?"

Dan knew Hines from e-mail exchanges. Code N2 was Surface Force

Intelligence, deputy for Admiral Olivero, commander of Surfaces Forces, Atlantic. Olivero was Captain Mullaly's immediate senior, which made Hines the representative of his boss's boss. "Yessir. What can I do for you, Captain?"

"I'm not interrupting? Saw you at the game and figured you'd be staying here. Got a minute? Can you come down to the bar?"

Across the bed his wife was getting up. Dan eyed her nude buttocks, her long tapering legs as she bent to pick up clothing. The shine of moisture where he'd just been. How could any man leave something like this? How could he want to go to sea again?

"Commander?"

"Be right down, sir," he said into the phone.

THE bar was modern and intimate, and was packed with alumni catching up. He stood in the doorway until an older man gestured him over. He was in slacks, a sports shirt, and a blue N-star Academy sweater.

"Beer?"

"A Coke, thanks."

They discussed the game first, Dan wondering what this was about but figuring the intelligence officer would tell him when he was ready. The ambient noise was deafening, though, and got worse every time the TV showed a clip from the game. Finally Hines suggested they take a walk.

"Sir, is this official? My wife's upstairs. We don't get much time together—"

"The deputy undersecretary? Wouldn't want to keep you two apart." The captain gave no clue how he meant this, though. "Yeah, official. Just a couple minutes. It's the high-speed torpedo issue."

Dan figured this meant the Shkval. Outside, they headed toward the lights of the nearby mall. Not a star was visible above them. He remembered when this had been green fields. Hines said, "On the tasking? There was a working group, Navy/DIA/Commerce/Defense Acquisition Agency, to coordinate how we go about meeting it."

"Uh, TAG hasn't passed that to me yet."

"The decision points are in Mullaly's in-box. Short version: Since Shkval-K's being advertised for export, Commerce suggested we were making this harder than it had to be. Maybe the Russians would sell it to us, if we offered a deal—say, a joint venture to manufacture Shkvals for the USN."

"You mean, just buy it?"

"Sometimes that's the easiest way."

"Well, that sounds reasonable," he said cautiously. "Do you think they'd go for it? This is supposed to be the most advanced weapon they have."

"They need the cash. It's worth a try."

"I, uh, I assume we wouldn't actually be putting Russian weapons in U.S. tubes? The safety issues—"

Hines waved that away. "We'll get Lockheed or Hughes to safe up the design, then charge us ten times as much. But that's many exits down the pike. Right now we're just talking about buying five or six for testing and evaluation."

"Uh, exactly who at Commerce suggested this? I know some of those folks from when I was at the NSC."

"All we got was the minutes and actually just our part of that. Well, the Russians put millions of dollars into this thing. Like you say, it might not be designed to NATO standards, but hey, it works. And Commerce says the more we buy from the Russian Federation, the more they can buy from us. That'd make their constituency happy."

"From what I saw in the White House, we're too eager to sell certain things," Dan said.

"Above our pay grade, son. I've talked to the development shop at SUB-LANT. Consensus, not only would we remove a threat to the carriers, our subs could use something like this hunting diesel boats in shallow water. Get a one-ping solution and clobber them at close range."

"Whatever. So, Commerce is going to buy it?"

Hines waited till a teenage couple buzzed past on motorbikes. "No. *They* don't want to get involved. They want *us* to buy it. From the Ministry of Defense."

Dan waited for the punch line. But apparently this wasn't a joke, because Hines went on, "CNO's willing to commit funding from his acquisition pot. So, rather than whatever Norm had you set up to do, Admiral Olivero wants us to try to get to this system legally first. You're already backgrounded. And as it happens there's a major arms exposition opening Monday. Day after tomorrow." Hines gave it a beat, then added, "Short notice, I know. But working at TAG, you're used to travel, right? We had our office cut the paperwork."

They stopped by a dark blue Mercury. Hines glanced around the lot, then popped the trunk and came up with manila. "Orders, tickets, a briefing package—you can read in on the plane. An invitation from the Russian Federation state corporation for military export. It's not made out to you by name, but it does invite the U.S. to send a rep, in case there's any question on their end. Who you can call up at the Building to work out the contractual end, if you get that far on the first visit. Which you probably won't, so don't sweat it.

"We don't expect you to come back with a finished deal, all right? Just talk to them, let 'em know we're interested, but only if it's reasonable—don't act like we're hot for this thing, they'll triple the price. Your assistant, we overnighted his package yesterday. But they said you'd be at the game this weekend, and since I was going, too . . . the personal touch . . . flight's at zero-seven tomorrow. So actually that works out, you can go right to BWI from here."

Dan hefted the envelope—it was heavy—then tucked it under his arm. He was still trying to get his head around the switch in direction. Hines wheeled back toward the hotel. "Any questions?"

He'd already planned his week, and it hadn't included travel. But everything else Hines had said made sense. Especially the part about it being easier to buy what you wanted, than get it under the table. "Well, this is sudden, like you said, sir. But I guess we can give it a try. Uh, you never said where exactly I'm going?"

"Didn't I? ARMINTEX—the International Armaments Exhibition. In Moscow."

Dan stopped at the hotel entrance. "Wait a minute. I thought San Diego, or Toronto, but—we've got to be in *Moscow* Monday? And I'm leaving tomorrow morning?"

"Not a problem, is it?"

He tried to recall how many pair of socks and underwear he had with him. "Uh, I don't have uniforms—"

"Not a problem. You'll be representing us in civvies," the captain said. He added, "Enjoy your evening." Then turned back once to call, "Remember, zero-seven tomorrow. And my very best to the undersecretary."

II

PLAN A

4

Moscow, Russian Federation

T HE oversized, full-color Komponent brochure, no, more like a
magazine, had been waiting on his bed when he checked in. But he
hadn't opened it. Not after eighteen straight hours in the air, or twid-
dling his toes in terminals. During the last leg in from Finland, just
before the doors closed, a party of drunken women had staggered
aboard the aircraft and loudly demanded his and Henrickson's seats.
Henrickson had shouted back in Russian, and after an argument that
had nearly come to blows the harridans had moved on forward, pausing to scream back abuse. They'd kept drinking all during the flight,
and from time to time, along with an alarming creaking from the wings,
screams and the crash of breaking glass had ripped back through the
smoky air.

They'd checked in at 0300 local, so tired he'd barely registered the little
beige cube of a room, just spotted the rack and stripped and fallen onto it.
In no time it seemed his watch had gone off. Now he flipped through the
brochure in the gray light from the grimy window that comprised one
wall, trying to glean the salient points as he stepped into slacks and
pushed his feet into shoes.

The three-day International Armaments Exhibition showcased the latest technical developments for sea, air, and land forces. It billed itself as
"most prominent and greatest European event in the field of ensuring national security." Three hundred companies from fifty regions of the Federation and twelve foreign countries were participating. The schedule
included seminars and round tables, presentations on doing business in
the new Russia, press conferences, and demonstrations. The coordinating authority was the Russian Federation State Corporation for Armaments Export and Import. A long list of new designs were listed for sale.

Dan noted nearly all were Russian. They included tanks, infantry fighting vehicles, small arms and artillery munitions, a new armored airborne fighting vehicle—he guessed this meant one designed to be air-dropped—and the list went on.

He found naval systems: fire control radars, missile systems, and the Shkval-K "high-speed underwater missile." He dropped his already-tied tie around his neck and two-blocked it as he read.

High-Speed Underwater Missiles

The underwater speeds of water-to-water missiles exceed the speeds of any known torpedoes for many times. This is reached by sharp drag reduction due to optimum body profile and the usage of high effective missile motors.

We offer production know-how for the development of assembly units of high-speed underwater missiles including propulsion systems. The missiles can be manufactured in different sizes and adapted easily to a variety of different launch platforms; surface ships, submarines, and other carriers. The operational readiness of stored missiles kept in launches is maintained. The missiles offered for the development will possess the high accuracy of damage because of disability of target-ship to carry out antimissile manoeuvre. The known antitorpedo defensive system are not effective against high-speed underwater missiles.

High kill capability of missiles achived by the combination of several factors including power warhead. We offer not only propulsion system licenses, assembly unit licenses, but also technical help, advices including the development and supply of test missiles, and instruments needed for their prestart installation.

We are ready to discuss the proposals for joint-venture production of missiles within laws accepted at the international market.

"You ready?" Henrickson's balding pate poked in from the adjoining room. "We missed the opening ceremony."

"I don't think that counts as a major loss, Monty. I need coffee. And the Shkval demonstration's not till this afternoon."

"Maybe not, but we should get over as soon as we can. Meet up with this guy Dvorov."

Dan pulled on his suit jacket. He wedged passport, wallet, visa, and a xerox of the official letter from Rosvooruzhenye in the inside pocket. He checked his other pockets. Camera, handheld, his official TAG cards identifying him as the Director of Special Projects. "I'm ready. Let's pull chocks."

"Uh, before we go. Slight problem. Well, not exactly a problem. But it could become one."

"Focus, Monty."

Henrickson blinked, then pointed to the ceiling. Dan stared at him. Monty cupped a hand to one ear like someone listening.

"What are you—oh. Sorry, I didn't get any sleep on the plane."

"Care to step into my room?"

"Sure."

Henrickson's was as shabby and cramped as his own, like an Eastern European version of a Super 8, but the analyst's bed was made up with hospital corners. He pulled a soft-sider out from under it and oriented it to open away from the window. He glanced at the ceiling again. Dan thought he was being a little overdramatic. This was the new Russia, after all. But when he unzipped it and held it open, Dan blinked.

He reached for a pad by the telephone. Wrote, HOW MUCH IN THERE? THIRTY THOUSAND.

WHY $?

HELPS DOING BUSINESS HERE.

WHO SIGNED FOR THIS? WHERE'D IT COME FROM?

DON'T WORRY. I SIGNED FOR YOU.

"Jesus Christ," Dan muttered. He scrubbed a hand down his face. Started to speak, then grabbed the pad again. HOTEL SAFE?

PUT IT THERE IF YOU WANT. BUT THINK IT'S ACTUALLY MORE SECURE HERE.

He rubbed his face again, torn between what he'd do at home—in the unlikely event he found himself in a cheap hotel with a cubic foot of crisp new hundred-dollar bills—and what Henrickson was saying, which was that putting it in the hotel safe might mean saying good-bye to it. Finally he scribbled, OK, LEAVE HERE. He tore the pages out, hesitated, then tore out more pages, till he couldn't see the indentation of his printing. He tore the paper into scraps and went into the bathroom, feeling like a character in a spy film as he flushed. Just as Henrickson stood from beside the bed, someone knocked on their door.

When he opened it a tall, dark-haired man in a European-cut suit and silk tie held out his hand. His heavy chin looked both freshly shaven and stubbled dark. He smelled very good and his shoes gleamed. "Commander Lenson? Capitaine de Vaiseau Christophe de Lestapis de Cary, Marine Francaise. At your service."

"Uh, Capitaine? *Je regrette, monsieur, mais je ne vous connais pas—*"

Wincing, de Cary held out a letter. "As you see, I am part of your delegation. This must be Monsieur 'enrickson?"

Dan asked him to step in while he read. The letter was from the U.S. Department of Commerce to the Chief of Naval Operations, asking that a C. L. de Cary, French Navy, be attached to the Special Purchasing Delegation to the Russian Federation Ministry of Defense between the dates of 5 and 11 October. M. de Cary would be representing the Défense Conseil International, NAVFCO Branch.

He lifted his gaze to see de Cary examining the curtains with distaste. "They have not put you in a very good hotel," he observed. "I am at the Balchug-Kempinsky myself."

"I've been there," Henrickson said. "Swanky. What's that go for these days—about four hundred a night?"

"I am not sure. I simply sign for it."

Dan held his letter out. "Uh, sir, this is—awkward. This looks fine, but no one told me we were being joined by a third party. Let me talk to my compadre for a minute."

In the bathroom Dan muttered, "How did the *French* insert themselves into this? They're not even in NATO."

"I don't know. But it looks like a real letter."

"It's *real*, but it's from Commerce. We don't work for Commerce, Monty. Remember?"

"It's the same government."

"With all due respect, you've obviously never worked in the Pentagon."

"So, what? We blow him off?"

Dan snuck a look, saw de Cary peering out the window, holding the grimy smoke-smelling curtains carefully away from his suit. "We can't just blow him off. For one thing, a capitaine de vaiseau's pretty senior—I think that's an O-6 equivalent, our captain or colonel. And he's obviously got somebody in DC on his side. But rule number one's gonna have to be, we don't discuss anything sensitive in front of him. Till we can clarify just what the hell he's supposed to be doing with us."

DE Cary had a taxi waiting. At one point they were on an embankment along what Dan figured to be the Moskva River. The last time he'd been in Russia they'd flown into St. Petersburg aboard Air Force One, with a motorcade, an official reception, the works. Now here he was again, less posh, but still, a Mercedes taxi on his way to an international exhibition. Not bad for a kid from smalltown Pennsylvania.

Actually he was looking forward to it. Getting rights to this thing, so the labs could devise countermeasures, might save lives the next time the Fleet brushed up against a rogue state in the littorals. But his mood darkened as he contemplated a suitcase of cash signed for in his name, and a Frenchman who'd barnacled himself to them out of nowhere. He glanced at the capitaine, who was riding shotgun with the Chechen-looking driver. Though de Cary seemed like a nice enough guy. Even an aristocrat, if he was reading the name right.

The exhibition center's modernistic concrete was flaking. They followed the ARMINTEX CHECK-IN signs. Stood in line to enter a lavishly carpeted hall, showed their IDs. Dan's badge read that he was a member of the United States of America Delegation. De Cary's, interestingly enough, read the same, but the Frenchman pinned it on with aplomb. A buffet held breakfast pastries, a huge baked fish, coffee, chocolate, tea. Dan skipped the food and settled for coffee, craning around. He wanted to find their principal and set up a meeting.

PAVILION 1 was the biggest conference space he'd ever been in. The ceiling was high as a cathedral apse, and every square foot of the immense arena was both immaculately clean and looked new, which wasn't what he was used to finding in Russia. Avenues fully thirty feet across were spaced along sparkling tile floors. He trailed de Cary and Henrickson as they moved from display to display, each of which was labeled in Russian, English, French, Chinese, and Arabic.

A booth displayed rubber-armored frequency-agile infantry radios. Another, a massive missile battery that on closer inspection was inflatable, a dummy, to trick aerial or satellite reconnaissance. Next to it a Swedish company better known for its cars touted a system for instant identification and destruction of "targets" within densely populated urban neighborhoods. A Canadian company offered upgrades to aging MIG airframes to let them "identify and engage the most modern First World aircraft." A Swiss-Taiwanese partnership offered "fixed-site control centers" to "coordinate joint operations in expeditionary environments." Russian companies displayed "man-portable antiarmor systems" that showed soldiers in unmarked uniforms destroying U.S. Bradley armored personnel carriers.

Flickering screens showed missiles erupting, tanks charging, artillery bursts walking across desert, but never a hint of blood or wounds. Acronyms and buzzspeak spun across languages: UKMFTS, ITAR, JLCCTC, I/ITSEC, EO/IR, C5I, net-centric, federative algorithms, austere environments, next-generation visualization solutions. He examined stabilized optical sights, unguided rockets advertised as "easy to fire, hard to neutralize," high-mobility excavators, stabilized remote laser designators, training aircraft that could be converted to "counterinsurgency roles," artillery shells that offered "increased trauma-production capability," bomb after shell after missile, each promising ever increased mortality at ever lower cost.

He walked aisle after aisle. Smiling women served vodka, wine, and hot hors d'oeuvres at linen-covered tables. They handed out crystal paperweights, Cuban cigars, bricks of Swiss chocolate, even curved daggers shining with silver inlay and engraved with the names of arms companies. Hard-edged spokesmodels pirouetted on elevated platforms like lap dancers, brandishing black-stocked rifles with glowing reflex sights, pouting as they struck poses in the latest infantry load-bearing equipment.

Gradually his attention shifted to those around him who, less eye-catching than the vendors, were the reason they were here. They drifted from booth to booth. They seldom smiled back at the salespeople, who seemed to cringe as they displayed their wares. Though nearly all wore suits, their complexions and beards and the murmurs he caught made clear most of the putative customers were from east of Morocco and west of India, south of Russia and north of the Horn of Africa.

De Cary murmured beside him, "Pakistanis, Chinese, North Koreans, the Taliban—they'll sell to anyone with cash."

"Sometimes we feel that way about the French."

"Then you don't know the history of ITAR."

"I don't even know what it is."

"International Traffic in Arms Regulations. Look into who sells the most arms, year after year. You will find it is almost always the United States." De Cary seemed to rein in. "But we are never far behind. Yes, we are competitors. Still, in this issue of supercavitating weapons, we find ourselves on the same side."

De Cary told him supercavitation was classified as a dual-use technology, rather than military-only. "That gives both purchasers and vendors more latitude, under the ITAR regime. The other point is that we may have better contacts with the company we will be dealing with. The Russians always perceived you as the main enemy. It's hard for them to think of you as a customer. That's where I may be able to help."

"And you obtain the technology, too?" Dan asked him.

De Cary shrugged. "We provide our good offices; you provide funding. We both increase the security of our respective fleets."

He broke off, nodding to a small Asian woman who emerged from the crowd. They fell into French too rapid for Dan to follow, though he caught an occasional word.

THE Komponent booth was at the east end of the main avenue. It was neither the glossiest nor the shabbiest. Two statuesque blondes handed out brochures. He flipped through one. Unfortunately it was all in Russian. At the booth a screen displayed an animated image of a supercavitating vehicle being driven through the water. The gas cavity was a wavering spheroid of pink and red; the surrounding sea, dark blue.

He stood and watched the flow patterns coming off the stern and slowly realized this wasn't a cartoon, but the output of a computer-driven model. Especially when the body went into a slow, corkscrewing turn, radically distorting the cavity on the off-yaw side. The vortices coming off the thing aft made clear what Boscow had been talking about, how modeling turbulence was so difficult.

But if this was what it seemed to be, the Russians had solved that problem. Studying the roiling screen, he saw how the tail-yaw was counteracted as the body rotated. Plumes of gas, etched in green, flickered on and off in brief bursts. He stared, understanding for the first time, as opposed to all the theoretical discussion, how difficult this gas-veiled, high-speed dance really was.

"*Voi ponemaye kto vizu*?" said a voice behind him. Then repeated, this time in a succession of heavily accented languages, "*Verstehen sie? Comprenez?* You understand what you see?"

He turned to face a bulky, white-haired Russian in a black suit decorated with cat hair. From an orange cat, it looked like. His gaze climbed the suit to a puffy, spotted, unhealthy-looking face, hazel-green eyes magnified by thick lenses. "Uh—some of it."

"You are interested in high-speed underwater travel?"

"Yeah. Yeah, you could say that."

Whoever he was, this man had presence. Dan found it hard to break their locked gaze as his interlocutor waved toward the screen. "Is not classic Newtonian fluid. Around the body surrounding. Is what I call biphase flow regime. Where is both gas and fluid. In some ways behaves like gas, other ways like liquid. Interesting connection to methane venting at

sea. But that is other project. The difficulty here is to make sure gas cavity ever sheathes body of rotation. Where cavity is pierced, wetted surface
induces asymmetric drag. You following?"

"I follow, yes." Dan offered his hand. "You wouldn't be Yevgeny Dvorov,
would you?"

"Academician Dvorov, yes. Do I know you? You am English I think. Dr.
Bennett?" Dvorov adjusted black-framed glasses, trying to zoom in on his
name badge.

"No sir. My name's Dan Lenson. I'm from the United States. A letter was
sent in advance, setting up a meeting with you on behalf of our government. Approved by Rosvooruzhenye—if I'm pronouncing that right. I'm
hoping to set up an interview, discuss a contract for technology sharing,
perhaps even license production."

Behind the smudged lenses the overmagnified eyes slid away. Dvorov
was still holding his hand, in his big, soft, warm one, but something had
changed. "Dr. Lenson. That would be in Russian Daniel Leonartovich, no?
Ochyeen priyatna. Very good to meet. But you understand, this we are
speaking of here, originally very sensitive weapons technology. Highly
valued by CIS Government. You understand? But, United States? You said,
United States?"

"Yessir. I did. Uh, and France."

Dvorov shook his head, and this time Dan read his body language as
the opposite of welcoming, though his voice was still soft as his hands.
"We did not expect interest from this quarter. So advanced in all matters
of technology. Tell me more, Doctor. Your government wishes to license
production? Precisely, production of what? Or is this perhaps private entity, some big American company you represent?"

Dan wondered if this was the prelude to a high asking price. But what
"high" might mean to a post-breakup Russian scientist, well, that was
what he was here to find out. What was more puzzling, though, was Dvorov's obvious revulsion or suspicion. Maybe he should have let de Cary
make the first approach? Had he screwed up?

But this *was* Dvorov, the man Hines, and through him Admiral Olivero,
had sent him to see. He cleared his throat. "Well, that's what we have to
discuss, uh, Academician. What arrangements we might come to. Two
others with me would like to meet you, get to know you and your team.
One's from the French Navy. We'd have to see if we're in the same ballpark
in terms of price. And by the way, I'm not a doctor."

"In the ballpark—"

"If your price is not too high. You understand."

The old man's grip tightened; his eyes seemed to grow closer, larger. "And *you* understand this: government, Communist government, yes, but still representing Soviet people, put billions of rubles into development of extremely powerful weapon. Rubles poor Russian people did without spending. Now the West comes expecting, flea market, pick up valuable jewels for pennies. This advanced technology. Important weapon to challenge control of the seas. Yes, I can see how United States is interested."

"I hear what you're saying, sir. But—well, we'll have to talk it over."

But the Russian had stepped back half a pace. He spoke rapidly to one of the blondes, who turned instantly back to the booth. Dvorov's gaze skated over Dan, then flicked to the screen. "So first you see demonstration, no? On Moskva River tomorrow. Twelve o'clock, noon. High noon, eh? Important announcement afterward. Then we meet, yes. There could be expenses, however. Our time is valuable. Very highly educated personnel. Also to prove you are serious about negotiate, yes?"

"We can discuss meeting expenses," Dan told him. Yeah, this was a different style of negotiating. He looked around for Henrickson, even de Cary. But they were nowhere in sight amid the crowd.

"Maybe you have question now, while I am at booth. I do not come here long." At last the guy dropped his hand, leaving Dan's damper than was pleasant. He wiped it unobtrusively on his trouser leg.

The issue he wanted to know about was guidance, of course, but instinct warned him not to approach directly. So instead he asked about vectoring. Dvorov turned cagy. Pulling out a note pad and pencil, he got down into the weeds on nozzle design. This Dan knew was well-understood engineering, nothing new about it, but he listened and nodded at the right places. At one point Dvorov used a number that seemed familiar. Dan frowned.

"Uh, Professor? This gas you're using to thrust-vector—it's superheated steam?"

The Russian hesitated. "This is correct. You recognize?"

"Which means your power source is a metal-water reaction?"

After another hesitation Dvorov said, "I believe this information is no longer classified. Early in program we tried rocket motor but power density too low. You are correct. Reaction is aluminum and water at nine thousand degrees. Celsius—I can never remember what is your Fahrenheit. One thinks of both as inert at room temperature. But with molten metal and superheated steam, power yield higher than even strong explosives. We bleed off waste heat in steam to prevent meltdown of vehicle and warhead. Some of steam serves as working fluid for thrust vector."

What Dvorov was describing was what Chone and Pirrell had referred to as hydroreactive metal gas generation. Dan was getting a feel for this thing. It wasn't a mystery anymore, though it was still a long stride ahead of the torpedoes he was familiar with. Actually it was more like a missile than a torpedo, which was what the Russians had called it in their literature—an "underwater missile." He craned around again for Henrickson. He could use someone who spoke Russian. But again the passing faces were those of strangers.

"I assume there's a guidance wire aft," he said in a matter-of-fact tone. "To carry steering commands from the launch platform?"

Dvorov's gaze turned hostile. "A wire? No wire light enough to spool out could endure turbulence. There is no wire. Not even glass strand."

"Well, I've wondered how a weapon like this, impressive as it is, could be made more effective. The best way would be—"

"There are many ways to improve weapon," the Russian broke in. "Tomorrow we will tell you about one of them."

"What's that?"

"We have talked enough for now. American, eh? Interesting. That you should be so curious. You will be at demonstration, eh? Then we will talk about possibly a meeting. And expenses. For our time."

De Cary and Henrickson arrived from opposite directions just as Dvorov spun and stalked off. "Who was that?" Monty asked as he looked after the professor.

"The guy we're supposed to set up our deal with. Dr. Yevgeny Dvorov."

De Cary raised his eyebrows. "That was Dvorov? I've seen pictures of him. A lot younger then. But one says he never comes to these shows. Actually I was briefed that he was dying. Of the cancer."

"He has cancer?" Dan said.

De Cary blinked. "They didn't tell you?"

"Tell me what?"

"In 1961, Yevgeny Dvorov was an enlisted man on one of the first Soviet nuclear submarines. Her name was K-19."

Henrickson sucked in breath. "The one that had the reactor leak? The 'Widow-maker'?"

"He's fighting bone cancer. You should have been better briefed, Commander. What did he say? You talked?"

"Just a couple minutes. He didn't say much."

"Is he open to a deal?"

Dan was still pondering. The former crewman of a Soviet submarine, who'd seen so many of his shipmates die . . . yeah, he might feel strongly about selling a new weapon to his former adversary. Maybe that was what he'd picked up on.

"No," Dan said, looking back over the immense carnival of the wares of death. "He didn't really say that. Not in so many words. But he invited us to a demonstration."

5

THEY found a decent restaurant not far from the Mir, and agreed over dinner it wouldn't be a late night. Dan set his alarm for seven, hoping to get his body clock on local time. Then he lay awake for hours, replaying the scene at the exhibition. There'd been something off in Dvorov's attitude. It had happened after he'd said he was an American. Should he have just handed de Cary the ball and stepped back? At last he told himself to stop. Tomorrow would answer all his questions, and usually whatever he dreaded didn't happen. Or at least, happened differently than he ever anticipated.

He woke to a banging on the door and the realization he'd slept through the alarm. And that he was due to meet with the assistant U.S. naval attaché in half an hour. He'd decided it might be smart to touch base with the embassy, find out what they had to say about dealing with Russian companies in general, and Komponent in particular. He shaved quickly as Henrickson leaned against the jamb, translating the headlines from the morning paper. Fortunately the embassy was right across the street, and they got there only a few minutes late.

Al Siebeking was paunchy and combed his thin dark hair over. He took them through a security area, then upstairs to his office. He set them up with coffee in a conference room, then closed the door. "Lenson. Lenson. Know a fella named Greg Munro?"

"Uh—Munro. Yessir, met him when he was on the DESRON Twelve staff. Former enlisted, wasn't he? What's Greg doing now?"

"Oh, retired—he does some kind of valuation agency out on the West Coast, appraises old armor, that kind of stuff. But we stay in touch. I mentioned I was meeting you and he said to say hi. Guess you made an impression, whatever you and he did together. Which I gathered I wasn't supposed to ask. How can I help you fellas? I did get an e-mail from Admiral Olivero's staff, by the way. He said you're approaching Dvorov. Subject: Shkval."

"Basically correct, sir," Dan told him. "NUWC's aboard, ONR's aboard, the tasking's out of the CNO's office."

"And you boys are from TAG." Henrickson nodded and Siebeking looked thoughtful. "Aiming to, what? Buy it?"

"If possible."

"Manufacturing rights?"

"Well, sir, that hasn't been decided yet. This is sort of a fact-finding mission, so far, at least." Dan debated telling him the ultimate goal was the guidance system for the K variant, but decided not to. He might be out of bounds even telling him this much.

"It's almost an intel mission, then."

"I guess there are elements of that. But our direction's to keep everything legal."

"Considering the state of the country right now, anyway," Henrickson put in.

Dan nodded agreement. "So we thought it was worthwhile to touch base with you."

Siebeking tented his fingers, then began explaining what not to do when trying to do business in the CIS. "The essential thing to remember is, yeah, everything's murky right now—not least to the Russians themselves. It's supposed to be this new era of openness and free enterprise. But the only people in the USSR who ever had any savvy at making a buck were the *blatnye*—the thieves. And the only fellas who were really organized were the KGB. So it's hard to tell, and somebody else might see it the other way around, but what we might actually be witnessing is a slow takeover by the Russian Mafia of the security apparatus. The KGB was officially disbanded, but most personnel lateraled into this new FSB—the Federal Security Service, it translates as."

"Commerce pointed us at something called Rosvooruzhenye—if I'm pronouncing that right."

"They're Ministry of Defense. But stay tight with them. Don't go wandering off, like to some private company, offers you a good deal on the side."

"Actually we're talking to an outfit called Komponent."

"That's how we get to Dvorov, right? Now, that's a name I know. The fella who basically invented the Shkval, I heard. Former submariner. Former engineer captain, first class. Now a member of the Academy of Sciences."

"I'd been told that," Dan said. "That he started in subs, I mean."

"After he retired he worked for the Rubin bureau. Submarine weaponry. Komponent's his new outfit. Him and a couple of *former people*, like they're

calling the ex-Communists now." Keys clicked and Siebeking's printer went
to work. "I'll hard copy you what we got on them. It's export oriented. Interesting, though, to date most sales are not to what we'd call the West."

"China? Korea?"

"Uh, don't have specifics. You might find more behind the green door,
but we try to keep the diplo/intel firewall in place. Not that we don't look
around when we can, but the attaché function's divorced from the spooks
these days. Understand?"

"I understand and fully agree," Dan said. "Stay as far away from them
as you can." Siebeking nodded and handed him inkjet pages, separated so
they wouldn't smear.

Henrickson said, "Any advice on dealing with these people?"

"Well, watch out for shakedowns. Just about anybody you talk to here,
they're going to have their hand out. Fella from Lucent was trying to buy a
new battery technology. He paid two hundred thousand dollars and got
absolutely nothing. Turned out the guys he was meeting with had no connection to the ones who actually developed the batteries. He never saw
them again. Or his two hundred K."

"Yeah, but this is the Defense Ministry," Dan told him.

"And what I'm saying is—this is all off the record, okay?—it's like every
year there's less of a membrane between the government and the crooks.
It's like a carnival midway out there right now. Want the Moskvoreskji
Bridge, cheap? Just let the word get around. There'll be a knock on your
door at dawn. Be *very sure* who you're dealing with. Cover everything
with paper. It'll take more time, but at least you'll have your ass fire-
proofed when the deal goes up in flames."

Siebeking's phone rang; he excused himself for a few seconds, during
which Dan asked Henrickson, "What do you think? He can't be talking
about the same people we are."

Henrickson shrugged.

Siebeking hung up. Looked at his watch. "Okay, what else can I do for
you?"

"Well, we've been invited to a demonstration."

"This the one on the river? At noon?"

"Correct."

"I've been invited, too." The attaché looked around for his cap. "Need
a ride?"

TO the south rose the iconic spires and domes of the Kremlin. A parking
area—it looked like a ferry stop—was solid with cars. The air was crisp,

and Dan turned up his coat collar as they got out and the wind hit them.

They looked from the embankment down twenty feet at a gray slowly eddying river a quarter mile wide, and on it, a very large double barge rig. One barge, perhaps a hundred feet long by fifty beam, was freshly painted in bright green. White awnings screened scores of spectators. The other, smaller barge was moored about twenty yards outboard, and technicians in bright orange coveralls moved about it with purposeful concentration.

A metal gangway slanted down from the embankment to the spectator barge. At its head two broad-faced men in black overcoats and black leather gloves checked passes. Dan, Henrickson, and Siebeking tailed on to the queue. The wind off the river was even more bitter than it had been in the lot. Dan caught a familiar face above a medium-blue uniform top-coat, and waved.

De Cary saluted with a flick of a white glove. "Good morning."

"Capitaine." Dan caught sight of what he carried, and grimaced, realizing he'd forgotten his own. "See you brought your camera."

"Me, too," said Siebeking.

"I'll be happy to share the photographs. We are all on the same team here."

"Works for me," said the attaché.

The barge smelled of paint and old fish, but the buffet made up for it, though the wind kept snuffing the flames in the chafing dishes. The menu leaned to Asian cuisine. Few of the spectators, muffled beneath overcoats and mufflers, partook. The Stoli booth, though, did a brisk business, the bartender dispensing shots by running the lip of the bottle down a meter-long rank of glasses, finishing the last with the final drop; then tossing the liter bottle into a bin with an ear-shattering clank, reaching for another, and going the other way left-handed. It was the most skilled and graceful performance Dan had yet seen in the whole country. The reek of raw alcohol reached him and he turned away. He didn't get the craving often anymore. Thank God. And when he did, there were ways to cope. He'd been doing it one day at a time so long now, there were whole weeks when he didn't think about a drink at all.

A video crew was setting up on the embankment. Amid shouts and the clatter of wind-tossed canvas the crew on the outer barge was snapping tarps off equipment, consoles, racks of compressed-gas bottles, a maze of piping around a ten-meter-long bronze gleam.

"Torpedo tube," Henrickson muttered. Dan turned to see if de Cary or Siebeking was taking pictures, and found himself face to face with a dark-skinned man in a gray topcoat it took him a moment to recognize.

"Commander Lenson."

"Uh, Captain . . . Khashar. Great to see you, sir."

The Pakistani took his hand, but with reserve. He and Dan had "co-captained" an ex-U.S. frigate years before, on its turnover voyage to the far East. They'd clashed on the bridge, and Dan had finished the voyage restricted to his stateroom. "It's, uh, great to run into you again, sir. Are you still in the Navy?"

"I'm now the deputy chief of naval operations. And you?"

"Oh, still in, yes sir. Congratulations."

The wind was growing bitterer. He and Khashar caught up as de Cary and Siebeking took pictures and Henrickson made notes. Then the techs moved to the far side of the barge and took off a last tarp, and Khashar moved away, and the rest of the spectators quieted and aimed binoculars.

"That's our baby," Henrickson muttered.

Dan frowned. The dull green taper was shorter than he'd expected; not much bigger than the lightweight torpedoes U.S. Navy ships carried. A white plastic or nylon split ring circled the tapered nose. Hard to judge its diameter at a distance, but as best he could estimate, maybe eighteen inches. Its skid was floored with small wheels, the same sort of transport cradle he'd seen in torpedo magazines. The rapid clicking of cameras sounded like a meadow full of crickets. Another video crew Dan hadn't noticed up to now gunned their boat's engine, out on the river, moving up on the barge, and were waved back by guards brandishing AKs.

To a shouted command, the techs put their shoulders to the skid. A second shout sent the cylinder gliding forward. The supervisor's fingers guided the white ring, which Dan guessed was a sabot, into the bronze tube. Foot by foot the vehicle was lost from sight, except for a cable. Dan squinted and murmurs rose behind him as the supervisor clipped this into a receptacle inside the door of the tube. A moment later the *whump* of the door sealing came to them.

"Wire guided," he muttered to Henrickson.

"Not necessarily. Could just be launching commands, swim-out power." The analyst blew on his hands and shivered. "See in a minute, I guess."

The test supervisor spoke into a radio. Shading his eyes upriver, Dan saw boats taking position, strung from shore to shore. About two miles north, where the Moskva took a bend to the right, a red flag fluttered from a third barge. He made out a white panel atop the black hull, no doubt to make it more visible to the distant spectators. As the banner stiffened in the wind, the guard craft wheeled and made for their respective banks. Aside from the target barge, the river lay empty.

Beside him Siebeking peered down, adjusting his Nikon. One of the men in overcoats pushed through the crowd distributing handbills. Taking one, Dan saw a layout of the test site and another diagram of the weapon itself. The latter was the same graphic Mullaly had shown him the first time he'd mentioned the Shkval. Turning it over, he ran his eyes down paragraphs of maladroit promo prose. There was also a diagram of the barge. It showed a heavy plate mounted from just above the waterline down to the turn of the bilge. It was marked *HY 80 30 CM.*

He frowned. HY 80 was a shipbuilding steel. High yield strength, 80,000 psi to be exact. It had been used in U.S. submarine hulls for years. And thirty centimeters was nearly a foot thick.

The black overcoats linked arms and began herding the guests away from the buffet. Some around the Stoli booth resisted, but were shepherded back toward the gangway. The crowd turned and began streaming up onto the embankment, Dan and his associates with them.

"Not a risk-free launch," Henrickson muttered.

"I'm thinking, this isn't the real thing," de Cary put in.

"What do you mean?" said Dan.

"That's not the Shkval. Can't be. It's only half the size."

"Demonstration vehicle?"

"Reduced scale. A test bed."

Dan had to admit, it made sense to demonstrate on a reduced scale, especially in the middle of a city. No Western capital would have permitted live ordnance testing smack in the middle of its downtown, where an errant turn could send a couple of tons of high-speed weapon up a slanted bank and down a commercial avenue. He looked around for Siebeking, but the attaché was gone in the crowd.

The audience spread out along the riverside, staring down at the launch barge. Which the techs, too, were leaving, jogging across a quickly lowered, bouncing gangway, taking their prospective customers' places near the buffet. Putting a few more yards between themselves and the launch platform. Where now only the supervisor, and one orange-suited tech remained, the latter at a stand-up console, the former a few feet aft of the tube, talking into a cell. Then he flipped it closed and stuffed it into a pocket. He swung himself onto the gangway and jogged shoreward.

A prolonged hooting came from the distant guard boats. The spectators fell silent. The orange-suited tech clamped on a hard hat, ear, and eye protection. He looked over his shoulder, down the river, then crouched. His arm moved once, to the right, then suddenly back to the left.

With a sudden deep thud, then a hiss of released air, the whole barge recoiled. A cloud of vapor shrouded the tube, cloaking but not quite obscuring the burrowing splash of something long and heavy wallowing deep into the river. The water closed again in a clashing swirl of foam. A half-ring of white plastic skipped across the surface, somersaulting through the air in slow motion. For a moment there was nothing more.

Then something ignited, deep below.

The light came up like a glowing apparition beneath the river, turning the chill gray a murky, tropical, opal-hued green. Within it a lance of pure white radiance burned beneath the Moskva. Dan felt heat on his cheeks and forehead, and only just kept himself from stepping back. Instead he leaned forward, straining his eyes for every scrap of information he could gather.

But the heat-pulse lasted only a second. The white-hot light began to move. Then from one instant to the next vanished, absorbed by the turbulent river as the angle between it and his gaze increased.

A creamy froth surged up, boiling and spiking queer peaked pyramids of water that blew apart, showering the barge. The wind picked up the spray and carried it over the audience, which recoiled from the river's edge, shouting and slapping at their coats and faces. Dan and Henrickson and de Cary stood without moving. He sniffed, trying to extract information from the mist, but it just smelled dank, like steam and river. No; there was an undertone. For a moment, almost like coffee beans. Then hot iron. Metallic? Or more like dirty old socks? It slipped away even as he sniffed again, the freshness of new sensation vanishing as nerve endings accommodated.

The spectators surged again, aiming cameras and field glasses up the river. Dan blinked through the spray. But so far, nothing. The river rolled on. The barge, the red flag stiff in the wind, the motionless boats, the distant golden spires, all were the same.

He lifted his Seiko and caught the sweep hand. A little over thirty seconds. He raised his eyes to the river, then returned them to the watch. He did this again, then lifted his head, and stared at the faraway barge.

A brilliant point ignited, so overpowering his legs dropped him into a hunch and his arms jerked up to shield his face. All he could think was: *nuclear*. De Cary flinched, too. Behind them others cried out as a double crack like the earth splitting rolled over the city and then echoed, rebounding from hundreds of buildings, and across the whole center of

Moscow birds whirled up crying·and darting as if to escape the sudden advent of an apex predator.

"Holy smoke," Henrickson muttered. "That wasn't RDX."

Dan straightened to see distant specks of debris raining down over a two-hundred-yard-wide circle, above which a white mushroom hearted with orange fire rolled upward. It lofted like a balloon till the wind took it, driving it off the river and off over the city, still rising, still milling, but rapidly thinning, so fast he suddenly grasped what it was: not so much smoke, though it contained smoke, as a cloud of superheated steam, condensing into microscopic droplets as it hit the cold fall air. And beneath it, behind it, no trace of the barge, the flag, the panel, whatsoever. Only that roiled foam, rocking and steaming.

A murmur ran along the embankment. As one, the faces, swarthy, dark, pale, turned back to the guest barge.

Aboard which, at a word of command, the techs stood aside. A middle-aged brunette with wind-blushed cheeks stepped to a microphone and began reading from a clipboard. Russian first, then what sounded like Chinese, Arabic, and other languages. She seemed to be fluent in them all. Then she got to English.

"You have just witnessed live demonstration of underwater missile weapons system. The warhead detonated is small demonstrator model. Full size 'Shkval' export model double this size with much larger warhead. Komponent Corporation offers underwater missile for sale or lease. Discuss with us terms. Full system is available with credits through special program Ministry of Defense.

"New announcements from Komponent, maker of advanced underwater weaponry for national defense. Shkval-K is armed with shaped-charge warhead designed to burn through submerged armor, backed with rods of depleted uranium as incendiary. You see effect of quarter-sized warhead on moored ship today. Full sized warhead will burn through one meter steel or five meters reinforced concrete, not counting fracture effect, with shaped charge penetrator permitting entry of uranium rods two meters long. These combust upon contact with air, water, or petroleum fuel. Optimally effective weapon against even the most difficult target at sea."

Beside him Henrickson sucked a breath, de Cary stiffened. A cold wave propagated up Dan's spine.

Depleted uranium was the heavy metal left over when fissionable isotope was extracted for use in weapons or reactors. Relatively inert radiologically, though there were those who disagreed, it was twice as heavy as lead. The U.S. packaged it in antitank rounds, in place of conventional explosives. When a "magic bullet" slammed into a tank, it, it burned its way through solid steel, then sprayed apart inside the turret in an inferno of phosphorouslike flame that ended any possibility of life.

But what she was describing wasn't a tank killer. This combination of speed, penetration, and terminal effect could only have been designed to penetrate the carefully crafted, highly classified combination of heavy underwater protection—mainly of HY-80, though other steels were used, too—and empty voids evolved over decades to protect U.S. Forrestal- and Nimitz-class carriers from torpedo attack.

Up till now, modern carriers had been so fast and maneuverable, well defended, and heavily armored, that nothing short of a wave of supersonic cruise missiles, or a nuclear weapon, could achieve a serious probability of kill. But being hit with three, or two, or maybe even one of these warheads—he'd have to run the numbers, discuss this with Monty—even the newest carrier would be crippled, if not destroyed from within by unquenchable fire and the toxic smoke and fragments that had made U.S. ordnance so effective against Saddam's tanks.

He tuned back in to the translator as she announced it was possible to upgrade existing contracts for earlier versions to the new K version, for only a modest additional sum. And that one customer had already done so. Dan wondered who. China? Iran? This was sounding worse and worse.

"We're gonna have to crunch some numbers on this thing," Henrickson muttered. "This could really be—this could really be something."

Dan just nodded, aware, as Henrickson probably was, too, of all the nearby ears. From the murmurs around them, the same conclusion was dawning on other minds. Minds not well disposed to America.

He stuffed the flyer into his pocket. Threading among the earnestly talking buyers, he plowed toward the gangway down to the barge. Behind him he heard de Cary. "Commander! Wait." But he didn't slow, just kept on. He got to the brow and was halfway down it before one of the overcoated heavies caught up. He shook the guy's hand off and kept going.

But not for long. Strong arms seized him. "Stop, you. Wait in line," one of them growled in his ear.

And it was true, a queue was forming. A sign-up line, it looked like. Aboard the barge the guys in orange suits were getting a chance at the vodka. They looked relieved as they tossed back shots. A few feet from the brow, flanked by more guards, stood several older men. One was Academician Dvorov.

De Cary, at his elbow. He murmured, "We operate carriers, too."

"Yeah?"

"I said, we operate large-deck carriers, too, Commander. In the same waters of the Mediterranean and the Middle East. What threatens your Nimitz-class ships threatens *Clemenceau* and *Foch*, and will shortly threaten *De Gaulle* when we commission the first non-American nuclear-powered carrier. This is as much a threat to us, as it is to you."

He looked at the Frenchman, understanding now exactly why he was here. The British had backed off fixed-wing carriers years before, going to the lower-capability, but cheaper, Harrier-operating ski-jumps they'd fought the Falklands War with. The Russians had almost gotten there, then their economy had fallen apart. The Italians, the Indians, Argentina, Spain, and a few other nations operated older, smaller classes; but only the U.S. and France fielded modern carrier task forces, able to travel great distances, defend themselves, and project air power inland from the sea.

Any possible enemy would love a weapon tailored to neutralize that capability.

Which explained the lengthening line behind them, a line that even involved some shoving. Looking back, he saw nearly every spectator in it. And looking forward, that he was being ushered forward, up to the waiting phalanx.

"Commander Lenson," said Dvorov dryly, before he had a chance to speak. "Have all your questions been answered?"

He cleared his throat. "A very impressive demonstration."

"Thank you. And now, as you see, we have others who wish to—"

"Yes sir; I do see. But I'd like to make some arrangement, that we meet privately."

"You wish to discuss a purchase?"

"I do."

"Then we can meet, yes, but I warn you, we will discuss details of purchase only. Not of the system itself. You pay the price, you receive what you buy. And not until then. And now, these others behind you—"

The overcoat beside him had his arm, but Dan shook off his hand. He felt as if he was about to step onto a hostile deck, sword in hand. He was taking a risk no one had ordered him to accept. "I don't know what else you expect of me, sir, but I just want to make an honest deal," he told Dvorov. "You've created something that doesn't exist anywhere else and we want it. In fact, I want exclusive rights."

This brought swift translation by the brunette and scowls from the others, but a surprised and, Dan thought, respectful look from Dvorov, as if he'd had one opinion of him and now had to revise it. "Exclusive?"

"We can pay you more than anyone else. And it would be to both our advantage. Think about ten years from now. All right? The Russian Navy will be back. It will go to sea again, strong once more. Is it to Russia's advantage to have a weapon like this in the hands of the Chinese? The Turks? What would this weapon do to your Typhoon submarines? Let's keep this between us. And maybe, the French."

The other Russians looked skeptical, but Dvorov didn't. The bushy eyebrows knitted. "You are serious? You have power to do this?"

This was the rub. He had no mandate for an exclusive buy. But face to face with what this thing could do, he had no doubt it was a brass ring worth trying to grab. Olivero would see it. Maybe Nicky Niles, too, though Dan had never been one of his favorite officers.

And Dvorov must have caught that hesitation, because he reached out. Slapped his shoulder and said gruffly, "You need time, eh? You wish you had asked me this before, eh? Well, right now we must talk to these others. But we will get together tomorrow, eh? I promise, I make no commitments until then. Marina, put Daniel Leonartovich down for tomorrow evening. To discuss a—*comprehensive* arrangement."

The soft hand came down on his shoulder again, Dvorov's gaze eased past him, and Dan stepped aside, looking behind him for de Cary, to tell him it was taken care of, he'd made their appointment.

He was standing by the rail when he saw a half-familiar face glowering behind the engineers, salesmen, translators, and goons around Dvorov. It must have been there all the time, but he'd been too focused on the scientist to notice.

He'd met Vice-Admiral Yermakov his last time in Russia. The reception had been at Petrodvorets, Peter the Great's "Great Palace." This time Yermakov looked sober, not reeling drunk; and now he was in civvies, a gray suit and silk tie, not Russian Navy blue and three-starred shoulder boards. But he recalled their conversation then, the vice-admiral's aggressive blustering.

Yermakov hated Americans. What was he doing with Dvorov? Was he part of Komponent now? And what did that mean?

He shook off sudden disquiet. He just had to push on, and hope he saw any cliff edges before it was too late.

De Cary, eleventh back between two excited-looking Middle Easterners. Dan jerked his head toward the shore. Looking concerned, the Frenchman followed him up the shaky, vibrating ramp, toward the attaché, waiting above them beside the embassy sedan.

6

H E spent the next morning sightseeing. He felt guilty about it, but there didn't seem to be anything else to do until the meeting that evening. Henrickson had gone to the embassy after breakfast, saying he wanted to get on their computers.

He'd always been interested in World War II history, so he went to a museum the Mir's concierge recommended. It turned out to be brand-new, just opened, a massive expanse of slightly uneven paving blocks surrounding Socialist-style statues and disquietingly abstract monuments. He wandered among the dioramas, but the place seemed grandiose and sanitized. It was also empty, aside from dispirited platoons of grade-schoolers.

When he'd seen enough he caught a taxi across town to the Armed Forces Museum. This was older and smaller, but more Slavically down to earth. Out front were parked tanks and missiles that when he'd first joined the Navy had been only blurred photos in binders with bright red plastic covers. They looked rusted and worn and small, and he remembered how each had seemed such a threat, with capabilities beyond what American industry could produce. The interior was packed with banners and displays, less glossy than the new museum, but the real thing. A toppled eagle from the Reichsakanzlerei. Captured Nazi weapons. He stopped at a display of human hair and mounted tattoos on human skin from a Polish village called Maidjanek. The Red Army had liberated the camp there on its way to Berlin.

He remembered another village in eastern Europe, and another massacre. Srebrenica. Now it was happening again, in Somalia, central Africa, the Sudan. Was hate and murder embedded in the human heart? For a time it had seemed humanity was making progress. Instead it had just learned to process mass death more efficiently.

Armageddon had started on a hot August day in 1914, and never stopped; just lumbered on through a century, an uncontrollable behemoth of war and revolution and terror. For a few years, after the Wall fell, its engine had fallen silent. Now the starter was grinding again.

He shook himself. He wasn't here to magnify the Shkval into a threat to sell countermeasures against. It was to keep an already developed weapon out of the hands of those who'd use it to wreck what little order existed.

He strolled down the boulevard toward the Kremlin. Walked through it, not entering any of the cathedrals or museums, feeling he'd better get back and see what Henrickson had turned up. He came out on the river embankment and turned south.

He was stalking along, stewing about how he was going to convince Dvorov to give up profits from selling his wonder weapon to half the rogue world, and how he was going to persuade the U.S. government to back his brainstorm, when a hiss grew at his back.

He spun, to watch a sharp prow peel up the river as it knifed past. It was followed by four bending and straightening backs, four close-cropped, sweat-soaked heads, four pairs of eyes that flicked to him, then refocused on that inner reality athletes saw during a supreme effort.

He shaded his gaze, watching as the crew went by. The shell was long and low, its gunwales centimeters above the surface. It was bright cherry red, like a hand-rubbed finish on a classic car. The rowers were all wiry, all in black and red Spandex and black tights. The cold didn't seem to bother them. They rowed like pistons. Dan couldn't see how they knew which way they were headed. He lifted his eyes to another razor prow, another torpedo-shape. The two shells were matching stroke for stroke, perfectly aligned as they sliced down the river. Their speed was astonishing, even given that they were moving with the current. He stood with hands in his pockets, admiring them.

"A coxless four," de Cary said, behind him. "Interesting."

"Capitaine! Uh, what did you say?"

"I said, it is a coxless four. A four-rower shell, with no *barreur*—no, ah—cock-swain? Yes, I think that's right."

" 'Cox'n', we pronounce it. You row?"

"I have done some time in double sculls. In Brest and elsewhere. And you?"

Looking up the river Dan saw there were other rowers out as well. "Looks like a fun sport. I sail, myself."

"You own a boat?"

"Actually I just bought one." He hoped she was all right; the marina manager had promised to keep an eye on her. "Going back to the Mir?"

"I don't stay at the Mir."

Dan said lamely that was right, he'd forgotten. They made arrangements to meet precisely at six at the address Dvorov had given them, shook hands, and parted.

HENRICKSON got back a little after he did. They were about to leave for lunch when there was a knock. Dan opened the door to find a well-built black guy in a close haircut, down jacket, jeans, and spanking-new bright-red running shoes. They stared at each other.

"Commander Lenson?"

"Yes. Who are you?"

"Gunnery S'r'n't Moale, sir. From the embassy."

Dan checked the proffered green ID. Moale was a Marine. "Come on in, Gunny. What can I do for you?"

Moale nodded to the sliding doors to Dan's balcony. "It's awful warm in here, sir. Don't you think?" For a moment Dan stared; then understood.

The wind was cold. Moale slid the door closed behind them and turned to face the railing, looking down on the street. Henrickson fluttered behind the glass like a captive butterfly. Dan turned up the lapels of his jacket. He didn't feel like leaning against a Soviet-era railing, four stories up, but stood close to it as he dared. "What's going on, Sergeant? I'm assuming something's wrong?"

"Hand-delivered message, sir."

Dan tore the envelope open, wondering what would happen if the wind got it. He held it firmly as he read. Moale moved a pace away, as if to be sure not to see the text.

There was no header and no salutation. All it said was SEE ME AT ONCE. DO NOT CONTACT DVOROV OR ANYONE ELSE FROM KOMPONENT.

"This is from who?"

"Captain S. At the Embassy? Wants to see you. Right away."

"Yeah, that's what it says. Just let me grab my coat."

WITH Moale at his side he got a swift pass through embassy security. Siebeking was on the covered phone when Dan came into his office. The first thing he said when he hung up was, "Where's that other guy who was with you?"

"Henrickson? Or de Cary?"

"Crap. Both, I guess—I forgot about the French guy. Sergeant!"

"I didn't, sir. Corporal Difilippantonio's over at his hotel now."

Siebeking nodded for the sergeant to leave. Dan waited till the door closed. "What's up, sir?"

"We have a complication. It seems that unknown to you, and unknown to me, too, up till about ten minutes ago, there's a parallel effort underway to yours. With the same target in mind."

"Uh-oh."

"Yeah. Uh-oh. Because you're overt, but they're not."

"That *is* bad. Who is it?"

"The covert effort's being run by Naval Intelligence and an allied secret service. You don't need to know more, okay? Obviously they compartmented you out, and me, too. Not a good decision, but that's the cookie. They've apparently got something going with somebody on the inside. So they're trying to buy the guidance system documentation from him."

Dan considered. Could this seller be the source of the original intelligence that a guided Shkval existed? Mullaly had said that source was in the Admiralty. He decided to start with a simpler question. "Okay, but—I don't understand. The missile's on the block. For sale. They just demonstrated it in the fucking Moscow River, with free vodka and two TV crews. Why would we, or these allies, whoever they are, screw around with covert action when we can just buy what we want?"

"Well, let me ask you a question back: Why bother with the metal when we can just get the documentation?"

Dan frowned. Siebeking went on, "Maybe it's not immediately evident, but take my word for it, we'd be better off with just the specs and circuit diagrams, and let them keep the hardware. Especially if they don't know we have them. It's one of those spycraft things. Make sense?"

Dan said slowly, "It's not just because getting the specs would be an intel coup? And buying the missile free and clear, wouldn't?"

"Boy, *there's* a cynical comment." The attaché rolled his eyes. "Let's just forget you said that, okay, Commander?"

"I didn't mean that, sir—"

"Like I said, I forgot you said it. But when you take delivery on a weapons system, especially something cutting edge, you don't typically get complete specs. We sure don't furnish them with our foreign military sales. You get operating documentation, enough to do fault analysis and board-swap repairs. But not what you need to engineer countermeasures. You buy iron, you're committing yourself to a lot of reverse engineering, a lot of guesswork and testing—by the time you're finished you might as well have done all the R&D in-house. What they're trying to get is exactly what we need. Are we straight now?"

Dan judged it best to nod. Siebeking explained that the planned purchase was via a Dr. Leopold Cecil. Siebeking didn't know Cecil, but assumed he was either British or Canadian. That evening, Cecil was supposed to meet with his source, one of Dvorov's people, apparently, to swap a briefcase of cash for complete schematics and copies of two classified reports: the official Russian Navy submarine handling and safety evaluation of the Shkval-K, and a top-secret countermeasures vulnerability evaluation the Northern Fleet had staffed out the year before.

"As soon as I heard that, I said, 'all stop,' and buzzed Moale to get you. I was afraid you were already on your way to Komponent. Which could have put a serious crimp in the operation."

"No, we weren't supposed to go over till later." Dan hesitated. "Uh—can I ask you something else?"

"You can *ask* me whatever you want. Whether I can answer, depends."

"You said somebody who worked for Dvorov was furnishing the data. Can you tell me who?"

Siebeking shrugged. "I guess, why not. An ex-navy guy."

"Who?"

"Who? Who? You sound like an old hooty owl. An engineer, okay? Somebody named Yefremov."

Dan felt a chill. "You mean . . . Yermakov?"

"I think that's it. Something like that."

"We have to warn whoever's meeting with him."

Siebeking frowned. "Yeah? Why?"

"It's a trap."

"A *trap?* Why do you say that?"

"Or a sting, or whatever you call it in intel circles. Yermakov's not an engineer."

The naval attaché's eyebrows cranked downward as he peered into Dan's face, then up again. "Now, how would you know that? And what would he be?"

"Never mind how I know, but he's no engineer. He's a vice admiral—retired now, working for Komponent, or with Dvorov—but he's no huggy bear, sir. If he can screw us, he'd be more than happy to."

"You serious?"

"Deadly serious, Captain," Dan told him.

Siebeking nodded, and reached for the phone again. "You sit tight. If that's true—"

"It's true, all right. I met him last year. I saw him again, yesterday, on the test barge. If he's part of the deal, it's not going to turn out the way we want."

When he hung up the attaché slid open a desk drawer. For some reason

Dan thought he might take a gun from it, but instead he shoved across a cell phone. "Here. They quit listening to the land lines for a couple of years, but what we're hearing now, they're back at it again. But we're pretty sure they're not up to intercepting cell calls yet. There's a commercial encryption on this one that's supposed to be tight. I want you back in your room. Don't let anyone in, don't go out to eat, don't use the hotel phone. Understood?"

"Aye aye, sir," Dan said. He slid it into his pocket and stood. "But what about our meeting? Our deal with Dvorov? Seems to me, we'd be better off buying exclusive rights to this thing. That way, none of the rogues gets it. I think—"

"Just hold your horses on all that. We'll get back to you when this situation resolves," Siebeking told him. He raised his voice. "Gunny!"

The marine poked his head in. "Sir!"

"Commander Lenson's ready to leave."

HENRICKSON had trail mix, granola bars, and instant oatmeal, and there was a coffeemaker in the room to heat water. They managed to make do for a late lunch, but Dan found it hard to sit and watch Russian game shows. He paced back and forth between the bed and the balcony window. Maybe he was wrong about Yermakov. Even vice-admirals must have a price. And afterward he could push his idea again. Maybe they'd end up with the specs, and the weapons, *and* an exclusive agreement. The best of all possible endings.

Somehow, it didn't seem likely.

A soccer game was blaring and Henrickson was on the carpet cranking off sit-ups when the cell phone chirped. He was little, but it looked like he could do sit-ups forever. Dan grabbed it off the coffee table and searched for the right button. "Lenson here. Hello? Hello?"

"Dan? Al Siebeking here. Bad news."

"Turn up that soccer game," he said to Henrickson. To Siebeking, "What is it, sir?"

"The meet was busted by the FSB."

"Oh, no. Did they get—"

"Yeah; they got Cecil. And it's gonna be ugly. Have you got alternate passports?"

He searched his brain: *alternate* passports? Did he mean *false* passports? "Uh . . . all we got were the official passports, the ones we usually travel on. The red ones. And our blue ones, our personal ones."

"In your own names?"

He *did* mean false papers. "Yessir. They're all in our, uh, real names."

"Here's what I recommend: Better clear out. You might have only minutes."

"Get packed," Dan snapped to Henrickson, who'd been listening to one side of the conversation without stopping his exercises.

"Why? What's going on?"

He covered the phone. "I didn't know about this, Monty. Not till today. But the FSB just picked up a spy who was trying to buy data about the Shkval."

"Really? I wouldn't want to be in his shoes."

"Me, neither. But the embassy says we could be, if we don't get the hell out of Dodge."

The analyst jumped up and dashed into the adjoining room. Dan muttered under the TV's clamor, "Captain? We can check out. But how are we going to get out of the country? Our tickets are for next week."

"Trying to work that out. Might have to pull you back inside the compound and sort it out then. See, any Americans in Moscow will be suspect. Especially guys who're sniffing around the same system, like you. I know, you were overt, but they'll see it as part of one plot. Hold on—"

Siebeking's voice went muffled, speaking to someone else with his hand over the cell, Dan figured. Drawers slammed next door. He tucked the phone between ear and shoulder and started throwing clothes into his suitcase, not bothering to fold them or separate clean from dirty. He made sure his passports were there, though, and the envelope with their orders and tickets.

Siebeking came back on. "Get your asses over here. Don't bother to check out. Leave your clothes and shit—we'll send Moale with your keys to pack it and bring it back. Just get over here, and bring anything with the word 'supercavitating' on it. If anybody tries to stop you on the street, keep going. If a car pulls up next to you, go the other way. I'm hanging up."

"Monty!" Dan yelled, cramming the cell in his pocket and grabbing his coat. "Forget packing. Get in here!"

But the phone was ringing in the other room. Dan stuck his head in to tell Henrickson not to answer it, but he already had. He glanced at Dan, eyes wide, and held it out.

"It's for you."

7

WHEN the voice said, "Dan?" he frowned, knowing he knew it before recognition itself arrived.

"Uh . . . Jack? Jack Byrne, right?"

"Pretty sharp, Dan. It's been a while."

Images rose from the past. John Anson Byrne had been the squadron intel officer on Dan's first staff duty, the Med float that had ended with the incursion into Syria. Dark-complexioned and distinguished-looking, the N2 had kept his tan current with sunbathing on the flight deck, eyes hidden behind tinted aviator's glasses. They'd met again years later, when Byrne, now a captain, had been on the staff of COMIDEASTFOR in Bahrain.

He recalled a bright morning in the Gulf when he and Byrne had exchanged winks on the quarterdeck as USS *Turner Van Zandt*'s new CO was sworn in. Byrne had briefed Blair before she and Dan had met on the deck of an Iraq-bound tanker. Later, Jack had been best man at their wedding; the bridesmaids had nicknamed him "Captain Wonderful."

He hadn't seen him since, but that didn't mean they'd drifted apart. You often ran into people you'd served with before, in the Navy, and picked up where you'd left off. Dan cleared his throat, snapping back to the present: on a phone in a Moscow hotel room, and needing very much to get out of there. He didn't wonder how Jack had tracked him down. Byrne always seemed to know everything, the story behind the story. Which was probably as much an illusion as anything else.

"Uh, Jack, great to hear from you. What're you doing these days? We were just going out the door. Super-important meeting. Can I call you back? Where you calling from? We're due at the embassy—"

"Heard you were in town. You're working for, let's see, you're at TAG now, right? What's Steamin' Dan Lenson doing in a shore billet?"

"Oh—special projects. Logistics, mostly. I'm hoping to get back to sea next tour. How about you?"

"I was over Krasnaya Presnya, too. The exhibition center. Didn't see you—"

"Guess we missed each other. Look, I've really got to—"

"Just give me a minute, Dan. How's Blair? You two starting a family yet?"

He'd been vaguely aware from the first moment of someone talking behind Byrne, some sort of background murmur. At first he'd put it down to crosstalk; you heard it a lot on lines with older switching equipment. But Byrne's voice was different. He always sounded relaxed. Now, though, he didn't, not at all. Dan motioned to Henrickson to leave, go, and sat on the bed. "Uh, right, yeah, it's been a while. She's okay. We're both doing okay. How's Rosemary?"

"Great, great, she's holding up. Look, Dan, sounds like you're busy, but I'd like to see if we can get together in the near future. Long's we're both in town. Sound good?"

Henrickson hovered by the door, tapping his watch. Dan grimaced and put his hand over the receiver. "Get over to the embassy, Monty. Be there in a minute."

"You said we had to go *now.*"

"We do—it's an old friend—I'll be right there, okay? Tell Siebeking I'll be right over."

As he was speaking his gaze roved to the television. The soccer game was over. An impeccably coiffed anchor was announcing a western-style news show. Now he froze, hand over the mouthpiece, as Henrickson walked out, then back in again, and stood in the door, watching, too.

Two burly men were hustling another out of a building. The man between them was swarthy and distinguished-looking. He wasn't wearing aviator glasses, though. Without them his face looked naked.

The scene changed to an office, cameras, lights, a pushing and shoving. Documents were spread across a table. A small camera was being held up and examined by another suit. The announcer intoned grave statements. Text bannered across the bottom of the screen. Dan wasn't too hot on Cyrillic, but it was perfectly plain some of them read Cecil.

Byrne was Cecil. Not some anonymous Canadian. John Anson Byrne, U.S. Navy. He rubbed his mouth, seeing but not quite registering Henrickson staring at him, then at the TV. Then the analyst disappeared.

A click; someone lifting a receiver on the same line. In the next room? Henrickson? Or someone else?

"Dan? You there?"

"Uh, yeah, Jack . . . I'm here. Sounds like . . . like somebody's there with you."

"What? Here? I'm callin' from a bar. Yeah, there's some asshole in the other booth."

"Sounds like a Russian asshole."

Byrne seemed to relax. "What can I say, country's full of them. So what do you think? How about we get together? We might even figure out we're in the same line of work this time."

Dan balanced the handset, feeling like his brain was just too slow. He stuck his head around the door, and saw indeed it was Henrickson on the other extension. Byrne's fate might depend on what he said next. Or didn't say . . . or half conveyed . . . he tried to game it out while not pausing too long. Byrne would be calling under coercion. His captors—the FSB—would be coaching in the background. But Byrne hadn't just played along. Instead he'd managed to warn him, with the comment about "the same line of work." But probably he actually knew more than Byrne knew he knew. So the first thing to do was get that across. "Uh, Jack, ran into a mutual friend. Over at the embassy? Al Siebeking. Know him?"

"Oh, Al? Sure, I know Al. You been talking to Al?"

"Yeah, interesting guy, knows a lot about a lot. Really up to the minute." He hesitated. "Jack, you okay?"

"Okay? Sure, I'm okay. Never better. Everything's hunky here."

A disturbance on the other end; by pressing the receiver close to his ear, Dan could almost make out the words. They were in Russian. "Jack? Jack?"

A note pad by his elbow. WHO IS THIS GUY?

Dan took the pencil from Henrickson. FRIEND. NAVY INTEL. CUSTODY FSB.

SHKVAL? THE COVERT ACTION?

How had Henrickson known that? Dan scribbled angrily, RIGHT.

Byrne came back. He was breathing harder, but still sounded perfectly self-possessed. "Sorry . . . sorry. Well, look, if you can't make it—"

"Wait a minute, Jack. Hold your horses. Where are you?"

"Where? Uh, Moscow. Didn't I say that?"

Now he had it. It was the next stage in the sting setup Siebeking had described. Byrne, AKA Dr. Cecil, had shown up to buy schematics and official reports. Instead the FSB broke in and took him into custody as soon as he had the classified materials—that was what the clip on the news had shown. Now his captors were forcing him to make this call, and maybe others, to suck more Americans into the trap. Dvorov must have given them his phone number here at the Mir. Yes, he'd given that to the academician.

The smart thing to do was to hang up instantly and hightail it across the street. Siebeking had warned him: every second he stayed meant the cops might be in the elevator.

But then Jack would still be in *their* hands. Maybe it wouldn't be as bad as if they were still called the KGB. But maybe it would. Whatever, it wouldn't be fun. Jack could be in prison for years.

Would they leave *him* here, if he'd been set up? He hoped not. He'd spent enough time with the Marines to know: You didn't leave your people behind. Was Jack Byrne his people? The hollow sensation behind his navel was his answer.

Henrickson was signaling desperately. Dan waved him off. "Jack? Still there?"

"Yeah . . . yeah. Look, lad, I don't want you to—"

"I've got to go do some stuff, but yeah, we can get together. How about tonight?"

"Tonight?"

"Yeah. That all right? Too short notice?"

"Well, tonight . . . wait one, Dan. Don't—"

Another disturbance on the other end. He spoke through it, knowing what Byrne was trying to do, suspecting what he was going to try. "Jack? Still there?"

He was breathing hard again. "Yeah . . . still here."

"Where you want to meet?"

A mutter. "Under the Kremlin walls," Bryne said, and his voice sounded dead. "Under the walls . . . no."

"No?"

He was thinking as fast as he ever had in his life. A glitter of sun winked in his mind. A knife slicing green silk.

"The Kremlin? Okay. But you know me. I'm a water kind of guy."

"What're you saying, Dan?"

"Let's meet by the river. Seven o'clock. It'll be dark then, right? We'll meet up and go for a walk along the river. Like those long walks we used to take in Bahrain, right?"

They hadn't taken any walks together in Bahrain, but Byrne didn't disagree. He just said, the warning behind the false bonhomie ringing clear, "If you can spare the time. If you're sure—"

"Seven. By the river. Remember. No sooner and no later—I've only got a little time before I have to leave town."

"Copy. Seven sharp. By the river."

He hung up and sat motionless while Henrickson fidgeted in the doorway. "We going?"

"We don't need to now," Dan told him. "We're going to the Balchug-Kempinsky instead."

"What for? What was that about the river? You set up a meet?"

"That's their idea. Use him as bait. Have us show up, then gaff us all in at once. Then it's show trial time. On television, a season series."

Henrickson stuffed his hands in his pockets. "So what's the plan?"

"That's what I need to talk to Captain de Cary about," Dan told him. "And I'm going to need a little help from you, too."

"Whatever you say, Commander."

"Still got that briefcase full of money?"

"I think I just spent most of it," Henrickson said.

8

I T was dark. Dan, de Cary, and Henrickson hiked along the embankment
toward the towers of the ancient fortress. Great red stars still lit their
spires, which surprised him. He'd thought that with the fall of the USSR,
they'd come down. They loomed ominously against the pinkish city night.
Beyond them another column of molten white and gold towered, one of
the huge mock-Gothic Stalin skyscrapers. To their left the lights from the
far bank of the Moskva glittered on black chop. The wind was cutting, no
doubt the reason there weren't many other people out.

He pulled his coat tighter, wishing he had a scarf. Under the coat he
wore his running gear: shorts, and T-shirt, and over them his Naval Academy Gore-Tex running suit. He felt the same dread as before battle, a race,
or a lacrosse match.

"We're gonna be early," Henrickson muttered, studying his watch. Dan
checked his Seiko and forced his steps to slow. A drunk swayed toward
them, spewing slurred Slavic. Henrickson said a few words and held out a
banknote; the man bowed nearly to the ground, and staggered away.

They'd all been busy in the few hours between Byrne's call and this
chilly night. First, of course, had come packing up and sending everything they wouldn't need over to Siebeking at the embassy. Dan had included a note explaining what they planned to do, and made clear in it
that he wasn't acting under orders of any kind, but that Henrickson
was—in case the worst happened. De Cary had vanished for a time with
the analyst, Monty taking along his suitcase of cash, while Dan had taken
a taxi into the central city.

He'd sauntered down the riverfront sidewalk between the ancient fortress and the river, scrutinizing every projection and culvert-mouth. The
crenelated brick walls of the ancient Kreml paralleled the river, with

guard- and bell towers every hundred yards or so, bare spindly treetops peering over it. Outboard of the wall was Kremlyoskaya Road: five pot-holed lanes of fast traffic, lit by lofty ornate streetlights, the standards green-tarnished bronze, the lamps drooping like bluebells. Thick power cables catenaried between them. Looking up, he guessed it was because they were so close to the river; underground cable-runs would have flooded.

The embankment itself was vertical stone, and he'd looked down at the greasy-looking river-chop from a narrow cracked sidewalk that deserved cleaning. At one point, not far from the largest tower—the Spassky? He wasn't sure—temporary barriers were set up where the railing was being repaired. The old stonework had given way and was collapsing into the river. No, he wouldn't want to put power cables here, either.

He stood there for some time, looking at the highway as grimy shoebox cars, huge-tired diesel trucks, and double-decker tourist buses zipped and rumbled past a few feet away. It wasn't rush hour on the Beltway, but it was steady traffic, and they went fast, fifty or sixty miles an hour. Each car rattled like pennies in a can as it went over joints in the road, and the uncatalyzed exhaust was choking.

As darkness gathered lights had snapped on inside the walls, bringing up the bulbous gold domes of the Arkhangelskiy, the Italianate facade of the Grand Palace, the tacky modernism of the Supreme Soviet. Then, all at once, floods powered on all along the wall, highlighting the whole exterior. The brilliance was staggering, like a set lit for filming. He'd stood shivering, watching it and then the river, and at last had stepped to the curb and waved down a cab.

And now they paced three abreast through the darkness toward the light and he was shivering again, even his thighs trembling. Henrickson reached out and gripped his arm. After a few steps the analyst dropped his hand, and they walked in silence.

SOME time later the ancient fortress came into view. The lights were still up and the traffic was still fairly heavy, though less so than that afternoon. A light cold drizzle began to fall. It soaked them but Dan decided to take it as a good omen. They were walking west along the river, a glittering onyx expanse to their left. Only once did a set of lights move out there: a barge and tug, forging slowly upriver. A powerful diesel throbbed across the water.

He watched the honeylit squares of the tug's high pilothouse cruise past and wished he was in it. To know what he was doing, and simply do it. Stand a watch, maneuver a ship, fix one of your sailor's pay problems; something straightforward and clean.

He might never go to sea again. They'd said he was being put out of the way to protect him. But it seemed more and more like the Navy had forgotten him, squirreled away in his obscure stash billet till mold grew on him and all memory of him evaporated.

Henrickson squeezed his arm again. "You okay?"

"Peachy, Monty. You guys stop here, all right? See you in a little bit."

"Yeah. In a little bit."

Henrickson slowed and fell behind. Dan walked on, forcing each step. A truck tore past, trailing whirling rain-mist that swept over him. It smelled of mud, and sulfur, and cold metal. He straightened his shoulders, trying to get a grip on the dread. As he did so he noticed a group on the far side of the road, near the fortress walls. One beefy figure in coveralls was pushing a broom along the sidewalk. Three others were on their knees, apparently taking up bricks; a small pyramid of them, and a portable cement mixer, stood to one side. They didn't look his way but he had no doubt who and what they were. After seventy years of socialism, he couldn't envision a city repair crew at work after dark.

He glanced surreptitiously riverward, suppressing a shiver. But what he'd feared most wasn't out there. Or if it was, it had its lights out. He looked over his shoulder. Monty was already out of sight.

When he squinted into the rain there he was, a trench-coated figure in a gray hat. Jack Byrne stood with hands sunk in his pockets by the railing. Alone. The glare of the floods showed a bulky case at his feet. As he saw Dan, Byrne turned to face the river, putting his face in shadow and hiding one hand. With that hand, he motioned him back, flicking his fingers as if flicking off water.

Byrne was warning him off. Trying to clue him in. Shit! Granted, Dan was a line officer, an 1100, and Byrne a 1600, intelligence. But just how dumb did he think he was? He kept on, glancing casually left and right, trying to pick up any other watchers.

He did: a stir of motion atop the Kremlin wall. For a moment his brain said *sniper*, and he nearly ducked. But the black tube that tracked him was more likely attached to a videocorder. He'd be on the news tomorrow himself. This time when he looked over he caught one of the pavement repairmen talking to something in his cupped hand.

"Dan, that you?"

"Hi, Jack."

Five more paces. Byrne was still gesturing him away, more urgently now. Dan shook his head slightly, trusting to the distance and the falling rain to mask the motion from the observers. He went up to Byrne, put his arm around his shoulder, and pulled him into a hug. "I know it's a sting," he said into the older man's ear. "Ready to go?"

"Dan—you know? Go where?"

"What's in this big fucking satchel? Anything you need?"

"Bulk paper. Moscow phonebooks."

"Just for the cameras, huh?"

"Right. For the cameras."

Dan turned them both to face the river. Behind him tires sizzled on wet pavement. He pumped air in and out, charging his lungs, while a clot of oncoming traffic neared. Headlights grew brighter in the mist, lighting them up as if to be machine-gunned.

"Take a deep breath, Jack."

It was the first time he'd ever seen Jack Byrne at a loss. His jaw dropped as Dan kicked the temporary railing aside. He grabbed Byrne's shoulders, braced his Adidas, and hurled them both through the gap, over the embankment, and out into the river.

The blackness was instantly freezing, numbing, shocking the breath out of his lungs. He'd let go of the other man on the way down, and immediately, even before he came up, was kicking off his running shoes, stripping off his overcoat. It was wool, but wet it was a recipe for drowning. He clawed at the darkness for what seemed like minutes but could have been only a second or two. Then his eyes broke the surface and he shook off the river like a wet Lab, looking quickly back above them.

The top of the embankment was floodlit empty. It wouldn't stay that way long, but it would take their watchers a few seconds to report and react. And more seconds—he hoped—to play Froggy across six lanes of fast traffic in the rain.

He craned around, treading water. There was Byrne's hat, a shadow bobbing a few feet away. Something else floating—a plastic bottle, trash. But where was Jack?

He was sucking air to dive when the intel officer broke the surface. Byrne spluttered and choked, fighting some undersea beast that had him in its tentacles. Dan stroked over and started working the trench coat off. "Kick off your shoes," he told him through a wave that leapt up into his mouth. The Moskva tasted like it had run through Russian fields, Russian factories, Russian kidneys. It was like chewing chemical-flavored worms.

Coughing, he got an arm under Byrne's shoulder and began stroking out into the river, orienting by sound rather than by sight, angling away from the whir and whine of tires on wet asphalt. Was that a head bobbing above the railing? The FSB were pros; it wouldn't take them long to re-orient. He kicked hard, wishing he had fins, a mask, snorkel. A scuba diver had to be prepared to swim long distances, but usually you had fins and at least some flotation.

But this river was fresh, not salt; he had no fins, and they were strug-gling just to stay afloat, burdened with increasingly heavy clothing. His fingers and feet were going numb, and he was gasping. Byrne was older and no great swimmer, as far as Dan knew. He had a side stroke going, but it didn't look like he could keep it up long. At the end of each reach his face disappeared beneath the waves.

A flash from the embankment. A beam, sweeping the black breast of the Moskva. A shout.

He and Byrne were being swept downriver, so they were already farther from where they'd gone in than they'd managed to swim. But still, not far enough. He concentrated on keeping their heads above water. He couldn't land them on the near shore. Running, their pursuers would be on them before they had a chance to haul themselves up, even if they could get a grip on the slimy, vertical, finely fitted nineteenth-century stonework.

The far shore? It was two hundred, maybe more yards away. Judging by Byrne's increasingly frantic struggles, they weren't going to make it. He could probably get to shore alone, if he didn't lock up from the cold. But could he leave Jack? He couldn't. If it wasn't for Dan, he wouldn't be in this particular deep shit now, beating the water to keep his nose in the air.

"Jack. Jack! Relax! Just float."

In fact, Byrne's clothes had held some air. But only at first. It was leak-ing away as they tired. Dan thought of jerking off his trousers, fashioning flotation, but that had been hard enough in the Academy natatorium; he didn't think he had it in him tonight, with fingers he couldn't feel any lon-ger. Instead he grabbed the other man and twisted, getting behind him. Byrne went under. Dan hauled him up again, submerging himself in dark-ness and cold as he shoved, kicked. A hand groped for him, missed, but came back, clutching at his chest. If Byrne panicked, tried to climb him, they'd both drown.

The beam steadied, a white dazzle that tracked them as they gyred in a waterlogged waltz, hitting an eddy as the turn south approached. Then the light lurched and started to bob. It jogged along the embankment after them.

The FSB were in pursuit. Even with the current, they could make better time than Dan and Jack could through the water. All they had to do was keep pace till they gave up.

Or went under. Dan felt fingers grapple in his sweatshirt and lock tight. Byrne began hauling himself up on his chest, thrusting him under. He kicked and sculled, but felt himself being gradually dragged under in a horrible slow grapple. Byrne was heavier. Byrne was desperate. The cold penetrated his brain, made him want to give up.

He fought back to the surface for a snatched breath, then was forced under again in a welter of bubbling black shot now with a red glare he didn't think was from anywhere but inside his own racked lungs, his oxygen-starved, panicking brain. He straight-armed Byrne in the chest but the other didn't flinch.

A flailing knee caught his groin and he saw red for real. He fought his way back up one more time, sucking air so hard pain snapped through his head like barbed wire being dragged through his cortex. He was paddling with stiff pieces of waterlogged lumber. He felt guilty, not that he was about to die, but that he'd taken a friend with him. In the world he'd made his life in, what mattered wasn't how hard you tried, but whether you succeeded.

He hadn't, not in anything. Not with his first marriage. He hadn't been much of a father. His career? A couple of times he hadn't done badly. Stood up for what was important.

Only what a stupid, *stupid* idea he'd picked to go out on—

A black shape hissed through the water toward them. A low voice chanted syllables that did not cohere into sense. He ducked as a shadow flicked over his head, sharp and fast and close as a guillotine blade, and knifed into the water and flicked back and cracked hard into his ear.

The side of the racing shell rushed past above them, dragging a rushing burble and the deep sucking breaths of trained bodies giving enormous effort.

Byrne went suddenly motionless. Dan took advantage of it to twist the other's fist out of his clothes. He oriented after the passing shape and struck out with five or six desperate crawl strokes. Something hard and small whacked his arm lightly. He twisted after it, felt nothing. Lunged in sudden terror, and felt another whack along his ribs. This time he twisted his numb arm into the smooth, swiftly fleeting line. It twitched out of his grasp and slid quickly away until his groping hand hooked into a bight.

A terrific jerk, and all at once he was being hauled through the black water so fast his head went under, and he fought to keep from twisting like a trolling lure. Byrne shouted as Dan crashed into him. He seized him with his free arm, nearly dislocating it before they were both on their backs, gasping, snorting, fighting on the end of the towline.

He yelled and after a moment it slacked. A voice called something, and he reached for a splash and got Byrne's arm into a second bight. He waved and the lines came taut again, the dark blades flashed, the chant resumed.

The light, which seemed weaker now, steadied on them again. Angry shouting followed it. Then a reddish flash and an echoing pop came from the embankment. And after a short interval, another.

It sounded like pistol fire, but though he waited there were only the two reports, two flashes. The chant went on from ahead and above, rhythmic and lulling. He forced himself awake. That sleepy comfort was hypothermia, the cold dropping his core temperature. He concentrated on holding tight and staying awake. But it was growing harder. For an indeterminable time he lay in a soft warm bed, then bungeed back to awareness as his head went beneath the river again and he was dragged along willy-nilly, fighting to right himself but feeling only that terrible lassitude. He came up choking, coughing. He tried to haul himself forward on the line but his hands wouldn't cooperate. He let himself be dragged, eyes frozen open.

The oars wove and dipped like dragonflies. Orangeish globes slowly rose above the far shore, became pedestal sconces at a waterfront bar. A slant of wet black stone rose to pilings. Across the narrowing water came the shouts and screams of a rowdy crowd and the bass bumping from a not very good hard rock screamer band.

The chant stopped. The low torpedo they followed curved smoothly and slid beneath an overhanging structure hung with arcs of vibrating scarlet luminescence. The drag against their wet clothes lessened as something slid over the sky. Then came voices and the hollow clunk of fiberglass against wood.

When hands reached down and voices called he could not move or speak in response. The hands found the nylon towlines and unwrapped them. They dragged them up from the black water into air that had to be chilly but felt tropical. He crouched shuddering on all fours, panting and trying not to lose consciousness. Concrete was rough under slime beneath his hands. Something hot ran down his neck. He heard Jack Byrne's voice, low and unnatural. "Who the fuck are you?" and de Cary's answer, "Lafayette, I am here."

"Jack. Jack?"

A grunt, then hacking as if Byrne's pancreas was coming up. "What the . . . what the *fuck*, Lenson?"

"That was for the bridesmaid."

"Never *touched* the fucking bridesmaid . . . was all over me, though . . . Just fucking drown me. Fucking swallowed half the river." More coughing, then, "*Jesus*, that's cold. Where the . . . what just happened?"

"We bought the Moscow Rowing Club a new shell."

"And where . . . we going now?"

"Figured you'd have a suggestion. Someplace the FSB doesn't know about." He had to stop, he was gagging. Boone Clinic had insisted his shot card be up to date. He hoped it covered whatever he'd just swallowed.

"Right. Out of country ASAP. I know a . . . a safe house. Just got to . . . make a call."

Headlights came on. An engine started. Henrickson trotted toward them from a parking lot, carrying blankets. Dan tried to get to his feet but halfway up his muscles seemed to lose power. The concrete came up and slammed into the side of his head. Then the black river rolled over him, freezing, smothering, and he didn't think any more at all.

III

PLAN B

9

Warsaw, Poland

THE first thing he did at the apartment was pull off his clothes and head for the shower. Their night swim had been two days before, but he still felt filthy. In those forty-eight hours they hadn't had more than quick spongedowns with toilet paper in the rocking, jolting W/C compartments of a series of local trains.

He ached all over. His feet were so swollen from sitting up for two days he had to pry off his shoes. Fortunately there were three bathrooms in the apartment, which was beautifully furnished with polished parquet floors, Afghan rugs, and modern paintings that looked real, not prints or reproductions. It was in a secure building with its own guards. The other tenants, Byrne said, were expats or Poles, all wealthy.

The marble-lined shower was big enough to play handball in. The fixtures were gold-plated and the water exquisitely hot. He lathered from head to toe, and when it was soaked through he carefully peeled the bandage off his ear. It itched, which was good. He let it air. He found a woman's razor in a cabinet and shaved.

When he came out, wrapped in a heavy bathrobe—it was tight in the shoulders and short, and he guessed it belonged to the same woman as the razor—Byrne and Henrickson and de Cary were sitting in their underwear in the kitchen eating cheese and bread. There was a bottle of white wine, too. The kitchen was filled with shining German appliances and tall bottles of peppers, onions, and olives, floating in saffron-tinted oil. "How's the ear?" Byrne asked him.

"Okay. How's the hands?"

"Skinning over. Anything in the place, help yourself. I know the girl who lives here. State Department. Air Force Reserve, flies to London every month for her weekend drills."

"She mind if we smoke?" Monty asked him.

Dan said, "I didn't know you smoked, Monty. Wait a minute. You don't."

"I might start."

"For a Polish cheese, this is not bad," said de Cary.

Byrne scratched his crotch. "I guess you could. Only thing to watch is—see that balcony?"

"That one?" de Cary turned.

"No, the far one. See the roof below it? The gray pebbly one, with all the antennas? No, don't look!"

"We see the antennas," Dan said. "What about it?"

"That's the Russian embassy. Right next door. So the balcony's off-limits, okay?"

"Thanks for getting us out, Jack," Dan told him. "We'd probably still be locked up in the Embassy."

He'd come to with the raw fire of brandy in his mouth, someone's undershirt tied over his bleeding ear, and his head lolling in the back seat of a Lada. He'd sputtered and spat out the taste, as all the tension and terror had swept back in a rush.

Their first stop after the rock bar had been a hole-in-the-wall flat five stories up in what smelled like an old brewery. Byrne said it was a joint safe house, shared by several agencies. This use would burn it, but there were towels and canned food, bottled water, clean clothes, money, and most important, false passports. The airports would be watched, so they'd have to go by train. Security was laxer on rail travel.

So for two days they became drunken Polish vodka dealers. Byrne spoke Polish, Henrickson broke up his Russian to sound foreign, and Dan and de Cary simply sat with bottles in their laps looking stone drunk. This was an excellent disguise on a Russian train; the only difficulty was when another drunk wanted to share. They'd headed east first, then north, before turning west again, buying local tickets at each change, and staying in third class with the farmers and families. They'd crossed the border near Pskov, handing over bottles of Wyborowa with their documents; the border guards spent more time examining the labels than their passports. They'd felt safer in Estonia, but still kept to themselves in first-class compartments through Riga and Kaunas. Dan was impressed with the trains. They looked romantically old-fashioned, with wood and glass and velvet curtains, but were clean, cheap, and on time. Byrne found an Internet café at one stop, and a van was waiting for them at the Wschodnia station. It had taken them to the Embassy clinic for exams and shots, then to this apartment.

"Thanks for getting *me* out," Byrne told him. "I'd be in the Lubyanka, sweating out how much I could take before I told them—well, I've had access to data we wouldn't like to become public knowledge. By the way, they're apeshit over there. The Russian government is enraged. We're being portrayed as escaped spies."

"You *are* an escaped spy," Dan pointed out.

"*Un espion echappe,*" de Cary put in. "Unfairly we will be tarred with that same brush. By the way, I should very much like to inform my superiors of my location. So far as they know I am still in Moscow."

"No calls from here . . . not with those antennas next door."

"Those are comm antennas, not surveillance antennas," Dan told him.

"Not that I don't believe you, but let's play it safe, all right? I'll take you over to the main building. There are secure phones there . . . or would you rather go to the French Embassy?"

"Anywhere will do." De Cary shrugged. "It will not need to be on a secure line."

The bread was fresh and crusty. The cheese was wonderful. He got up and searched the fridge and came up with apple juice in a cardboard box. He munched and took a sip of juice. He closed his eyes and felt like melting through the chair and running all over the Italian tile.

"When you guys are ready, I'll take you over," Byrne said, getting up.

THE Embassy was a warren, with shabby covered walkways connecting small back buildings. Their contact's office was in one. Byrne hadn't said what the bald man's job was, but since he'd picked them up at the train station in civvies, Dan assumed he was the Agency resident. Adding to that impression was the huge Rottweiler that had sat in the back of the van with them as they edged through the streets of Warsaw. Bone, the man called him. Bone didn't bother them, but he didn't beg to be petted, either. He carried himself like a professional; courteous, but detached. The kind of dog a man owned when he had reason to carry a gun but wasn't allowed to. Today when Byrne knocked, the bald man was sitting at a terminal, in a sweater vest with his collar open. A suit jacket hung behind the door. "Hey, Jack. Dan, right? Look better than you did this morning. Coffee, guys?"

Dan said sure.

"Where's *le capitaine?*"

Bryne: "At his embassy. Any news out of Moscow?"

"Merle says they declared two of our guys non grata. Out of the attaché's office."

"Not Siebeking—"

"No, no, two others—actually one was sort of tangentially involved. With what Jack was doing, not what you were doing."

If the expellees were from the attaché's office, and Siebeking hadn't known what they were doing, somebody wasn't telling the whole truth. But there was no point going there with this guy. Later, though . . . "Speaking of that, I'd like to figure out who let us go in overt at the same time a covert mission was working the same tasking," Dan told him. "I realize it's probably beyond my need to know and over my pay grade, but I'd just like to raise the issue."

"It's not uncommon, to run two ops," Byrne told him, in the tone of a dad explaining to a six-year-old how the motor makes the car go.

"Without letting your right hand know?"

"Even that."

"My guess, and it's only a guess, is that the FSB set you up with Komponent from the start," the bald man mused.

"They were never in earnest about selling?"

"Not to us. They make the kind of deal you were suggesting, which by the way I don't have any idea where you got the blessing to offer Dvorov that—" He waited but Dan didn't say, so he went on, "—they agree to that, and bing, they lose downstream sales from every rogue regime that fronts a seacoast."

"They'd never have passed that up," Byrne said. "They'd have agreed to Dan's deal, taken the money, then sold it to the others under the table. Or set up a subsidiary company, a cut-out."

"Oh, not only that," the bald man said. "Now they have this big spy scandal, they can double their price. Now it's super-secret technology even the U.S. wants."

Dan rubbed his face, reveling in the feeling of clean skin, but suddenly depressed. He'd been naive. Dangerous secrets had a way of bleeding through any barrier, like virus particles passing through a filter. The money passed it, going the other way.

"Anyway, Jack said you needed a secure line?" The Agency guy powered down the computer and took the jacket off the door. He pushed the red Tri-Tac phone toward Dan. "Going over to Visas. You can close the door. Jack?"

"I'll go with you."

Dan thanked him again for the use of the apartment. When they were gone he punched in his access code, then numbers from memory, computing the time in his head: it'd be about 07 in Virginia Beach. His CO answered on the first ring. "TAG, Captain Mullaly."

"Good morning, sir. Commander Lenson. Can we initiate and go secure?"

Hiss. *Beep.* When they were scrambled Mullaly said, "Dan. I got a message saying you were out of Russia?"

Beep. "Yessir, I'm at the embassy in Warsaw."

He filled Mullaly in on what had gone wrong. "There's a possibility Komponent was playing us from the start. So you might want to question whoever gave you the word that they were willing to sell. To us, I mean. Bottom line, sir, Plan A's not going to work. With all the outrage they're putting out, the Russians aren't going to lease us anything with super-cavitating technology. They're treating this like a major spy case. The intel resident says they've expelled two of our staff in Moscow."

"What about unexpended funds?"

He frowned, not following. "Unexpended funds, sir?"

"The money Henrickson put in for. The thirty thousand."

"Oh. Um, Captain, I'm afraid all those funds were . . . expended."

Silence. Then Mullaly said, sounding exasperated, "Well, I'm glad you're both okay, but Monty told me you weren't going to spend that. That it was for a bona fide."

"Well, sir, if we hadn't used it—say, maybe we could charge it off to Navy Intel. Get reimbursed. Should I ask Captain Byrne how to do that?"

"Maybe. But if I take the hit, that gives me a chip the next time I need something from . . . I'm thinking out loud, sorry . . . let me think about that. But right now we're at the end of the quarter and that puts me over budget."

"Sorry, sir."

"Well, you did what you thought you had to. You're probably right, we're not going to make any time with Dvorov. So we'd better cut our losses and bring you guys home. See if there's Space-A out of Warsaw, okay? If there isn't call Dawn and have her cut you four tickets back."

"Four, sir? There's just Monty and me—"

"Got another call coming in. See me when you get back."

"Aye, sir." He hung up and sat gnawing his lip. "Shit," he muttered.

A tap on the door, and Byrne put his head in. "Done?"

"I guess."

Byrne came in holding two pastries. "Raspberry." He put one in front of Dan and got himself fresh coffee from the maker. "Merle come back yet?"

"No."

"Everything okay?"

"It'll work out. My CO's ticked about my spending all our walking around money. He's thinking about asking your guys for reimbursement. It's thirty grand."

"Hell, he can have it out of my pay," Byrne said. "I owe you, Dan. I could have been behind those charges for ten, fifteen years." He added, "Though I wasn't too happy about it out in the middle of that river."

"You'd have done it for me."

"I'd certainly have tried."

They sat together for a few seconds. Then Byrne cleared his throat. "In fact, thinking about it, seems to me you're in the wrong end of this business."

"What end?"

"Yeah, the Navy always needs ship drivers. And I know, backbone of the Fleet, iron men in wooden ships, all that. But basically, any idiot can drive a ship. Left rudder, right rudder, all back full. Not a lot of nuance. Ever thought about the intel community?"

Dan decided not to respond to the blackshoe taunts. He said patiently, "I know you can put in for it. At least, when you're a jaygee, or a lieutenant."

"The rules say that, but the nice thing about spookdom is, the rules are not always the rules. If you know what I mean."

"I'm starting to guess."

"That's the spirit. Now, I've followed your career, okay? You're technically savvy. I mean, the Tomahawk program, you found out why they were crashing. You work well in mixed teams. Like the black ops thing in Desert Storm, going into Iraq. Like Korea—yeah, I heard what you did in the Strait. You're better known than you think.

"We could do better for you than the surface line community is doing. We'd send you to Defense Intelligence College, get you your master's in intelligence policy. Then put you in operations. We lost a lot of the old guard when the Wall came down. People felt like, well, the Soviets are gone, I can take early retirement. And we downramped our accession pipeline then, too.

"Now the mission's global again, and we're stretched thin. The current DNI'd be real interested in somebody like you. So interested—" Byrne gave it a beat, "—I'd guarantee you'd make captain on your first board."

Dan blinked. Captain was more senior than he'd ever expected to get, even as a dreamy-eyed mid fresh out of Annapolis. He made himself take a minute. Because it was a tempting offer.

"Jack, I appreciate it, but I'm not sure I'm cut out to be a pookah spook. I know the job you guys have to do. And that you only get noticed when something goes completely to shit. But, call me an idiot, but I'm still hoping for another command."

"Another destroyer? You already had one, Dan."

"Well, a deep draft next, I guess. A cruiser, or one of the new Burke class. I miss going to sea, Jack."

"We go to sea. Half our billets are large-decks, task forces, strike groups. We play in mission planning and post-strike analysis. You'd be on a carrier . . . but you'd be at sea."

Dan regarded him, knowing the one thing Byrne hadn't mentioned, that he couldn't without prejudicing his argument. The line Navy guarded no privilege more jealously than ship command. Over the years, rather than yield it to such Johnny-come-latelies as engineers and oceanographers, it had created separate promotion stovepipes for medical officers, legal officers, meteorologists, intelligence officers. They called these "the restricted line." Restricted line types competed among themselves for promotion, and led their own organizations. But they didn't command.

"So you're thinking . . . let me guess. That the difference would be that you wouldn't command."

"You took the words, Jack."

"Let's get realistic. Are they ever going to trust you with a ship again? After what happened to *Horn?*"

He tensed in his chair. "She's still afloat. I brought her back."

"She *glows in the dark*, Dan. She'll stay behind that wire at the Navy Yard for twenty years."

"I stopped the—"

"I know, you're not supposed to talk about it. But you and I know they haven't forgiven you for that, or for the Congressional, or for second-guessing them on a few other occasions. Including what happened at the White House. You know Niles is being talked about for CNO. It was Nick Niles who put you out to pasture at TAG, right? You think he's going to give you another shot?"

"He'll do what's right. I trust the guy."

It was less than the truth. Niles had said more than once that another command was the last thing he had in mind for Dan. If Niles became Chief of Naval Operations, he could forget ever going to sea again.

He took a slow breath, quieting his yammering mind. What you couldn't change, he'd tried to learn to accept. He'd seen too many men let their ambitions warp their actions. Each time it had sickened him more. "Jack, if the Navy offers me another command, I'll take it. If they don't, I'll do what they give me to do. I'd just rather not wall off the possibility, okay?

I appreciate the offer. I know it's well meant, and you can do everything you say. But no thanks."

BYRNE took it well; he probably had expected the refusal. And maybe Dan was just being blind turning down the opportunity. He'd stick till the O-6 board met. If he didn't make captain then, it'd be time to think about what to do with the rest of his life.

He had lunch in the compound cafeteria with the bald man and Byrne. They thought it'd be just as well if none of the recent escapees went traipsing around town. He borrowed the phone again to call Blair at Manpower and Personnel. Then the bald man and Bone escorted them across the street back to the apartment. The dog trotted quietly at their side, glancing alertly at the passing cars, the passing pedestrians. Dan watched the windows of the Russian embassy, but saw nothing out of the ordinary. No one seemed to know they were right next door. Still, he'd be glad when they were on their way home.

Letting himself in, he heard voices in the kitchen, the clink of glass on glass. Faces turned toward him. Two were new since this morning. One he knew, but hadn't expected here. The unfamiliar one was huge, well-built, solidly muscled. The new arrivals were in casual clothes, slacks and jackets over black muscle tees.

"Obie," he said, surprised. "What the hell are you doing here?"

HE hadn't seen Teddy Oberg since shotgun training at the GrayWolf compound. The Team Charlie member came to his feet with a lazy respectfulness that was almost arrogance. "Sumo, this here's my team leader at TAG, Commander Dan Lenson. A blackshoe, but he's seen action. Iraq. Srebrenica. A diver, too—right?"

"Just a sport diver, Teddy. Just scuba."

"Monty told us how you got the guy out, hitting the river, paying off a rowing team to do the snatch. Pretty slick. Buddy here I'd like you to meet: Jeff Kaulukukui. Young, dumb, and full of come. Sumo Man's from Team Two, been in Bosnia hunting PIFWCS."

"Hunting what?"

"Persons indicted for war crimes," Kaulukukui said. His smooth features looked Polynesian, or more probably, Dan guessed, Hawaiian. His arms were as thick as Dan's thighs, but despite that he didn't look threatening.

"I hope Ratko Mladic's on that list."

"He is. You run into him?"

"I ran into him once," Dan said. "Yeah."

"You're lucky to be alive."

"I know. Did you get him?"

"Not yet," the big guy said, and his smile dimmed. "He travels with a big PSD, but it's low-key, hard to pick up. I was in a bar with him in Belgrade and I couldn't do a thing but try not to get made myself. So, you know Teddy Bear, huh? Know there's a restraining order out against him? Part of him, anyway."

Dan played along. "Which part?"

"His hand. For self-abuse."

As an answer, Oberg got Kaulukukui in a headlock. The two of them nearly demolished a couple of chairs. They reminded him of two lions playing. It got pretty realistic at the end, finishing with Oberg lashed into one of the now-shaky chairs with his hands zip-tied behind him.

The mention of teams, of course, meant Kaulukukui was a SEAL. The East Coast even-numbered teams, two, four, eight, and ten, were based out of the fenced compound down the road from TAG. He was in his late twenties, probably a second-class or first-class petty officer. But rank structure didn't work in the SEALs the way it did elsewhere, Dan knew that. "Well, good to meet you, uh, Sumo. See you found the Polish beer."

"No, brought that with us." Kaulukukui left the "sir" off, but Dan didn't get the feel it was usually there.

"So, what are you doing here, Teddy? I thought you were back at Little Creek."

Oberg sat hunched forward, arms still behind him. His face was going purple, but he wasn't making any progress on the zip ties. The creased seams on his face turned darker than the rest, suffused with blood. It occurred to Dan, not for the first time, that he didn't know that much about Oberg. The man joked, but he didn't reveal. "We staged out of there when you dropped out of sight."

"Oh, yeah? Captain Mullaly didn't—oh, wait a minute, he did. *Four* tickets. Now I get it."

Oberg explained that when they got the message Dan and Monty were missing, after having met with someone presumed to be under FSB control, he'd organized a reaction team. "Jeff was in off deployment. He didn't have anything to do other than get drunk and hop anything that moved at Hot Tuna, so we pulled some gear together and flew to Helsinki. I figured we'd get word where you were, and see what we could do. Then we heard you were headed for Warsaw, and caught a commercial down here."

"Pretty flexible scheduling," Dan said. "TAG cut your orders that way?"

Oberg gave him a funny look. "We don't need no stinkin' orders, sir. Ticketing, orders—they're not the problem in the spec ops community they seem to be for the rest of the Navy. We just slap it on the Visa and sort it out afterwards."

"Monty tell you about the Russki embassy?"

"Yeah. We're staying off the balcony." Oberg looked at the window. He twisted, holding out his wrists to Kaulukukui. "Okay, take 'em off. Or you're really fucked, when I get out of 'em."

"Say, 'I'm an asshole.' "

"You're an asshole. Now take them off."

The Hawaiian produced a knife that Dan didn't see how they'd gotten on a plane and flicked apart plastic. Oberg rubbed his wrists as the bigger man sat forward, smilingly waiting for the blowback. Instead he just said, "Monty, how about you and the Commander and me go get a bite?"

THEY had *stek mexicaja* at a café, then strolled through Lakenki Park as the chill of night arrived and the lights of the palaces winked on through the trees. Dan observed how Oberg watched everything around them without seeming to. It was the same unobtrusive watchfulness the Recon Marines he'd gone into Iraq with had had. Not a big man, especially compared to the Hawaiian, Oberg now gave an impression of quiet resourcefulness that wasn't there the first time you looked at him. But then, he hadn't seen much of the guy on their first mission, to Korea. He'd ridden one of the other ships in the task force.

Henrickson said, "Something you wanted to talk about, Teddy?"

"Yeah. I haven't gotten the full download on what happened in Moscow, but I heard enough to figure we won't be getting our Shkval from there."

"I'd say that's accurate," Dan told him. "About all we really did was get to see a model demonstration. That, and raise the price for their third-country customers."

"I thought we came close," Henrickson said.

"There's some feeling they had us on the string the whole time, Monty."

"Well, sorry that didn't work out. It would have been the easy way."

"That it would," Dan said. "Unfortunately, I don't think we're going to be talking to Yevgeny Dvorov again. So what's on your mind?"

Oberg looked around at the trees again, at distant couples walking the winding gravel paths. "Who's the Fifi?"

"De Cary? He's French Navy."

"Yeah? What branch?"

"An outfit called NAVFCO. I'm not sure what that is. The Department of Commerce fixed us up with him. The French operate carriers. Shkval's a threat to them, too."

"He cleared?"

"Well, I haven't seen any documents yet. Have you, Monty?" Henrickson shook his head. "So far we haven't had to get into that because we've been operating overtly. Why?"

"He was asking me who I was, what I was doing here."

"I don't think there's anything wrong with that. But to answer your question, we haven't seen any clearance on him—no. That what you wanted to talk about?"

Oberg did the casual 360 search again and came back to them. "Not exactly, sir. Question in my mind even before you left was, What's Plan B? If Moscow didn't pan out. So while I was sitting there at TAG with nothing to do, I got on the SIPRNET and did some searches, made some calls. Komponent's apparently not the only ones involved with Shkval. There's something called Ros-voor-u-shenya—"

"Rosvooruzhenye," Henrickson said. "Komponent's the design bureau, Rosvooruzhenye handles the sales."

"Like our Foreign Military Sales directorate," Dan said.

"Makes sense. But I asked a guy I know, he told me a name, and I pulled on that thread, you know how that works, and finally found a dude at NMIC, National Military Intelligence Center, who tracks high-tech sales. It took a while to get the blessings lined up but I finally talked to him. He sent me a list of Shkval-K buyers and how many units and sometimes, even the itinerary."

Oberg paused. A small bridge over a canal came into view. A man stood on it aiming a camera at the palace. They turned and walked back the other way, the gravel crunching under their shoes. Dan felt weak, shaky. He kept falling behind, forcing the others to slow their pace. "Okay," he said. "Go on."

"Three countries have orders in so far. Iran, Ukraine, and China. But NMIC says Ukraine's a cut-out. They only have one sub anyway, and it hasn't been to sea for years. The real end destination for every unit the Russians ship to them is China. So actually, numberwise, the Chinese are buying at least two-thirds of all the Shkval-Ks Komponent's exporting."

Dan wondered why China needed so many anticarrier weapons. He saw from Hernrickson's glance he wasn't the only one. "Good detective work, Obie. So what have you got in mind?"

"I had him put in an RFI for the route of the Shkval-Ks leaving Ukraine for China."

An RFI was a request for information, a tasking for the intel shop. Now they were both looking at the petty officer. "Go on," Henrickson said.

"I call it Operation Kalashnikov," Oberg said. "I've got the ship operator and the schedule they're going out on. That operator routes via the Malacca Strait."

Dan knew that narrow passage between Singapore and Sumatra. A vista lit in his mind: an endless procession of tankers stretching from one horizon to the other, low green hills on either side. He'd often reflected that a single torpedo into one of those deep-laden hulls would double the world spot price of crude. "Okay," he said again, feeling a frisson up his spine as what Oberg was proposing took shape. "Go on, Teddy."

"The Straits are full of pirates. They come out of the islands in small boats."

"I don't like this," Henrickson said.

"Why not? You've seen the pirates out there," he told Dan. "Haven't you?"

He was never surprised by the omniscience of Navy scuttlebutt. "We had a multinational task force there at one time, patrolling to suppress them. But Teddy—are you serious? We'd have to—"

"We'd board as oil bunkerers, sir. That's new since you were out there. Difference is, pirates just bust the safe and rob the crew. Bunkerers take the whole ship, run it inshore, and pump the fuel off into barges."

Henrickson said, "You're proposing we hijack a ship—"

"Whatever you want to call it. We rob the crew and leave them in the lifeboats."

"Nobody gets hurt," Dan put in.

"Nobody, no sir. And if you want, we don't even have to rob them, just blow the safe for show, and that'd be covered by the shipper's insurance."

He felt like grinning. Oberg's eagerness was almost funny. "Okay, we put them in the boats, you say—"

"Right. When we're over the horizon we offload—to a boat, maybe a sub, whatever we've got. We set the ship on fire, to cover the theft, and nobody ever sees us again."

"I don't believe this," Henrickson said. "It'd be an act of war."

"Who with?" Oberg asked him. "The shipping line? It's Chinese owned, but the crews are mixed, Nigerian, mostly. The captain's Italian and it's flagged Panamanian. Panama's going to declare war? I don't think so. Anyway, they'll never know it was us."

Dan was strolling with hands in his pockets. Their steaming breaths drifted ahead of them, like spirits departing their bodies. He'd nearly laughed. But now he was turning over the idea. Henrickson was right, it was illegal. And would probably be a lot riskier than Oberg was making out.

But wasn't that what TAG Charlie was for? Covert operations, in support of Navy requirements? They'd tried the legitimate route, and gotten nowhere—worse than nowhere, and he recognized the shaky feeling now: despite the shots he was feverish. From swallowing half the Moskva River, no doubt.

It might also be a chance to poke a sharp stick into the Chinese. His grudge against them dated a long way back. He'd found Beijing's fingers in too many dirty pies, from selling weapons to people who shouldn't have them, to backing the pirates he'd hunted, to suborning a president he'd tried to serve.

The Great Game had always been bare knuckles and knees to the groin. But the Chinese didn't feel bound by even the few rules they'd agreed to.

"Mullaly'd have to get it cleared. Mention it to him?"

"No sir. Figured it'd sound better coming from you. You've got the Congressional. That gives you clout, right? And your wife—"

He bit back an angry retort. Why did people assume that because Blair was in the administration, that gave him access, influence? The only thing that influenced this president were votes and money, and of the two, money spoke louder. He glanced at his companions and thought, But why disillusion them.

He almost spoke, then thought again. About guys who'd died with him, maybe even for him: in Iraq. The China Sea. Aboard USS *Horn*. Women without husbands. A little girl without a mother. He wasn't going to let that happen again.

That was what command meant. You were responsible for whatever happened, good or bad, foreseen or unforeseen or even unforeseeable. That was how the Navy had run things since before there'd been a United States.

A hard rule, but one he understood. And one he'd tried to live by from the moment he'd stepped aboard his first ship, years before.

"We'll look at those files of yours when we get home. But Monty's right, too, Teddy. There'd be major grief if we screwed up. It'd have to be approved all the way. And we definitely wouldn't go to Mullaly until we sandboxed it, the whole team, till there's no question he could ask we couldn't answer."

"Absolutely, sir. Success through planning."

"Another thing. No matter who's on it, no matter how good they are at what they do, I'm doing the risk analysis myself. If it doesn't look good, we don't go, I don't care how much the CNO wants it."

They were both watching him now, in the sparkling darkness beneath the trees. He didn't think they saw it, he tried not to show doubt or weakness to those he led, but he was trembling. His knees were shaky. He felt nauseated. It had to be fever. He didn't think it was from fear. No. He didn't think it was from that, at all.

10

Arlington, Virginia

H E jerked awake, uncertain whether he'd actually cried out. This time he'd known about the bomb. Had known the trawler they tracked was not what it seemed. They'd tried to stop him, after all. Forbidden him to cross into Egyptian territorial waters. This time he'd obey. This time, he'd steer clear.

The well-known faces surrounded him on *Horn*'s bridge. "Left hard rudder," he said, in the hard tone that meant *I have the conn; obey this order instantly.* But no one moved. The bridge team looked through him.

His terror mounted. They had to listen. This time, he could save them.

A screaming started, distant on the wind—

Beside him his wife stirred, and the jostle of the queen-size stole him back from sleep again. He was home. They'd flown back into Andrews, and he'd called in to TAG for a Friday off and a weekend with Blair. Who for some reason had been snoring all night, and when she snored, he never seemed to lie easy. Not only that: they'd been uncomfortable with each other the night before. An argument over something so minor he couldn't remember it now. He'd wanted her all evening, but something had told him it wasn't mutual. And after the sharp words, they'd gone to bed, him first—he was still weak from the fever despite the Embassy clinic's antibiotics. He must have been out when she came to bed.

"Bad dream?" she muttered sleepily.

"It's okay."

"Was I snoring again?"

"No. Not much, anyway."

"So I was. You weren't having those as often. Are they coming back?"

"No. First one in a while."

He lay still, trying to recapture it, then wondered why it seemed to matter.

As if a lost dream meant losing a part of who he was. How could you lose a memory and still be who you were? For a moment, half asleep and half awake, he'd glimpsed something significant about memory and self. But like an eel it slipped and twisted, and finally when he grabbed his hands were empty, and he was back in a world where little that mattered could be understood. He propped up the pillow and opened his eyes . . .

. . . to early-morning brightness lighting the sheers and gilding the intricate ironwork of the queen-sized bed Blair had ordered custom made. It glowed on the portraits of her father and mother, the matching wardrobes, the maple built-in that was always littered with her novels, hairbrushes, cosmetics, and, incongruously, the red secure phone of the OSD communication system. And on his side another table, not quite so bookladen but with a few, and the drawer he'd had to keep a pistol in just to get to sleep not long ago. He still had it in the house, but didn't need it in arm's reach anymore.

The house was across the river from Washington, in the suburbs that had grown up along the Metro line. It had been built years earlier, so there were lawns and maples and elms and yellow poplars. A brick colonial with flagstone walks, and three bedrooms, and a family room in the basement though they didn't really have a family. Blair had done most of the furnishing. Some pieces had come from her Crystal City apartment. Others, from the antique stores she made him stop at when they drove out to visit her parents. And some were from her family's estate, pieces her mom and dad had let go when they redecorated.

A bigger, nicer house than he'd grown up in, and it felt strange having so much room, so many things he didn't need. But when he hinted at that she'd raise her eyebrows as if he were from another planet. Once she said that if his father hadn't beaten him he wouldn't feel that way. He wasn't sure if this was insight or psychobabble, but he felt like an imposter and figured he always would.

She rolled over toward him. "Remember what we were arguing about last night?"

"Capital punishment, I think."

"I didn't mean to be a butthead."

"Neither did I."

"That doesn't mean you're not still wrong. But I shouldn't have gotten all bent about it. Sorry."

"That's okay." He opened his eyes to hers, and his hand found her hip under the comforter. "Those the PJs I gave you?"

"I didn't think I'd like black silk. But maybe I do."

"That mean you'll take them off for me?"

"The bottoms, or the tops?"

"The bottoms *and* the tops."

"I'd have taken them off last night. All you had to do was ask."

"It didn't feel like the right time."

"It's pretty much always the right time. As long as the press isn't around, I mean."

He wasn't sure this was accurate but it didn't seem the time to contradict her. Not with her leg thrown over him and every crevice of her pressed against every projection of his. He felt around under the covers and found silk and flesh beneath. The silk flowed down skin smoother than silk, and his hands gradually penetrated regions explored before but still not yet familiar. His erection was like a third person between them, and when they fused, pulled into her as if into a perfect vacuum, she tightened around him instantly. From nowhere Oberg's words echoed. *Young, dumb, and full of come.*

She said into his shoulder, "I miss you when you're gone."

"Miss you, too."

"Tell me about that Russian woman."

"She was terrific. The Polish one, too. She had braided armpits—"

"Don't talk anymore. Just fuck me."

He felt her widen and soften and then focus down. He rode the first wave out, then kickstarted it again. If he timed it right and caught the monster she'd surf it for minutes, crest after crest rolling in and tumbling them over and over till they panted for breath.

He plunged and it built again, then they were over the top and headed down. She gripped him the way Byrne had, deep beneath a dark river. There was no way back. She was arched and bucking, her expression like that of a terrorist being tortured. He was a dark river reaching deep into the land. Two electrodes touched, and a stream of white fire connected separate consciousnesses, flesh and bone and blood filled with the shattering roar of the void.

THEY sat in bathrobes over breakfast, listening to the morning news. A gang shooting in Montgomery County. A freight train of chlorine derailed in Iowa. Two evangelical missionaries missing in the Philippines, probably being held for ransom. Her hair was damp from the shower and she had it twisted in a towel to dry. He felt damp and twisted, too. She'd gotten the dark roast he liked, and it tasted good after airline coffee. The bay window looked down on the backyard. Almost everything was winter dead now but in summer they had azaleas, and peonies, and tulips, and hollyhocks he thought too tall but that she loved. The yard was backed by a screen of trees so that with the leaves gone you could just see the houses on the next street over. He murmured, "Woodpile's getting low."

"I like a fire at night. Seems less lonely. Not that I get to spend many nights here."

Her travel schedule was as bad as his. He wondered what would happen if they ever got to spend a whole month together. "I'll call that place out on Lee Highway and order another half a cord."

"Did you see the *Post* out front?"

"Want me to get it?"

"Never mind. I don't want to see what today's idiocy is."

"Speaking of that, what are you doing at the Building?"

She told him she was in another political fare-thee-well. This time she was battling Treasury and a good deal of her own party, trying to add a light infantry division while the White House budget people were trying to cut the Army to fund the new foreign aid initiative. "Which is dead, in my opinion. I even offered them a carrier battle group. They liked the idea, but not the trade."

"Presidents usually get more middle of the road toward the end. This one seems to be getting more liberal."

"This isn't a matter of liberal or conservative. That's the point I was trying to make at the committee. The Right calls us antimilitary when we're just really antiwaste. Or anti, at least, spending so much on their pet donors. But we really need more manpower. Unfortunately we don't have the numerics to help us anymore with our force sizing. The way we used to back in the Kahn era. Who exactly are we deterring? And who are we going to have to fight? I know you think China's the main threat—"

"I never said that—"

"Well, not in so many words. But I understand your focus. That'd be a naval war, unless it went horizontal to Korea. But that's not all we have to be prepared for. Things could get bad in the Mideast very quickly. East Africa. Venezuela. We're just not ready for sustained ground operations anymore."

"You don't have much longer with this administration, anyway."

"No, he's quacking and limping. The court fight didn't help." She got up and poured more coffee. "Warm up? Then I've got to get dressed."

"Okay, I get to ask you what you're always asking me. Where's Blair Titus go from here? Is the Vice going to run?"

"He'll try but I don't think he's got a ghost in the primaries. I'm not sure who I'm going to work for this time. Actually I can't while I'm still at DoD. But Dad said he'd put my name on their Central Committee donation. If the radical wing captures the nomination I won't be welcome. I've kicked too many ankles on better enlisted housing and TriCare for retirees. The same thing that makes me anathema to the other party—putting the bucks against the people who actually serve."

"I'm new to this political behind-the-scenes. What happens if the other guys win?"

"Not likely. They've had Congress sewed up all this time and what have they done?"

"I think there are some strong candidates there."

"Unfortunately they've got your friend advising them."

"My friend? Who?"

"Doctor Edward Ferenczi. They've all but named him the national security adviser, if they take over the White House."

"Ferenczi'd be a great choice. He's objective."

"He's a technocrat in love with big weapons systems."

Dan wasn't sure this was fair to the guy who'd been his mentor years before, back when he'd been working on the flying torpedo that became Tomahawk. He thought about bringing up the Chinese and how influential they were in the administration, but he didn't need another argument. "Yeah, maybe."

"Okay, I'm getting dressed now."

He finished the pot and took the cup into the bedroom. He could hear her in the bathroom, finishing her makeup. Her voice floated out. "I was thinking. Would you have a problem if I ran for the House?"

He stopped, one leg in black jeans, one out. "Uh—that's one I haven't heard before."

"Well, we're exploring it."

"Who's 'we'?"

"I've discussed it with Dad. And some other people in Montgomery County."

She came out in her slip and glanced over as if she wanted to ask something, but wasn't sure she should.

"What?"

"I was just wondering . . . Dad thought you'd make a good campaign manager. I said I didn't think you'd go for it."

She was fitting herself into a dark blue dress. She was right, he didn't go for it. Radiation, spying, and politics, three things he tried to stay as far away from as possible. He'd be first to admit that was short-sighted. If everybody felt that way, it just guaranteed the scum would rise to the top. But trying to live in that world himself . . . "I don't know . . . actually I don't think they'd let me."

"Who? The Navy?"

"Right." A cowardly out, but he'd take it. "You serious? About Congress?"

She started brushing her hair. "Not yet. But we've got an incumbent who's vulnerable. I wouldn't want to go back to being a committee counsel. I guess I could hide out at SAIC or one of the other think tanks. Or take the revolving door out to Lockheed Martin and make some real money, general counsel or something—ha ha."

"I don't see you there, either."

"But I really don't think the country's going to go with the other guys."

"This president's ticked off a lot of people. Could be a backlash."

"I don't think the American people operate that way, Dan." She took her cell phone off the charger, checked it, tucked it into her purse. She reminded him of a Marine prepping for battle. Uniform, gear, attitude. She wasn't the same woman he'd had under him an hour ago. God help anybody who got in her way today.

"What's on your plate?"

"Not much. Call Nan and see if she can break me out a couple hours."

"A daughter needs her dad. What else?"

"Get the car inspected. Then start on those bookshelves downstairs." He flexed his fingers. He'd had the wood a month now, smooth seasoned poplar. He planned floor-to-ceiling units, to fill with the hundreds of books he'd accumulated and never been able to winnow down. A display cabinet for things he'd picked up over the years. It'd be nice to build something he could put his hands on. Too much of what you did in the Service was over and forgotten the next year. If not the next day.

"Well, have fun. How do I look?"

He ran his gaze up and down, then spun her around. "You look . . . very businesslike."

His arms went around her from behind, and his lips found her neck.

"Oh, no." She wriggled out of his grasp. "We know where *that* goes. Home around seven. If you're still interested."

"See you then, honey."

She turned at the door. "Almost forgot. I've been asked to speak at Davos. Next spring. It'd be great if you could come."

"Davos . . . where's Davos? Colorado?"

"That's Aspen. Davos is in Switzerland. A week long. And they hardly ever invite administration members at my level. It's a good sign." She hesitated, not meeting his eyes. "Will you try? It'd mean a lot."

"I don't know . . . what would I do there? I could try to get leave. If we didn't have an exercise scheduled."

"Will you? Would you?"

He hesitated, then nodded. But his heart wasn't in it and her gaze turned flinty. "All right. I go to your Annapolis reunions, but you don't go to Switzerland with me."

He started to open his mouth, to say that they weren't the same thing; an hour's drive to Maryland wasn't a week in Switzerland. But before he could muster words the door slammed.

He thought about going out and catching her car, but the way the tires sounded going down the driveway he'd as likely get run down. He'd catch her tonight, after she got over it.

Okay—Nan. He tried his daughter, but her line was busy. He stood irresolute, wondering if he should call Blair at the office. Try to make up. Or let it ride.

Instead of making a decision he took the remote phone down to the rec room. Flipped the table saw on and off beside the stacked lengths of smooth white wood. Looked at the pencil marks on the wall where the shelves would go.

He thought about boarding a merchant ship, putting innocent sailors adrift in lifeboats. Setting the ship afire. Could he do that?

He flicked the saw on again and off again, watching the blade turn invisible as it spun up to speed. If he put his hand in there, invisible or not, the teeth would slice skin and sinew and bone. Blood would spray over the walls.

He hit redial. Still busy.

Putting it all out of his head—Blair and Nan and Congress and the Shkval—he picked up a length of poplar. Taking his time, he measured it. Measured again. Then with a flick of his wrist scored a pencil mark.

There. That would be his first cut.

11

Southern Mindanao, the Philippines

WHOEVER had the control had set the day to broiling before morning. They lurched and banged along in the Cherokee, the air-conditioning so cold it made Dan's teeth hurt.

They'd been on the road, if it could be called that, for two hours, mostly on a side track that was supposed to lead around a downed bridge. Obie and the local guy were in the lead car. The local guy wore his hair down past his shoulders. He sported a little Uncle Ho beard and reflective sunglasses, a Walkman, cheap black sneakers, and a black Chrono Crusade tee he wore untucked with camo pants. Maud'dib Sosukan had said so little when they'd met that morning Dan still wasn't sure if he spoke English. As they drove he glimpsed him now and then in the car ahead pointing or sometimes just nodding where he wanted Oberg to turn. Not that there were any off ramps. They'd been in four-wheel-drive and low gear, going up and down through a mountainous jungle that had only grown thicker and darker.

Now, again, the Cherokee ahead pulled over. Beside him Henrickson plucked at his short-sleeved shirt and muttered, "Fuck. We lost again?"

Dan lowered the window as they eased off the track into thick edge-of-the-road brush. The rot-heavy stink of the jungle rolled in, wrapped in fever and wet fur. Within seconds his guayabera was sweated through. The air felt heavy, like some hot transparent oil. Oberg snaked out of the SUV ahead. He crouched beside it, as if expecting incoming. The SEAL looked carefully around, then motioned to them to dismount.

Dan stepped out into an overpowering shade of green that enveloped everything, and suffocating heat. The Jurassic must have been like this. He half expected a tyrannosaurus to come crashing through the canopy that blocked the sun and sealed the smells underneath like a greenhouse. They were organic, earthy, setting off alarms in primeval layers of his brain. His boots sank ankle deep into the churned-up red-yellow mud of what was less a road than a razor-cut where the jungle was not quite always master. He listened to the sounds that had gone still when they stopped the engine. Suddenly the world seemed very loud, and at the same time hollow silent. Flies buzzed in shrinking orbits. He waved them away, but they didn't take a hint. Nor did the mosquitoes.

"This it?" he called. Keeping his voice low.

"Our boy says so." Oberg glanced in at Sosukan, who was basking in the air-conditioning. The SEAL jerked the door open and hoisted a thumb.

The teenager unfolded himself like a sulky deck chair. He stood in a wheel rut, unbuttoned, and began pissing, only slightly turned away. Dan and Henrickson moved a step farther off. Wenck and Carpenter were back at the hotel; he hadn't seen any reason to risk more men than he had to on this first trip in. Beside the lead vehicle, Kaulukukui stood with fists on his hips, peering around. The darkness cupped a steady chatter now, distant shrieks like women being murdered alternating with clicks and hisses Dan hoped were just insects.

The kid hitched up his pants and nodded to Oberg, whom he seemed to have fixated on as the leader. Then stepped through the green wall and was swallowed, not so much as a swaying leaf marking where he'd been. The SEALs traded impressed looks.

Dan cleared his throat. "Jungle time, Monty."

Henrickson looked aghast. "I told you," Dan told him.

"I know, jungle—but I didn't think you meant, *jungle.*"

Oberg squished down the ruts toward them. His sweated-through olive-drab skivvy shirt clung to his chest, outlining his pectorals. "Commander? You two better stay here, is my recommendation."

"Who's going to do the negotiating, Obie?"

"That's going to take time, sir. Could take a long time." Oberg scanned the jungle again. "It'd be better if we scoped the situation. Set up the meet, do the psychology, find out their bargaining position. Then come back and bring you in as the VIP who closes the deal with their head man over a cup of tea. That'd be the smart way."

Dan looked around, at the silent, noisy jungle, then directly up. The canopy had grown together above the ruts, showing only a transient gleam far above, as if it was a single enormous organism that quickly scabbed over even the cruelest incision. "All right, Teddy. We'll do it your way."

He rubbed his head as the SEALs moved off after the Filipino. He said to Henrickson, "I hope that was the right thing to do."

"Teddy's sharp. They train for this."

Dan rubbed his head again. He checked his Seiko. Slapped gnats. They were tiny, but they bit above their weight class.

Far overhead, something mocked their thin whine. It grew slowly, though still far away. He shaded his eyes, and caught a glimpse as something raptorial passed slowly over.

"Drone," said Henrickson under his breath, as if it could hear them. It banked slowly, then disappeared over the trees. The chain-saw whine faded.

He hoped Oberg didn't take too long.

A week ago he'd been sitting in his office. The Navy's riverine force, small boats to take wars up rivers and inland, had been disbanded after Vietnam. But somebody on the E ring wanted the manual dusted off. It looked okay tactically, but he'd tabbed on scores of yellow stickies where new equipment and new surveillance and targeting capabilities might require updates.

Was the Navy getting serious about brown water operations again? It did occasionally. The Civil War, World War II, Vietnam. But in the intervals, the blue water strategists, the big-ship advocates, let everything learned at such expense wither away. Monitors, for example, had had to be reinvented to cover troop landings in the Mekong Delta.

He hefted the manual, tossed it on his desk and stretched, frowning. And as usual, after not updating it for twenty years, they wanted the rewrite by next month. Usually when you got an order like that you turned to and did the best you could. But it shouldn't be done that way. They should set up a development schedule. Run a CPX, a command post exercise, using the old procedures. Use the lessons learned to design a live joint exercise—Army craft from Fort Story, Marines from Little Creek, Air Force surveillance, Coast Guard shallow-drafts for inshore work. No service operated alone anymore. Maybe he could work an exercise in as part of the workup for a deploying amphibious group. That way they wouldn't need a major chunk of funding. It was always hard to push cooked spaghetti up a ladder, which was what trying to implement any kind of change from the bottom was like in the Navy.

On the other hand, he wasn't exactly on the bottom anymore. And that was TAG's business, to develop new tactics.

He pulled his keyboard toward him and booted up Word.

He was midstream in a memo when it occurred to him that maybe he could work through Blair. Riverine had always been low-tech, but maybe she knew of something that would make it high-tech. The easiest way to advance a project these days was to make part of it involve buying huge numbers of computers. That was the Navy's definition of stunning innovation—buying more computers.

"Or are you getting cynical?" he muttered.

His phone rang. "Lenson," he grunted, phone in the crook of his shoulder, still typing.

"Dan? Oh, you're here. Step in a minute?"

His CO didn't seem to be ambitious for flag, which made him easier than most O-6s to get along with. Dan front and centered on the desk. "You called me in, sir?"

Mullaly leaned back. "Close the door, Dan. And sit down. What are you working on now?"

"The riverine manual, sir."

"Almost done?"

"Well, sir, it's been twenty years since it was revised. And with the new emphasis on littoral operations in the CNO Guidance, the time's right to update. Only I think it needs more attention."

As he explained Mullaly looked thoughtful. "Maybe so, maybe so. I might be able to find a hundred thousand for that. And we could get our reserve unit to run the exercise. Can you give me a memo?"

"On my screen, Captain."

"Okay, new subject. Just got a call. Your Philippine mission's approved. The orders are on their way by courier."

He took a second to reorient. Then felt his hands go numb. "We're talking—this is the hijack, right? On the freighter? For the Shkval?"

"A covert operation. In every meaning of the term. Including the legal one. Covert, clandestine, and deniable."

"Covert," Dan repeated. He was getting that old sinking feeling. He stirred, suddenly feeling trapped in the chair's padded embrace. "Uh, sir, I'm still not totally up to speed on the terminology. I understand what 'covert' means. But what do you mean by 'clandestine' and 'deniable'?"

"I'll give you the official definition. A 'clandestine' action is one sponsored so the operation itself is secret and concealed. A 'covert' action conceals the identity of the sponsor. So it could be clandestine but not covert, or covert but not clandestine. But in this case, of course, it'll be both."

"And 'deniable'?"

"That means you'll have orders, but they'll never leave my safe."

"Unless we get into trouble?"

"Dan. There's no way the Navy could ever be connected with what essentially's an act of piracy." Mullaly gave him a moment, then added, "So, we all clear?"

"Not quite, Captain. What I'm hearing is that if things go to shit, we're out there in the wind."

"Not if we could help you, pick you up—that's not what I mean. There'd be forces on tap. Secure comms throughout. But if the cover blew off—no."

Dan came to a seam in the logic and cleared his throat. "I get that, sir. But another question. My team. They'd just be following my orders, right? They wouldn't know whether I was off on my own, doing something out of bounds."

"Well—not necessarily."

"Will they see these orders?"

"No."

"Then as far as they know, there *are* orders. Even if later, the government announces there never were any."

Mullaly touched his fingers together. "I follow you. In that case, yes, I could probably cover them. As far as any court-martial proceedings, their pensions, insurance and so forth."

Dan added the unspoken part of this chain of reasoning: *But not you.* "Well, sir, all that aside, and I have more questions along those lines, let's slow down a minute. On the action itself. I passed along that idea mainly because Teddy Oberg surfaced it. I don't believe I actually recommended we pursue it."

"True. You didn't. I didn't, either. You don't 'recommend' things like that. You just put them in a list of options and pass it along. But Higher likes it."

"Uh, what other options did we pass along?"

"Basically it was do this action, or torpedo or otherwise sink the freighter, or wait for the spooks to come up with something better than what they tried in Moscow."

"Which could take a while."

"Longer than whoever's driving this train can wait," Mullaly said. "They ran several iterations of the sink-the-freighter idea, but it always came out with too many worst-cases."

Dan could see that. "Uh, do we know specifically who Higher is?"

Mullaly hesitated. "It's SecDef level."

"The SecDef, sir? Or just his office?"

"Well, I assume it'll be his signature on it. What's the difference?"

He let that go for now. "Do they actually understand what we'd have to do, sir? We're talking about seizing a ship on the high seas. Then scuttling it. I don't have a problem with seizing these weapons. The fewer of these things some people have the safer we all are, themselves included. But the team would be at risk. And as you say, if the news the Navy was in that business got out—"

Mullaly pointed a finger. "Mind if I talk? Commander?"

"Sorry, Captain."

"I'm sensing an argumentative mood, but I'm not sure I see the reason for it, frankly. Your people can be tasked with covert missions, when required. We agreed on that?"

"Yes, sir. That was made clear when you gave me Team Charlie."

"Well, that's what you're being ordered to carry out."

Dan sat gripping the armrests. Finally he got out, "Sir, I know I'm not responding with much enthusiasm. But I can't pretend to be gung-ho about this. It's illegal, and it could be very dangerous for my people."

"Really? You've made a career out of crossing the line. In ways that, frankly, a lot of senior people didn't think was warranted by your orders. True or false?"

"Those were situations where there was no other choice."

"You had another choice: obey your orders."

"When they were stupid orders? Not to be non-Joint, sir, but that sounds like Armythink to me. I thought the Navy had a different tradition. Right back to Nelson and his blind eye."

"You're not Nelson," Mullaly said. "But my point was, you've crossed the line before. This time, you're going to do it to carry out an officially assigned mission."

Dan tried to think it through. This was no time to get angry. No time for emotion. He reached for that clear cold detachment he sometimes reached in extremis, and maybe got a little of it. Because he'd made it his business to carefully read the regulations and rules of engagement that covered what Team Charlie could and could not do. Unlike the movies, you didn't get orders for a secret operation on a self-destructing tape. He'd read National Security Decision Directive 286, and the requirements for covert action notification and approval by Congress. "Well, sir, I'll look forward to reading those orders. When they come in. Did the oversight committee get prior notice?"

"You're better off if they don't. Sensitive contacts have been made, with groups we're not officially speaking to. The fewer people know, the less chance of leaks while you're in the field."

"But that's part of the oversight process."

"By law. Correct. And those entities will be informed in the proper manner. Which is all they're entitled to, and all you need to know." Mullaly pushed back his chair and got up; Dan rose, too. His CO nodded, his manner cooler than when Dan had come in. "The courier will be here this afternoon. Start setting up your transportation and getting your guys notified. Remind them: close hold. As far as their families are concerned, this is just another SATYRE exercise."

He nodded again; Dan stood by the door. But for some reason he didn't want to leave, as if leaving meant it would all happen, and if he stayed, maybe it wouldn't. "I'd feel better if we had some sort of cover story. Just in case it really does go wrong."

"My advice is, don't waste time worrying about it," Mullaly told him. "You're just going to have to hang your butt over the edge. As you've done before. Now put that riverine shit on the back burner and get your team ready to go."

CROUCHED, letting his eyes adapt to the dim beneath the trees, Oberg bent to check the Glock in his leg sheath. The knife, not the pistol—a heavy-duty thin-blade he'd used in Iraq to cut truck tires off their rims. It was sturdy and lightweight, and he could sharpen it with a file. Then he straightened, and followed Sosukan's black tee. He kept his gaze moving between the trees, probing the shadows. He didn't trust this guy, and wasn't sure he trusted the people who'd sent him to them.

The Filipino was MNLF. And the Moro National Liberation Front was supposed to have made a truce, or at least a temporary cease-fire, with the Manila government. So far, so good. But when an insurgent group compromised, it had a way of splintering. An op was only as good as its intel, but on this one, they didn't have Team intel.

He trusted the people who'd passed him to Abu Pula. They said he'd been on the right side in Afghanistan, against the Soviets. But the contact had gone through several hands since, ending with this goofy-looking kid. Who didn't impress him a hell of a lot, although he did know how to navigate jungle. The Chrono Crusade tee slipped through the dim like a dancer jerking to unheard music.

Hard to tell when your visibility was about twelve feet, but he'd thought the road had been running along the side of a ridge. This seemed to be proved true when fifty yards on from where they'd left the cars the ground plunged away into green like deep water. The rotting wet leaves of the jungle floor suddenly changed into a mud-slope. First he went down on his ass, then Kaulukukui rocketed by like he was on a toboggan. Sosukan watched them shoot past, eyes unreadable behind the reflectives, like some cracker prison guard.

At the bottom of the ravine huge dead boles lay rotting, interlaced over a motionless stream. Enormous live trees with gnarled, twisted buttress roots made their progress even more difficult. Some looked like they were covered in ghillie suits, the kind snipers wore. Thick vines snaked down from above to seek the soil. With the interlocking triple-canopy over them it was like navigating the bottom of a long dark tunnel. The Filipino gave the ghillie trees a wide berth, as if they were poisonous. The fallen ones he ducked beneath, weaving and scrambling. Within minutes they were dripping with sweat, itching, and burning with stings and bites. He felt like he was fighting off narcolepsy. Also nervous: some of the rebel groups paid the bills with kidnapping. He wished he'd come armed. Still, you could do a lot with a good knife. He pulled out his GPS to check that it was working.

Sosukan took it out of his hands. Oberg was so astonished that at first he didn't react. Then he grabbed him and bent his wrist back. The kid dropped it, then stood there smirking, rubbing his wrist, but not going anywhere.

The Hawaiian came up. "What's going on?" Kaulukukui said.

"Bastard took my GPS. I got it back. But now he's not going anywhere."

"He's got you by the balls, Obie. Better go along. Unless you want me to fuck him up?"

He didn't think that'd be productive, to show up at the rebel camp with a terrorized guide. He turned his head, spat, and handed it over. The kid grinned. He held it up, flourishing it like a trophy; opened it, removed the batteries; dropped them and the device into his pocket. Still without a word, he turned and headed off again, ducking and wriggling through vines and creeper that looked impenetrable. Oberg looked after him, frowning. There wasn't a path or any blazings he could see.

Kaulukukui plucked at his cheek, then held up a tiny green worm. "Careful of these guys. I run into them before out here. They burrow in. And don't let them get anywhere near your eyes." He flicked it into his mouth. "Tasty, though."

"Thanks, Sumo Man."

TWO hours after leaving the road, the jeeps, Lenson and Henrickson, Obie heard quiet voices. Sosukan dropped to a crouch beside a tree with yellow spikes growing out of the trunk, motioning for silence. The SEALs

froze. The kid listened for a few minutes. Then angled left, around whoever it was, before coming back to his original bearing.

An hour later they came out into what was less a clearing than just
huddle of thatched huts at the lowest level of the jungle. By then Oberg
had no idea where he was, and Kaulukukui looked just as lost. His legs
ached from scrambling up and down the ravines, he'd scraped the shit out
of his back when he went down, and he was muddy. Leeches squished in
his boots, but it felt good getting out in the field.

Kids scrambled in from all sides, pointing and staring. Roosters strutted. Bowlegged, skinny, long-muzzled brown dogs slunk away. As they
hiked past nipa-and-bamboo huts he started cataloguing weapons. A
worn-looking carbine. An old Vietnam-style M16. Two Garands, rusty.
The rest were shotguns and antique bolt actions that might even be Japanese. He didn't see any grenades or RPGs, but you usually didn't even
when they had them; insurgent groups kept their heavy stuff hidden except when the photographers came calling, for the same reason he himself would be burying the satellite phone the team had been issued until it
was time to leave. Any machine guns would be dug in; they'd probably
walked right past them during the approach.

Sosukan led them to a central hut and for almost the first time spoke,
calling out in what Teddy guessed was Tausug. A voice answered, and
Sosukan waved them in, smiling at Teddy. *Some time soon I'll wipe that
smirk off your face*, he promised himself.

They arranged themselves around a smoky fire that made the heat
twice as thick, but kept the gnats out. Blinking, he made out four guys
across the flames. Weapons leaned against the woven bamboo walls. The
men were all dark-haired, most with beards, but scraggly, spotty ones,
like junior-high boys trying too soon. They wore a ragged assortment of
what looked like Philippine Army camos and weirdly random civilian
tees—one said "Ohio State National Championship Chess." Some had
black do-rags, others civilian ball hats worn backward hood-style. One
sported a Che beret.

The Agency had briefed him. Rebels, of course, but they made their nut
from kidnapping and quick raids. There was a connection between them
and certain elements of the Army, some of whom seemed to be trying to
set them up as informers against the MNLF, and the provincial governor,
who was playing a deeper game.

But he wasn't interested in the politics. *"Salaam aleikum,"* he opened.

"As aleikum salaam."

"Any of you guys speak English? Spanish?"

"We will speak English," said one.

Oberg got out a bottle of Tanduay, the local rum, and offered it around. Politeness cost nothing, and people who owned little valued it most. They didn't take any, which he found interesting. But they brought out cold tea and sweetened rice. They sipped and nibbled, using their hands.

Oberg glanced at Sumo. He looked comfortable, even somnolent, sitting big-thighed on the platform with eyes half closed. So far this was all SOP. Linking up with your hosts. Taking each other's measure. Too bad they didn't drink, it usually warmed things up. He took out a pack of cigars, a pack of cards. "Guys like a smoke? Play some poker?"

Two looked interested, but when the guy in the beret frowned Teddy saw who was boss. "We don't smoke. Or drink. The Prophet forbids it."

"Well, we certainly wouldn't want to go against the Prophet, peace be upon him." He put away the tobacco, the cards, the rum. So much for warming things up.

Che Beret tilted forward. "It is said you want one of our boats. What for?"

Okay, they didn't want to do the traditional getting-to-know-you stuff. "Training our operational people."

"You are Americans? CIA?"

"You don't need to know who we are. Do you?"

"You are right. We know. We have worked together before."

Sumo said, "You actually have this boat?"

Che examined him. "You are very large. Where are you from?"

"Hawaii, man. So, the boat?"

"The boat, the boat. Friends have this boat."

"Pirates?"

Che's lazy shrug was all his question deserved, Teddy guessed. "Fishermen. Sometimes, smugglers. Why not? But everybody wants something in this life. You want a boat. The question is, what will you pay?"

"We'd like to look it over," Teddy told them. "Before we get into the price. If you don't mind."

Che told Sosukan something in a peremptory tone. The kid, who'd been sitting a few feet off combing his hair, jumped up at once. One of the men around the fire handed him what Teddy was pretty sure was a Sten, a weapon he'd seen pictures of but never actually met. Sosukan racked the bolt casually. He slung it and motioned to them to follow.

THE beach was another couple of hundred yards, through low brush with only a few palms clattering overhead now. Oberg could smell the sea, and it smelled good. Rock formations towered. This would be a good place to evade aerial surveillance. The automatic weapon he spotted set up under a palm-frond screen would discourage any helicopter that ventured too close, too.

The boat was moored in among the rocks, with fronds scattered over its decks. He followed the kid down to it and waded out through the warm water till they reached where it swung to lines leading shoreward. As he heaved himself over the gunwale something rustled in the fronds. He hoped not rats. He didn't like rats. They acted too human.

Around here the boats tended to be plywood and bamboo outriggers, and for a motor, a motorbike engine with a steel rod for a drive shaft, and a pathetic little hand-hammered propeller. This one was about forty feet long, fiberglass, camo-painted in brown and green, with three huge four-stroke Honda outboards bolted on at the stern like swollen silver ticks. The SEALs had done a lot of VBSS—visit, boarding, search, and seizure—ops during the war. Teddy didn't figure this made him an expert, but he'd done over fifty boardings, sometimes two a day, and a goodly number had been on hostile decks. He tried to look at the boat from that point of view. It wasn't new, but it wasn't that old, either. Still it had seen hard use, with scuff marks along the gunwales, a crushed-in section aft bristling with yellow glass fibers beneath the gelcoat, and a charred place in the well that looked as if someone had built a cooking fire there. Small-caliber bullet holes were patched with what looked like shoe-repair glue.

He tapped the fuel gauge, then followed the gas lines to the motors. He turned the wheel to check the linkage. "Feels kind of loose."

The kid said nothing. Kaulukukui came back from an enclosed cubby in the bow, dusting his hands. "Smells like they used it for the head. This the only boat you guys got, brother?"

The kid shrugged.

"Kind of small," Kaulukukui added. "How far we got to go in this?"

"You know how far. And we don't need to discuss it in front of him."

"All I'm wondering, has it got the range? Will it make it?"

"Hell, it's a boat," Oberg said. "Let the commander tell us if it'll make it or not." He glanced at Sosukan, who was watching casually. He strolled over, took the Sten away from him, and doubled his arm behind him. He applied a little pain. "My GPS," he said into the kid's ear.

The boy hung from his hands. He tried to hook Teddy's leg. Oberg applied more force. Not too much, he didn't want to break anything.

"In my pocket," Sosukan muttered.

"Good boy." He patted him, dropped the magazine out of the Sten, ejected the one in the chamber, and stripped the cartridges out with his thumb.

Just five, all green with corrosion. He spun, throwing them far out into the bay. Then handed it back and patted the boy's cheek.

Who turned a slow burning red, and gave him the sort of look Oberg remembered from his own adolescence. When the assholes who hung around his mother, hoping for a producer credit, for money, for whatever glamor they could rub off her, used to patronize him, or worse, tried to be his Daddy Buddy. And those had been the good ones.

Yeah. He remembered that look. The one that said, *I'll kill you, motherfucker. Just as soon as I get the chance.*

12

Southern Mindanao

IT was raining again. For the third day straight. Monty sat by the rutted mud track, jungle boots off, picking the leeches out from between his toes. They'd chowed down good, leaving bloody stains on his socks. He pinched the head off a fat slick brownish-red body, shuddered, and flicked it into the brush as the gate squealed down on rusty hinges.

The hinges were rusty, the gate was rusty, the old Chevy truck was orange with the rusty frost that grew in the tropic heat and rain the way mold grew on his shoes and scum on his teeth. He liked to keep himself clean, but it didn't seem possible here no matter how often he sponged off and brushed his teeth. He scratched his crotch. Something was growing there, too. But when the rebels—he was sure they were rebels, now, if not bandits—began skidding the cases over the tailgate, down to the churned-up ground, he stopped scratching.

It was "the delivery." But what were they delivering? He'd asked Oberg twice, and both times gotten a half smile and a shrug.

In the days past they'd gotten to know the Filipinos a little. Some of them, at least; there seemed to be about sixty or seventy of them in the camp, counting women and kids. The guy in the black beret, the closest thing they seemed to have to a leader, was Captain Abu. Abu stood beside him now, watching the others sweat around the tailgate. The squat smelly guy in the black head wrap was Izmin. Another, in a checkered Palestinian-style headdress, said very little; Monty thought he'd made out "Ibrahim" when they addressed him.

What was interesting was that he hadn't so much as spoken to a single woman so far. He'd caught glimpses of them on their way in and out along the trails, and going down to the sea. Sometimes they carried water, or what he guessed was food, tied in banana leaves. But they kept out of sight, and even when you caught a peep they drew cloths across their faces, though their brown, scab-pocked legs were bare from the knees down.

He flicked away the last leech, for now anyway, and reached for his wet socks. The long-haired teenager, Sosukan, and Izmin, and others Monty didn't know the names of, short wiry guys with knotted muscles from years of hard physical labor, were working on the crates, prying at the lids with knives and machetes. With a little dying shriek of reluctantly extracting nails, one came off.

The dark metal was coated with thick caramel grease. A rime sheened the wood, too. The weapons were scarred, heavy varnish over dark wood. They looked as if they'd been banged around in trucks, or thrown against something hard. Curved magazines covered the bottom of the box. A dusting of fine sand clung to them like brown sugar on fresh doughnuts.

Sosukan held one up to the gray-green light. Abu spat something angry, and he flinched and handed it over. The leader fingered a knob and jerked a lever up and down. Then looked around.

"Obie?" he called into the jungle.

TEDDY Oberg hadn't shaved since they got to the camp. He'd told the rest of the team not to, either. He'd traded his pants for the same camos the rebels wore, and found a black T-shirt with a ripped pocket and cheap dark glasses. With a green do-rag, he was starting to look like them, though he was bigger than any of the Mindanaoans. Monty rubbed his chin. His was growing in, too. Kaulukukui, though, didn't show the slightest fuzz. Maybe the Hawaiian couldn't grow a beard?

"What's he got, Monty?"

He nodded toward Captain Abu. "Wants you to check out the shipment."

Oberg took the weapon the way a postal worker might reach for the next piece of parcel-rate. He pushed something in and with one jerk pulled the whole back off and then the inner mechanism out. Looked it over, slapped it back in, ran the bolt back and forth. Looked down the barrel, and said something in the language that the rebels didn't speak between themselves, but that they apparently all understood. Henrickson figured it was Tagalog, or maybe, Bisaya.

"What kind of rifles are those, Teddy?"

"These?" Oberg sounded surprised he had to ask. He thrust it into his hands, and Monty flinched at its greasy weight. "AKs. Seven-six-two by thirty-nine." He frowned up into the truck. "Yeah, there's the ammo. Mikhail Kalashnikov's finest. You don't know AKs?"

"I guess. Russian?"

He pulled another one, squinted at the stock. "Hungarian."

"Where'd they come from?"

Oberg didn't answer, just pulled out another rifle and gave it the same jerking apart, examination, and reassembly. By now Abu and Izmin and the others had theirs, too, and were jabbering and pointing them at each other. Triggers clacked. Monty backed off, hoping whoever had carried them last hadn't left one loaded.

He'd been wondering how they were going to move the crates, it was a long way from camp and there wasn't even a trail, but over the next hour a silent train of women emerged from the jungle. Loaded with four or five rifles each, or boxes of ammunition, or jerricans of fuel, they melted soundlessly, bent over, back into the green. Out on the road the rain speckled the water in the ruts, but not once did one of the Abu Sayyaf—he'd picked that name up from Oberg; they apparently didn't consider themselves part of the MNFL anymore—move out from under the cover of the trees.

Of course; the recon drone they'd heard pass over that first day. He'd heard it again last night, waking on the rickety floor of the hut to hear its mosquito song vibrating above them in the dark.

Finally Kaulukukui swung himself out of the empty truck. He looked at the trampled, muddy ground. Rubbed his big flat hands together, then pushed grease off them onto his jeans. His broad face was friendly. Henrickson wondered how this guy had gotten into the SEALs. He looked like he'd be more at home behind some food counter. But probably that had helped him doing the undercover drug thing he'd mentioned once. "Hey. Sumo. Can I ask you something?"

"Sure."

"Does it strike you that these guys, this Abu Sayyaf outfit—don't they seem kind of isolated out here?"

"Isolated?"

"I mean, they act more like bandits than fishermen. Should we be giving them guns?"

The SEAL stared. "We get their boat. And we got the AKs for free."

"That's not what I mean. Uh, what I'm trying to say is, I feel like I'm with Castro in the hills, or the Viet Cong, or something."

Kaulukukui smiled. "These guys aren't Communists."

"I didn't mean Communists. Guerrillas, I guess. Why are they hiding out here in southern Mindanao? Why's someone surveilling them with drones? Why—"

The Hawaiian's big soft hand engulfed his biceps. It squeezed gently, like a padded set of hydraulic shears. "Be cool. All taken care of, Monty."

"What do you mean?"

"Teddy cleared it. With the Army here, the governor, everybody. Don't worry your little head about it. Okay?"

He went back to the front of the truck as the engine started. Monty hadn't seen the driver at all. The guy had never gotten out of the cab. Now he gunned it, rocked back and forth to free the big tires, then snorted the vehicle around, smashing down small trees. Soon it was a fading growl, then not even that.

He looked around. "Sumo?" he said, not very loud. Then, a little louder, "Uh, Sumo Man?"

Fifteen minutes later Kaulukukui was there again, all at once, preceded by no noise whatsoever, as if materialized out of the dripping green. He held one of the AKs like a big pistol. Henrickson looked from his broad splayed brown feet, to the machete in his belt, to the gun. Kaulukukui was still smiling, but now he didn't look quite so much like a displaced sushi chef.

BACK at the village he found Oberg sitting in the middle of a rapt circle, showing the locals how to clean the rifles with rags and the kerosene they used in their lights. He started to edge past, but the SEAL waved him in. "Monty, you're gonna be carrying one of these. Grab Rit and Donny, get them over here, too."

"Me?"

"We don't have a lot of guys to do this with. Don't worry, I won't make you a shooter. But you're gonna be carrying."

Kaulukukui brought Carpenter and Wenck over from their hut to join the cleaning session. Oberg joked with the Filipinos, making them laugh uproariously. He took the guns apart one after the other, till they were piles of parts on the blankets, then slapped them back together so quickly it looked like a magic trick. The rebels oohed and aahed. Henrickson sat trying not to scratch his balls, his unease growing.

When dusk came Oberg put the last weapon aside and stretched. The rebels rose, each picking up his new rifle, and ambled off. No, strutted; they stuck out their legs like the scrawny village roosters. Sosukan lingered, smiling at Oberg, but finally he left, too. The smell of roasting meat and the women's lilting songs drifted from the cook fires.

Oberg turned to him. "Learn anything today, Monty?"

"I've got a problem with this."

"Yeah, you look like you ate something bad. Let's get it out in the open. Let's get some of that beer, too."

"All that trucker brought was Gold Eagle, Teddy. No Red Horse. No San Miguel."

"Fuck. Well, beer's beer."

Carpenter came back lugging the case. There were already several bottles missing. Monty didn't like warm beer but he took one. He shifted on the blanket, hoping his crotch wasn't rotting away. Oberg hand-signaled them to sit close together. Monty noticed both SEALs had their rifles where they could reach them, and pulled his own closer. Oberg toasted them and wiped his mouth. "Okay, Monty. Shoot."

"These are bad guys, Teddy. Why are we arming them?"

"Sumo Man said you were bellyaching. Why don't you get with the program?"

"Running guns to rebels, pirates, whatever these guys are—that's not part of our mission." He asked Carpenter and Wenck, "What do you guys think? This feel right to you?"

The sonarman shrugged; Wenck just looked at him with big puppy-dog eyes. He turned back to Oberg. "What about the Commander? What's Lenson say about it?"

"Lenson ain't here."

"Right, but does he know you're doing this?"

Oberg said, "No reason he should. The guy's a Shoe. Not just a Shoe, a fucking *Annapolis* Shoe. We need a boat, I get a boat. We need weapons, I get them. Why bother him with details?"

"What if these guys start robbing banks with these guns? Or shooting up some village? Aren't these Moros?"

"Morons," Carpenter cracked.

"Shut up, Hooters."

"Shut up yourself, Coconut Head."

"I told you, it's cleared with the Philippine Army," Kaulukukui said.

Oberg cleared his throat. He sat forward, and Monty almost couldn't meet those blue blue eyes. "Henrickson, you been at TAG longer'n I have."

"Damn right."

"And you're a hell of a good analyst. But TAG Charlie's new to you, right?"

"It's new to everybody."

"Fair enough, but stop shittin' kittens, okay? And stop acting like we're stupid."

"I never said—"

"Yeah, you did. Didn't he?"

"Yep," said Kaulukukui. He wasn't smiling now.

Oberg leaned even closer, breath to breath, and tapped his knee. "When you go operational, you're crossing into spec ops territory. You don't just analyze shit, you got to get your hands dirty sometimes. Which is why Sumo and me are here. Okay? And from what I hear, there was some reluctance to release us to you. We didn't ask for this mission. That's not how we operate. The Army, the Rangers, they'll bust their asses to get a mission. We got more missions than we got SEALs. But we're the guys got handed the job: join up and make this Team Charlie concept work.

"Now, the way we work is, tell us what you need, and we'll get it done. We get the intel, rock-drill the shit out of it, then we do it. Sometimes that means working with local groups that aren't the kind of people the U.S. wants to snuggle up with. I'm not gonna get into the politics of Mindanao, but shit, you're right—these are not good guys. They're pirates—that's why they've got the kind of boat we want. It just makes better cover. Okay?"

Henrickson scratched his groin and fidgeted. The men opposite were liaisons to what the military called the "black community." "Black" in the ancient sense of "black arts"; arcane, unrevealed, and most likely, evil. Usually the uniformed services avoided it, but now they were reaching out. Involving TAG. He wasn't sure if they were supposed to, or who they were reaching out to. The CIA? He didn't think the Navy wanted to get close to the Agency. This Filipino rebel movement, whatever it was? He shifted again, but couldn't get comfortable.

"How about it, Monty? We on the same page now?"

"I guess so," he muttered, wishing Lenson was there.

"Jesus," the SEAL said. He took out a notebook. "Now listen up. We've got a lot to do. And here's the plan."

RIT Carpenter was carrying fuel down to the boat that afternoon when it happened. Nobody else on the trail, just the two of them, and the declining sun shining softly through the jungle—hazy, like it was shining through smoke, or maybe milk, through the trees down by the water, but night already almost here on the shadowy trail. The air so hot and close you ran sweat just standing still, and the hum of the insects like a room full of tiny clocks all clicking and ticking and once in a while alarms going off.

He came to a bend in the trail screened by the banana trees, where it was nearly dark, and there she was gliding toward him, in one of those sarongs or whatever, blue with a pattern of flamingos or egrets. The moment their eyes met something clicked, like a misaligned vertebra snapping back where it belonged. No mistaking that. Just a word or two, a murmur; a touch.

Then they were slipping through the whispering waxy leaves of the bananas, pushing aside webs bearing huge yellow-and-black spiders, into the dimness. She let the headscarf drop as soon as they were out of sight of the trail.

She didn't kiss like an American, or like the Korean girls who'd learned it from TV. In fact she didn't open her mouth at all. That wasn't what lifted him out of his shoes, and it sure wasn't her perfume. She smelled of fish and hard work, but her hand knew the way to third base.

"Whoa! Been there before, huh? What's your name, honey?" He pointed to himself. "Rit."

"Reet." She smiled and pointed to her left breast. "Um mali."

"Umali? That your name?"

She didn't answer, just brought her face close again. And not long afterward, they were stretched out on the blue and white cloth. She was no *Maxim*-cover model. Her breasts hung pendulous, and her skin was going leathery. He figured her at forty, which meant she was probably about thirty. But who was counting, when she was rubbing his cock between her legs? She wasn't as ugly as some of the tail he'd woke up next to in twenty-two years in the Navy. She giggled as she pinched a green worm off the tip of his dick and flicked it away.

Until she pushed him away, gasping. "What's the matter? Did that hurt?" he murmured, cleaning her ear with his tongue. A sure-fire way to drive them crazy.

She placed a finger before her lips. Glanced toward the trail. A moment later he, too, heard the voices.

Male voices. They ducked and held their breaths. His heart was going like a coal truck climbing a steep hill.

When the voices passed he slicked back his hair and sucked in his gut. Tried to pick up where they'd left off, but she pushed him away. Motioned at the sky; made a curve with her hands. He frowned. "What?"

"You take me States?"

"You want to go to America? That what you said?"

"Take me States," she muttered, hiding her face against his chest. "I go, you marry me. I love you, do what you say. Take me States, Reet, okay?"

He patted her, wondering what to say. Like he was really going to take her back? But, shit, couldn't blame her for asking. He'd never seen a woman here who wasn't working, butchering chickens, hoeing in their little gardens, wiping snot off kids' faces while two or three others hung on them, while the guys lolled around shouting for food and telling stories and drinking, at least when Abu or one of the other chiefs wasn't around. A dog's life, as far as he could see.

She laid her head over and mimed sleep. Then waking. Then pointed behind them, to a screened glade by a ring of rocks he recognized after a moment as a well. The air was cooler here and there didn't seem to be as many flies. He tried to take her hand again but she slipped away, miming the curve again. She looked hopeless and desperate, but she was forcing a smile. He felt sorry for her, but hell, what could he do? Maybe a little romance was just what she needed. He showed her his watch, tapped it. "When?"

And she'd brought her fingers together, like a pair of scissors closing, before looking quickly both ways, then pulling up her face-cloth and melting back into the green. Which he figured, turning the dial to study it, must mean midnight. Not too far away, now that the sun had gone down while they'd been lip-locked playing touchie-feelie.

Whistling under his breath, counting the hours till then, he'd buttoned up his trou. Looked carefully around, just to make sure none of the rebel assholes was waiting to jump out at him. It was getting dark, all right. He was about to step back out on the path, when footsteps crackled.

The shadow walked past as Rit crouched, stone motionless in the bush. It wasn't one of the Sayyaf. They slipped through the jungle silent as smoke. Henrickson? Wenck? He wondered what they were doing up.

But not for long. When whoever it was was gone he stepped back onto the path, rubbing his palms on his thighs and smiling, a huge shit-eater stretching the skin of his face. Nobody'd believe this. Even if he told them. Which he had no intention of. At least, till they got back to Norfolk.

It would make a hell of a sea story.

"FUCK," Donnie Wenck muttered, wincing as another web caught his face. Full dark now and he was afraid. For a while he'd thought everything was okay, that he knew where he was, even though it was late.

Now he knew: He was lost. Pretty clueless, duh, to get lost on his way to the well to wash. He had his towel and the bar of soap from the Holiday Inn Manila, the last place with running water before they'd gone native.

The last with air-conditioning, a shower, or anything cold to drink . . . Oberg had gotten him fucked up in the bar, kept egging him on to chug the rum drinks . . . shouldn't have had that last shot out of the bottle of that native shit, either . . . he stopped, catching his breath as something rustled in the bush. Then growls and thrashing and something small screaming as it died.

Totally. Fucking. Lost. In the middle of the fucking jungle. He felt like screaming himself, but if he did, whatever that thing was might come after him.

Get a *grip*, dude. You're still on the trail, right? It's gotta go *somewhere*. He turned one way, then the other. He'd come that way . . . no . . . by the time he swallowed his panic, he couldn't tell where he'd come from. He turned right, then left, but walked only a few steps in either direction before he was convinced he was going the wrong way. He stopped dead again and listened to the jungle night.

This is nutty, Donnie. Trails lead places. You just got to go until you get wherever it's going. Then if that's not the huts, turn around and go back.

But it's dark.

Just keep going, jerkoff, he muttered to himself. And ran full tilt into another gross sticky web. He fought it, making little noises like whatever had just gotten eaten.

Then suddenly he felt calmer. Like he'd stepped through the horror and fear, and was back on the trail again. Dark, and narrower than he'd thought judging by how he blundered from one side to the other. But still, a trail.

Then he came to a fork. He didn't remember any forks, just that the track went from the huts, past the well, down to the water. He wasn't at the water, and the jungle was thicker here than he'd ever seen it. The ground was wet, but at least the mosquitoes were gone. Teddy had said that the ones they had here in the daytime, with the white and black bodies, carried dengue fever. And that they didn't even want to get dengue fever.

Was that a light? He rushed forward but suddenly tripped, banging his shin so hard he almost howled, like hitting it on the knee-knockers on an aircraft carrier. He figured it was the buttress roots of one of the huge trees. He almost turned back, but got courage from somewhere and pushed himself on. He was pretty sure now this was the wrong way, he wouldn't come out at the hamlet, but he'd see what was down here.

Voices. A dim light, one of the lanterns the Sayyaf hung in their huts. Some had battery-powered fluorescents, the portable kind, but most just used kerosene lamps. The light was soft and he was close enough to see huge moths orbiting it when he stopped.

The voices were in English. And they weren't Oberg's, or Kaulukukui's. It was a woman. An American woman. She was singing, in a soft, sweet voice. Midwestern by the sound of it. He stood stock still, listening. Then took a quiet step forward.

It sounded like a hymn, low and musical, but he couldn't quite make out the words. He moved in again, and one line came through the leaves and dark boles, and then another, before the longing voice was overwhelmed once more by the million-voiced jungle night.

> *. . . I surrender all, I give my self to thee . . .*
> *Fill me with a love and power, that your blessing follow me. . . .*

He stood unable to move, not understanding. Then, all at once, he realized who she must be, and who must be with her, and why small motors buzzed past above the jungle canopy now and again.

He took a step back, not daring to breathe, knowing that not far away, maybe only yards, someone was guarding her and whoever was with her, maybe drowsing but there, cradling a weapon, making sure no one penetrated this isolate ravine to its secret heart. And that anyone who did would have to vanish, and never be seen again. He stepped back again, and again, then turned and ran, sobbing for breath, tripping on vines and roots, splashing through fetid invisible streams.

He had to tell Oberg. Oberg would know what to do.

SINGAPOREAN ARMED FORCES YACHT CLUB, SEMBAWANG, SINGAPORE

"Don't even come aboard my ship," the captain had said on the phone. Which was a frank and direct statement, Lenson had to give him that.

As the sun vanished and night came Dan crossed his civvy-clad legs on the cabana deck, enjoying the first cool and watching lights wink on one by one on the moored-out yachts. The club looked out over the narrow strip of sea between Singapore and Jahore, Malaysia. A hundred years ago this had been jungle. Now it was the most heavily industrialized island in the world. To his right huge floodlit white warehouses and cranes marked Sembawang, a shipyard, freight terminal, and naval base that dated from British times. Now it was not only a base for the Singaporeans, but a stopover for the U.S. and other navies. Blazing yellowgreen pierside floods picked out a containership, patrol craft, gray hulls flying Australian and U.S. flags.

The single white hull belonged to USNS *John McDonnell*, T-AGS 51. Whose commanding officer, if Dan wasn't mistaken, stood now a few feet away, scowling around the cabana deck. He was in a short-sleeved knit shirt and blue slacks. Dan lifted a hand. The guy frowned, then reluctantly slid between the tables of chatting diners.

"You Lenson?"

He got to his feet, determined to keep this cordial. Considering he was essentially hijacking the guy's command. "Good evening, Captain. Dan Lenson."

He got a handshake and a grunted name, and then the waiter came. The other grumpily recommended the rice dishes, but warned him to order it "mild." They ate in near-silence, though Dan tried to start a conversation. The guy didn't play golf. He wasn't a sailor. He turned down the waiter's offer of dessert. Dan got the tab, but that didn't seem to warm the atmosphere.

The other officer wiped his lips and threw down the napkin. "All right, I had to meet with you. I've met with you. Thanks for dinner. Good night, Commander."

"Just a moment, Captain. I was hoping to get some time aboard with you to go over the operational requirements."

"You're not coming aboard. And this is the only time you're getting with me. *McDonnell*'s on a surveying mission. I understand you have some sort of covert, spec-ops-type requirement. I don't believe it's an appropriate tasking for a USNS ship. Nor is it worth seven hundred extra miles of steaming time. I've made my position clear in a message to COMLOG, MSC, and the Oceanographer of the Navy."

COMLOG was navspeak for Commander, Logistics Group Western Pacific, the captain's immediate boss. MSC was the Military Sealift Command. Dan leaned back, considering how to reorient the guy.

Sealift Command vessels were civilian-crewed and civilian-captained. They sailed on federal business: hydrographic surveys, laying cables, transporting fuel and ammunition, missile flight test support, counterdrug surveillance, escorting submarines on test dives. A lot of ex-USN people worked for Sealift, but it wasn't part of the Navy, strictly speaking; it was part of the Department of Defense, in the Transportation Command.

Which meant that even though he was pretty sure he had the whip hand here, it made sense to try sweet reason first. "Sir, how about some coffee?"

"I'll pass. We done?"

"No sir, we're not. Correct me if I'm wrong, but MSC's mission is supporting U.S. forces."

"My mission's *hydrography*. We have no intel function. We *can't*, Commander. The access various countries give our charting missions is on our ironclad assurance there's no intel function attached. In *any* way."

"What are you doing in the Banda Sea?"

"A sea bottom survey."

"I don't see the distinction, Captain," Dan told him. "That survey might let us find a sub transiting in shallow water someday. That's not an intel mission?"

"It's not covert, that's the distinction. It's cleared by the host government and they have full access to the output."

"Well, what we're asking for will take place on the high seas. There won't be a host nation involved, and if we do this right, no one will ever hear about it. So your argument falls."

The other's lips set. He pushed his chair back. "That all you got for me? Commander?"

"No, sir." He got his briefcase out and unsnapped it. "You can kick the directive up your chop chain if you want, but it'll come right back down. So while I've got you here, I need to make sure we're on the same page. Lifting capacities on your cranes. Boarding ladders. Stowage requirements. Security. The transfer's got to take place after dark, so—"

"How stupid do you think I am?"

Dan felt like belting him but just said, "Not very, sir. Okay? Now let's get this over with like the professionals we both are, all right?"

BASILAN STRAIT

Oberg stood on the bow as darkness grew above them, a black iceberg slowly eclipsing stars as brilliant as any he'd ever seen in the hills above Beachwood Canyon, when he'd sneaked out his bedroom window during one of his mother's all-night cocktail parties. When he'd hiked so far up there were no more houses, no more lighted pools, he'd build a mesquite fire and smoke whatever he had and lay back and watch the stars. That was what the sky looked like now. This far out from Southern Mindanao it was as if the electric light had never been invented. He balanced as the surf rocked the boat. The burble of the big Hondas sounded very loud. He hefted the long supple pole at its balance point, making sure it was ready to go.

Captain Abu had told him how the Sayyafs operated. It wasn't the way SEALs boarded oil platforms, a silent inchworm up from surf level. Or, the other alternative, the way he'd done it in the Gulf: run alongside in the inflatable, get a grapnel over the deck edge, and muscle your way up hand over hand. Some of the Iraqi ships had greased their sides. Others put barbed wire and busted glass on the deck. And some had even shot at them as they boarded, which hadn't turned out very well for them, given that the SEALs always went in with either a ship or an armed helo on backup, along with their organic weapons. The way he figured, anybody who shot at them deserved what he got.

These guys didn't operate like that. They ran in close behind the target ship at night. Matched speeds, and edged in until they were running right alongside.

The shadow was close above them now. Behind him he heard Sumo Man curse softly as he wrestled throttles and helm. Oberg crouched, eyeing the angle the shadow made against the stars. The seas dropped them, then they rose again.

At the crest he swung the pole up. Abu had sold it to him for his spare knife. The springy bamboo was light but strong, sixteen feet long, like a pole vaulter would have used in the Olympics before fiberglass. An iron grappling hook was carefully bound to the end with light line. It looked like Captain Ahab had lashed it on, but it was tight. Halfway up, he twisted it. He'd practiced this scores of times and was starting to get it.

A faint ring of iron on steel echoed from above. He put his weight on it, then leaped.

He put all he had into the jump, getting as high on the pole as he could, and went up the smooth slick bamboo hand over hand. He wasn't carrying a rifle. Or a pistol. Just his blade, and coiled over his shoulder, the real weight: a caving ladder, light cable and aluminum rungs, but still bulkier and heavier than he wished it was. The pole oscillated, then spun and smacked him against the black. Rough rusty iron whanged his back. He kept going, though the pole started to slip through his gloves, and got to the rail and pulled himself over and oriented, knife out. He pulled the goggles up—he needed binocular vision to climb, but he'd want night vision once he got aboard—and swept his gaze across the deck. Ready for anything, the way he'd have to be when he came over the rail for real.

He relaxed. Resheathed. Leaned, to call down to the idling cutout of the boat, the glitter of stars on black sea: "All right. Let's try it again."

The ship wasn't a ship; at least hadn't been afloat for many years, to judge from its dangling rusty plates, the huge hole in its side through which the surf rolled. An old cargo tramp, piled up years before on this shoal, it was being gnawed back into its component molecules by sea and salt air. Not a large ship, either. The stern was only twenty feet up.

He wasn't looking forward to doing this for real. Shinnying up a bamboo pole in the dark, dangling over the screw . . . if he lost his grip things could go to shit fast. But if he and Sumo practiced it should go okay. He'd drop the ladder for the others after he made sure there was no after lookout. Or at least, that any lookout wouldn't be warning anybody they were there.

Back in the boat, they idled in again. This time he nudged Kaulukukui. "Get farther over to starboard, Sumo."

"Centerline, we'll have less turbulence to fight."

"Yeah, but most of these freighters have one screw. If one of us hits the water, we'll be better off to starboard or port, rather than centerline. Maybe we can swim clear before we get turned into fish-flavored tomato paste."

"Mm, sounds yummy."

"Yeah, anything fish flavored, right? You guys ready to try it this time?" Teddy called back to the silent forms behind them. Christ, he hoped none of them froze on the ladder. Better to find it out now than on the mission, though.

The stern loomed and he crouched. Hooked on, and swarmed the pole again. If it was raining, he wasn't going to make it. Maybe roughen it with a file, that'd give him a better grip if it was wet. He hit the top, swung, and almost went over backward as the rusted lifeline snaked out through the stanchions. "Fuck," he muttered, and barely saved his balance before plummeting backward into the boat, tossing and growling below. *Good way to break your fucking back, Oberg. Then you can drive that new Samurai from a crank-up bed.*

He did the night-vision goggles check, then swapped the knife for the rock gear and kicked the ladder over. Sumo came up second, handing the helm to Carpenter, hulking up the swaying ladder with both their Kalashnikovs, extra ammo, and the tape-wrapped bricks of plastic explosive.

Wenck came up next. The gangly kid was pretty fast, considering. Wenck had wakened him the night before last nattering about hostages, a woman in a hut, hymns in the jungle. Teddy had told him to zip it. The Sayyaf did ransom snatches—everybody knew that. If they were holding missionaries, it had nothing to do with the Team. Maybe after they left, they could pass the word to somebody who could do something about it.

Now Kaulukukui grabbed the kid as his head reached the deck-edge, hauled him up, and set him on his feet. Oberg watched as he oriented, swept the deck with the muzzle of his weapon, took position at three o'clock looking forward. Good.

Henrickson. The little guy was fast up the ladder, but went wide when he came off it. Oberg hauled him back and pointed him the right way. He wondered if he wanted Henrickson behind him with a weapon. The guy was fine at a computer, but Oberg could see him turning tail if the going got tough. But they only had so many bodies. Just enough to secure a ship, if they all did their jobs. Carpenter was hopeless on the ladder. He'd been looking more and more bushed since they got to the camp; said he was having trouble sleeping. The submariner seemed to be able to handle the wheel, though. He'd have felt better with two guys in the boat. The old SEAL saying: "Two is one, one is none." But if he didn't have them, they'd still have to do the job.

"Okay, heads together here. Let's go over who goes where again."

The wreck wasn't much like the ship they were going to board, plus, there was a big hole forward; anybody who wasn't paying attention would go down twenty feet onto jagged steel. So he'd laid out rocks and boards on the beach and run them through it a dozen times.

He put the red spot of his Pelikan on the photo. A shot of *Fengshun No. 5*, taken from directly above. Labels identified the deckhouse, forecastle, walkways, and where they'd find the one piece of cargo they wanted. RUS U 8789032 would be a forty-eight-foot container, painted green. It would be double locked and isolated by empty containers on either side, above, and below, to protect the Shkval in the event of collision or fire. Unfortunately, 8789032 would not be the top stack, but one layer down. Before he'd left for Singapore, Lenson had pointed out this was probably a precaution against it being washed overboard in a storm, not to make it more difficult to steal, but the effect was the same. Since *Fengshun No. 5* had no cranes, they'd have to move the containers above it to get at the one with the weapon.

"Any ideas on how to get those containers off?" Oberg asked them.

"Like I said, blow 'em off," Kaulukukui said.

"I don't think so," Henrickson said. "From what they told Mister Lenson at NUWC, the guidance system may be pretty sensitive. We don't know how it's packed. We don't know if there are live explosives in the warhead. Given all that, I don't think we want to set off explosives that close to it."

Teddy didn't like how the little guy said this. Henrickson seemed to think he was number two to the commander's number one. The guy might be a GS-13, but he was still just a fucking civilian. Nobody else said anything and Henrickson added, "If nobody has a better idea, why don't we just use the boat? Grapnel on to the containers above it and use the boat's engines to drag them off."

"This T-AGS Mister Lenson's getting us. Won't it have cranes?" Wenck put in.

They looked at him. Henrickson said, "Sure, Donnie, it'll have cranes, but the less time we spend alongside the better. It'd be smarter to have everything ready to go by the time we rendezvous. The more containers we can clear away before we go alongside, the better. Right, Obie?"

"I guess," Oberg said reluctantly. "We're gonna burn the fucker anyway. We can dump all the cargo we want, far as I can see." He gave it a moment's more thought—there was something there that didn't sit right yet—then shrugged. "Okay, ready to play firebug?"

"Me first," Wenck said, hands out.

They'd brought the thermite grenades and the night-vision goggles in separately from the rifles, and kept them out of their hosts' sight, just so nobody got sticky fingers. He went over the procedure again—setting one off inadvertently could wreck the mission—and at last backed off. Took a final look around. Far off and low on the horizon a quarter moon was rising. No other lights; nothing but the stars, and the reddish, faintly shimmering moon. "Okay, Donnie, have at it. Just go slow. And, where do we plant these?"

"Right on top of the fuel tanks," Wenck said breathlessly, fondling the grenades. *Fuck me*, Teddy thought. *Got to keep an eye on this idiot.*

"And where are the fuel tanks?"

"Lower deck, forward, level with the aft end of the forecastle."

"Okay, just go forward and set it just a little behind that gap in the deck. Here, use the flashlight! And don't fall in!"

Wenck came running back, panting. His grin was a green leer in the emerald gaze of the night-vision goggles. "Fire in the hole. Fire in the hole!"

Oberg turned off the goggles and hit the deck as night turned to noon. The column of smoke and flame roared upward, pumpkin-colored fire blended into black smoke like some enormous scoop of mandarin-chocolate ice cream. Rusty steel shuddered under his hands. A horrendous chemical stink caught in his throat. "Shit, Wenck! Where in the fuck did you put that thing?"

"Next to some old oil drums up there."

"Oil drums?" Kaulukukui coughed. "That wasn't no fucking oil. That's gonna bring everybody here in for twenty miles around."

Choking, brushing off greasy flakes that fell from the night and stuck to their clothes, they piled aft and down the ladder into the waiting boat. "You fucking awake, Carpenter? Haul ass out of here," he grated.

"The fuck was that, man?"

"Just *drive!*" Fucking blackshoes, fucking retirees, fucking *civilians*. He was supposed to take *these* guys on mission? "Just fucking drive, all right?"

MUCH later, the moon stood above huts and trees. Firelight swayed. Figures lay sprawled, snoring, some wrapped in blankets, others in mosquito nets stenciled USAID. Broken glass sparkled where Kaulukukui had given an unasked-for demonstration of terminating bottles one-handed with an AK.

Rit sat up very quietly. When no one stirred he crawled away from the flickering circle of ruddy light. He fingered the hard long lumps in his trousers. The flashlight in one pocket, the bottle of the local rum in the other. He slung his blanket over his shoulder. Umali liked something to lie on. He did, too, considering what was probably crawling around on the jungle floor by the well. Their regular meeting place, now. He was both eager and getting fucked out. Whichever of these assholes she belonged to, she wasn't getting enough at home, that was for sure.

Well, never let it be said Rit Carpenter let down the honor of the sub force. He oriented by Polaris and headed between the huts. Past another fire, lighting Lenson's face as he sat with Captain Abu. The commander had just gotten back to camp when the team had come back from drilling out at the wreck. Abu was shaking his hands up and down, talking rapidly; the American was listening intently. Rit faded past, and neither looked his way.

Sighing as he left the last hut behind, he headed down the path that led to the sea, looking not directly in front of him but using the edges of his sight to stay between the dark towerings of jungle on either side. As the firelight faded he gradually made out the white glow of the foot-smoothed path. His mouth began to water. He fingered another lump in his trousers.

There were always women. And some were always open to suggestion. You just had to be tuned in. When you were, it was all around you. When you weren't, you'd bop on past and never even notice. Like fucking Donnie. The kid was so nervous around women, even girls his own age, he wasn't going to ever get any. He wondered if he should ask Umali if she had any friends.

The path turned this way and that, perfectly visible now under the moonlight. He hummed under his breath. "Rolling home," he sang softly. "Rolling home, by the light of the silvery moo-oo-oo-oon; happy is the day, when a sailor gets his pay. . . ."

"Reet?"

The half-whisper came from the darkness to his right. He stopped short, peering. Was he there already? He'd thought it was another hundred yards.

"Umali? That you?"

Was that a whispered yes? A moving shadow; was that her, beckoning? Maybe this *was* it. He swung the blanket off his shoulder. Touched the bottle in his pocket, then the hardness next to it. This wouldn't take long.

"Here I am, baby," he murmured, stepping into the dark.

13

ABU looked up from the fire when the shouting started. Dan had been sounding him out on his plans, but the Sayyaf chief had been evasive. He tilted his head, listening to the distant yelling. Then suddenly rose.

"What is it?" Dan said, getting up, too.

"You come with me."

When they reached where the path left the hamlet to head down to the well and then the beach, four men were headed toward them, shining flashlights and carrying torches. Dan grinned at the torches. They looked like the villagers from *Young Frankenstein*. He quit grinning when he saw who they were dragging.

"Carpenter, you didn't," he breathed. "Not again."

The submariner's eye was swelling closed and blood was running down his temple, dripping onto his bare chest. He didn't meet Dan's eyes. He started to speak, but was kicked into silence. Behind him, not beaten but plainly terrified, was a slight woman who hugged a head wrap, though she was naked from the waist up.

Abu shouted at them, and the men shouted and shook their fists back. Izmin, the squat, ugly little man who'd sat with the Americans in the headquarters hut, kept shaking the woman and spitting on her. She looked fixedly before her, gaze unfocused.

"Okay, okay, what's going on," Dan said, but no one paid any attention.

Oberg burst out of the hut area, Kalashnikov muzzle-down along his leg. Kaulukukui followed, also armed. Without a word each went to a knee, flanking Dan. Behind them the Abu Sayyaf were boiling out, rattling the bolts on their new weapons. Whatever the guys dragging Carpenter were shouting was heating the others to ignition point. Amin grabbed one of the torches and started beating the woman with it, scattering sparks over her hair and clothes. One of the others got the torch away from him, and someone else beat the sparks out. But they didn't act eager to do it, and there was a lot of muttering.

Abu and Ibrahim were pushing the crowd back, shouting questions. They shoved the woman forward, gesturing angrily at her.

"Teddy? Can you understand what they're saying?"

"Not a lot, sir. That's Tausug they're spouting. Looks like they caught Izmin's wife, I guess maybe his senior wife, with Carpenter here."

"Anything we can do about it?"

"Christ." For the first time since Dan had known him, Oberg looked uncertain. He rubbed his mouth with the back of the hand that wasn't holding the AK. "Well . . . she's dead meat, that's for sure. My take, him, too. The rest of us, we're gonna be golden if we can get out of here with our heads still attached."

By now Abu and Ibrahim, Ibrahim especially, had brought some order to the uproar. At least no one was being flailed with lit torches. But Dan didn't like the way the team was surrounded. There were at least forty Abu Sayyaf bunched close around them, each with some type of rifle and almost all with machetes in their belts as well. The women stayed to the fringes, faces veiled, keeping well back from the firelight. Their eyes shimmered in the torch glare, but they said absolutely nothing. There were kids, too, big-eyed, hanging on their skirts, and a dozen mangy dogs plunged about, tripling the din with frenzied barking. Abu was still speaking at length, questioning the original four who'd brought in the couple. Then he turned to Izmin, who'd gone berserker. He kept trying to burst out of the armlocks two of his buddies held him in. He howled at his wife, spittle-spray gleaming in the firelight.

"This might be our only chance to break out," Oberg murmured.

"Break out?" Dan glanced around. "Where to?"

"Hit 'em hard and bust through. Lay down covering fire and head for the road."

Dan doubted a fighting retreat through rough terrain, in the dark, outnumbered six to one by men who knew every tree, would have much chance. His anger boiled up again. "We might have been able to do that before you fucking armed them all, Obie. Couldn't you have waited to weapon them up, till after we left?"

"No way to keep 'em locked up, Commander." The SEAL shook himself. "Sumo! Monty! Breakout to the north. Stand by—"

"No. Belay that," Dan snapped. "We're not going there, Oberg! Ground your weapon!" The SEAL had it aimed at a villager who'd shoved him. *"Ground that weapon!* And stand fast. I'm going to talk to Abu."

"Standing down, boss," Oberg said unwillingly.

Dan pushed his way through the throng, getting furious glances and punches to his back. He ignored them and got to the little chieftain. Abu looked different without his beret. Less artistic, more like a thug. "Captain. What's going on? I am this man's leader. I must be involved in the discussion."

To his surprise, this seemed to go down perfectly. "Yes. You his leader. So. You speak for him?"

"I'm not certain—you mean, like a lawyer?"

"No. Like the head of his family."

"Uh, yeah. Sure. The head of his family." He hissed to Carpenter, "You stupid son of a bitch, don't you ever learn? You did this in Korea, too!"

"Sorry, Commander. She hit on me first—"

"Goddamn it, who gives a shit about who hit on who first! I've seen you operate! This time I hope they cut it off!"

He was sorry the moment he'd said it. Especially since it looked like that was exactly what the men milling around them had in mind. Carpenter looked shocked, as if he'd never expected to hear an officer use that kind of language. Dan rubbed his face, feeling the beard prickle. How instantly a mission could go to shit.

"Excuse me," said a quiet, nasal, but beautifully modulated voice next to him. It even had a Scottish burr.

Dan glanced up in surprise. He'd never heard Ibrahim speak before. "I didn't know you spoke English."

"Oh, yes. I studied at a madrasa in Scotland."

"Is that so?"

"Yes, that is so. In Dundee. Now, Mr. Carpenter," the imam said pleasantly. "Did you lie with this woman? These witnesses say you were found together."

Carpenter mumbled something.

"Excuse me?" Ibrahim enquired gently.

"I said, yes."

"Did you rape her?"

"More like the other way around."

"Really," said the imam, deadpan. "That is a joke, I take it."

"Yeah. Sorry. A joke."

He turned to Dan. "Your soldier here. He is married?"

"Uh, no. Divorced."

"Did you knowingly have intercourse with her?" Ibrahim asked Carpenter, courteously. "With Amin's wife?"

"I *said* I did. But I didn't know whose wife she was."

"I see. Did you know it was unlawful?"

"Unlawful? Fuck. I suppose so," said Carpenter. He seemed to be trying to buck himself up, which was probably, Dan thought, not easy, surrounded as he was by heavily armed outlaws howling for his blood.

"So you laid with her, knowing it was unlawful, and that she was married?"

"Uh—affirmative."

"And you had sexual intercourse with her? Was this the first time?"

"No."

"How many times previous?"

Carpenter hesitated. Then squared his shoulders and said, louder than his previous answers, "Fifteen or twenty. Maybe more."

"Oh, you fucking bullshitter," Oberg muttered.

"We need to defuse this," Dan told Abu and Ibrahim. "All three of us, or we're going to have a bloodbath."

"There is not other possible," Abu said.

"Meaning what?"

Ibrahim said oh-so-sadly, "He means that unfortunately, this is what we call a *hadd* offense. The punishment is defined; we cannot alter it. He was caught with the woman by four men. Four witnesses—as the law prescribes. And unfortunately, he has just admitted his deed four times. Also as the law prescribes."

So that was why the imam had kept asking the same question over and over. It sounded like entrapment, but Dan had the feeling "entrapment" wasn't going to be a defense. "Okay, assuming he did it. What's the punishment?"

"This that they do, is hated by God. It gives bad example to other women. If she has child, it will be hated by all. Therefore what *shariya* prescribes is what is best for the community." Ibrahim smiled fondly. "If she is found guilty, she must die."

Dan looked at the woman. Her gaze was still on the ground. He honestly didn't see anything he could do for her. "Uh . . . and for him?"

"For a non-Moslem? It, too, is death."

"*Death?*"

"Correct."

"Uh, right . . . but . . . there's no trial?" He was groping now.

"Of course, there will be a trial," Ibrahim said, sounding shocked. "Who do you think we are? We shall have it right now."

BACK in the hamlet, with fresh torches planted in a ring around the dusty chicken-scratched patch at its heart, and fresh wood stacked on the previous evening's embers to stoke up the fire. Dan had asked for a few minutes to talk things over. He motioned Henrickson and Oberg in, too. "Guys, we've got a problem."

"That's an understatement." Henrickson looked as worried as Dan had ever seen him.

"Teddy, we're going to need a plan in case they actually condemn Carpenter."

"Well, I say, fuck his ass," Oberg said. "Screwing around with the host group's women? A *Moslem* host group? Leave him, he's that fucking stupid."

"We're not leaving anybody. You think we'd leave you?"

"If I ballocksed up like that, sure," Obie told him. "If it means we lose the rest of the team, can't accomplish the mission—fuck, yeah. Leave the silly fucker. Maybe if they cut his empty fucking head off, he won't do it again."

"Well, we're not. So I need you to help me figure how we're getting him out of here. Is the boat ready to go?"

Teddy squatted, flipping up a bit of soil with the tip of his Glock, over and over. He was wondering if he should tell Lenson about the Americans in the hut. The man and the woman. He still hadn't seen them, but when he'd crept in to check it out, after Wenck had told him about his discovery, he'd heard the distant murmur of their talk. Midwest, by the flat vowels.

"Well?"

"It's running, sir. Had to get the heads off and clean some crap out of the cooling system, looks like they ran it through a bed of kelp. But she's ready to go now." Fuck it, if Lenson knew, he'd figure he had to do something about it. Then they'd really be up shit creek.

"Fuel?"

"Half a tank, and the jerry cans that came in on the truck. I did a fuel-consumption run, put the clock on her. We're good for about four hundred miles."

Dan went over what they had and where it was. The extra fuel was hidden among the rocks, down by where the boat lay. The food still hadn't arrived, though, and the water tank was only half full.

"Okay, listen up. I want Donnie down there, getting all those gas cans aboard. *Quietly.* I want anything we can find filled with water. And food, anything we can lay our hands on without attracting attention."

"We're not gonna be able to snatch him, if that's what you're thinking," Oberg said. "We might have been able to when they brought him out of the woods. Now they're loaded for bear. We try to shoot our way out, we're gonna get hit, bad."

Sumo said, "You give the order, we'll do it. But Obie's right, we'll just all go down."

Monty had been listening, wondering if they were missing a simple answer. "Look, these guys are supposed to be bandits, right?"

"Someplace between bandits and rebels," Dan said. "Why?"

"Well, what are bandits in business for? The *money*. Can't we buy Rit off? At this trial. Can't you pay like, blood money?"

"Good thought," Dan said. He sucked air through his teeth. "I'll try Abu. This Ibrahim guy, he doesn't sound buyable."

"Yeah, he comes across as a true believer," Oberg said.

Dan started to get up, but they were still waiting. He lowered himself again. "What?"

"In case none of that works out, we need an execute signal," Kaulukukui muttered.

"Teddy? Help me out here."

Oberg scraped the blade off on his boot. "Not much to say, sir. Group on you, blast our way to him, take out as many of them as we can. Grenade the huts. Then head for the boat and rear-guard the hell out of it on our way down the trail. If we're still walking."

Abu was calling him. Dan dusted off his trou and got up. He scratched in his beard. "Okay," he muttered. "Okay. Tell Wenck to get the engines turning over as soon as he hears firing. If we can make it down there, we want to be out past the reef before they can get their machine guns down to the beach."

"The execute order, sir?" the Hawaiian said again.

"Ambush," Dan said.

" 'Ambush,' sir?"

"Yeah. If they understand English, it might confuse them for a second."

"Not bad." Oberg got up, too. He squinted.

"Let's go to trial," Dan said.

They headed back toward the fire.

TWO hours later they were still sitting around it. Dan was in the guayabera, the most dignified shirt he'd brought, though it was filthy. Under it he was coated with sweat, and his legs were cramping.

They sat in a square. On one side sat Carpenter and the woman. She still hadn't said a word, and Dan hadn't caught her name clearly enough to be sure he knew it. Someone had thrown the blanket over her shoulders, and she sat without moving or looking up, hands in her lap. Carpenter fidgeted, pale under his stubble, sucking on a beer bottle of water the imam had ordered brought to him. Behind the defendants stood armed men. Dan, Sosukan, and Oberg sat on the second side. Across from him Ibrahim sat cross-legged, cool in a white robe that looked like something you'd get baptized in at a Pentecostal church. The imam had a book open in front of him. He kept quoting from it to the five men who finished the square, stone-faced rebels, apparently the oldest in the camp, most, though not all, with gray in their beards. These were the judges, the imam had explained in the incongruous Caledonian burr that made him sound like Scotty in *Star Trek*. The Abu Sayyaf could not comply with all the requirements of *shariya* law. After all, they were warriors in the field. But they'd do the best they could to render Islamic justice.

For two hours straight Dan had labored to penetrate what was going on. The language arrangements didn't help. Ibrahim would read something in Arabic. Then he'd translate it into Tausug for the "judges." Beside Oberg, Sosukan would translate it and the ensuing discussion into Tagalog, which Oberg turned into English. Dan suspected serious losses in meaning at each interface, but it was the best he could do; Ibrahim refused to translate what he was reading directly into an "infidel" language. Such as English, apparently.

So far, they'd established that four "upstanding" men had witnessed the act, that Carpenter was not a Moslem, that he'd known his deed was unlawful, and that he'd admitted his crime aloud four times before being confronted with the witnesses.

Dan rotated his head, stretching the kinks out of his neck. He was getting the drift of the process. It wasn't like a common-law trial. Actually, it was more like a court-martial, with its panel of judges instead of a jury, its limited representation, and the way evidence and admissions, matched scrupulously against a code that set down in black and white exactly what had to be proven to constitute an offense, were weighed against testimony about the character of the accused. He figured this was nothing like a real *shariya* court would be, say in Saudi, where it was the law of the land, but he could see where, if you kept to the letter of Islamic law, an accused might get something resembling a fair hearing.

The penalties were another question. He shifted on his blanket and tried to catch Ibrahim's eye.

"Commander Lenson?"

"I'd like a recess, please."

The older judges and spectators lumbered up gratefully and headed for the dark, fumbling with their trousers. Dan followed. Specifically, he followed Abu. The chief wasn't one of the judges, but he was definitely a player. He lined up next to the guy as urine rattled against leaves. Dan edged in; the guy sidestepped away.

"Uh, Abu? A word?"

"Oh. It is you. Yes, Commander."

"How do you think it's going?"

"We will have justice."

"Uh, right. You know, where we come from, we don't punish people for adultery."

"Really? Fucking other man's wife, is not crime in America?"

"I guess it's still on the books, but we quit enforcing it quite a while ago."

"Then you must have much adultery," the Sayyaf murmured. "How else will women have honor? Tempting is everywhere. Well, your road is your road. But we have Qu'uran."

"Uh-huh. Well, I was hoping you could see your way to letting me make restitution. For Amin's uh, dishonor."

"Restitution?" Abu murmured, pointing his stream this way and that. "You mean, pay?"

"Right." Dan cleared his throat. "How much do you think would be appropriate?"

The bandit took his time. He finished, shook, tucked away. Finally he sighed. "For five thousand dollars, I would speak to one of the judges."

"*One* of them? There are five judges."

"He maybe speak to the others."

Dan cleared his throat again. This didn't sound like a winning hand. On the other hand, he wasn't going to walk out of here missing one of his guys to some kangaroo court. Simple bandits? Right. They'd gotten guns out of Oberg. Now they were screwing money out of him. "All right. Five thousand. One of my men will give it to Amin."

"Not to Amin. He is not inclined to mercy. Give to me. I will give to him later. Afterward. As his friend."

Some friend, Dan thought. But what the insulted husband finally took in, or didn't, he could care less about. As long as it got them out of there with an unbeheaded Carpenter. "I'll get it to you right away."

The rebel chief sighed again, turned on his heel, and walked away, fingers digging deep into the crack of his butt.

BACK to the fire, and the "trial." Dan checked his watch. Four A.M. Carpenter jittered a boot, looking like he was about to tear out his hair and run shrieking across the embers. The woman sat in the same motionless suspension. Dan wondered if she was even listening, if she'd just given up when rough hands had grabbed her, back in the glade.

Oberg had been whispering with Sosukan while he'd been pissing and bribing. As Dan settled again he leaned and murmured, "Might be a loophole."

"Yeah?"

"The kid here says he heard, that if a guy's on the road, on travel we'd say, so he doesn't have access to his regular wife, he's like exempt from the code. From back when they did camel caravans for a year, or whatever."

"That's in the book?"

"He doesn't know if it's in the one Ibrahim's using. He doesn't think Ibrahim's reading all the passages."

"Great. But yeah, if it says that, we could drive a truck through that." He took a deep breath. "I put the fix in with Abu, too. He says he can get to one of the judges."

"Can only help. Good job, sir."

"This sucks."

"Copy that, sir. Thought about snatching Abu?"

"Snatching him?"

"Or Ibrahim. Or both. Take them hostage. They let Carpenter go, or we off 'em."

"I don't think so. Once these people start shooting, we're all going to be a lot worse off. Let's stick to the plan. Until there's no other way."

Oberg nodded and settled back into his attentive posture. Ibrahim cleared his throat, spat, and began reading in a singsong drone, rocking forward and back. The translation limped and hobbled: Tausug, Tagalog, English. A scraping came from over by one of the huts. Looking over, Dan saw two kids digging a hole. As he watched more came up the path, arms loaded, and dumped rocks into a growing pile.

"What's he saying?"

"The evildoers are invited to repent."

"Will that mitigate the punishment?"

"Wait a minute . . . uh . . . it would have, if they'd done it before the evidence was presented. Now it's too late."

He swore. How could he defend his guy, if he didn't know the rules? But Ibrahim did, and he was using that knowledge to twist them deeper into the barbed wire. If he wasn't actually making them up himself, as he went along. Their gazes met across the fire. The guy gave him a sly smile. Message: *fuck you, infidel.* "Uh, I have an objection," Dan called. "Point of order."

This went up the translation chain. Ibrahim smiled. "The Commander will speak in defense of his man. Commander Lenson."

Dan rose. He noticed Abu just behind the judges. The chieftain gave him a microscopic nod. Then put his hand lightly on the shoulder of the judge with the longest beard. The one who'd sat with a stone face through everything. Dan bowed to them, all five. They bowed back as they sat. All but the eldest, who stared with what looked like outrage glittering in his gaze.

Fortunately he'd spent enough time in the Middle East to make a stab at this. "Honored judges," he began. "We came to you as guests. Has not the Prophet, blessed be his name, instructed all true believers to be hospitable to the guest?"

He waited for the translation. It wasn't the United Nations, and the translations weren't simultaneous. He hoped they got the gist of what he was trying to put across. "I deeply apologize for the wrong actions of my soldier. Mistakes happen. I personally do not believe my . . . subordinate fully understood how wrong his act was."

He tried not to fidget or look impatient while this was turned into language after language. The judges stared, the flames leaping in their pupils.

"You must also take into account how far from home we are, and how long we have been away. Is there not an exemption, in the law, for men separated by duty from their wives? Men are men, and Tausug women are beautiful. Surely they would tempt even angels, much less simple sailors."

He searched his mind. Moslems honored Jesus as one of the prophets, didn't they? It was worth a try. "Jesus of Nazareth, uh, blessed be his name, once asked a group of men, who were ready to stone a sinning woman: Who among you is truly righteous? Let him cast the first stone. And no one stepped forward. They turned away, one by one, and left."

None of these guys looked like he planned to slink away. They looked like a stoning jury. Dan rubbed his sweaty palms on his trousers. Carpenter was yearning up at him with desperate hope. Yeah, you sweat, too, you cunt-happy son of a bitch. He groped, unwilling to sit down. He'd spoken at many masts for many of his men, but never for their lives. *So do it, Lenson.*

"And, finally . . . uh . . . finally, I ask your mercy on both this man and this woman, and offer to pay any fine the judges may think right. Uh, in Allah's name, as your guest and friend, I ask this. Thank you."

He sat down disappointed, as if he'd had his chance and blown it. But

Oberg leaned and whispered, "That was pitched just right, Commander. You shoulda been a JAG."

"Yeah, well. At least I got the fix in." He had a sudden flash of fear: Had Henrickson actually made the payoff? He twisted where he sat as the imam droned on, rocking over his book, and searched the flickering dark for the analyst. Who signaled back from the direction of the huts. Dan frowned; surreptitiously scratched his palm. Henrickson looked both ways, then laid one hand firmly in the other. Dan breathed again. He turned back and tried to look as though he was concentrating on the imam's monotone.

Which finally came to an end and was succeeded by silence. Then, after a stir among the judges, they clambered to their feet, one after the other, and moved off away from the fire. Where they went into a huddle, heads together.

Dan took advantage of the break to massage a cramp out of his calf and get a dipperful of water from the ready bucket. He checked his watch, then the sky. Gray light percolated behind the black cutouts of the palms. He hitched up his pants and ducked into his hut. His AK was under his blanket. He loaded it, slung it as unostentatiously as he could, and went back out and settled into his place again, laying it carefully beside him. Oberg had his handy, too. They exchanged glances. Carpenter called something to them but the guy behind him sank the butt of his rifle in his spine, and he gasped and sank back. Dan took a deep breath, trying to still the trembling in his knees. In five minutes, he might be dead. They all might be.

The flames were translucent pale in the growing dawnlight. The woman still hadn't moved. No one had spoken for her at all, nor had she shown any reaction to the testimony. He couldn't decide if it was shock or resignation, or maybe the final transcendent peace a mouse was supposed to feel, in the jaws of the cat.

Ibrahim droned in his pedantic monotone. The oldest judge creaked to his feet again. The graybeard coughed into his fist, obviously relishing being the center of attention. Then made a wide gesture that ended at the accused couple, and spouted a couple of sentences.

Beside him Oberg whispered, "Well, *that* I understood."

"What'd he say?" Dan tensed.

"The verdict: guilty."

"Fuck."

"The punishment: Each is to be placed in a hole and covered with soil. He, up to his waist. She, to a line above her breasts."

"Then?"

Oberg muttered, "Then, they're to be stoned to death." His hand fell casually to the blanket.

There didn't seem to be an appeal process; the rebels were tugging Carpenter to his feet. They pulled him toward where the kids were digging, shouting at them. They mock-screamed and ran. The rest of the spectators began getting up, feeling around for their weapons.

Dan's fingers found his own. He pushed the safety off.

He had his mouth open to shout when a far-off *bonk* echoed through the jungle. Then another.

The rebels froze. Their heads cocked. Their mouths came open.

The first mortar round exploded on the far side of the village. Then, in a ripple of flashes, a cascading roar, dirt and logs leapt up into huge black airborne mounds. They began walking inland, toward where judges, accusers, spectators broke, scattered, screaming, arms clasped over their heads.

Dan's reflexes had driven him to the ground at the first explosion. He hugged it, clawing down into it, as the mortars walked over them. The sky went dark. Trees, beams, cookpots, smoking tree stumps hurtled into the air. Shock waves slammed his face into the soil, then whammed his chest into the ground like a giant staple gun.

Abruptly the barrage ceased. He started to his feet, then changed his mind and scrambled baboonlike through smoke and pattering dirt to the hole the kids had dug. He knew what came next. Kaulukukui hurtled in on top of him, driving the breath out of his lungs again.

A rising roar began off in the hills. It grew till it was on them, over them.

A black shape darted out of the sky, twin engines howling. Black streamlines tumbled from it. Where they hit, the jungle erupted into long smears of orange flame. A second jet. A third. Thought oozed through frozen terror. A-10s. Warthogs. They were laying a careful pattern of seething flame, boxing in the low valley leading to the sea.

A crackle broke out uphill, on the far side of the burning jungle. Around them the rebels jumped to their feet. Fumbling with their new weapons, they began firing wildly into the smoke. Dan squinted, searching for what they were firing at.

Something grabbed his arm. He flinched away, then caught Oberg's shout through the ring-tones of the explosions. "Philippine Army. They're after the hostages."

"Hostages? What hostages?" One of the moments-ago judges stumbled past him, trying to jam a Kalashnikov magazine into a rusty Garand. Dan glimpsed Carpenter leading the woman, hand in hand, toward the smoke cloud. "Carpenter! *Carpenter!* Get your ass back here!"

"Fall back!" Oberg was yelling. "Fall back on the boat!" The SEAL set his AK to his shoulder and hosed a burst uphill. Dan was about to shout at

him to stop when he noticed the rebels were all firing in the same direction, and moving forward, but that Oberg was falling back a step with
each burst. The effect was to gradually separate the Americans and the
Abu Sayyaf.

He fell back, too, pausing twice to trigger a burst in the direction of the
hills. Something was wrong with his leg, but he didn't look down. Another
thunderstorm of mortar shells walked across the hamlet like a titan with
a bad swing hooking up huge divots. Kaulukukui hulked out of the smoke
and hanging dust, carrying a kicking Carpenter. He set the submariner on
his feet, slapped a pistol in his hand, and shoved him toward the beach.

Dan fired till his magazine ran dry, spun, and sprinted down the trail.
Gasoline-stinking fires crackled along it. Red stringy things hung from
the burning palms. He vaulted a woman's smoking body, her back laid
open like a split hog at a barbecue, clothes aflame. Ahead he caught Henrickson's diminutive figure, bowed in an all-out sprint. He sucked air, trying to keep his legs moving.

The jungle fell away. There were the vertical rocks, the gritty sand, and
the boat. The rumble of engines. Wenck, standing to toss a line free, then
spinning the wheel, bringing her stern to as Dan and the others hit the
water and waded in, holding their rifles high. The smoke blew off the land
low and dark. Dan hoped it would screen them. "Cast off!" he screamed,
voice squeaky in a smoke-blistered throat. "Cast the fuck off, Donnie!"

A machine gun, a fifty by the sound of it, riveted slugs over their heads.
Dan reached the stern, threw his rifle in, and pulled himself over the gunwale. He fell on top of someone else, wheezing, as the big Hondas snarled
up to full throttle. When he recognized his own hand in front of his eyes it
was black with soot and coated with blood and dirt.

14

The Kepuluan Tambelan (Tambelan Islands), South China Sea

THE islands were surprisingly high for such small specks of land, so far from anywhere. Dark green, sheathed with thick jungle and built on white foundations of surf. Parrots, at least he thought they were parrots, trailed long yellow tails, wheeling in noisy flocks. Surf seethed along the rocks at the base of the smallest, supposedly—according to the *China Sea Pilot*—uninhabited.

Dan lowered the binoculars and squeegeed his hand down his face. The heat rose in clouds around and under his clothes. It melted his face and ran down his cheeks. His eyeballs were liquefying. He worked his dry mouth and spat a slimy paste over the side, where it slowly uncoiled in the clear faintly rocking water.

He couldn't enjoy the sun. Not as short of water, sunburned, and hungry as they were. He wondered if there were any wild pigs, anything edible, in that coarse green verdure. Didn't really matter, they couldn't take the risk, but he still wondered. He leaned back, rubbing what was now a respectable beard. But he was careful to keep his gaze averted from the other eyes staring at him.

He wondered if he was really safe turning his back on them.

IT had been a long voyage down. Five days, all in all, though they hadn't spent that entire time under way.

That first afternoon out, fleeing, he'd kept the boat close inshore, under cover of the smoke-pall from the burning huts and jungle; then, as it thinned, turned sharp and angled out to sea. He kept their speed down to minimize their wake. Five miles out he angled again, to join a half-mile circle of fishing craft drawing a net tight. He pulled up alongside one of the fishermen. The boat was weatherbeaten, handmade, strewn with nets, cooking pots, and clothes hanging on lines to dry; the family stared open-mouthed, like the children back in the village. Who were probably, he thought, being shot and burned even now . . . Kaulukukui and Oberg grabbed the net with boathooks and hauled a corner aboard.

They watched the jungle burn. And the fishermen watched them, but made no move either to welcome or shoo them off. Maybe their rifles had something to do with that. And their masquerade must have worked, because although the A-10s howled back and worked the rebel hamlet over again, with high explosive this time, they didn't seem to notice the boat.

Around nine o'clock, as the sun started to get really intense, the fishermen pulled in their nets. He kept the one they had hold of, and again, no one objected. The little fleet cranked up their put-puts and nosed west in a loose gaggle, some leading, others trailing, drawing wide glittering vees across the calm sea. Dan started one Honda and ran with them, staying in the centroid of the group, neither one of the leaders nor the tail end charlie.

All that day they headed west, across the Strait and through a narrow unmarked channel of clear shallow green water, reddish-brown coral heads, and white sand bottom between what the chart called Sangboy and Teinga Islands, out into the Sulu Sea. He kept a close eye on the coral heads, but mainly just stayed in the wake of the fishermen. They cleared the channel as the sun started to dip, and turned north. Dan made a sweep of the horizon, clicking all the way around ten degrees at a time; then another, checking the sky. Clear. He pointed for Kaulukukui, at the helm, to keep the bow headed west.

"We keep poking along like this?"

"You can nudge her up to ten. That speedometer's working, right?"

"Ten? That's all?"

"Long way to go, Sumo. Let's keep it slow till we see if we've got the fuel to make it."

The other boats sank slowly beneath towering white clouds, leaving them alone on a sea like an old mirror. After half an hour Dan took his binoculars, which he'd managed to save, and checked the horizon again. Once he was sure there were no boats, no aircraft, and as far as he could tell, no drones tracking them, he took out his nav kit and the rest of the charts and went forward, behind the windshield, and began planning their route.

He'd expected to do this before they got underway, but now he perched on the gunwale and tried to do it on a folded chart with a pencil. He worked at it for an hour, checking and rechecking his intended course and fuel consumption figures. Then put it aside and stared down into the slowly passing sea, the purr of the four-stroke resonating across the flat water.

He figured the total distance to the intercept point at a little under a thousand nautical miles. Running at just below hull speed, they'd make about 230 nautical miles a day, which would make it 4.3 days in transit.

Unfortunately, when he compared that to the fuel/mile curves Oberg had worked up, it meant they'd run their tanks dry three days out. The Philippine Army attack had forced them to cast off with low fuel, hardly any food, and nowhere near enough water.

On the other hand, they were underway two days early. So there was no hurry, but there was a real danger of running out of everything, fuel first, leaving them rocking and baking in the South China Sea till they died of dehydration and sun poisoning.

He scratched in his beard again, combed it with his fingers. He went through the charts, then the *Pilot*, then his other references, looking for a favorable current or a bright idea, but came out empty-handed. He had no wind, no sails, and no oars, so that ruled out any assist.

"Crap," he whispered. He sucked on the divider-points and thought.

OBIE was on the wheel the next day when they saw the plane. Teddy caught the first glint far off over the rugged humpy lushness that was the coast of Borneo. Malaysia, over there. Or maybe Brunei—he wasn't sure. He'd been here a couple of times before, but he wasn't sure of the borders. And Lenson didn't seem to want to let the charts out of his hands. Control. Control. Control. There it was.

He glanced back to where they'd rigged a tarp against the blazing sun. The commander was huddled under it in jeans and his dirty shirt, asleep. Or at least, with his eyes closed.

They'd run all night, navigating by sight and guess between Malaysia and Balabac Island and out into the warm open blackness of the South China Sea. Teddy had been surprised there'd been so little traffic. Only two sets of running lights all the way through. As soon as Lenson had figured they were clear they'd come to port and headed down the coast. There were little islands ten or fifteen miles offshore and he wanted to stay inboard of them, stay as close inshore as they could. Teddy didn't see the point. Who knew they were here? Who cared? Lenson kept complaining they didn't have a fathometer. It would have been nice, but they had the spare GPS. They weren't running a fucking destroyer here. Just a piece of shit pirate boat. They were lucky the engines even ran.

Thinking about that, he told Kaulukukui, "Hey, Sumo, that engine sound okay to you?"

"I don't know. Sound good to you?"

"Hear that chatter? Sounds like a timing belt. We ought to pull the cover off, take a look."

"I say long as it runs, leave it be."

"Yeah, you'd say that. Fucking puddinghead Hawaiian."

"Fucking rich boy hao'le." Kaulukukui dipped his skivvy shirt over the side and wrapped it around his head.

"Hey, a real raghead. I pull on the end of that, does your head spin around?"

"Try it and see, asshole."

Teddy didn't come back. He kept his attention focused where he'd seen the glint. And pretty soon he saw it again. He looked aft to where the guys off watch were tumbled along the gunwales. The fat one, the submariner, Carpenter, was awake and looking at him. "Rit."

"Yeah?"

"Shake Lenson up there."

"He was up all night."

"Get him up, Carpenter."

Lenson rolled over, maybe he hadn't been asleep after all, and crawled out from the shade. He rubbed his face. "What you got?"

"Air contact."

He pointed, and they watched together for some minutes. "Heading our way," Lenson said at last.

"Airplane," Teddy yelled, and around the boat figures flinched and started to move. They crawled under the tarp or into the cuddy, with the anchor and line and the crates they'd stowed the weapons and ammo in to keep them out of the salt. Teddy snapped, "Sumo, grab somebody to help and get that fucking net deployed. We're supposed to be fishermen here."

They grabbed the net and started wrestling it toward the side. It was damp yellow twisted nylon, very heavy, and stank of rotted fish. They had the heavy rolled bundle up on the gunwale when Lenson turned from the plane. He saw what they were doing and recoiled. "Get that back inboard," he barked.

"We're fishermen, we need a—"

"I said, get it inboard! Cut that engine!"

They looked at Teddy. Who hesitated. Then pushed the throttle to idle and the shift to neutral. "You heard the commander. Get the fucking thing in."

"Soon as they have it out of the water, put us back in gear. Same course."

"Fuckhead," Teddy muttered. But he obeyed.

The plane came in on them. A little high-wing prop job, single engine. It flew over them five hundred feet up and droned off to the north in a straight line. They watched till it was out of sight.

"Monty, take the wheel." Lenson turned to Teddy. "Come on back here a minute."

They stood beside the running engine. Teddy noticed again it sounded funny, a sort of chatter. Right now though he had to handle this guy. He crammed fists into pockets. "Beard looks good on you, Commander. Got a problem?"

"You got one, Petty Officer?"

"I'm here to make problems go away."

"I don't want any question about who's in charge of this team, Oberg."

"SEALs think for themselves, sir. I thought looking like a fisherman was a good idea. If we're supposed to be a fisherman."

"How many missions you been on that had two guys in charge, Oberg?"

Under that gray stare he didn't feel as assured as he had before. He took his hands out of his pockets. "Not many."

"If that plane was looking for us, a smooth sea like this, he had his eyeballs on us miles away. Long before we saw him. It'd be a dead giveaway to slow, alter course, and put out a net. Just the kink in our wake would show him that."

After a moment Teddy said, "Okay. Copy that."

"I'd prefer 'aye aye, sir.' And another thing, I want you to set up a lookout rotation. So if there's another plane, or a surface contact, we see it before it sees us."

Teddy watched a muscle jump under the commander's eye. The guy was wound tight. Maybe not that far from losing it. "Aye aye, sir."

Lenson turned away. Oberg contemplated the back of his head, then went back to the wheel. "I got it, Jeff."

"We gonna have trouble with this guy?" Kaulukukui muttered.

"Just blackshoe bullshit. Setting up watches. Making sure I know who's boss." He spat over the side, looked at the compass, then back at their wake. "Jesus, man, can't you even steer?"

THEY drank the last of the water the next day. Another blazer and no wind, or to be exact, what little there was blew from directly astern, making the exhaust travel with them for hours. Neither SEAL commented on it, but Wenck and Carpenter complained incessantly, and Henrickson vomited despite the calm seas. He seemed disoriented and lethargic, slumped under the shade of the tarp. Dan figured it was either sunstroke or dehydration, maybe both.

He'd hoped for rain, but there weren't even any clouds. At last he said reluctantly, standing by the wheel, "Okay, we're going to have to get fuel and water. We could use more food too. Come left to 180 and run in toward shore. Look for a village, piers, cell or microwave towers. Run in *slow*. I keep seeing reefs that aren't on the chart. We bend a prop, we're not going to be able to catch that freighter if she comes down the Strait at full speed."

Wenck hummed to himself, dancing at the helm. He came slowly left and managed for once to steady up on the right course. Dan went forward and balanced on the bow, watching for coral heads. After a while Oberg handed up a pair of sunglasses. "Polarized," he said. Sure enough, they helped.

He squatted. Took a GPS reading and matched the longitude against the chart. It showed marsh along the shore, with two small settlements and no roads leading inland. He didn't feel great about going in, but if they had to, he wanted to keep their interaction as brief and anonymous as possible. "Could you ask Sumo to come up here?"

When Kaulukukui came up Dan said, not taking his eyes off the flat sea, "What languages you speak, Sumo? Any Arabic?"

"Arabic? I can tell a guy to drop his gun. Why?"

"Need you to do some shopping. You're the least identifiable dude, by sight, as American, we've got aboard."

"Copy that, sir. Water, food, and gas?"

"Since we didn't get a full loadout, back in Mindanao."

"What are we paying in?"

"Uh, dollars. But that doesn't necessarily point to us as Americans, does it?"

"No, sir. Seen dollars used lots of weird places."

"See Henrickson for the money. But don't flash it, okay? Buy at different places . . . use your good judgment. Speak whatever language gets the message across, as long as it isn't English."

"Yessir. No problem. Want me to swim ashore?"

"No, no. We'll run in to the beach. There's got to be an inlet or pier or a landing. If there's a village there."

He had Henrickson get a list together as the land slowly rose. The mountains farther north had gradually dropped and receded toward the horizon, then vanished as they'd run westerly.

He remembered the last time he'd sent men ashore in tropical seas. Years before, when he and the orphaned *Oliver C. Gaddis* had been on the loose not far to the north. On their own, without a country or flag . . . now he was a pirate again.

A shudder traveled his spine. At least he didn't have any serial killers aboard this time.

HE didn't like putting Sumo ashore alone. Especially when there turned out to be no sign of an inlet, just endless bright green salt marsh and mangrove. They motored along it, making it clatter eerily with their wake, and finally made out a huddle of rusty roofs a few hundred yards beyond. He edged in as close as he could, probing for the bottom with one of the boarding poles, and at last dropped Kaulukukui overboard to wade ashore. Dan turned and ran out to deeper water and put the anchor down. Then they sat and baked, slapping stinging flies that came out to them and watching the beach through the binoculars.

The SEAL came back four hours later in a dugout canoe, paddled out of the mangrove by a dwarfish, skin-over-bones oldster who chanted without stopping in a high singsong. Dan kept everyone under cover except Henrickson, and told him to speak anything but English, but the Malay didn't even look up. Kaulukukui handed up blue plastic jerries of water, red plastic containers of gasoline, and cloth-wrapped bundles of cooked fish, rice, plantains, and flat bread. When the Hawaiian heaved himself out of the dugout he folded bills into the outstretched hand. The old man dug in his paddle and angled away, still chanting as he merged again with the mangroves. Kaulukukui said he'd walked into town, found a store, pointed to what he wanted, then made signs for a boat to run it out. Everything had been very low-key.

Dan started a different engine, figuring to give each one some run time, make sure they could all be depended on, and headed ten miles out to sea, out of sight from shore, before resuming his original course.

They ran westward into the afternoon and then the evening and then the night again, the motor singing a steady burring drone. The only traffic was a few native lateens, miles off. It was perfect tropical weather, the sea nearly flat, the faintest swell lifting and dropping them; at sunset a few fluffy clouds hovered near the dying sun. He wished he could enjoy it.

Henrickson seemed better once he had some water in him. The analyst even managed to keep some of the rice down. But he still looked weak.

The coast gradually left them, dropping away to the southward until it vanished, and they ran in the open sea all night, a boundless desert of water under the gazes of millions of stars. Dan lay staring at the Pleiades. His eyes would drift closed to the hum of the engine, but he never quite lost consciousness. Just too much going on in his head.

When the sun heated the sky red again it backlit a peninsula and two high islands stark against the horizon. Far beyond them a shining white hull that might be a passenger ferry was heading west. He made the islands as Tanjung Datu, Pulau Serasan, and either Pulau Panjang or Pulau Subi Besar. "Pulau," he figured, meant "island." He took a round of bearings—he didn't trust the GPS alone—and ran out his dead reckoning line from the visual fix as the ferry dropped below the brightening rim of the sea.

He straightened, kneading his neck, exhausted. "Teddy. Monty. Let's put our heads together."

"Feeling any better?" Oberg asked Henrickson. They were sitting up on the bow, the boat rolling slowly as swells from some far-off storm heaved them up and then dropped them. The sun was glaring already and it was only seven.

Henrickson shrugged. "I'll be okay."

"Okay enough to climb a boarding ladder?"

"Do it if I have to."

"These guys need to know how to shoot these AKs," Oberg said. He watched Lenson carefully.

Dan thought about it, balancing what was incontrovertible about that statement with his misgivings about the mission. He didn't want any wild shooting. On the other hand . . . he leaned to dip his ball cap in the passing sea, fitted it to his head. The evaporating water felt good. "Uh, all right. Take them one at a time and fam fire off to port.

"Okay. Now. We're catching up to the schedule, but we're still a couple days ahead of the freighter. We need to find someplace to hole up."

"Someplace there's no natives or residents to report us to the Malaysian authorities," Henrickson said.

"Indonesian," Teddy put in.

"Correct," Dan said. "We're in Indonesian waters, anywhere to the west of Tanjung. I've operated with the Indonesians." They were an ally, but even allies didn't need to know about covert actions. Especially those involving hijacking, theft, and arson. "Now. Here on the chart. The Kepuluan Tambelan group. Distance . . ." He dividered it off. "I make it fifty-five miles from the intercept point. And the *Pilot* says it's sparsely populated. Which means, if this weather holds, we could get underway after dark and just have a short run to intercept."

"How do we know the freighter's still on the same schedule?" Oberg asked.

"Because they haven't called us on the sat phone."

"I'd feel better if we had a positive confirmation."

"That's a good point. Monty, ask for confirmation when we report in at noon."

Teddy sat darkly pondering this whole lack of preparation as Lenson talked about the chart. This wasn't the way SEALs operated. This whole thing should be a Team operation anyway. He should have just backed out. But then, the way they were doing this, they really needed help.

Wenck stood at the stern, youthful features screwed into concentration. The crack of a Kalashnikov set to single shots whacked across the water, bursting up white fountains each time the rifle jerked.

THE Tambelans pushed over the horizon the evening of their fourth day out from Zamboanga. By then everyone was sick of living aboard forty feet of boat with five other men. Dan had made them sponge off in salt water every morning, but they still smelled, the boat smelled, the fuel smelled, and they were all so scraggly, bearded, and burned they looked as if they'd spent their lives out here. Still, he kept them offshore that night, unwilling to close without a fathometer. The charts said he could have gotten in, but he didn't trust them. He couldn't anchor because he didn't have enough line for a proper scope. Fortunately the weather was still friendly. He hove to and let a current migrate them north during the dark hours. Then restarted an engine at 0400 and ran slowly westward, toward the smallest, most remote, and westernmost island, keeping a sharp lookout for lights or the outlines of boats. The *Pilot* said it was uninhabited, but even uninhabited islands had visitors.

Which was where they were now, anchored over coral heads on the east side of an islet too small to have a name on his chart, shielded from the swell and any storms that might come down on them, though he hadn't seen any storm sign and the met report at their last sat phone checkin had been for five-knot winds. He stood and stretched, then picked up the binocs and once more checked the horizon. They were alone.

He lowered the glasses, then lifted them again, focusing on the island.

The far side had looked like bare rock or earth as they'd approached. This side was a thick, deep, threatening green, jungle and undergrowth and along the beach palms above a chalk-line of surf. He thought he glimpsed movement under them, but it was probably just shadows. Colorful yellow and blue birds wheeled and dipped. Their harsh cries piped faintly over the sigh of the breeze, the seashell-whisper of distant surf.

He lowered the glasses, hawked, and spat over the side again, noticing fish moving down there, above the multicolored, fissured coral heads, slowly finning in and out of the shimmering shadow the boat printed over the reef, as if that shadow was protection or safety.

Kaulukukui squinted toward the island. "Think there's any pigs over there?"

"Thought I saw something moving. Under those palms."

"An AK'll take down a pig."

"No shooting," Dan said. "And nobody goes ashore."

"We been on this boat four days, sir. At least, swim call. Doesn't that water look great?"

Kaulukukui rooted out mask and fins from his gear bag and held them out. Dan considered. He tugged on the anchor line. Then looked down into the clear again. He really ought to get some sleep while he could. It would be a long day tomorrow, a long night after that.

"Watch out for sea snakes," the Hawaiian said. "One of those suckers starts gnawing on you, you'll be sorry."

Dan nodded. He pushed off his stinking, hot boots, strapped the mask on, and stepped over the side.

THE surface rocked silver above him; the powdery blue surrounded him. He pulled himself down the smooth braided nylon of the anchor line, paused, cleared his ears, then kept going down. To the sugar-white sand between the coral heads, where he tugged on the chain pendant. The anchor held. He let go and floated upward lazily and broke the surface beside the boat.

Wenck, pale-chested and bony in shorts, cannonballed over him with a whoop and hit with an enormous splash. Dan sucked air, jackknifed, and surface dove, into the blue once more.

The top of the nearest head was only about five feet down. He leveled off and coasted along its crest. Finned over it, and came face to face with a huge green parrotfish. The fish eyed him and angled off, casually, not panicked. Not many divers here, then.

Suddenly he was at peace. The endless demands of keeping a team pulling together, the looming danger of the boarding seemed a million miles distant. All around him fish darted, intent on tiny missions probably just as important in the grand scheme of the universe as his search for the

Shkval. If only he could stay here forever, drifting in the powdery blue . . . but he needed air. He turned his face up reluctantly, and finned upward, toward the golden light.

As he surfaced he caught the flicker of someone else going overboard. He turned away and swam for a hundred yards, enjoying the water on his skin and the sun on his back. Looking down on the colorful teeming life of the reef, he tried again to forget what they had to do tonight. The closer he was getting to the attempt, the less he liked it. But it had to be done. Taking the carrier task forces off the board would skew the whole calculus of deterrence, all around the world. Ever since the days of Morris and Decatur, sea power had been the only answer to those who considered their contiguous seas their own, and traffic on them lawful prey.

It had always struck him that a world in which violence was the price of existence had not been well designed. But he had to accept it, just as every wrasse and damsel scurrying from his passing shadow had to accept the conditions of their own watery lives. Without security, the predators would rule.

He went deep, as deep as he could, right down again to the white fine powder between the coral heads. He stayed alert for sea snakes and lionfish, and actually saw one snake, a black and white banded one, zigzagging some distance off. He finned in the opposite direction. That'd be a great way to go, paralyzed from a neurotoxin.

He came to a hollow in the reef. Chunks of bleached dead stone lay scattered across the bottom. He hovered, gradually understanding some explosive had gone off here. Some errant shell or bomb? Or, more probably, blast fishing? That was how some of the locals fished. With dynamite. Destroying an entire intricate universe, for a day's catch.

He was sculling on the surface, sucking breath for another dive, when a shot clapped from the island.

WHEN he pulled his fins off on the beach, shin weeping blood from painless razor-cuts from the coral he'd bumped on the way out of the surf, Oberg was crouched over something in the undergrowth. The birds whirled over their heads, keening warnings. Glancing his way as he came up, the SEAL held aloft a large green reptile, blood pumping slowly from where its head had been.

"Lizard sushi, Commander? Guaranteed fresh."

"I said no one goes ashore, Obie."

"Didn't hear that order, sir. Figured we could use fresh meat. A boar or something."

"Who's on the other side of this island?"

"Other side? I haven't checked the far side."

"Exactly. Fishermen. Tourists. A dive boat. Or an Indonesian patrol. That's why I wanted no one ashore. And no fucking *shooting*." Dan pointed to the boat. "Get your ass back there, Oberg. Right now."

He held up the lizard. "Yes, take the fucking thing," Dan told him. He picked up the rifle and threw it at Oberg. "Find your brass. Take it with you, too." He stood breathing hard, till the SEAL angrily bent.

HE lay awake again that night, waking from time to time and looking at his watch. Around the boat the others slept or tossed, cramped into corners and cuddies. Their snoring waxed and waned.

At last his Seiko beeped. He rolled over, scratched himself, and got up. Across from him another dark figure stirred against the stars.

"It's time?" Henrickson sat up.

"Let's go," Dan said.

15

"Point India,"
the South China Sea

THE sea heaved darkly; a quarter moon silvered the waves. The boat rolled with a wet slapping like a snapped towel. Their lights were off, and around the deck dark shapes lay like long-dead corpses. In the hours they'd tossed out here several sets of running lights had passed. None had been on *Fengshun No.5*, but larger vessels, tankers, Dan judged, by their length and their laden-low lights.

Merchant ships weren't Swiss trains. They could run early or late, so he'd wanted to be in position well in advance of when she was scheduled to pass. Sitting on the gunwale, he reviewed their gear, each man's assigned tasks, how it would go and what could go wrong. Unfortunately, almost always what *did* go wrong was something you'd never anticipated. Murphy was alive and well.

"Petty Officer Oberg. Anything else we need to do? Set up your climbing gear, anything like that?"

"Been ready since we got here, Commander."

The SEAL had been frosty since their set-to over the lizard, but Dan could not care less. He checked again that his weapon's safety was on. The chamber was empty anyway, he'd ordered chambers empty until they were actually aboard, so no one would get shot by mistake, but it gave him the illusion of something to do.

He sat for a few minutes, then checked his watch again. Then again.

By 0400 he was worried. Would she arrive before dawn? He didn't think they could approach, grapple, and board by daylight. They'd be seen at once, and if she started to weave, no way they'd get aboard.

Wenck grabbed his hair, making him flinch. "Something out there," the Carolinian muttered, sounding like he was choking. Dan put up a hand and Wenck pulled him up with him on top of the cuddy and thrust the glasses into his hands.

A distant green spark, two white lights in a near vertical line. Heading: a little east of them. "Start one engine," he muttered, as if they could hear him from here. "Ahead slow. Course two-zero-zero magnetic. Everybody out of sight, except the helmsman."

"Why are we running toward?" Carpenter wanted to know. Dan looked at him. Since his trial, the sonarman had barely opened his mouth, just jumped to it whenever it looked as if something had to be done. Seeing Dan's look he added, "Sorry, sir. Just wondered."

"We want to look like a crossing contact. See if they react in a closing situation; that tells us how well the bridge is manned, how alert they are. When we get in tight, they'll lose us; we'll be below radar coverage. Then we can alter to drop in astern, but we want to look like a fisherman till the last minute." He noticed a shadow behind the sonarman. "Obie, this'd be a good time to tell me if I'm doing something wrong."

"Really want my input, Commander?"

"Yeah, I do."

Teddy tried to master his growing dislike for the guy. Their asses would be on the line in a few minutes. "Okay, sir, no argument with that. But once we get alongside, it'd go smoother if you just let me call the shots."

"You're the pros. Just remember, these guys aren't our enemies. Just merchant seamen, doing a job. We can restrain them. We can scare them. Even threaten them, but I don't want anyone to get hurt."

Teddy grinned in the dark. Like they were going to take over a ship and burn it, and nobody was going to get hurt? Shit, if that's what the fool wanted to believe . . . he made his voice gung-ho earnest. "Hey, you got it, sir. Just make sure your guys are behind us, and everything'll go great."

"There's no 'mine' and 'yours' here, Teddy. We're all on the same team."

Oberg gave him another "yessir." And that seemed to finish the conversation.

THE lights rose from the sea, glimmering out toward them like reaching hands. Behind them one engine burbled, driving them along at a trawler-like eight knots. Kaulukukui was sprawled on top of the cuddy with the night-vision goggles, watching the oncoming ship. "Get me an ID," Dan called. "I'm not going in till we have a positive ID."

He bent, shielding the lit numerals with his body, and switched his handheld to the bridge-to-bridge frequency. He had no intention of answering any calls, but it might serve to tell them they'd been detected.

It didn't seem that they had. The massive shadow drove steadily on.

They crossed its bow a thousand yards ahead of it, the bulging froth at its stem glimmering in the moonlight. He made out a shadowy mass aft, probably an accommodation block. But now he was closer this ship looked bigger than what they'd been briefed to expect. Which was a 900-TEU, feeder-sized containership of about ten thousand gross registered tons and a hundred and sixty meters long.

But he couldn't hang around while he decided if this was it or not. It was really tearing along. If they were going to make it into position without a long stern chase, he had to tuck himself in. "All right: Lights out." Their running lights snapped off. "Come left, angle in toward the stern as she passes," Dan told Carpenter, on the helm. "Come on, kick her in the ass, Rit! Full RPM, let's get up on plane."

Sumo turned his head, the protuberant muzzle eye of the night goggles making him look inhuman against the lights of the ship. "I don't think that's Feng Shui."

"It's *Fengshun*, not 'Feng Shui.'"

"Right. But that's not the name I'm reading on the bow."

"Oh, shit," Dan muttered. "Angle in more," he told Carpenter. "All engines, flank— What's it say? Can you read it?"

"*Van Linschoten*, it says."

"That doesn't sound Chinese," Henrickson muttered.

"No, it doesn't. More rudder, Rit. Look at the stern, Sumo. Can you get a home port?"

"A - m - s . . . I think an R—no, a T—"

"Amsterdam." He could make it out himself now. Along with the white tumult at the base of the black hull-cliff, where the screw lived. He shivered, envisioning falling into that frothy doom. It would be like diving into a tank of hungry sharks. The bow wave hit them with a rushing crash and they grabbed for handholds as the boat climbed under their feet, then aimed her nose for the bottom.

He grimaced and glanced to the east. The horizon was not yet visible, but it was getting there. Back when he'd been a navigator, he'd be already dressed and shaved, up in the nav shack deciding which stars to shoot. He slammed his fist into the gunwale and felt skin peel off it. "Sheer off. Lights on! Monty, they said it was coming through the Strait tonight? That was firm intel?"

"I don't know about intel, they said it was from VTIS."

VTIS was the vessel traffic information service, the maritime safety ship reporting system that tracked traffic through major straits. "That should be good dope, then."

"Then where is it? Broken down? Running behind schedule?"

"I don't know," he muttered. He slammed his fist into fiberglass again, felt blood trickle. It seemed like this whole Shkval-hunt was Jonahed. Every time they got set up to actually *do* something—

"More lights, sir," Wenck called.

He sucked breath. There they were, another set of red and green and white. He checked behind them; the Dutch ship dwindling, already low to the horizon. It had gone past faster than he'd expected, huge, towering, a freight train. Getting up a ship's stern in the dark, the black cliff moving at fifteen or twenty knots, would not be easy. He wiped sweat and blood off on his pants, checked his gear again, checked it again.

The oncoming ship grew even more swiftly than the one that had just creamed by. She seemed smaller, but maybe that was the rain-colored half-light that was gradually filtering up out of the sea, the unearthly radiance that seemed to come from nowhere and not really even to be light. She was stacked deep with containers and he could make out the outline of cranes forward, or maybe just one.

The boat rocked again, crossing the wave system the Dutchman trailed behind him. Dan made out streaks of creamy foam lying parallel to their course. He could almost see his guys now, see the team's weapons, the bamboo poles, the boarding ladder rolled up in the bow. They didn't have much longer, if they were going to pull this off. He swung back and focused. This sucker was really roaring along. Was it the right one? He couldn't wait. Not with dawn coming. After the molasseslike hours out here, suddenly events were moving so fast he felt overwhelmed.

He keyed the VHF and tried for an accent. Fortunately ship-to-ship commercial comms were nearly always in English, or at least, something resembling that language. He said slowly, "Motor Vessel *Fengshun*, Motor Vessel *Fengshun*, this is Motor Vessel *Van Linschoten*, ahead of you in eastbound channel, over."

"This is *Fengshun Number Five*. Over."

"This is *Van Linshoten*. Be advised we have lost rudder hydraulics. Advise you proceed with caution as we are slowing and do not have steering control."

"This is *Fengshun*. Hear you loud and clearly. We are slowly. Are you need help? *Fengshun, Fengshun*. Over?"

He clicked the transmit button on and off quickly, giving the effect, he hoped, of a broken signal. He caught Oberg squinting at him. No time to interpret. He said urgently to Carpenter, crouched at the wheel, "Same drill as before. Down her port side. Lights off as we close. Then cut in tight under her stern, *tight,* line up and match speed. Got it?"

He said he did. Dan watched the pilothouse as they neared. Dim yellow lights glowed behind the large square windows high above the container-crammed deck. They had to be there. *Someone* had answered up on 12. He still couldn't see anyone though.

"Chinese characters," the Hawaiian said from the bow. "This might be our boy."

Dan looked back at the horizon, at the men lying on the ceiling boards, at the swiftly approaching vessel. He stared at the white water at the stem but couldn't tell if it was lessening, if they were shedding speed. He could almost make out the large white letters that marched along the black wall. It was still dark, but the day was coming. "All three engines," he snapped to Carpenter. "Hold your course . . . hold your course . . . now. Lights off."

Carpenter flipped a switch and spun the wheel. The boat was only just starting to turn when the bow wave hit them. They rose, tipped crazily, almost went over. Dan crouched, butt tight against the gunwale, clinging to the helm console. Spray shot over the side and drenched them. The Hondas spooled up, bellowing together in a chorus of power. Beside him Oberg turned his ear as if to hear them better. The boat shot past the swiftly moving steel wall, now only yards away, and hit a slick patch. "Cut left! Cut left and line up!" Dan shouted.

"Son of a bitch—"

Oberg grabbed for the wheel but Dan pushed him back. The chunky sonarman hunched over the console. The boat bounced, snarled, canted hard as it came hard left again. The stern loomed alarmingly close. "Cut power! Cut power!" Dan nearly screamed, but kept it to a gutteral shout.

"Jesus Christ," Henrickson shouted. "He's gonna slam into—"

"Why don't all you fuckfaces just shut the fuck up," Carpenter said between gritted teeth. He pulled two throttles back and left the middle one all the way forward. "She's slowing down. Get Oberg ready."

But when Dan turned the SEAL was already on the bow, holding the long thin shadow of the bamboo pole like a harpooner about to thrust. Kaulukukui stood behind him, holding a coil of line out of the way. They crouched tensely, staring up at the gigantic stern swaying above them, like figures caught on a heroic frieze. Dan pushed back from the helm, willing himself by main force not to grab the wheel as Carpenter wrestled it this way and that. A pale luminescence played down from the stern light, swaying high above. The pulse of the freighter's screw hammered at the soles of his feet through sea and fiberglass and leather like the repetitive pounding against its bars of a maddened panther. He balanced as the boat tossed in the screw wash, as the bow swung crazily, lurching and bouncing in the turbulence.

Ahead of him, Oberg was reaching up.

TEDDY cursed between clenched teeth. The idiot on the helm couldn't keep it steady for even a second. Behind him Sumo had his hand in his belt, trying to brace him, but he still staggered, trying to keep from falling overboard, while riveting his attention on the deck-edge above. It was higher than he'd expected. Subtract the boat's and his own height, he might have just enough bamboo to hook on, but not a millimeter to spare.

"Can you get it?" Lenson yelled.

"Wait one—gonna have to—"

The bow surged and he lunged with it, thrusting with the pole to his tiptoes. The grapnel skidded off, the point grating on metal. The bow dropped away and the pole came back down and nearly took him into the water with it before he and Kaulukukui got it under control. There didn't seem to be any lip, or water channel, on the deck edge, the way he'd expected, for the hook to lock on. That wasn't good.

"Can you make it?"

Lenson, sticking his fucking oar in from back by the helm. Teddy didn't bother to answer. He crouched, watching the edged silhouette above them move away. The Hondas picked up speed and he heard that chatter again. Just so it held up until they got away, that was all he asked. The boat fell, rose, and he lunged again, grunting with effort. The hook clanged and grated and fell away. "Keep it fucking steady!" he shouted over his shoulder. His shoulders and arms burned but he blocked it. They could hurt when he was on that deck. If he made it.

Lenson, at his side. "Want me to give it a try?"

"Get off my back, Commander. Just give me room."

The boat roared forward. He staggered to his feet and had the pole halfway up when fiberglass crunched into steel as the prow slammed into the freighter. He lost his balance and shot forward. Just as his feet left the deck he pushed off, stretching upward and twisting in midair to get the hook turned backward, not sideways, the way he'd angled it the first two tries. It clanged into something hard, vibrating down the pole, and all at once he was swinging free, dangling through the dark air at what felt like a terrific speed, boots kicking. He struggled to get himself up the pole. But it was slick with the spray and his gloves slipped as he swung back and forth above the roaring maelstrom below him. The bulky weight of the rolled boarding ladder was like two full packs dragging him down. He stared upward. All that fucking hook had to do was make a quarter turn and it would come right off.

He got his knees locked on bamboo and started inching.

WHEN he reached the deck edge he got an arm over it and hung there while his eyes decided whether to come out or stay in their sockets. When they stayed he raised his head slowly.

No lookout came out of the shadows to kick him back overboard. That didn't surprise him. The ship might have posted one going through the Strait, but that lay miles back. A merchant could do a lot to discourage boarders. But the only antiboarding measure he spotted here was barbed wire, already salt-rusty, wound perfunctorily around the top liferail.

He got an arm over the lower rail, pushed the rolled-up caving ladder through, then followed it, wriggling under. He backed instantly into the shadow of a large winch and crouched immobile, waiting for an alarm, a shout, a probing beam.

None of those things came. He gave it fifteen seconds, counting it out and trying to work the cramps out of his long muscles, then pulled the lashings off the ladder. Staying low as he rolled out from behind the winch, he locked two large stainless carabiners around a lifeline stanchion and kicked it over the side. He got out his Glock and sawed through the barbed wire and let it drop overboard.

Kaulukukui came over the rail and handed over Teddy's AK without a word. Obie checked magazine seating, safety, sight position. He felt better armed. He pointed to a light burning above a doorway, what looked like a starboard side passageway. Gliding from shadow to shadow, they took position.

Teddy turned his attention back to the ladder as another head bobbed above the liferail, followed by a boot. The way the guy came over it he'd have castrated himself if the wire had still been there. When he stood Teddy saw it was Lenson. The commander oriented and joined them. "Where's Sumo?" he whispered

Teddy pointed. "Perimeter. Till we're all aboard."

"Going to be light soon. Got to get moving."

As far as he was concerned, they weren't going anywhere until everyone was aboard. "You got comms with the boat?" Lenson nodded. "Check it. Then tell me you got it. Sir."

Dan hesitated, then nodded. He put the radio to his mouth and made sure the earbud was in. "Carpenter?"

"Here."

"Donnie and Monty coming?"

"On the ladder."

"As soon as they're aboard, drop back half a mile and follow us. Zigzag, so it looks like you're not keeping station, in case anybody's got you on radar. Singaporean patrol craft, or anybody. I'll check in when I can, but I can't tell you how often that'll be. If we call, or you see a flare, come in fast."

. Carpenter aye-ayed and Dan clicked off. He started forward, but Oberg pulled him back. "Let us lead, Commander. This is our job."

"Okay, but I don't see you leading."

Oberg fought to keep from backhanding him. "We got two more men to come. Just keep your pants on, Commander."

Dan looked anxiously back. It was getting lighter with every passing minute. Where in the hell were Donnie and Monty?

DONNIE was halfway up the ladder when it just got to be too much. His eyes squeezed closed. His hands cramped. He hunched in as it swayed. After a moment Henrickson, below him, slapped his boot. "Donnie! Wenck! You okay?"

He couldn't answer. The dark was all around him, rushing in his ears. He felt ashamed, but he still couldn't move. Like pushing the buttons on a disconnected game controller.

"Donnie!" The hand again, shaking his foot. He kicked it off savagely. "Jeez—you almost got me in the head!"

"Wenck!" From above. "You're holding up the program. Get the fuck up here!"

"I can't." His voice sounded choked and high even to him.

Something long came down and cracked across his back. He flinched, then gasped as something sharp hooked into his ass. It jerked upward, stabbing him painfully an inch away from his balls. "Get the fuck up here!"

Oberg, that was who was jabbing him. Donnie let go with one hand and groped wildly for whatever it was he was jabbing him with. "Knock it off," he half screamed, half whispered.

"Get up here or I'll tear you a new asshole for real. Now, dickhead!"

The pain jabbed again, he felt the hook tearing skin, and he yelped and suddenly his hands moved and he scrambled the last few reeling feet and a hand came through the lifelines and got the back of his collar. "Oberg. What the fuck you poking me with—"

The SEAL laid the bamboo aside, and the cruel steel clanged on the deck. "I'll fucking ream you up the ass with something sharper than that, you don't get with the fucking program. Get that AK in your hands and follow me."

"Fuck you," he muttered, but not out loud. His legs were shaking even worse than at the range in Virginia. Something warm and wet was trickling down his leg. He couldn't tell if it was piss or blood.

"Get moving!" A shove, and he stumbled after a shadow, starting at every sound, fingering his rifle and trying desperately to remember if up was "safe" or if it was "fire."

MONTY Henrickson followed Kaulukukui, making sure he kept his rifle pointed away from the Hawaiian's broad back. They'd gone over this again and again on the printouts. Once aboard, divide into three teams. Oberg and Lenson to the comm room and bridge. Wenck to the engine room, and Kaulukukui and Henrickson to the crew's quarters.

So he knew where he was going, but it was different drilling it and actually running in the dark through passageways and up ladders you'd never seen before. What the layouts didn't show was how spooky they were, how grimy, the white paint probably the original paint, never touched or even washed probably since the ship had left the builder's. It had the air of a hospital fire-exit stairwell, a space that belonged to no one and no one took care of, just transited on his way from here to there. But the big man ahead of him went up surefooted and silent. He hugged the edges of the passageways and "sliced the pie" on the corners, covering his advance with the muzzle of his Kalashnikov. Monty followed in the combat crouch they'd learned at GrayWolf, trying to work spittle into a dust dry mouth.

A man turned the corner so suddenly he ran into Kaulukukui. The SEAL had him down and was zip-tying him before Monty understood what was happening. The crewman rolled to look up at them and Monty instinctively covered his face. Then lowered his hand. With the beards, black scarves over their mouths, camo paint, and the dirty, ragged clothes they'd traded for with the rebels, he didn't have to worry about being identified. As long as they remembered not to speak English, and whatever Kaulukukui was shouting at the guy, it sure wasn't American. The big Hawaiian hauled the sailor up and shoved him on ahead of them.

They came to a narrow passageway walled with doors. The crew's quarters. Monty started pulling doors open, pointing the gun, yelling at startled Asian faces in random Russian. *"Davai! Ponemayite? Kto rukkava'ditiel?"* Their cabins looked like rooms in a frat house: cluttered with beer cans, porn mags, snack wrappers, crammed with the tinny noise of cheap CD players and the flicker of VCRs. They stared back terrified, putting their hands up at once. Ahead the SEAL was shouting, too, herding men out into the passageway and zip-tying them. When they had them all out and lying on their faces Kaulukukui mouthed: *search them.* Monty bent and started patting and slapping bodies. They were little men, most of them, about his own size. They acted passive, as if they didn't want to resist. Maybe he and the SEAL were pretty frightening.

He remembered they were supposed to be thieves, and went back and got wallets and watches and stuffed them into a cheap red Marlboro tote from one of the rooms. Two had cell phones and one a knife and he took those, too. When he signaled they were clean, Kaulukukui gestured them to their feet.

The plan was to take them to the crew's dining area, one deck down, and hold them till they heard from the bridge team. He kicked the closest sailor. *"Davai, tep'yer!"* he shouted, waving the rifle, trying to look as if he wanted nothing more than to mow them all down. They shrank back, palms up to placate him, then scrambled where Kaulukukui pointed, his normally placid face the snarling mask of a Polynesian war god as Monty urged the last shaking kid along with his rifle-butt.

Look at me, he thought. He tried to grin, but his lips were so dry they cracked. Childhood fantasies fulfilled mingled with utter fear. This was no joke. If they got caught doing this, it was an act of war. But it was still every boy's fantasy, and he was living it.

Look at me. Mom! Look!

I'm a pirate!

DONNIE headed through the portside door. He swallowed, fingering his AK. The Commander had said not to chamber rounds, but as soon as he'd turned away Oberg had locked and loaded. Donnie hesitated, then did, too.

All at once, he was alone. He hesitated, not wanting to do this. Wishing there was somebody with him. Then made himself head for the ladderway down.

He crept down two decks through echoing brightly lit ladderwells whose turns were too sharp. His steps echoed. His breath echoed, too.

The ladderwell ended at a watertight door. Machinery-roar vibrated the air. After a second he reached up with the butt of the AK and smashed the light over the door. Glass tinkled and pinged.

Inside the air was much hotter, the roar much louder. He moved along steel catwalks between huge engines. The reek of hot lubricants boiled off them. He tried the combat waddle they'd learned at GrayWolf, but finally just jogged along, bent at the waist.

He found one guy in that whole huge space, ensconced in a glass-enclosed booth overlooking the engine floor. Heart pounding so hard he quivered, he eased the door open. Cold air flooded out.

The watchstander sat at a control panel reading what looked like an Asian version of *Hustler*. His pants were around his ankles. He had something pink on his lap. A tube ran from it to a bulb in his hand.

Donnie stared, then cleared his throat. The engineer looked up. His eyes grew round. He squeaked, reaching for an intercom.

His snap shot was deafening in the little booth. And to his utter and complete astonishment, it connected. The intercom exploded. The engineer recoiled, crashing his chair over backward, sending the pink apparatus flying. He crawled across the deckplates, trying to pull his pants up, pleading in Chinese.

Donnie gained confidence, hearing him sob. He spread-eagled him across the control panel and patted him down. He zip-tied his hands and pushed him out of the booth. He looked at the magazine, then tucked it into the small of his back. A souvenir. The corner of the pink thing peeked out from under the console. He hesitated, then kicked it out of sight.

SEVEN decks up, Dan and Oberg were zip-tying the bridge team. One had made no attempt to resist, just dropped his eyes and stood waiting to be told what to do. The other, an older European who'd come storming up in a terry bathrobe, had begun shouting at them in Italian. Dan made him for the captain. Oberg pushed them both into a little nav compartment behind the bridge, after checking that there were no radios in there, and shut them in after waving his gun in their faces.

Meanwhile Dan was studying the helm console, the autopilot, and the radar. He checked their course: 035. About what he'd made it as, when they'd been maneuvering to board. He found the RPM indicators for the main diesels and the speed log. Both held steady. If they stayed that way, *Fengshun No. 5* had three hours on this course before they ran afoul of another high island. Past that was the open China Sea.

Oberg was hunting along the bulkhead. He threw a switch. Lights came on down on the deck. He flicked four more. The whole foredeck lit up like a stage set.

They looked down over a square mountain of containers. Some new, others rust-stained, painted all the colors of a clinical depressive's rainbow.

"Okay, which one is it?" Dan muttered.

Oberg took out the overhead shot and oriented it with the walkways. "Standard length container. Green. Double locked and isolated by empty containers all around it." He pointed to the port side, a third of the way forward from the bridge. "One down from the top. If it's where this says it is."

"We've got to get the crew off. Get them in the boats and shove them off." Dan looked at the radar again, then at his chart. "As soon as they're out of sight we alter course. Come left and head for Point Juliet."

Oberg rubbed his beard. "You don't want to check first?"

"Check what?"

"That it's there."

Dan's turn to rub his face. Yeah. He was both sick to death of it and violently eager to run his hands over it, this deadly Grail that had gotten them bombed, shot at, and nearly drowned. "Okay. I'll hold the fort here. Go check it out. But hurry. We've got a lot to do, before we set fire to this tub."

JUST like old times, Obie thought, wiping his palms on his pants and gazing up. He'd done so fucking much of this, busting seals off containers, holding weapons on angry crews as they stewed in the sun. At least he wasn't eating gritty sand, the red fucking powder that got in everything. He'd had his own climbing gloves then, his own beeners and chocks and slings . . . He slung the AK and started climbing.

The stack was five containers high. So U 8789035 from RUS for Russia, should be third up, second from the top. He spotted it. It looked gray, not green, but in this light, maybe that was what green looked like.

The trouble was, it was butted solid against the ones fore and aft and above and below. He didn't see any way inside until they were cleared away, and they weren't going to do that without the crane on the T-AGS. He hung there, feeling the burn in his thighs and calves. He wasn't in climbing shape, the way he'd been in the Gulf. "Crap," he muttered. He searched for the next handhold, wondering if he should've set a grapnel up top, and pulled himself up another couple of yards.

Which put him level with the stenciling on the container. Not only did it still not look green, the number in front of his face wasnot 8789035 but 4589040, and the alpha ISO wasn't RUS U but FTC U. Who knew where it was from, but it wasn't what they were looking for.

Two possibilities, he thought, hanging by one hand while he got his knife out. One: it was the right container, but disguised. This didn't seem likely. You might not think weapons, ammunition, got shipped in containers like this, but he'd seen it, in the Gulf. Containers full of RPGs, artillery rounds, one even of the military-grade Czech plastic explosive called Semtex—that had made the ensign shit his drawers. But the papers had been valid for Iran, for "industrial uses," and they'd had to let it through. If you put something in a container marked as something else, you ran the risk of losing track of it, ending up with a box of cacao beans or plastic doll heads instead of a high-speed rocket torpedo.

The second possibility was that it wasn't where intel said it was, one slot down on the port side, but five down in the middle. Or anywhere else, just not *here*. On a 900 TEU ship, that meant it could be 899 other places. He grimaced, envisioning trying to check nine hundred containers looking for the right one. Even just all the green ones, it'd take a full day. Which they didn't have.

The third possibility was that it wasn't here at all. He spidered down, hung, and dropped. Then jogged back toward the deckhouse, circling as he went to sweep the horizon. No lights. Good.

But he didn't think Lenson was going to like what he was about to tell him.

DAN felt like clutching his head and screaming, but a naval officer did neither. At least, not in front of his team. He allowed himself a tight smile. "That figures. Not there . . . okay, first thing, we need to blow that safe."

"Sumo's on that. But it's not going to be in the safe."

"I know that, Obie. I'm talking about our cover. See how Sumo's doing. I'll talk to the captain."

Teddy hesitated. "Want me to take that, sir?"

"You can sit in if you want. The safe?"

Just then a thud below told him it was probably done. He told Oberg, "Break him out of the nav shack and bring him down. And if he arrives in a cooperative frame of mind, that's a plus."

The door to the captain's cabin was open. An ammonaical haze of explosive fumes was eddying out into the passageway. The porthole was open, air was blowing in. The big Hawaiian was ransacking the space, throwing pictures to the deck, smashing a table lamp. The safe was still smoking, and still closed. The charge had punched out the locking mechanism. Dan turned the handle and it swung open and more smoke whiffed out. "Good job, Sumo. I'm gonna need this cabin. Can you take the bridge? Yell if there's any closing contacts, or anybody calls us on twelve."

Oberg pushed the Italian in. Blood ran down the side of his head. Dan frowned past him at the SEAL, but let it go. The captain froze as he saw the open safe. Dan waved the heavy envelopes of money. He'd used the time waiting in camp and in Singapore to brush up on his Italian, memorize the sentences he thought he'd need. Unfortunately his use of it now was probably not going to make him savor the memory.

"*Capitano. Parlate italiano?*"

"*Sì. Sì, sono italiano. Chi sono voi?*"

"*Non faccia le domande. Obbedisca appena e velocemente. Che cosa è il vostro nome?*"

"*Il mio nome? Siniscalchi. Alberto Siniscalchi. Provengo da Palermo. Conoscete Palermo? La Sicilia. Non desiderate nuoc.*"

Dan was only getting part of this. "*Dove è la vostra polizza di carico, Capitano? Mostrilo me. Immediatamente.*"

Whatever Oberg had done—busted the guy's ear, it looked like—it had made an impression. The middle-aged man was shaking. He hesitated, then turned and collided with Oberg. He wheeled back to Dan, white-faced. "*È nell'ufficio del purser. Posso andare là?*"

Dan wasn't sure, but he made that to be that the document he wanted was in the purser's office. He scowled, motioning for Oberg to accompany them.

Siniscalchi led them to another cabin off the same passageway. He fumbled in his pocket for keys and let them in. Then fumbled some more and unlocked a drawer. Held out a sheaf of computer-generated print. "*Ciò è la polizza di carico. Sto cooperando, signore. Che cosa progettate fare con la mia squadra?*"

Dan caught "cooperate" and that sounded good, but the rest went past him. He tugged up the black scarf and turned the light on over the desk and started flipping pages. He'd gotten familiar with commercial documentation in the Red Sea aboard *Horn*. So it didn't take long before he reached an unpleasant conclusion. He led them back to the captain's cabin, then jerked his head at the door. "*Soggiorno qui,*" he told the captain. "*Sia calmo. Non si muova.*" The man nodded quickly and groped his way to a chair.

Oberg followed Dan out and eased the door closed behind them. He muttered, "It's not there?"

"It's on the list. Along with two other containers with the RUS prefix."

"Great," Oberg muttered, looking as enthusiastic as Dan felt. "Has he got a stowage chart in there?"

They paged through the sheaf and didn't find one. Dan checked his watch, biting his lip, feeling time peeling away as he tried to think this through. So far, the captain and crew thought they were bandits. The rag-tag looters that hit random ships in these waters and farther south. That's why they'd blown the safe, taken wallets and watches: mimicking their MO. But if he started asking about specific containers . . . Oberg must have reasoned along the same line because he said, "We don't have time to look at every fucking one of nine hundred containers. We've got to get these guys in the boats before we join up with *McDonnell*."

"I know that. What I was thinking, our intel's not serving us well here."

"No shit, Commander."

"Their location's wrong, where the container's supposed to be. And they said there'd be empty ones around the one with the weapon. That'd mean seven containers prefixed RUS, not three." Dan rubbed his face. His palm came away wet. "Okay . . . I hope Alberto's got some answers."

The man looked terrified when they let themselves back in. He hunched forward, breathing with stertorous rasps. His gaze was nailed to the floor. When Dan followed it he saw the broken frame, the shattered glass, the family picture. He squatted next to him and made his voice menacing. *"Capitano. Vi farò questo problema una volta. Come possiamo individuare un contenitore, se conosciamo il relativo numero?"*

"Che numero desiderate?" Siniscalchi started to reach for the binder, but of course, his hands were bound. He smiled pleadingly. Dan glanced at Oberg. The knife he always carried came out, gleamed. Siniscalchi rubbed his wrists, glancing at the blade, then smiling again at Dan. He flipped through the binder, hands shaking. *"Che numero desiderate?"*

"Contenitore numero, uh, otto, sette, otto, nove, uh, zero, tre, cinque. È russo."

Siniscalchi blinked. He carefully did not meet their eyes. He wet his fingers and leafed through the pages. Found the number Dan had found and cross-referenced it to another section farther back. Then looked up. *"È stato tolto."*

"Che cosa?"

Siniscalchi made a cupping motion, then fluttered his hands away. *"È stato tolto; ha scaricato il giorno prima che navigassimo. Quell'unità non è a bordo."*

Dan wasn't a hundred percent sure he got all of that, but what he understood was not good. The gist: It wasn't aboard. It had been taken off the day before "navigassimo" . . . perhaps "sailing" or "sail date." He started to ask why, then didn't. He'd said too much already. Looking at the slumped, sweating Italian, he realized he'd said far too much.

Siniscalchi seemed to be struggling with himself. Finally he muttered something. *"Che cosa?"* Dan said again.

Siniscalchi's tongue darted, wetting his lips. *"Non parlerò,"* he said again. *"Non so da dove venite o chi lavorate per. Ma non dirò, mai, che avete chiesto notizie su quel contenitore. Giuro sulla tomba della mia madre. Signore."*

Dan said slowly, trying to get this right: *"Capite? Sarete uccisi."*

"Sì, sì, capisco. Sarò per sempre silenzioso come la tomba."

Dan looked at Oberg and nodded. The SEAL pulled the man backward and pinioned his hands again. Duct tape snarled. Siniscalchi's eyes widened as it went around his ankles, around his chest, taping him to the chair, over his mouth. But he didn't struggle. Just kept his eyes locked to Dan's as the door closed behind them.

TEDDY waited till they were in the ladderwell back up the bridge. "What was that about? I speak Spanish, I got some of it, but—"

"He says it's not aboard."

"Does he know why?"

"I didn't ask because I probably wouldn't have understood. But it *was* aboard."

"It was on the manifest."

"Correct. And I *think* he was telling us it was here till right before they sailed. The day before, if I understood him. My guess, it was pulled off and sent some other way."

"By air?"

"I don't know. Maybe somebody thought sending it by ship wasn't secure enough."

"Or they knew we were planning to hijack it," Teddy said, watching the commander's eyes.

"Maybe."

"And what was that at the end?"

Lenson shrugged. "At the end . . . oh, he was saying he wasn't going to talk. Wouldn't tell anyone what we were asking about. *'Silenzioso come la tomba.'* Silent as the grave."

"So he knows who we are."

Lenson gave him another unreadable look. "I don't see how he could. But my guess is, he knows who we're not."

Teddy started to ask another question, then shut his mouth on it. Lenson turned and resumed his climb.

Kaulukukui was in the pilothouse. Lenson said, "We're terminating the operation and extracting to the boat. We've got to leave everybody here thinking all we were after was the cash and their CD players. Sumo, you blew the captain's safe and the purser's. Where's the payroll?"

"Here." The SEAL patted a buttpack.

"The crew's wallets and shit?"

"Henrickson's got them in the messroom. He threw them in a gym bag."

"Great. Donnie, go back to the engine room and shut down. Fire a magazine into the engine controls. Make sure there's lots of brass lying around for them to pick up. Then go to the mess room and help Monty get tape on everybody. Do it fast.

"Then go through the cabins again. Take anything that'd look valuable to a Basiliano pirate. Shoot things up, but make sure nobody's on the other side of the bulkhead. Ten minutes, tops. Then meet me back aft where we came aboard, at time"—he checked his watch—"zero-five."

They grunted and left. Dan considered the wheel, then spun it. The gyro began ticking over. He waited till it registered 090, then met the rudder. When it was steady on the desired heading he pushed a black button on the console. Released it, and waited. The autopilot held the course. He searched across the console, peering to read the lettering, then punched in zeros and pushed another button. He looked at the radar one last time, then charged his AK. A burst turned it into fizzing sparking junk.

Teddy jumped back. "Watch for richochets, you do that again, Commander."

"All right, let's go."

"Where you want me?"

"Collect the guy in the nav shack and the captain, and take them down to the mess decks. Make sure everybody's restrained. I put them on a safe heading and Donnie's shutting the engines down. Sooner or later somebody'll work himself free."

"Aye, sir."

Lenson headed for the ladderwell. When the door closed behind him

Teddy blew out noisily. He looked at the door to the nav shack. Then headed down the other ladder.

He came out in the passageway between the captain and the purser's cabins. Waited a moment, head cocked. He heard Lenson's steps, fading away. Then, just the creak of a ship rolling, no longer under power, picking up the rhythm of the swells.

DAN stood by the ladder, gripping the radio and feeling more and more anxious. Where was the boat? Where was Carpenter? He leaned over and tried to judge their speed. It was dropping, but it would take a long time to get all the way off ten thousand tons of steel and cargo. "I still don't see you," he said into the handheld. "Flick your lights."

"Flicking."

He picked it up, maybe half a mile off: a single scarlet throb though what still, surprisingly, wasn't yet full dawn. "I got you . . . come on in. Speed's dropping. Don't run into the stern."

Carpenter double-clicked in return. Dan leaned again. Maybe three knots. Wind off the port bow. Really it was a lovely night. A lovely sea, beautiful stars. Just too bad they hadn't gotten what they'd come so far to find.

A stir forward. He raised the AK, but it was the team, carrying bags and totes, their tawdry loot. Wenck. Henrickson. Kaulukukui. He felt bad having to steal from seamen who had precious little anyway. "Where's the bag with the wallets?"

Henrickson held one up. "Here."

"Leave it there. Behind the winch. Like we forgot it, as we were going over the side."

He felt bad about the skipper as well. Scaring the guy. Threatening him. It had turned out a fiasco. He waved for Wenck to go first. He felt low. She wasn't much of a ship, but she was a ship, and he'd almost burned and scuttled her and set her crew adrift.

He missed a face, and looked around. "Oberg. Where's Teddy?"

"He'll be here," Kaulukukui said.

WHEN the door eased open the Italian was looking right at Teddy. Big drops stood out on his forehead. He heard me come down the ladder, Teddy thought. He didn't feel angry at the guy. They couldn't let him live, though. Not after what Lenson had asked him. Nobody's fault. Just collateral damage.

He picked up the family picture and set it on the desk where the man could look at it. Siniscalchi made a smothered sound, heaved his shoulders. Trying to talk through the tape. The chair jumped, but stayed put. Taped to it ankles and chest, hands wired behind him, the guy wasn't going anyplace. Before either of them had too long to obsess about it, Teddy ripped another strip off the roll and pasted it down tight over Siniscalchi's nose.

It didn't take long. He looked away, giving the guy his privacy. When he stopped jerking Teddy tore the tape off his face and left him sagging, cheeks the color of port wine, staring at nothing now. He looked around the cabin once more, making sure none of them had left anything. He eased the door closed behind him.

IV

PLAN C

16

Naval Base Coronado, San Diego, California

THE TAG West office was in a bright modern building in a new compound at Coronado, all pale brick, and dark glass, and meticulously spaced azaleas rooted in bright ocher mulch. Not unwelcoming, and a long step up from the shabby crumbling cinder-blocks shore commands usually tenanted, but anonymous as a medical center. The lieutenant who met Dan in the atrium checked his ID and handed him a pass. He said the compound was part of the new Fleet Antisubmarine Warfare Center. PAC-FLT was trying to revive the ASW skills that had gone neglected since the Cold War had ended. He even used the phrase "the rising Chinese threat." Dan liked the sound of that. Somebody was paying attention, even if the White House wasn't.

They wanted him at 0830. He'd had time to shave and eat, and even felt fairly rested. He'd washed and dried a set of khakis at the Q before he went to bed, and though they felt loose—he must have lost a few pounds, on Mindanao and at sea—he looked okay in the mirror.

McDonnell had docked back in Singapore the night after the raid on *Fengshun No.5*. Without the Sayyaf's boat. Oberg had blown its bottom out as soon as they were aboard the T-AGS, so it and their tawdry loot rested two thousand fathoms down in the China Sea. The team had broken up there, some flying west, others east, each on a different itinerary and airline. His tickets had taken him to Guam on a Continental Micronesia twin-engine Fokker, where he picked up a Navy C-9 to San Diego, and actually managed a nap in the air, something he'd almost never been able to do before.

Which was strange, because somewhere in those burning days down the Borneo coast he'd begun to nurse a gnawing anger, and a savage determination. He'd led twice, and failed twice. But neither time had *he* made the plans. This time, he was going to make the decisions. Or throw the whole mess back in Mullaly's lap, and tell him to get another boy.

The first thing he'd done at the BOQ last night was call Blair. She wasn't in the office, but he gave her the number at the quarters, figuring that's where he'd be that evening, unless they sent him home direct from the conference. Then he called the marina. The manager, a retired Marine, said yeah, his boat was fine, he looked her over on his walkdown every day and snubbed up her lines if she needed it. When would he be back to take her out? Dan said he didn't know; soon, he hoped.

The conference room was on the second floor. As they climbed the stairs he reflected how much time the Navy spent in conferences. Or maybe it was just that as you got more senior, you spent less time carrying out orders, and more time figuring out what those orders ought to be. Things certainly didn't seem as clear-cut as they once had. He felt like he'd been groping in the fog ever since the start of this whole Shkval tasking.

A once-seen face glanced up as he came in. Calvin Carroll Hines, the intel officer from SURFLANT. Hines nodded, but didn't offer to shake hands. Behind him and already seated around the usual table were Ted Mullaly, Dr. Pirrell—the young scientist from NUWC—and an older man with close-cut gray hair in a civilian suit. Dan knew him from somewhere but couldn't place him. His CO said, "Dan. Good to see you. Nice tan! Coffee?"

"Thanks, sir, pass for now."

His gaze fell to the bandage. "Problem with the hand?"

"Just coral cuts, sir. They cleaned them out, nothing serious."

"I think you know Captain Hines and Dr. Pirrell."

"Yes, sir. Captain Hines. Doctor."

"This is Rear Admiral Levering Spangler. Admiral Spangler is Force Defense at AIRLANT."

The name supplied the connection. Dan shook hands. "Good to meet you, sir. I heard you speak at the Surface Navy Association symposium in Crystal City. Last July, I think. You spoke on how the shift to the littorals would affect strike warfare."

"Actually those remarks were written for me by a very bright young woman who knows you. Claudia Hotchkiss. Served under you, I believe."

"Uh, yessir. She was my XO aboard *Horn*. How's she doing?"

"I believe she has a future. And she speaks highly of you."

He couldn't help remembering a different Claudia Hotchkiss than the one Spangler obviously had in mind. A night in his stateroom, in the Med, when the distinctions and demands of rank and duty had fallen away, and the creak and sway of a destroyer in a seaway had covered any noise they might have cared to make. He'd never told anyone about that night. He'd resolved firmly that for her sake as well as for his, he never would. "Glad to hear that, sir. She's the real deal, Claudia is."

Mullaly cleared his throat. Dan looked for a chair and found he was at the foot of the table, with them all looking down at him. "All right, let's start . . . we'd do this by message, or e-mail, but Admiral Olivero wants as thin a paper trail as possible. Everyone's heard the news from the Gulf. Right?"

"News?" Dan said.

They looked at him. "Iran's closed the Strait," Hines said. "I guess you *have* been out of touch."

Dan swallowed and sat back. He hadn't stopped for a paper that morning, nor had he seen a television for days. He tried to get his head around it as his skipper went on.

"That's why Admiral Spangler's with us." Spangler leaned back, not responding; Mullaly went on. "Iran continues to build up surface and air forces opposite Hormuz. So everyone's concerned about the security of the carriers should we have to surge. Dan, I don't want you to feel this is aimed at you, or that you're on the hot seat. But the issue's getting notice. Admiral O thought we had this situation in hand. He doesn't like having to tell the Chiefs we wasted two months we didn't have."

Great, Dan thought. He'd been around long enough to know that when they started by saying you weren't on the button, you were *really* on the button. He tried to look as if he cared. "Well, sir . . . I understand this is a priority. But we made two attempts to get our hands on the weapon. The first, the Russians didn't cooperate. The second, we were not well served by our intel. The team gained the objective, the receiving ship was standing by, but the target wasn't aboard. According to the ship's captain, it was removed just before sailing. Almost two weeks before our raid."

The intel officer said, "Was it necessary to kill him?"

That stopped him. "Sir?"

"It's a simple question, Commander. The captain. Was it necessary to kill him?"

"I understand the question, sir, but he was in good shape when we left. Zip-tied. Scared. But not dead."

"He was when *Fengshun* docked. Maybe you'd better read this."

Dan looked at the fax. It was from the Asian Shipping News Web site.

Pirates Strike Again in South China Sea

SINGAPORE-An increase in pirate attacks is undermining commercial confidence in security in the Malacca Strait area.

After the formation of the Territorial Neighbor Task Force several years ago, marking the beginning of security coordination between the Philippines, Malaysia, Indonesia, and Singapore, attacks fell markedly. But recent occurrences have reversed that trend, raising insurance rates and shaking the confidence of shippers.

"Our attempts to keep the area east of the Malacca Strait safe for commercial traffic continue and will be increased. We are implementing aggressive patrolling, but the problem is Malaysia's refusal to cooperate in providing refueling facilities and basing rights for aerial patrols," said Waluyo Suriadiredja, who retired last year as commander of the Indonesian Navy's Antipirate Task Force.

The most recent attack saw an estimated twenty pirates hijack the 900-TEU containership *Fengshun No. 5*, owned by the China Foreign Transport Company. CFTC sources announced that the intruders, armed with automatic weapons and rocket-propelled grenades, boarded from small boats, robbed the crew, and blew open safes. They destroyed radios and navigational equipment, headed the ship for a nearby shoal, and restrained the crew so tightly the captain died of a heart attack.

Dr. Soong Mei Guo of the International Maritime Bureau commented that if pirate and terrorist activity rebounds it may be necessary to place armed escorts aboard ships transiting the Straits. "Authorities must take this renewal of lawless activity seriously," she stated. "If they do not, it is an open invitation for neighboring powers to send warships to assume security responsibilities. This would cast doubt on contiguous states' ability to protect those fishing and mineral resources they claim in the neighboring seas."

Chinese authorities declined to comment on plans to react to the attack with deployments of the increasingly assertive Chinese Navy, but did not rule it out. "Ideally those countries bordering the strait will provide the needed security forces," a spokesman said. "The question of sending the Peoples' Army Navy to assist in maintaining order is, however, under review."

But clearly China and Japan, the two countries most dependent on the Strait for trade and energy requirements, are watching developments very closely.

"Comments?" murmured Mullaly. "On the record, or off?"

"On or off the record, sir, same thing: when we left, he was alive. I'll give you my word on that. Heart attack? This is the first I've heard of it, but it's probably exactly what happened."

They exchanged looks. "Good enough," Hines said at last.

Dan didn't catch the handoff, but Mullaly took the chair back. "Dan, this was your first operational mission in charge of Team C. Here's what concerns me. Captain Hines assures me his intel was solid about the location of the container and it being aboard. And in fact, it's on the manifest."

"Yessir. It was on the captain's copy, too."

"Go on."

"The captain said—my Italian's not that great—but I'm pretty sure he said it was taken off the day before they sailed." Dan took a sealed envelope from inside his cap and floated it down the table. "I typed up my after-action report aboard *McDonnell*. Yessir, I know. I did it on an old Selectric, so there's nothing left on any hard drives."

Mullaly looked at Hines. Hines shook his head slightly. Mullaly tucked it into his shirt. "Then my question is: Could there have been a leak from within the team, or within TAG? Think about that before you answer."

Dan gave it a couple of seconds while they waited and the coffee warmer snorted in the corner. A jet passed over the building, turbines whining, coming in low. They hadn't taken Im along, so the North Korean wasn't an issue. Carpenter had his flaws, but he didn't seem like a leaker. Donnie? No. Monty? Again no.

That left the SEALs, and about them he had to admit he knew less than he liked. Where, for instance, had Oberg come up with the rifles? He'd been evasive when Dan had asked him. Was it possible Oberg had passed info on the mission to the Agency, in return for the guns?

Motive? The impression he was getting so far in this whole operation was that it was bypassing the CIA. Which might not like being cut out. Would they go so far as to sabotage a DIA/Navy operation, to defend their turf?

It was all speculative and he was taking too long answering. "Uh, sir, I don't have anything to suggest. As far as any possible leak. Our comms were secure. We took all the usual security precautions."

Hines said, "There's one outside agency that might have an interest in frustrating our efforts."

"Sir?"

"The DCI."

Dan looked from one face to the next. He'd expected Hines to say the CIA. But apparently they all understood the acronym. "What's that, sir? I'm sorry, I don't—"

"The Defense Council, International—the French national corporation for arms sales."

"Oh." The light went on. The outfit Christophe de Lestapis de Cary had said he worked for.

Hines said, blinking at the ceiling, "The information we have is that the DCI's preparing to market a Gallic version of the Shkval. To follow up on their success exporting Exocet, I assume."

"Uh-huh," said Dan. "But why would that make them pass information to the other side—I guess in this case, either the Russians or the Chinese?"

"We're just exploring possibilities," Mullaly said. "But I guess the idea would be, if the U.S. doesn't have a countermeasure, it'd make this new French weapon that much more attractive to third-world buyers."

Dan thought this was scant evidence on which to accuse an ally, and de Cary hadn't seemed like a back-stabber. They might not have gotten Byrne out of Moscow without his help. The French didn't always see eye to eye with the U.S., and they seemed abnormally concerned with demonstrating it, but that didn't make them an adversary. "That seems far-fetched, sir. They operate carriers, they need a countermeasure, too. De Cary seemed eager to help in Moscow."

"Well," said Hines, "That's all over the dam. Maybe the Chinese just changed their mind and decided to ship it by air, and we're obsessing over a nonproblem. The upshot is, what you tried didn't work. But the tasking's getting more urgent every day. Ted?"

Mullaly turned from the urn with coffee. He added creamer and swirled it. "TAG's not a well funded entity," he said mildly.

"You need more, we can sweeten the pot. But we already funded two tries and they didn't work."

"Blood in the scuppers?" Mullaly said mildly. Which was Navy for, Will heads roll?

"Higher wants the Shkval," Hines said.

"Dan, what are your thoughts?" his CO asked him. "What I'm hearing is, TAG's in the toilet, we failed to deliver. How do we get out?"

Dan sat so enraged he didn't dare separate his teeth. Team Charlie had failed? They'd done all they could. Taken too many risks, without any backup. They were in the toilet? And it was up to him to get them out? Fuck this.

He was about to say so when Spangler cleared his throat. The deputy pushed back his chair and rose. The others scrambled to their feet. "Thanks for the briefing, Carrol. Very interesting, but I've got to make a flight." He nodded to the rest of them. "Gentlemen."

They stood till the door closed. Dan sat slowly; Mullaly went to the sideboard and refilled; Hines leaned against the table, chewing his thumbnail. "Dr. Pirrell?" Hines said at last, to the civilian scientist, who up to now had said absolutely nothing.

Pirrell took a breath and sat up. "We've done some of the spadework at NUWC. After Commander Lenson met with us. OPNAV got the funding from CNO. PMS-415's asked us to do an initial countermeasure analysis."

"How significant's the funding level?" said Hines.

"Half a million for initial analysis, and we can go back when we need more."

"So, have you come up with anything?" Dan asked him.

"Dr. Chone and I envision a three-track approach. The first is to reverse engineer what you may recall his calling the simplistic solution—tuning passive transducers to low frequency noise in the water, primarily the 20–100 Hertz range where the main output from a carrier's screws falls. We did a couple of simulations. Remember we said the transducers would have to be either on canards or on some sort of deployable boom? To keep them out of the turbulent flow?"

"I think so."

"Well, now we're looking at putting them up front, on the cavitator. The flow always stays laminar there."

"You said, three tracks," Hines put in.

"The second track's the countermeasure. Which should be the same, we think, at least so far, no matter what the K's guidance system is. Our alternatives are hard kill, or a seduction system—a soft kill."

"Like a decoy?" said Mullaly.

"A decoy's a seduction system, yes. The downside to soft kills are that they don't work if the incoming weapon's unguided. The hard kill system nails the threat either way, so that might be the best bet. Now, bear in mind two facts: first, we have less than thirty seconds to react after launch. Second, hydroreactive vehicles are very susceptible to puncture damage. Anything that perforates its skin will stop it, from a propulsive standpoint, and probably in a very spectacular way."

"That's going to take time. To field, I mean."

"Well, sir, we're not starting from white paper. ONR and Grumman have a program to fire SCPs, supercavitating projectiles, from a helicopter, to destroy mines. We're looking at how to adapt those SCPs to the carrier's Phalanx self-defense suite. And there's a joint U.S./UK program, the Multi-Sensor Torpedo Recognition Acoustic Integrated System, that we've been evaluating in the Weapons Analysis Facility. So we've already got some of the building blocks.

"Our plan is to simulate our guided Shkval in the WAF. Then use the MSTRAIS to model the underwater fire-control system. The AN/SLQ-25 has a torpedo alertment capability we can add another acoustic processor to. We'll put the algorithms together and crank it through the mainframe and see how much of a P-sub-K comes out and whether there's any way we can bump up our localization. Lab-test it—we need in-water data to validate the simulation. Then proceed to a test-analyze-fix of the integrated system on a carrier."

He smiled as if apologizing for the blizzard of technical language. "If the concept's valid, we could have an interim capability out there in six months at around fifteen million dollars. Those are tight constraints, but technically it's medium risk. We'd only need to hand-build two systems; each carrier could turn them over to its relief as they outchopped—"

Mullaly said, "Do you still need the weapon itself, then? Are we trying to accomplish a tasking we don't need to anymore?"

"No, sir. I mean, yes, unfortunately, we do." Pirrell eyed Dan with regret. "We need at least a gross idea of the guidance system's sensor and maneuver envelope to design the predictive portion of the fire-control software. The more data we have, the more accurate our predictions will be. Right now our first run-through on the back of the envelope's telling us we can't pump out enough projectiles to guarantee a kill. So—I'm sorry, but the answer's yes."

"Thanks, Doctor." Mullaly checked his watch. "Okay, we should be getting sandwiches pretty soon. I figured we might as well eat here, get through everything so we can agree on what has to be done next. Because based on what I'm hearing, they still want us to proceed with the tasking."

Hines heaved himself up. "Smoke break for me."

"You can excuse me, too," said Pirrell.

When he and Mullaly were alone Dan cleared his throat. "I thought about this on the plane back, Captain. I have a proposal, but I'm not sure I should present it."

"Why not?"

"I'm sure Dr. Pirrell's cleared all the way up to Compartmented Ridiculous—"

"But he doesn't need to know this? All right. I'll tell him we're done with the technical side, he's free to go."

Dan got coffee. He looked out the window, down at the mud flats near ACU 5. Then at his hand. He tried to make it stop shaking. That wouldn't make a good impression, if anyone noticed it. But he was only partially successful.

* * *

NOW it was just him and the four-stripers. "All right," Mullaly drawled. "Dan's got a proposal for us. But he's not sure we're going to like it."

"Let us be the judges of that, Commander," Hines said. "In any case, whatever it is, we'd need SURFLANT and AIRLANT approval. Since your CO here seems to be using the requirement to squeeze more funds out of us."

Dan said, "My advice is not to tell either of them. Or put it on secure Internet, or distribute it in any other way, either."

Mullaly grimaced. "Enough drama. Let's have it."

It might not be the best idea. But it was all he had to offer, the only road that might get them where they wanted to go. He plunged. "I'm tired of having Higher tell us how to go about this. Go to Moscow. Go to the Malacca Straits. The way I figure it, the straightest line from not having a Shkval-K to having one is to go where we *know* there's an operational weapon."

"Which is where?" Hines watched him closely. "The Russian Navy?"

Someone knocked at the door; the lieutenant, carrying Styrofoam sandwich containers; Mullaly waved him off.

"No, sir. Iran. They're buying all the arms they can get. We know one of them's the Shkval-K. You've seen this on the secret JWICS. They're making the first installation in a Juliet-class submarine. A former cruise missile sub."

The intel officer frowned and sat back.

"You're proposing—what?" Mullaly shook his head. "I don't think—"

"Wait, sir. Think about what we'd get. The weapon. Plus any guidance computers, software that comes with it. And as an added bonus, it's a preemptive strike. Dr. P's just told us it'll take him at least six months to generate an initial countermeasure. *At least.* Which could mean a year, two years—who knows?"

"Right," said Hines, his tone the essence of noncommittal.

"For that whole time, Tehran's got our nuts in a vise; all they have to do is spin the handle. But if we got the testbed installation out of Iran's hands, we preserve the viability of our carriers in the Gulf until we can get a defensive capability to sea."

"You're not seriously proposing we hijack an Iranian submarine," Mullaly said.

Dan turned to him. "Not hijack it, sir—no. We don't need the sub. But we've got a team already trained to take over a ship and offload a weapon."

Mullaly looked to Hines. The N2 touched his lips, then shook out a cigarette. "Can't hurt to look it over. But that's the kind of thing we'd have to kick *way* upstairs."

"I'm glad you mentioned that," Dan told him. "That was my next question. Actually, I asked it before and I didn't get a straight answer. I'll ask it one more time. Has there been a covert action finding? Has the president authorized us to do this? Or are we tearing off on our own here, doing an Oliver North for you, or for Admiral Olivero?"

"To be perfectly honest, that's a VUCA situation," said Hines.

"A VU what?"

"It's volatile, uncertain, complex, and ambiguous. You ask, has there been a finding? The trouble is, I don't remember."

"You don't *remember?*"

Hines tapped his forehead. "I have a memory problem. Documented in my medical records. Head injury, Desert Storm. So, you ask me questions like that—"

"This is ridiculous." Dan stood. "I could have lost guys aboard that freighter, if the crew had resisted. We came this close to getting napalmed on Mindanao, when the Philippine Army hit the rebel camp. Looking for kidnapped Americans *I* wasn't told were there."

"There's no diplomatic way to say this, Commander. But the Navy's not being supported by the civilian intelligence structure on this issue. Including DIA."

"But that's DIA's mission," Mullaly said mildly. "How can they back away from it?"

Hines said, "Oh, there's very little our national intelligence structure can't back away from, Todd. But don't get me started on that. The current chief of DIA's a lieutenant general. An *Air Force* lieutenant general. Does that help?"

"I'm still not clear exactly what 'not being supported' means, Captain," Dan said. "Can you find it convenient to tell me? If you remember?"

"Sure. To the extent you need to know. Does it mean you have an official finding, a blessing out of the West Wing? You worked for this president. You seriously think he'd find for something like this? You and I both know the answer.

"On the other hand, is keeping Hormuz open vital to the national interest of the United States? It is. So vital, we'd have to send that carrier in whether there was a threat or not. So then what happens?"

Dan said after a moment, "We might lose it."

"Yeah. A carrier. And an air wing, and five thousand sailors, worse case." Hines looked at the door again, and his face was calm but his eyes moved this way and that. "I hardly remember half of what they tell me. But from the CNO on down, the Navy's squatting and straining to shit out a solution here. If that means we have to do it ourselves, our own intel, our own operations, and our own countermeasures, then the phrase that comes to mind is, 'Damn the torpedoes, full speed ahead.' "

"Dan, that answer your questions?" Mullaly murmured.

He didn't even need to nod. But he kept his hands away from his coffee cup. If he reached for it now, there'd be a real mess.

17

USS *San Francisco*, SSN-711, Off Naval Support Activity Diego Garcia, British Indian Ocean Territory

FIFTY feet down, Teddy Oberg floated in a turquoise haze that stretched lightfilled above, below, around, without bound or limit. Bubbles tumbled upward in silvery floods. The sun poured down golden torrents that shifted and shimmered across the flat black paint of the massive cylinder he was slowly hand-jockeying out of a black archway into the light.

He and four other divers hung like strange gourds from the slowly writhing loops of hookah hoses inside the Dry Deck Shelter. The nine-foot-wide DDS was bolted to the main deck aft of the sail. Below it, out ahead of him as he faced aft, was the far more massive curvature of *San Francisco*'s afterbody, then the towering black blade of its rudder.

The DDS's walls were high yield steel, built to take as much pressure as the submarine hull itself. Breathing fifteen times a minute, Teddy hung in the main compartment, or hangar, all the way aft. Forward of it was the transfer trunk, an airlock that mated to the after-torpedo hatch. And forward of that was a hyperbaric chamber, in case a diver had to be depressurized.

The black shape they were maneuvering out into the blue-gold shimmer on its track-and-cradle gear was a "Gator"-class submarine delivery vehicle. It looked more like a swollen, blunt torpedo than a submarine. But its smoothly faired aluminum was sausage-stuffed with ballast and trim tanks and pumps, fathometer, gyro, ahead-looking sonar, even a small inertial navigation system.

Starting two hours before, they'd flooded the hangar and equalized pressure. Wearing open circuit SCUBA, the DDS team had undogged the huge exterior door and extracted the tracks. Now they were slowly working the vehicle out of the hangar.

This was a drill, of course. Lenson and the SDV team commander had insisted on a run-through before they headed in to the Strait. This DDS was brand-new, just delivered, and longer than previous models, to accommodate larger teams for longer missions. They wanted to make sure nothing would go wrong. Not that you ever could . . . He had to admit, it was a lovely sea for a dive. Seventy degrees, so they didn't really need the wet suits.

He only knew a couple of the SDV guys. All SEALs operated with SDVs, but these were the West Coast team.

A grinding scrape dragged. He couldn't really tell where from, it was difficult to localize sound in the water. One of the divers pointed to the stern. He mimed getting a grip and pushing. Teddy finned around till he could brace himself against the inner wall. He grabbed the crossbar on the rudder and applied force. Not too much; underwater you just wanted steady thrust on something that weighed this much. With massive deliberation it hesitated against his gloves. Then began swinging the other way.

A few minutes later he clung to the outer lip of the shelter, watching the vehicle leave. The screw rotating so slowly he could make out each blade, it shrank gradually away into the blue. A single ping rang through the sea, jabbing a pick into his right ear.

He watched till it disappeared, then jackknifed, pulling himself back inside. Joining the line of other handlers, pulling himself down the length of the hangar into deeper blackness. A circle of light showed the hatch to the transfer trunk. He waited patiently, the dry gas hissing in through his regulator, bubbles roaring in his ears as he breathed out.

SIXTY feet forward, Dan perched on the single chair in the captain's cabin. With two men in it, both taller than average, there wasn't much spare cubic left under the curved overhead. He kept expecting the air to be close, but it smelled like white bread. Andy Mangum was sprawled on his bunk in blue coveralls, hands behind his head and one foot propped against the door. Andy and he had been classmates at the Academy. The year before, they'd met off South Korea, during a multinational exercise that had turned into the hunt and engagement of a covert strike force. Now Mangum was humming "Take My Breath Away," and staring at the overhead. Dan waited.

The sub's skipper said, "Those boots work out for you?"

"Yeah. Thanks." He looked at his feet. "Still wearing them, actually."

"You know, from what you say, this is an illegal operation."

"Covert's the official word."

"But you say there was no finding? You never got written orders?" Mangum shook his head. "We do black ops in the sub force. But there are orders. They don't travel outside the chop chain. But they're there."

"Do you have orders for this operation?"

"Matter of fact, I do."

"Who from?"

"SUBPAC."

"So what's your worry?"

"I guess I don't have one," the CO said. "Warm up that coffee?" He pressed a call button on the bulkhead.

"What do they say?" Dan asked after a moment.

"What does who say?"

"Your orders."

"Oh. Pretty bare bones. Like always. Pick up a DDS and a task element from SDV Team One in Pearl. Proceed to Diego Garcia and pick up elements of SEAL Team Three and TAG Team Charlie. Transit to Point X-ray and debark. Remain on station until SDV returns; high-speed transit to Diego Garcia for offload."

"That's all?"

"All that's my business."

"Nothing on our objective?"

"I don't need to know your objective. All I have to do is get you there, and pick you up when you're done."

Dan scratched his regrown beard, looking at his classmate's deliberately incurious face. He felt tempted to tell him. But he reluctantly concluded he had to act like a naval officer, even if sometimes he didn't feel like one. "All right," he muttered.

"Pretty clever, what the Iranians did. The spot market and all."

"What's that?"

"You don't follow the market?"

"The stock market? Not that close. Blair's got mutual funds, but they're in a trust or something. Since she's in a policymaking position."

"Get her into energy. Everything revolves around energy. Remember when they announced they were closing the Strait? Going to lay mines?"

"And then the next day said no, it wasn't closed."

"Right." Mangum sat up and pulled his notebook over, booted it up. "I had it here someplace . . . the *Wall Street Journal* Online . . . heck, this battery doesn't last very long . . . never mind. First they announced they were closing the Strait, warning mariners, threatening to sink tankers. The next day they say, oh no, our mistake. The actual effect? Can you guess?"

"To put the fear of God into us?"

"Better than that. The National Iranian Oil Company quietly bets long on millions of barrels of oil futures. Then, after the announcement, the spot price of crude doubles. They start selling. They ride the spike up to the peak, unloading all the way. They sell future deliveries of their own production in Europe and Japan.

"Then suddenly, hey, we're sorry, there'll be no mines, somebody in the Pasdaran got overzealous. But by then all the futures are snapped up, and they sold two years' production in advance, too. They figure the total take at around sixty billion dollars."

"A nice payday."

"Enough to fund their naval expansion plans for years. The North Koreans, now the Iranians—they're learning how to whip us without firing a shot."

Dan shook his head in mock admiration. But maybe it would recoil on them, maybe they'd been *too* clever. Because after that he hadn't heard a single doubt or problem about his operation, and every piece of equipment and resource he'd asked for had suddenly been his.

Someone tapped at the door. Mangum took his boot off it, and a young man in the same blue coveralls as Dan and Mangum thrust a hand in with a carafe. "You remember Cus," Mangum said. "Cus, you remember Commander Lenson."

"Yessir, sure do. Honor to have you back aboard, sir."

"Damn it, you didn't need to tell them all that stuff about me," Dan said when the door closed again.

Mangum looked at his watch, then at the bulkhead readouts. "Let's see how they're doing with the drill," he said.

THE Task Element Commander for the SDV team was older than an O-4 should be and though he didn't wear insignia other than his dive pin Dan figured he was former enlisted. He hailed from Pasadena, but he didn't act or talk like a surfer. In fact it seemed like an effort for him to talk at all. Dan didn't know much about the special ops side of the Navy, but he knew the SDV teams had split off from the SEAL teams in the eighties, half of what had been the Underwater Demolition world specializing into the operators ashore and the other half into the micro-subs. The TEC stood dripping at the bottom of the ladder, stripping off his gear. Dan smelled rubber, salt, urine, and the iron bite of compressed air.

"Everything go okay?"

"Went all right." The TEC frowned at his guys as they clambered down the ladder, shedding gear and water. One was bleeding from his nose but no one remarked on it. The bleeding guy spat onto the gratings.

"Don't spit on our boat," said one of the engineers. The divers and the sub crew looked at each other, then away.

"So it went okay? No hitches?"

"Pretty smooth," the TEC said. He scratched his wet scalp, then added unwillingly, "We ran the mission profile. Eight miles out. Shut down. Reboot everything, then eight miles back. All the instruments work. We have solid nav with the inertial. We'll have more weight with all your folks aboard, and the drag from the towed body, but since we stripped out that number three battery we should hit neutral buoyancy. But that brings up another problem, Commander."

"Sure," Dan said. "What?"

"Let's go back here."

He followed the TEC through the engineroom till they were as private as they could get aboard a 360-foot sub with nineteen more guys aboard than there were bunks for. The lieutenant-commander looked at a set of weights someone had bungeed to the grating. Not meeting Dan's eyes he said, "We don't have the capacity we thought. We can't take all your people back with us, Commander. Not with the tow you want me to calculate for. So you can't take them all in with you, either."

"Is this a SEAL issue?"

"How do you mean?"

Dan didn't feel like being stubborn, but he wasn't about to let a single seat go. "These guys have been drilling right along with Oberg and Kaulu-kukui. They've had CQB training. Oberg ran them through a SCUBA refresher. If you're telling me because they're not SEALs you don't want to take them in, forget it."

"Training ain't but training. If they freeze up, or freak out, they'll get people killed."

"I don't know your people either, uh, Chibbie. But my guys have been in on this mission from the get-go. How many drivers do we need?"

"They're pilots, not 'drivers.' And we need two."

"How many personnel's the vehicle have seats for? It doesn't matter if they're in each other's faces. It's only for two hours, three tops."

"It'd be more like face to buttcrack, but we can get eight bodies in. That's not the problem."

Dan rubbed his face, thinking it over. Oberg, Henrickson, Kaulukukui, Im, Carpenter, Wenck, and himself. Seven bodies.

During the planning phase they'd considered various methods of insertion—by helo or combat raiding craft, by submarine, even high-altitude, low-opening parachute insertion—but the known emitters around the Bandar Abbas base had indicated such heavy antiaircraft defenses as to rule out any insertion by air. Plus, once you inserted, you had to extract. The next iteration had Team Charlie inserting at night, via "combat rubber raiding craft"—CRRCs in SEALspeak; rubber rafts with waterproof outboards. But a careful plot of coverage of Iranian surface patrols in the Strait had pushed them off that square too and onto the last one—a covert, submerged penetration of the Iranian harbor.

The insertion itself should be fairly straightforward; what happened afterward might not be. Preparing for this had entailed three furious weeks of planning and training.

One major complication surfaced early: Juliet-class submarines had no torpedo loading hatches. It seemed strange compared to American practice, but there it was. To load, they ballasted down at stern or bow. The crew opened the outer and inner doors on the tubes and fed the torpedoes aboard through them, in effect reversing the launching procedure.

Eventually Dan had decided this was an advantage. Once they had control of the boat—assuming they got that far—all they'd need to do was ballast down forward, open the forward door, and let the weapon slide out, underwater, onto what a survey dating from back when U.S. ships had used Bandar Abbas, in the Shah's time, said was a soft sand-and-mud harbor bottom.

It wasn't what he'd call robust, but it was a plan. According to Hines, the Iranians didn't stay at high readiness. It should be possible to get in without being observed. But to get out again, they'd have to do so submerged.

So the extraction would be via SDV as well. The vehicle would settle to the bottom a few yards off the bow. The assault party would exit, using Draeger rebreathers, and take over the Juliet while the handling party— the two pilots—stood by. When the Shkval dropped out onto the mud, they'd wrap it in a buoyant jacket and attach a tow cable. The assault team would exit the target, swim back down to the SDV, and all hands would extract back to *San Francisco* safe from any Iranian lead that might be flying around by then.

Meanwhile, while they'd been thrashing this all out, the NUWC model shop had been building a sheet-metal-and-wood full-sized dummy Shkval. When it was done they crated it up, labeled it "wind-tunnel body," and flew it to Norfolk. Dan and the rest of the team practiced with it aboard *Spadefish* at the destroyer-submarine piers, coached by a master chief torpedoman from SUBRON Six who was the only soul allowed in the torpedo room with them when they were practicing. Hines had turned up one day with photos of the interior of a Juliet-class; Dan had no idea where he'd gotten those.

They'd eventually learned to move the thing around pretty rapidly. The question would be, of course, how well they could do it in a strange torpedo room, working with non-U.S.equipment. Dan hoped they'd find the Shkval already in the tube. That would make it simpler, faster, and so, a whole lot less dangerous. The less time they spent smack in the middle of a hostile naval base, the better.

He felt someone next to him. When he turned his head it was Mangum. "Problem?" the captain said.

"Not sure yet. What exactly are you asking me?" Dan asked the TEC. "I thought the plan was, nine guys go in. That's two helmsmen, or you're calling them pilots; and my seven guys, the assault team. While we hit the sub, the pilots stand by on the bottom. The shooters take the sub over and shit the thing out the tube, where your guys are waiting. Right?"

"Right."

"What's the problem, then?"

"The weapon. Coming back."

"Why's that suddenly a hard spot?"

"Drag."

"And why's drag suddenly the problem? Didn't we go through all the numbers already?" He exchanged glances with Mangum. Damn, he had to drag every word out of this guy.

"The hitch is, we're not getting enough energy out of the battery. Enough power hours. Kilowatt hours. That's like a horsepower is 746 kilowatt hours—"

"I know how batteries are rated. What's wrong with the battery?"

"What's wrong? It's old. They're talking about replacing these with lithium batteries, so they didn't do a rebuy on the silver-zinc. But now the new batteries are held up and we're still operating with the old ones."

"Bottom line?" said Mangum.

"We can't take everybody he wants to take. Either he cuts his guys to six, or I'm calling a no-go."

"This battery," Mangum said. "What's the storage cycle?"

Dan stood back while they went into the technicalities of recharge and reforming. Mangum kept asking if they could reform the battery. The TEC said they didn't have chargers that would do that. Mangum picked up a bulkhead phone. "Chief electrician, to my cabin. No, make it the wardroom—might as well sit down."

At the end of another hour's conference and much unfolding of diagrams from manuals and arguing, they had something set up. The chief electrician seemed hesitant, but said he'd give it a try; if they brought down the batteries into the engine room one by one, he'd discharge and reform them, bring them back to their original capacity. And finally the TEC agreed that, yeah, Teddy Oberg could serve as the copilot, thus meaning one less body to haul in and back.

So that was the compromise. Dan sat through it all as his butt went from torpid to numb. He kept trying to internalize that in just two days, they'd be back aboard, with their prize.

Either that, or they could very well be dead.

THAT night, in the torpedo room, Donnie Wenck punched the limp little pillow. The bunk they'd given him was unbelievable. Not even room above him to turn over, and he had to share it. It was only his till midnight, then one of the off-watch engineers owned it. And there were always guys going in and out, the lights were always on . . . But it was impressive, being aboard a nuke. He'd roamed the passageways with his mouth open, asking about the gear. This was his kind of duty. He should have been a nuke.

Instead of . . . whatever he was now. Some kind of nerd, pretending to be a SEAL.

They'd spent most of the day learning how to tear down, test, reassemble, and troubleshoot the oxygen rebreathers they'd be using on the mission. Oberg had made them all, even Mr. Lenson, check and lubricate the various O-rings and seals and canisters, while he explained how the Draegers worked, and what would happen if they didn't.

They wouldn't be pirate look-alikes this time. This time they'd be real commando types. He slid his hand under the pillow for the SEAL patrol leader's handbook Teddy had given him. He was memorizing it, all the detailed stuff about C-3 vans, and target analysis, and special boat capabilities. He wanted to know it cold.

He rubbed his arms, wincing. He'd been lifting with Obie and Sumo

Man. He couldn't do it the way they did it, clanging metal and shouting at each other, faces red and streaming sweat. He wished his arms didn't look so thin. He wished he could shoot better.

He wished he could get a girl like the one he'd seen Obie with in Virginia Beach. He'd been sitting at the bar in Croc's with his lonely drink, yearning after one of the waitresses, when he'd glimpsed Teddy's scarred hard face in the mirror, up by the hostess's station. And then, slowly, every male head at the bar had rotated, like so many radar dishes, to home and track on the woman hanging on his arm: so stunning she stopped all conscious thought; a gorgeous, gorgeous natural redhead, with long curly hair, and gorgeous tits, and gorgeous legs, and a gorgeous ass, and a face Donnie was sure he'd seen in some movie or TV show, so that when he reluctantly turned his gaze back to the waitress he'd thought so hot she seemed overweight, tired, somehow malformed.

Donnie closed his eyes, calling up again her legs in tight black capris and high heels, the way everything got outlined when she bent over. It made him want to whack off, but not here, there was no privacy. He felt lightheaded. Then he remembered the mission and felt scared.

He rubbed his arms and tried to focus on the manual.

THE next day. 1000. Oberg sat in the crew's mess, hunched over the game Sumo had brought, sluggish after a heavy breakfast of baboon ass, liver transplant, and battery acid. You couldn't work out all the time, you couldn't do briefbacks all the time, and on a sub, the crew never let the SEALs touch anything. They were protective and assholes about it, though they had it backward, they thought the SEALs were the assholes. Sumo had brought a folding bike but it broke the first time he got on it. Teddy didn't mind. His jump rope and weights were enough for him, and you could do those back in the engine room between the turbines, where it was over a hundred, get yourself a real sweat going.

Kaulukukui, though, was the Game Boy. He always brought games on missions. This time it was some kind of Japanese card-and-board thing that was actually pretty interesting. He wondered how Lenson was doing. He hadn't seen much of the commander since they'd come aboard.

"You think this thing's gonna fly, Obie?"

"Absolutely."

"We'll get our hands on it this time?"

"We'll grab it, shit it out, and run like a raped ape."

"With these guys for a team?" Kaulukukui said. "It's gonna be a fucking boodiddley goatrope. What if one of them gets his Draeger caught?"

"Deal the fucking cards," Oberg said.

RIT Carpenter felt perfectly at home. He hung out with the crew, not with the SEALs or the SDV guys or even the rest of Team Charlie. He spent most of his time in the sonar shack, getting smart on the gear that had come along since he'd gotten out. The 688s were like spaceships. Everything was solid state, digitized. The sonar suite was amazing and they could fire Tomahawks from the torpedo tubes. But a lot of the systems were pretty much like what he'd trained on, just faster and with more bells and whistles.

He hoped this went okay. He had the feeling Lenson was close to bouncing him off the team. So, maybe he'd slipped up once or twice. What of it? He liked to interact with the locals, see the sights, drink the beer. Was that anything sailors hadn't done forever? Everything was getting so fucking PC a guy couldn't scratch his ass without some lezzbo female JAG type calling him on it. It sure wasn't the old Navy, the one he'd grown up in.

He was thinking this when he came around one of the dogleg corners and collided with the man he'd just been stewing over. Lenson looked irritated. They dodged this way, then that, trying to get past each other in a space so walled with electrical cabinets only one could pass. At last he said, "Commander. We talk a minute, sir?"

"Sure. Go ahead."

"Not *here*."

Lenson glanced around. He seemed unwilling. "Up one deck," he said at last.

When they closed the door to his stateroom the commander waved at the chair. Rit stayed on his feet. "Won't take long, sir. All I wanted to ask was, you still got it in for me?"

Lenson took too long to reply. "Okay, you asked. You put us all at risk back on Mindanao, Carpenter. And before that, in Pusan. At the military cemetery. Where they caught you with that girl on the British soldier's grave."

"We weren't doing anything he wouldn't have cheered us on, sir."

"Everybody else in the team seems to be able to keep it in his pants. You're the only one who gets in trouble."

"All due respect, sir, but ever think, I'm just the only one gets caught?"

"Then that's just as good a reason. This is your last mission with Team Charlie, Rit. No prejudice. I was steamed in Mindanao, I admit that, but I've decided to let you go without an adverse report. I just think you're better off back at the Group, eight to five and weekends off."

Rit thought about trying to argue him out of it. Then thought: Fuck it. He'd almost had his head handed to him in the Philippines. He didn't like being patronized by Oberg and his oversized asshole-buddy. He didn't even need TAG. He'd had offers from Honeywell, Hughes, Loral. If Lenson didn't want him, fine.

Besides, he had a realtor in Virginia Beach and a base bunny in Norfolk. Nice clean American girls. Not that exotic wasn't exciting. Everybody liked a change.

FINALLY it was the last day. Then, the last afternoon. Mangum had bunked Dan in the executive officers' stateroom, a clone of his own, but no roomier. He went there after dinner and turned off the light. Then lay awake, staring at the overhead. They were tearing through the water, hundreds of feet below the surface, but only the faintest clues conveyed that reality. A repetitive tremor writhed through the steel around him. Something ticked beneath his bunk. Air sighed through the ventilation baffles. It smelled like oiled steel.

He turned his head nervously on the thin Navy-issue pillow. The light was dim but he could just see the photo. Nan and Blair together, taken at a deli in Alexandria. They were both laughing and though they didn't look at all alike Dan always thought when he looked at it that they might be mother and daughter.

He smiled. At any rate Nan would be taken care of. After one of the rehearsals, Kaulukukui had unobtrusively slid a form in front of him. Dan hadn't known the spec ops community had its own term life insurance program, over and above the group life every service member was eligible for. If he didn't come back from this one, she'd have no money worries. Not for the rest of her life, if she was careful.

But then his sight focused past the picture, on the heavy steel arch that spoke silently yet eloquently of the crushing force it resisted from microsecond to microsecond. No. He couldn't think about that.

Think about the mission instead. No, that wasn't any way to invite sleep either. Think about his daughter. His wife. Or his new boat, which he hadn't even gotten to take out yet.

That didn't work either, and at last he swung out of the bunk and folded the little desk down, and clicked the light on.

They'd held the last backbrief that morning. Gathered in the torpedo room, the crew locked grumbling out of their sleeping and work space. Perched on the racks, the Mark 48s, he'd gone over it again, making each man explain what he had to do and how he'd do it, and what would happen if he didn't. He'd had them bring weapons and gear, and inspected it himself.

Team Charlie was as ready as he could make it.

He just hoped nothing popped up they couldn't handle.

He tried to read, sitting in his skivvies, but his eyes wouldn't track to the ends of the sentences. At last he pulled out the tan briefcase and unlocked it. Fanned out the charts, the photos, the op order. The port layout. The bottom hydrography.

He'd memorized the distances from the entrance to the piers, and from one pier to the next. He'd spent hours visualizing their relationships, engraving into his memory where they'd lie relative to one another as seen from here or there. Just in case they had to do some swimming within the port. Or the SDV was forced to the surface. Or if, when they got there, *K-79*—the cruise missile sub the Russians had sold to the Iranians—had been shifted across the basin.

American contractors had modernized the ancient port of Bandar Abbas into a base from which the Shah's fleet could protect the world's energy traffic. Unfortunately it had turned out to be just as strategic a location under the mullahs. Also, secure; guarded by three islands between it and the Gulf of Oman, layered with radar sites, missile batteries, coastal guns, and surface and air patrols.

Assuming they got past all those, the charts showed a dredged basin shaped like a giant trident. Breakwaters protected the entrance, which was thirteen hundred feet wide and about fifty deep. Narrow for a submerged insertion, but doable. At night there were supposed to be lights on the ends of the breakwater—Bandar Abbas was a fishing port as well as a naval facility—but no one had been able to tell him if they'd be lit.

He kneaded his forehead in the humming light. Once inside, they'd pass an anchored guardship, then proceed for half a mile to the original harbor entrance. This was much narrower than the breakwater entrance, but deeper. Past it the harbor branched into its tripartitite flowering. To the west, the shallowest branch, was the torpedo boat harbor. Directly ahead, a dredged channel led to warehouses, loading areas, and the commercial fishing piers.

He studied a color photo. Congress and the President had prohibited overflights of Iran, but somehow he was holding several obviously taken from low altitude. So clear he could make out individual figures walking along the piers. Their shadows stretched west; taken about 0800 local, he guessed. The building with the ragged line in front of it had to be the mess hall. He'd examined photo after photo, and finally concluded the Juliet's crew either hadn't reported aboard yet, or slept ashore. Most likely the former; the Iranians had probably sent them to Russia for training.

To starboard—the direction in which the SDV would slowly pivot, assuming they made it through the entrances—they'd squeeze through another bottleneck, between piers to north and south. The northern piers served the frigates and corvettes left from U.S. and British support of Iran in the seventies. One had been sunk during Operation Praying Mantis, but had been raised and repaired. Intel doubted the effectiveness of their electronics and computers, but Dan had no doubt they had enough weapons still operational that if the team was detected, they'd not have to worry long.

Past them, at the far end of the right-hand branch—farthest from the entrance, of course—lay their target. He lifted the photo, squinting.

The oblate silhouette of the Juliet lay between two Kilos, one moored ahead, the other astern. The pier was offset from the shore and linked to it by ramps; this meant, he was fairly sure, that the bottom slope was gradual there. Looking closer, he noted a squared-off shadow between the sub's hull and the pier proper. It might be a camel, a floating balk of raw timber. That made sense. A Juliet drew a lot of water. She might even ground on the bottom during extreme low tides.

Once they had what they came for, they'd have to retrace their steps. Past frigates, corvettes, guns, out again through the narrows . . . was it realistic to hope to make it out unobserved? They had a diversion planned, even a rescue force; the USS *Nimitz* strike group was carrying out a joint task force exercise off Bahrain, along with the 26th Marine Expeditionary Unit aboard USS *Bataan*. But he'd need the sat phone to call for help.

Which meant he'd have to be on the surface.

Which would mean every Iranian with an AK would be shooting at them before he got to say word one.

Under the buzzing light he dug the heels of his palms into the sockets of his eyes. This felt like the night before the Looking Glass mission into Iraq. The one that had lost him so many people. So many good people.

What could go wrong? Maybe nothing. Maybe everything would go smooth. For once.

They'd go at dusk. Four more hours. He really should try to get a little sleep. But his guts felt like shitting out everything he'd eaten that day.

He'd have to look confident. He'd have to lead. But Christ, he didn't feel at all confident, and he didn't want to lead.

An icy sweat broke out all over his back, soaking his skivvy shirt. He took deep, slow breaths, digging his nails into his face, trying to dike the dread that burrowed like maggots within a corpse.

18

The Gulf of Oman

MANGUM shook his hand for a long while, at the bottom of the ladder in the engine room, then gripped his shoulder too, as if unwilling to let him go. "Take care of yourself, roomie."

"Just be here when we get back, Andy."

"Oh, yeah. Absolutely. Where else would we be?" His classmate slapped his shoulder and abruptly faced away. "Turns for one knot," he said to a talker, who repeated the order into his set.

Dan stuffed the fear into his belly and clambered up the ladder. With difficulty: He was burdened by nearly a hundred pounds of weapons, ammunition, knife, rebreather, and weights. It was a painful pull with his left arm, which he'd burned the shit out of one black night in the Arctic Sea. He reached the top and wriggled slowly through and up, into the transfer trunk.

A single bulb behind thick glass lit the white-painted sphere. Oberg and Kaulukukui sat bent over on the little circular shelf seat. The big Hawaiian looked even more enormous curled into the minuscule space.

Oberg leaned forward and tugged at Dan's Draeger. The LAR-V was a chest-worn black-plastic-coated oblong with a green oxygen tank the size of a sixteen-ounce Coke tucked under it. Inside were a breathing bag, an air scrubber canister, and a first-stage regulator. There was a pressure gauge for the tank on top, where you could look down and read it; it measured from zero to three hundred. A recessed manual oxygen-add button on the front. Two corrugated rubber breathing tubes led to the second-stage regulator in the mouthpiece. The tank dug into his diaphragm as Oberg jerked on the cylinder straps, twisted the valve closed, open again. "Just a little buddy check, okay? We good to go, Commander?" he said, looking deep into Dan's eyes.

Dan cleared his throat, trying not to look as nervous as he felt. He had a lot of hours underwater, but sport diving and penetrating a hostile harbor by night were orders of magnitude apart. "Let's do it," he said. He bit the mouthpiece into place and took a hit. Rubber and stale-tasting gas and a faint sting of alcohol.

"Only easy day was yesterday," Kaulukukui joked. "Right?"

"Sure, Sumo Man."

"It's gonna be just like on SCUBA, only there won't be any bubbles, and believe me, you won't miss them. Remember that bailout bottle on your leg. No reason to get hinky. You need more oxygen, hit the button. The bag collapses, suck in, you'll get more. This is a diverproof unit, long as you stay shallow. Always plenty of air." Beside him Oberg was going on his Draeger, too. His hand hovered over a big push switch on the bulkhead, giving him one last chance to back out, Dan supposed; then thumped it like a faith healer invoking the Spirit.

Water gushed in. It swirled around their feet, rising quickly. It felt cold at first, as it flooded down his booties and up into his wet suit bottom, then warmed. He sealed his mask, tongued the mouthpiece, and flexed his arms, trying to relax. Deep slow breaths.

The water came up over his chest, then over his face. Deep slow breaths. The two SEALs were watching him like hawks.

He breathed out, then blinked, surprised. No bubbles. It *did* feel weird.

TEDDY watched Lenson's eyes as the water came up. He looked tense, but the pupils weren't blasted wide, the eyeballs weren't jerking around the way they did when a diver was fighting the Monster. The last bubbles came up out of their wet suits and gear. They drifted between them, wavering upward, then vanished, sucked into the overhead vent. Up on the surface there'd a be a seething slick, just for a few seconds; then it would drift apart, vanish in the chop. That was okay. A moonless night, forty miles off the coast, there'd be no one to see. Which a cautious periscope sweep had already made sure of.

He spun the wheel on the hatch. It swung out, into the hangar. Kaulukukui was closer, so he bowed, made a courtly gesture: *You first*. And got a lifted finger in return.

BY the time Henrickson pushed himself through the hatch, gulping as he sucked on the mouthpiece of his Draeger, most of the others had exited.

He kept breathing shallow no matter how hard he tried not to. This thing on his chest was supposed to take the carbon dioxide out. Hydroxide to carbonate reaction. But he had a headache already. He felt for the oxygen add button, then forced his finger away. He shouldn't need more this soon, should he?

Blackness, so dense and enormous he lost which way was up. They'd told him not to stop, that it was "just like getting on the bus." But which way? He hovered, lungs pumping faster. Shit. Shit!

A hand grabbed him out of the dark. A hovering figure pointed him and shoved. Motioned to keep going. Instead he hovered, sculling slowly, oriented now, taking it in.

The lights were shielded, so they wouldn't glare upward. The effect was eerie, illuminating everything but only from above. Hoses drifted across where divers were herding a black flattened shape like a torpedo sat on from above. Another beckoned impatiently from the barely lit circle of the hangar opening.

Whoever was behind him—Im, he thought—bumped him. He gulped and swallowed and made himself let go the edge of the hatch. He swam down the empty hangar and out into the open night sea, toward the looming shape that slewed slowly out to the side.

Turbulence jostled him. They were underway, slowly, and the current was pushing him aft. Toward a slowly rotating shadow he realized with a squeeze of his heart was the sub's massive screw. He shrank instinctively. But he couldn't back down. The rest of the team was behind him, Lenson was in front of him.

No, he couldn't back out now. . . .

HANGING in the dark sea, watching the lights creep here and there, Teddy felt heavy, which wasn't good. The Draeger wouldn't burn off gas like an open circuit rig. But you always felt heavy going in. It was all the gear. And all the straps, and slings, and hoses, and shit.

Some guys got all jocked up for a mission. He preferred to keep it light. He didn't carry a pistol, for example. Just another thing to hang up. He took an extra HK mag instead. Less weight, and you got thirty rounds instead of fourteen, or whatever you felt comfortable with in your handgun.

He was carrying the standard SEAL close quarters weapon, an ugly little Heckler & Koch nine-millimeter just barely controllable on auto. They had special trigger groups for a three-shot burst setting and waterproofing and lugged barrels for suppressors and the waterproof Surefire flashes with the lithium batteries.

His free hand roved, touching each item as he checked it off in his head. The rest of his first-line gear: compass, watch, his Glock knife, a Maglite with red and IR lenses. A wad of dummy cord. Bailout bottle, in case his scrubber canister broke through, or he took a bullet through it—it had happened, on an Iraqi oil platform, though he hadn't been in the water at the time. Grenades—all frags, he wasn't taking any flash-bangs on this mission. Five thirty-round magazines. A liter of water. His med kit. A claymore, in case things got really ugly. No night vision or bone radios this time, they were supposed to be waterproof but tended not to be reliable after you spent a couple of hours at pressure, but Kaulukukui had the UHF SatCom in case things went totally to shit. And batteries for everything that needed them. They were all wearing unmarked three-color BDUs under the wet suits, in case it came to cross-country work. Though he couldn't see how this mission could turn into that. If they had to cross more than a couple hundred yards of Iran, they'd be already dead, their boots sticking out of the back of a truck.

Lenson was already aboard. Next up in the shadows was a small figure. Teddy still wasn't sure why they had a North Korean on the team, but Im kept his mouth shut and obeyed orders. He caught a flash of dark questioning eyes and pointed to the open door. Im grabbed the edge and hauled himself inside, his fins a flick of black flame.

Henrickson. The little guy moved slowly, but he kept going.

And Carpenter. When he was boarded Oberg stuck his head in to make sure they were taking the right seats. He wanted Sumo and himself nearest the door. They'd be first out, he didn't want some goatfuck developing where these guys got hung up on each other. They weren't Team guys and he wasn't sure how much dark-and-underwater they were rated for.

When it came to the door-kicking, he and his swim buddy would do that themselves.

DAN oriented himself inside the vehicle. He'd expected cramped, expected dark, but this was darker and more cramped even than he'd feared, and it didn't help that they were all packaged in gill to gill under water. At least his breathing gear seemed to work okay. He was used to open circuit SCUBA, but swimming with the rebreather was different. The gas was warmer and more comfortable to breathe. When he exhaled the bag swelled against his chest. Though the rebreathers produced no bubbles, they had downsides, too: they couldn't go as deep, and overexertion could produce carbon dioxide faster than the system could scrub it out—which could have nasty consequences.

Still, they shouldn't have to swim that far, or fast, on this mission. If everything went as planned, they'd only have a few yards to cover on the rebreathers. Into the SDV, then up to the Juliet; back to the vehicle, and the return to *San Francisco*.

If.

A red interior light snapped on, and Kaulukukui mimed taking the regulator on its hose off the overhead clip, securing the mouthpiece on his Draeger, and replacing it with the onboard supply. Dan got the one above him and thumbed the purge valve to make sure it had air. He took deep breaths, flushing his lungs, then twisted the valve on his second stage and switched off mouthpieces to the onboard system, sucking in the familiar harsh dry cold of tanked air. He helped Wenck, sitting across from him, who seemed awkward with it. He patted the data systems technician's knee, then gave a thumbs-up to the Hawaiian.

A beam came on. It flicked from face to face as Kaulukukui searched each man's expression, waited till he got a thumbs-up from each. It went out, and a moment later a *chuk-chuk-chuk* came through the water and Dan felt the acceleration.

He leaned back, tilting his watch to the scarlet light. So far, on schedule. And a short ride in to objective—only three hours. Piece of cake.

If only this team held together.

DONNIE peeked at his watch, then closed his eyes. Three hours! How was he going to keep it together for three hours? *Underwater?* He wished he had a Game Boy. Anything to take his mind off it. The SEALs didn't mind. They liked riding in undersea vehicles. And, yeah, it was cool. But he felt like he couldn't breathe.

Okay, he'd better start thinking over what he was going to have to do when they got there.

Which mainly was, download and suss out anything novel he could find in the combat system, the idea being to vacuum up anything that would relate to the Shkval-K's still-only-rumored guidance capability.

Which he had his own opinions on, but whatever. According to what limited intel the team had been able to get their hands on, the Juliets had the Russian MGK-400 sonar and an Uzel MVU-119 fire control system.

What he wanted would most likely be in the Uzel, a 70s-era digital computer based on the UM-2, a homegrown Russian computer more or less comparable with something like a DEC PDP-8, Univac 1219, or the old Navy Mark 152. An 18-bit machine that ran the inputs and outputs for the torpedoes and the cruise missiles through a digital-to-analog box, with a magnetic core memory of around 256K and a clock speed around 25 kilohertz.

Like most microcomputers of its era, the UM-2 had its read-only memory at the bottom of its addressable memory, with the interpreter, core functions, input matrix, and a little bit of mapped video—just enough to drive a little screen. The dinky memory and snail speed meant it wasn't going to do a lot, but on the other hand you could program it fast and run it with grade school grads. The Uzel could run three attack solutions at once. So, maybe, three Shkval routines too, unless they had two computers. Which might be possible.

Anyway, he wasn't that interested in the computer. What he wanted was the programming. It would probably be in a Russian version of AL-GOL called ALGAMS, which wouldn't be hard to compile once he got it into a can. In fact he'd downloaded a compiler that would emulate a PDP-8 in C on his notebook, and thought he had a good shot at making it run an Uzel too.

So he didn't think running the software was going to be a problem, but nobody was sure what media it was going to be in. If the system update for the Shkval had kept the original input devices, they'd load the programs on mag tape, or even paper. He hoped it wasn't paper, because it'd be impossible to copy. They'd just have to steal it, and if he got it wet, he'd end up with papier-mâché. But he couldn't see them putting new programming on punched tape. Maybe those big old computer cassette tapes. Or an eight-inch disk. Then it'd be easy, audio output to line in on the little recorder he carried in the waterproof case. If they'd transitioned to a PC add-on, he'd tap into the serial port and download into his PalmPilot; he had connectors and jumpers. Or it was just possible the whole thing was hard-wired in as an add-on, a separate computer that reformatted the Uzel's targeting output for the missile's brain. Whichever, fire control programs were generally pretty small. They dealt with straightforward calculations and data. Unless there was something no one had anticipated.

If the program was in ALGAMS he could write an interpreter to let the Palm run it statement by statement, like with the old BASIC language systems. This was slower than compiled operation but it should be easy.

Worst case would be if he had to modify the downloaded compiler. He hoped it didn't have any bugs, taking him back to his "finish the project the night before the final exam" college days.

Donnie Wenck sat motionless, bursts of bubbles coming up around his face, watery pale eyes focused far away through the mask.

OBERG sat with palms braced on the instrument panel, comfortable as he could make himself. Lenson had browbeat the TEC into letting Obie fly copilot. Which meant they only had one body along from the SDV team, a dude named Vaught that his teammates called "V-Dag," Teddy hadn't asked why. Bus drivers, the SEALs called the SDV guys. The steady cluck of the prop, the whine of the motor vibrated through the hull. Bubbles roared in his ears. He kept listening for the ping of a sonar, the rumble of distant ships. There was a port above his head, but he didn't bother looking. He'd see nothing, or at most the phosphorescent flare of drifting organisms, flashing blue or green at the bump of the pressure wave.

Instead he studied the forward-looking sonar, which unrolled a multi-colored tapestry of the rippled, gradually shallowing bottom ahead. Here and there metal objects glowed bright blue: trash, jetsam, iron from old wrecks. Numbers flickered, giving distance to the surface and to the bottom. The needle of a magnetic compass wavered.

Next to him, Vaught was fastened to a screen with a point centered on a green-outlined lane. The pilot had his hands off the joystick at the moment, which meant the autopilot was on. He and Teddy examined each other's eyes; then his mask turned back to its study.

When they entered the harbor, they'd switch to inertial navigation. It gave off no signal for harbor security. The rest of the instruments were mainly comms. They had encrypted VHF, Team Charlie's portable Sat-Com, and modulated ultrasound to communicate with *San Francisco;* but strict silence was the rule during a mission. Especially in the approach phase, when the slightest emission could alert the enemy.

They ran in for an hour. At one point a noise spoke flickered on one of the displays. He lifted his hood off his ear, and caught the faint thin whine of distant propellers. The pilot angled away, put the spoke on their stern, and it faded.

He craned back into the passenger compartment. The only light now was a dim glow near the overhead, more to keep guys oriented than actually let them see. Lenson and Sumo sat hunched, motionless save for every-few-seconds gouts of used air. Carpenter and Henrickson were playing rock, paper, scissors, with the attitudes of gamblers in over their heads. Wenck seemed to be in a trance, sprawled back, mask tilted, looking at the overhead. Im sat like a coiled spring.

Obie wondered again about the little Korean.

Another hour and a half went by with nothing changing, except for the sea bottom rising on the display, the numbers gradually dropping on the readout. Then Vaught nudged him. He pointed and Teddy switched to the selection screen and went to low power.

The display shrank as the screw-beat slowed. The pilot took the wheel and altered course, oiling it around. Two black bars took form on the sonar. The ends of the breakwaters.

Teddy toggled back to the command screen and hesitated, finger on the button, until Vaught nodded. His bubbles were coming faster. Teddy pointed to his mouthpiece with his other hand. The pilot nodded and his cheeks hollowed as he sucked air. He punched the autopilot back on for a couple seconds as he got his Draeger fired up. Teddy leaned so the guys in back could see him, thumped the bulkhead, and gesticulated to change to closed circuit. Sumo would take it from there, make sure they all swapped over.

Okay, let's get this fucking thing into the harbor. They weren't riding alone. All the other frogmen who'd swam and ridden into enemy harbors rode with them. The Italians had done it for the first time, way back when. Penetrated Austrian and British harbors astraddle torpedoes they called "pigs," slapped limpet mines on battleships, escaped or died, but had not turned back. Whoever thought Italians didn't have balls had never looked into the Decima Flottiglia MAS.

For the next few minutes he was too busy to think about anything other than his instruments. They were inside the breakwaters, but running blind. It was too dark for visuals, and they couldn't use the sonar or even a fathometer now because some late-at-night operator on one of the ships might pick up a strange signal. They were running on inertial navigation and a simple depth gauge checked against his own jotted dead reckoning on a slate, turn count against course and distance traveled. Every time they came up on a mark to turn the pilot would glance at him. Teddy would nod, then he'd put the helm over.

It seemed like forever before the last correction, in the middle of the eastern basin, that should take them right in to the submarine piers. He started getting concerned, but actually he trusted the inertial more than his own navigation. Finally the pilot brought it around. He lifted his left hand and flashed five fingers.

Five hundred yards? Five minutes? Whatever, they didn't have long. He flipped on the "stand by" light and gave Sumo five fingers, too.

DAN started as the man next to him stirred, and opened his eyes. He'd been almost out, asleep, when Kaulukukui had flicked his mouthpiece. His heartbeat ratcheted as the screw descended the scale, as he felt a bump and lurch, a skating hiss underfoot. His teeth tightened on rubber.

Everyone was inventorying gear, checking valves, feeling for the mesh bags that held what they'd need. His own fingers started doing the walking. Knife, pistol, grenades, spare C4 and detonators, the flat pack with his references, all printed on waterproof plastic. The Navy didn't have much on a Juliet's combat system, but that would be his main job, aside from kicking the Shkval out of the torpedo tube, if indeed they could do that: keep Wenck and Henrickson on task, make sure they got what they needed.

And bring all your guys back, he reminded himself.

Yeah, that above all.

He felt woozy. He couldn't quite make out the gauge. But he still felt as if he needed to breathe, when he already had. He fingered around and found the Add button. Gave himself an extra shot.

His brain seemed to rev, step up to a deeper comprehension. But only to realize more keenly how dangerous this was. Going under the enemy's radar, under his table, roaches scurrying in the dark beneath the chairs of giants with swatters, with cans of insect spray.

Another lurch, a sliding, canting bump. Wasn't this supposed to be a soft landing? On a mud bottom? The screw caught something and went *clacketaclacketa* before the pilot cut it off. A thunk. He grabbed Henrickson, next to him. Jesus, what were they hitting? The banging and scraping sounded like they were landing in a junk pile. If an enemy sonarman caught this, he'd jerk his headset off and start yelling. He tensed, bracing for whatever they'd smash into at the end of the ride. But it smoothed and they bumped once more before sighing to a creaking, rocking halt.

A red light went to green. Kaulukukui uncoiled like a moray. Hinges creaked as an access panel pushed open. He oozed out, fins licking, making the hull rock again as his weight left it.

Dan was next. He faced the black hole, counting the seconds off rather than checking his Seiko, which had burrowed up under his wet suit sleeve as if hiding from some sharp-eyed predator. The SEALs wanted three free minutes so they could make sure they were where they were supposed to be, then dig in the anchors so what Oberg called "the pig," the SDV, would stay put.

He counted, panting, but not wanting to hit the add button too often. If these things malfunctioned . . . the body couldn't detect carbon dioxide buildup. You just lost consciousness, instantly and without warning. The pilot was moving around in the cockpit, doing something that involved a repetitive, muffled thudding. Wenck suddenly started up; Henrickson grabbed the straps on his Draeger and hauled him back to his seat.

. . . Fifty-eight thousand, fifty-nine thousand, sixty, sixty-one thousand, sixty-two. . . .

The bridge of a destroyer—that was where he wanted to face the enemy. Not from under the sea, in the dark, crouched like an oyster in the forgotten muck of a harbor bottom, carrying enough plastic explosive strapped over his liver to blow them all into scraps of drifting fish chow.

He grabbed the jambs of the exit, sucked a breath of moist somehow earthy-tasting recycled gas, and launched himself into an inky void.

19

Bandar-e Abbas Harbor, Iran

ARMS going rock hard, putting all his strength into it, Obie took a final turn on the anchor, boring the stainless steel corkscrew deep into the mud and sand. He backed away, fins brushing the ooze, and felt for the line. Just right; so taut it wouldn't kink or coil, but with a little slack to accommodate tide or a passing boat. Though, this deep in the basin, he didn't think tidal current would be a problem.

It was almost completely dark, though random beams glittered down, probably from pierside lights. He aimed his Maglite down the line and pulsed it. An answering blink told him Kaulukukui had the aft anchor in place. He held his glove over the lens, shielding it from above, and sent out another blink.

A shape coalesced in the dark. A hand waved. Teddy restowed his flash and sculled around, orienting himself with the luminescent needle of the compass on his wrist. Due east. He checked his gear again, patting himself here and there, and began swimming.

Twenty yards on he collided with something massive covered with hundreds of razor-sharp edges. He backed away from the concrete piling. Felt for the sling of the HK, which had fouled on his rebreather. Then slowly, *slowly* finned upward.

His glove, groping above him, met a roughness. He finned backward, fending off, until there seemed to be nothing but clear space overhead. He took a deep breath, held it, and drifted upward.

He broke the water with the back of his head, so the black hood would be all that would show at first. Slipped off his mask with face still submerged. Then, trying to match his motions with the jostle of the waves, slowly raised his eyes.

He'd surfaced at the end of a massive baulk of timber. This must be the camel the overhead imagery had shown inboard of the Juliet. He was in the shadow it cast from a row of brilliant lights that stretched off down the pier. They were haloed by what looked like fine dust blowing past. The air was much hotter than he'd expected. Sweat began prickling under the wet suit. He took his time looking things over, despite Kaulukukui's meaty hand gripping his ankle. Stealth and patience. His heart was pumping hard but he felt good, alive the way you never did outside a mission. Probably how his dad had felt, closing some big film deal.

He shoved that away and finned slowly back, getting a better look down the pier. It lay deserted under the silent light, white concrete marked with black ribbons from tires. Pretty much like the old proposal from Bechtel had pictured it, though getting shabby. Still, every bulb was burning in the standards, which meant somebody was paying attention. There'd probably be sentries too. Cameras? It was possible. They'd have to stay in the shadows as much as they could.

Which was standard practice, anyway. He gripped the edge of the camel with both hands. With one smooth motion, staying behind the concealment of the piers he levered himself up and over.

He froze, prone on the splintering tar-smelling wood. A faint splash behind him as his swim buddy broke the surface and brought his weapon up to cover him. That was the thing about the Teams. Working with the same guy over and over, you didn't need to talk. You communicated with a nod, the flick of a finger, maybe just a look.

Slowly as a sprout reaching for the sun, he got first to his knees, then millimetered up into a crouch, until he could see over the concrete edge.

The pier was a thousand feet long, with four massive ramps bridging to shore. Across it, abreast of him, was a large metal warehouse surrounded by chain link. He squinted through the wind-driven dust. There it was: chain-link behind the warehouse, too.

Their escape and evasion route, if everything hit the fan, was through that fence and across a perimeter road to a canteen building for what intel said was a beach club. He'd memorized the topography for three miles around, but that was the shortest road home. Hang a right from the canteen and the beach was two hundred meters on, down a gully then over low dunes, with a half-obliterated and maybe abandoned emplacement of some kind on the right flank to watch out for. The oblique imagery hadn't shown any wire, and there were no signs of minefields. They'd squirt a call for help on the SatCom, swim out to sea, and hope the friendlies got to them before the Indians.

Feeling better with the escape route eyeballed, he returned his attention to the pier. A frigate at the far end, but no other ships. So the fleet maneuvers had, as they'd expected, pulled the other subs out to sea.

Now, finally, he turned his head, examining the sloping bullnose, the long foredeck, the massive black sail towering against the startlingly close Middle Eastern stars, visible even through the glare and dust. He searched for motion or human form on its deck, but saw none. Looked for a line, a fender, any way of getting aboard that didn't involve going over the brow, but didn't see that either. And the sloping sides were too smooth and steep to climb.

So, it was the pier. He examined it again. Perhaps a hundred feet away a couple of containers stood on what looked like foundation blocks. He took his time. Vitamin S, for stealth. If you had enough Vitamin S, you didn't need to be a shooter. The Invisible Man would have been the perfect SEAL. He didn't see any sentries, and after a moment more, beckoned to Kaulukukui to join him on the camel.

It rocked as the Hawaiian's weight came out of the water. They crouched, Oberg surveying their route up onto the concrete, across the brow, and onto the submarine.

Headlights gleamed, coming over the northern access ramp. The SEALs shrank back into the shadows. Just before the vehicle reached them, its beams silhouetted a figure that strolled out from behind one of the containers. It carried an AK. It leaned into the window of what Teddy saw was a pickup, then straightened. The engine gunned, missing, as if running on dirty fuel or too low an octane, and rolled slowly past as they froze. Then turned, tires squealing in the night air, and shrank off back toward the northern section of the base.

The sentry remained standing. Teddy cursed, feeling moments ebb away. They couldn't wait all night. They needed time to offload, then get clear. He turned his watch enough to make out the hands. Then stared at the sentry again. They hadn't been able to rock drill this. No way of knowing what level of security the base maintained. But he figured now, seeing it on the ground, they had at least an hour before the truck made its rounds again.

Neither reluctantly nor with eagerness, just part of the job, he decided they had to take the sentry down. The question was how. The HKs were suppressed, but they weren't soundless. The only quiet way was up close.

He watched for several more minutes, willing himself into immobility each time the Iranian turned his head. He stood smoking, from time to time hitching the slinged rifle up on his back. Finally he began walking toward them.

Oberg tucked under the lip of the pier. If the guy looked over, he'd see them. Then they'd just have to shoot, and hope he went down quiet. Unfortunately, in Teddy's experience, having a bullet hit you didn't shut up most people. Usually you got half a second as they tried to figure out what'd hit them, then they started hollering their heads off and shooting back. Unless you were close enough for a head shot, in which case it was as easy to use a knife.

But he hoped the guy didn't look. Like a lot of missions, this one would be fully successful only if no one ever knew it had taken place.

The steps dawdled closer. The guy hawked his throat clear and spat over the side. The spittle landed beside Obie. He brought the HK up.

A red ember flew over them and hissed in the water. The guy cleared his throat and spat again. Then walked on.

The moment his back was turned Teddy rolled up over the edge and curled down behind a bollard. He get an arm around it and stuck a hand down for Kaulukukui. The Hawaiiian came up with a seallike heave. The sentry was still pacing away. Teddy held his weapon muzzle down, shaking the last drops out of the barrel, and checked that the selector was on single shots.

The sentry suddenly turned back. He walked directly toward them. Teddy heard a jingle, like a sling coming off a shoulder.

"Pelvis," Kaulukukui whispered.

"Head. One, two, *three.*"

They leaned around opposite sides of the bollard and fired. The sentry was ten yards away, bending over a cigarette. The lighter-flash showed startled eyes. They must have caught him just right because he went down at once, the rattle as wood and steel hit concrete louder than their firing.

He choked as Kaulukukui cut his throat, and died convulsing in their arms as they patted him down for grenades or a radio. He carried neither. Teddy scrubbed his bootie over the blood until it blended with the oil-spotted concrete. The overhead lights buzzed. The dust spun in whirlwinds. Kaulukukui tried on the man's hat, then handed it to Teddy. They rolled the body over the side next to the pier, into the water. The splash was no louder than a fish jumping. It sank instantly and without a trace.

Without speech they rose and moved forward. When they reached where the brow leapt from the pier and passed overhead they paused again. Teddy stripped off his hood and put on the sentry's cap. He surveyed the pier once more.

Rising into the light, he turned calmly, ambling along as if it had been a long night on duty, and paced up the brow. He stepped off onto the sub and at once melted into the shadow of the sail. He waited. No one moved. No headlights showed.

After a few minutes Kaulukukui rolled up onto the pier, rounded the brow and sauntered up it. He made no noise, sure-footed as a tiger. He bent and wires snicked as they parted. Obie pointed aft, to a canvas tent. Sumo lifted a flap and vanished.

Teddy went forward, staying outboard on the narrow slice of deck by the sail. He'd hoped the forward hatch would be open, but it wasn't. He faded aft, swept the pier again, the light-dotted darknesses of the warships at the pier to the north. Had to be sentries there, too, but no sign they'd noticed anything yet. Okay, Sumo Man had the phone wires. He knuckle-walked to the canvas tent and slipped in.

The access trunk was a ghostly place, the wind moaning above, the dust grating under his feet on the rungs. He went quickly down and turned and went down again, following the muzzle of his MP5.

At the bottom, in the forward torpedo room, Kaulukukui waited. The night lighting was dim amber. The air was hot, stale, as if all the oxygen had been sucked out of it. Teddy took in leatherette-covered bunks, gauge panels, and, up forward, the stacked inner doors of the tubes. The Hawaiian brushed his ear with his lips. "Went aft as far as the control room," he whispered, less sounding the words than shaping them. "Two hostiles. Both asleep."

"You put 'em down?"

Kaulukukui nodded. "They're still in their bunks."

Once they had the Shkval in tow, a charge of C4 on one of the other torpedoes would blow off the sub's bow. Any bodies recovered would be written off to an accident. With luck, the Iranians would never realize their most advanced weapon was in American hands. "Let's check aft. I'll take the upper deck."

He winced at the squish his booties made. He peeled them off, bent through a circular pressure door, and padded aft in damp wool socks past a dimly lit pantry and officers' staterooms paneled in dark teak. He eased each door open carefully as a burglar, aiming the light on his weapon at each bunk. They were empty. Kaulukukui peeled off down a ladder to the lower deck.

Juliets were subdivided into eight watertight compartments. Next was another cabin area, with larger rooms, motor generators, a ship's office. So far he'd noticed six motor-generator sets, which seemed like a lot.

He found a man Kaulukukui had missed asleep in a large cabin behind a huge hydraulic assembly, possibly for one of the radars. Teddy didn't want to use the HK unless he had to. Recovering a bullet from a body would raise too many questions about the "accident." The thin blade of the Glock was fast and quiet, but left a mess. He pulled the sheet over it and kept going.

No question what this next compartment was; the periscopes and consoles said "control room" even before he saw the brightly colored ballast control valves. He checked what looked like a weapons control space, a sonar nook, and headed aft. Galley, showers, mess table, all bereft and spooky in the dim amber.

He ducked through another pressure door and found himself in engineering territory: engine and motor control stations, electrical panels. Aft of them were the engines. He paced the length of the space, making sure no one was flaked out on the deckplates behind the lube oil coolers, and came to a sealed door.

Not good. Just the grinding of the gears, the thump of the dogging bar would be loud enough to wake a sleeper. The aft torpedo room was on the far side, and probably more bunking as well . . . He hesitated, then quickly spun it open and stepped inside.

Into darkness. He triggered the light on his weapon.

The beam caught two startled pale faces dawning from sleep. Shading their eyes as they peered from pipe bunks. He double-tapped them one after the other, catching the second in the back as he rolled off the bunk. He checked pulses and used the knife again on one. By their pallor, and the words they'd shouted as he began firing, they weren't Iranian. Most likely Russian technicians, here to fix any problems during the turnover. Had the others, up foward, been Russian, too?

Kaulukukui, at the doorway. "All secure?"

"Two sleepers. Have to drag them forward."

"Could have made 'em walk."

"Shit. You're right." He wiped the knife and sheathed it. Looked around, and finally pulled a steel bar off the bulkhead. He hefted it, not sure what it was—a torpedo-handling pry, most likely—and took a good swing and whanged it into the pressure hull. Two more left his ears ringing and his palms stinging through the gloves. "Think that was loud enough?"

"Should be," said the Hawaiian, deadpan.

They grabbed the first body, it was in that fresh-meat stage where everything still lolls so loosely it's hard to carry, and headed forward, careful, despite everything they'd just done, not to strike its head against the coaming of the door.

DAN stood hunched in the sail's shadow, where the big SEAL had pointed him, until the last man was out of the water and across the brow.

Iran. The blowing dust, the dry heat felt familiar. Even since Operation Earnest Will, every time he'd deployed here he'd found himself pushing back against Iran. Now they were on a roll, with oil prices higher than ever before. Buying fighters from the French, missiles from the North Koreans and Chinese, weapons like Shkval from the Russians. Moving toward the ability to close the Strait of Hormuz, and cut off the lights and motors of half the world.

But maybe Team Charlie could put a thumb in their eye. Abscond with their carrier-killer, and buy time for the Navy to build a countermeasure.

A pop; he started as a pier light fizzed out, pulling a black cloak over the bow. Oberg slid around the sail. "Everybody here? Everything okay on the pig?"

"Vaught's set and waiting," Dan told him. "Anybody aboard?"

"They won't give us any trouble. Let's move." Oberg pointed to the trunk. "One at a time, and keep low. I don't know if there are any cameras, but I figure maybe forty minutes before the patrol comes back."

"Forty minutes?" Henrickson muttered. "I don't think we can—"

"Well, we better. You first, Commander."

Dan held his weapon at port arms. He ran in a crouch and slid into the hatch. He clambered down a narrow vertical trunk maybe fifteen feet long and stepped off into a subterranean Morlock-world of humming machinery and oil-heavy air. Where he stood motionless, waiting as first Henrickson, then Wenck, then Im, and finally a puffing Carpenter slid down the ladder.

His first impression of the Juliet-class submarine K-79 was of unexpected spaciousness. The passageways were wider than *San Francisco*'s, the door through which he peered larger. The bunks were positively spacious compared to the 688's forward berthing, and he didn't have to watch for sharp edges jutting from the overhead to open up his scalp.

But the paint looked faded, the moving parts on the hatch worn, the equipment looked like it was 1963 again. The smell was nothing like the nuke's: a deep gravy of unwashed bodies, diesel fuel, ozone, and—he sniffed again—burnt gunpowder. Nothing he didn't expect. But something in here was wrong. Missing. What was it?

"Dead guys," Carpenter called softly.

When he went over he caught the reek of blood and emptied bowels. "What happened?"

"Just clearing the objective, Commander," Oberg said.

Dan started to react, then put it aside. He headed forward, frowning and rubbing his mouth. Something *else* was wrong. The dead staring eyes were disturbing, but neither the first he'd seen nor, he suspected, the last.

Then he stopped. Turned back, and peered again. There were the racks, complete with rails, rollers, chain hoists.

But no torpedoes.

Nor were there any in the compartment he was in. Bunks, workbenches, test equipment, handling equipment, yes.

Don't tell me this, he thought. *Don't* tell me they took them all off and stowed them ashore. "Find the fucking Shkval," he snapped. "Monty, check aft. Rit, Im, let's take a look at these tubes."

He stood back, waiting as Carpenter and Im began checking. To him the tubes looked just like the ones aboard *San Francisco*. Probably they all descended from the same design, way back with Holland. Each heavy bronze tube and its dished-out inner door was festooned with drains, valves, hydraulic and pneumatic lines, gauges, and indicators like ivy grown tight around the trunk of an old oak. He looked at Carpenter, who was rubbing his head. "Rit? Know what you're looking at?"

"Oh yeah. Torpedo tube's just a big gun, with a lid on the end of the barrel. You open the inner door and load. Then flood, to equalize pressure, so you can open the outer door. Blow the fish out with compressed air. Close everything again, drain, and you're ready to reload. What we got to be careful of is the interlocks." He reached in to point out several levers painted bright red. "What we really don't want to do is open those outer doors, same time you've got the breech doors open."

"Are the muzzle doors closed now?"

The heavyset submariner bent and inspected all three port tubes, going up from the bottom to the top, then turned and did the same to the starboard ones. "Affirmative."

"Any way to tell if they're loaded?"

"Well, ours have a sight glass on them. But no glasses on these. And we used to hang a card on them, so we knew what was in each tube. No card, no load. No cards on any of these."

Dan bit back a curse as Im cleared his throat. He rounded on him. "Yeah? What?"

"What is bad, Commander?"

"Nothing's bad, Yeong-min Im. Just tell me this looks familiar."

"Is familiar." The Korean started pointing. "This indicator outer door open, shut. This hinge. This here you need wrench to fit and turn, unlock inner door locking ring. Wrench is on bulkhead . . . yes."

"Can you open these inner doors?"

He shrugged. "Sure. I open. Which one?"

"Open them all," Dan told him. "Just don't sink us."

While they got busy he took a deep breath and moved his personal indicator to the next task. But first, he reviewed the team's positions. Oberg: topside, watching the pier and road for unwelcome visitors. Henrickson and Kaulukukui—the latter with plastic explosive, for safes—were going through the staterooms and work stations, looking for manuals, circuit diagrams, anything with "Shkval" on the cover. Donnie Wenck, with the little computer he'd brought in a sealed Pelican hard case, would be in the control room, downloading the programming from the fire control system.

Which left Dan to deal with the ballast tank. He went through the shelves under the workbench and found a hacksawed-off stub of copper pipe in a scrap metal bin. He balanced it on the smooth steel surface of the workbench, waited a moment, adjusted it. Good.

He walked aft, searching the valves and indicators hanging from the curved overhead. They projected through what looked like cork, painted white on the inside. He came to a green handwheel a foot across, reached up, and started cranking. It moved stiffly, is if it hadn't been lubed for a long time, but it turned. He cranked it all the way open, listened, then went aft.

The control room, starboard side. He found the "christmas tree," the bank of indicator lights that showed valves open or closed, and searched around it until he found another panel with black Bakelite knobs with red and white arrows. It was marked НОСОВАЯ ГРУППА and СРЕДНЯЯ ГРУППА and КОРМОВАЯ ГРУППА. ГРУППА was pretty easy to spell out: "grupa"—group.

Forward group, midships group, after group. He clicked the upper and the lower knobs over. The upper would be the hydraulic vent valves on the two forward tanks. The lower would be the valves on the bottom of the tanks that admitted water. Something went "clunk-clunk" up forward and a light on the panel went from white to red.

So far, so good. He noticed a speaking tube and uncorked it. Put his ear to it, and heard only the wind. Murmured, "Teddy?"

A clank, a scrape. "Commander."

"Everything quiet up there? Where are you?"

"Top of the sail. Good observation position. Nobody moving. Where are you?"

"Control room."

"Hear me all right?"

"Yeah. I'll leave this open. Going forward now."

Dan headed back forward, ducking through the doorways, and stood under the green wheel. The indicator on the remotely operated valve, beside it, had moved.

The piece of pipe on the table suddenly began to roll. He caught it before it hit the deck, tossed it back into the scrap bin, and reached up to crank the green wheel closed again. He'd flood down the rest of the way as soon as they had the Shkval ready to offload.

First, though, they had to find it. As he got to the forward torpedo room again Carpenter was grunting, "Okay, pull." Im leaned back on the handle and the upper-left tube popped open. It was painted red inside, scuffed, with a black rail to guide the fish.

"Empty, sir."

Im finished spinning a crank on the next tube down. Carpenter reached forward, tripped the interlock, and unsealed the door. It, too, opened on nothing but an echoing tunnel.

Dan gnawed his lips. Tube two, port side, down almost in the bilge; Im had to hop down off the deckplates and crouch to crank the inner door unlocked.

It, too, was empty. "Son of a bitch," Carpenter muttered. He glanced over his shoulder at Dan. "Maybe it isn't here. Anybody check aft? After torpedo room?"

Dan felt a sudden jab of uh-oh. Then remembered. "No way. Shkval's a twenty-one-inch weapon. Tubes aft are smaller on Juliets. Fifteen inches, I think." He hoped that was right. He was getting tense, more rattled than he liked to be. Had to chill. Take deep breaths, think about something other than how little time they had left. He checked his watch: only thirty more minutes.

Then the patrol would be back. They'd wonder where their sentry was. And take a look aboard.

They could kill them, too, certainly. But then their headquarters would wonder why there was no patrol report.

The upper-right tube thunk-popped open. Nothing but a little water in the bottom, glimmering in the light of their flashes. "Shit 'n' Shinola," Carpenter muttered. "Did we miss something? Or is it our crappy fucking intel again?"

Dan didn't answer. He headed aft, swung through the door, past the torpedo racks, giving them another worried scan just in case; but they were still empty. Then nearly collided with a pale, sweating Henrickson. "Monty! You okay?"

The analyst lowered a seaman's duffel bulging with angular objects. He said in a hurried voice, "There's two bodies in after torpedo."

"And move up forward, Monty."

Henrickson pulled sweat off his face. "I've never, uh—seen one before. Ha, ha! You'd think—well, never mind."

Dan squeezed his shoulder. "Mind on the job, Monty. A guy told me once there's plenty of time to think about it, after it's over. But—I've got to see Oberg. I don't know if they, if this was necessary."

"I think he likes to kill." Henrickson avoided his eyes, lowered his voice even more. "Sumo, I don't think he enjoys it. Oberg does."

"Let's not overreact. Stay focused. What's in the duffel?"

"Manuals, test equipment. There's more, I just cherry-picked what looked portable." Henrickson looked past him. "Any luck up forward?"

"Not yet. Any of the stuff you got Shkval-specific?"

"Yeah, there's Shkval stuff. Like I said. Manuals. Tapes."

Dan grimaced. "So it was aboard at one point—"

"What?" The analyst went even paler. "It's not *here?*"

"Commander," Carpenter called, voice echoing. "Better look at this."

When he got back up to the tube faces it was hard to say which submariner looked grimmer, the North Korean or the American. Dan exhaled, ready for the bad news. "Okay. What've you got?"

Im put his hand on the grip for number three door. "Torpedo tube three."

"Yeah? And?"

"Open it for him," Carpenter said.

The door swung open in greased silence. It revealed something Dan didn't at first make sense of. A black rubber plug, pierced with scores of tiny holes. He stared. "What the hell's that?"

Im and Carpenter reached in. Their fingers hooked over opposite sides and they gave a coordinated yank. The material came back and out of the tube. When Dan bent and pointed his light in, the spot of brightness showed him a six-inch-diameter tube running forward to some larger body he couldn't make out, since it filled the cylinder it nestled within. All he could see was one large hole, circled by eight smaller holes around its perimeter.

Carpenter said, "It sure as shit isn't a torpedo."

Dan peered in again, not sure *what* it was. "What's this rubber thingy?"

"Probably a pressure plate. Protects the nozzle, then drops off after launch."

"Can you get it out of there? Or, wait. Check the lower tube first. See if that's the only one."

"Already," Im said. "Number one tube empty. This only tube with . . . thingy."

Carpenter was chaining up the bunks, throwing pillows and personal gear into the bilges. Im hurried to join him. Dan glanced at his watch as they pulled rails off the bulkhead and pinned them together, and helped them rig a chain hoist from the overhead lifting point. Im half crawled into the tube, head and shoulders vanishing in the maw, to attach a wire rope as Carpenter hooked a comealong to a padeye on the aft bulkhead. With a ratcheting click, he started throwing the lever. Inch by inch, the projectile emerged, shining with a thin coating of grease.

It was half an an inch smaller than the tube diameter, so tight a fit Im's little finger wouldn't go into the gap. Its greased length rode on lands on the interior of the barrel that fit it so tightly there was no play as it extruded smoothly into the light. Smooth, unpainted, polished metal, with a red stripe halfway up it. When they had five feet of it out Dan put his hand on it, hesitantly, as if it were a dangerous pet. Im glanced sideways at him, like a Christian trying to blend in at a Shabbat service; then put his hand on it as well.

It was greasy and cold, but Dan couldn't restrain a fierce smile. Their work and risk had not been in vain. If they could get it home, the Navy would be on the way to protection against a grave danger.

Carpenter was touching it, too, all three hands on it, only his moved in a slow up and down rubbing that Dan thought, with a flash of first irritation and then sardonic realization, had something almost masturbatory in it.

RIT caressed the thing's flank, way back in his mind now, to when he used to load Mark 37s aboard the old *Tiru*, before he went to the sonar shack, and he was single and didn't have to worry about anybody finding outthings she didn't need to know. He got a thrill handling a torpedo he didn't get from anything else. Almost as good as a woman. No, not quite. Nothing as good as that. But it was close.

This arrangement was like U.S. boats, but the tubes were different. The castings were bigger, rougher, the parts weren't as well machined. They used plain steel or bronze where a U.S. boat would have stainless. You could tell what everything was, it was even more or less in the same place, but there weren't as many interlocks and it looked as if it'd be easy to bypass the ones there were.

Right now though he had to figure out how to handle this. They'd discussed it and he and Im had brought some gear but the thing was different than he'd expected. He said tentatively, "Fucker's *tapered*. Nobody said it'd be tapered."

"We didn't know what it was shaped like. Only that it fit a twenty-one-inch tube."

"Tapered," Im repeated. Rit showed him with his hands. The guy seemed to know his way around, but communication could be a problem. They had to get this done fast. He didn't need Lenson looking at his watch every five seconds to know that. He didn't want to spend the next ten years in an Iranian prison. If they didn't stand them up against a wall and shoot them, yeah, that's what they'd do, for the fucking SEALs killing the guys they'd found aboard.

"That a problem?" Lenson asked.

"Could be . . . here's like a sabot . . . here's the nose. Jeez, look at that."

A sudden flash made him almost jump out of his skin. The commander had leaned forward and gotten a picture with a little camera he hadn't seen before. "Jeez, how about a warning before you do that."

"That plate on the nose is the cavitating disc. Can you get it out of the tube?"

"It *is* out of the tube."

"I mean going out, Carpenter. Can you reverse direction and slide it on out the bow end?"

"On it, Commander. Can you finish up getting us ballasted down?" He turned to Im, but the Korean already had their tool-roll unlashed and was laying gear out. They'd figured to find most of what they needed in the torpedo room, but there was one thing the Iranians probably wouldn't have.

The tube of super-special Teflon lubricant he'd come up with off an obscure Web site that catered to private investigators and paranoids. Not only was it Teflon, embedded in it were tiny nylon balls. It was supposed to be practically zero friction. Im handed it to him, and Rit handed it right back.

"Not me," he told the Korean. "It's for you."

IM peered into the tube, then back at the Americans. He understood what they wanted him to do, but still wasn't sure what was going on. The commander was studying his watch again. He looked angry. The fat American looked angry, too. He looked into the tube again, getting angry himself.

Because he had no choice.

He'd never had a choice, not since that moment on *S-13* when his captian had decided to spare his men and surrender, rather than killing them all. Since then he'd been a puppet. The Great Leader had always said the South Koreans were American puppets. Now he knew what he meant.

Raging, but keeping his face like stone, Im pulled off his wet suit top, shirt, and finally his undershirt. He kicked off his shoes. Carpenter meanwhile had taken the tube back and cracked the cap. The fat man squeezed the compound into his palm and began slathering Im's shoulders and chest with it. His flesh crawled at the man's flabby touch. He grabbed it and began rubbing it on himself.

"Hurry," Lenson said. "We should be back in the water in fifteen minutes."

"Just let our boy here grease those lands up," Carpenter said, giving him a push.

"Do not push."

"Get in there, guy. Quit stalling. Move it!"

He bared his teeth, but with face turned away. He bent and squirmed between the sharp plate at the nose of the weapon, on the temporary loading rack just aft of the tube, and the tube itself. Got angled right, hunched his shoulders, and forced his upper body into the opening.

The bronze walls were smooth and cold. Fortunately he was not fat like Rit Carpenter. The lands, the four straight rails that lined the inside to right and left, top and bottom, dug into his shoulders and back. He was face down staring at the lower one, right arm extended in front of him. He couldn't bring it back down. Nothing but dark ahead, with his body plugging the tube. He wished he'd brought a flashlight. But he'd have had to carry it in his teeth. He might drop it and jam the weapon. No, this was better.

Thrusting with his legs, he drove himself up into the tube. They were the same as on *S-13*, which the Russians had also built. They were 533 millimeters wide and almost eight meters long. Which meant, since he was only a little over one point six meters tall, he had a long way to crawl. He wriggled ahead, using the tips of his stockinged toes against the pebbly cast-bronze interior.

He progressed several feet in, before he came to something unexpected.

In the blackness he encountered a collar or fitted inner sleeve of what felt like smooth plastic. He explored it with his fingers. His nails found a thin seam, then another, opposite the first. It was a sabot, to support the forward body of the weapon within the straight sides of the barrel. Once it was launched, the halves would drop away into the sea.

Im hesitated. How far did the sleeve extend? To the inner door? But he had to remove friction, so the missile could slide out once the tube was flooded. They'd discussed ejecting it in the usual way, but decided that would be unwise. Even without an engine firing signal, a torpedo could run a hundred yards on launch impulse alone. In a murky, unfamiliar harbor, it would be all too easy to lose.

He exhaled, and forced himself ahead once more. Into the sleeve. *Within* the sabot. Now his greased shoulders were bound all around by the solid cold grip of the dense smooth plastic. He wriggled another inch forward, pushing with his toes. Then another.

He pushed again and didn't move. His toes skidded on the rough metal, and he felt nails bend and then tear off as he kept digging in, trying to force himself forward. Then he thought better of it, and tried to back out.

His toes scraped, but found no purchase. His arms were locked inside the narrow bore.

He tried again to push ahead, and couldn't. Tried to back out, and didn't budge.

He was locked in, a greased plug of muscle and flesh and bone.

He lay unable to move, barely able to breathe, right arm stuck out in front of him into the dark. His heart squeezed on itself, then fluttered in his chest. He started to struggle, but made himself stop. An officer of the North Korean People's Army Naval Forces did not panic. Not even a traitor to the Homeland.

A faint shout outside, ringing, as if he was trapped inside a bell. He couldn't make out the words. He dug his toes in again, but succeeded only in tearing another nail. He could feel the tube around him tilting, too. They were flooding the forward tanks, putting her bow down.

He felt something move against the soles of his feet and instinctively drew them up. But it kept moving and in another second he felt it again. For a moment he didn't know what was going on. Then he did, and screamed shrilly in the closed lightless plastic that enclosed him.

They were forcing him up into the tube, using the missile as the ram. The resilient smoothness against his bleeding toes was the rubber plug that had been behind it, and now was ahead. Preventing the sharp edges of the cavitation disk from cutting him; or more likely, protecting it from his kicking feet, if he panicked. He screamed but it kept pressing against his feet, as both he and the sabot, locked together, slid slowly deeper, following his choked cry, into the echoing darkness ahead.

"I don't like this," Lenson said, but he was looking at his watch again so Rit read it as: *I don't enjoy listening to hear him scream, but it's okay if you shove his ass in there.* Rit almost made a crack about it, but didn't. He was in deep enough. Maybe if he could bring this off . . . they'd practiced this back in Norfolk, him and the Korean. Im hadn't had any problem then; all he needed now was a little help.

"How are you going to get him back out?"

"Just pull the torp back out again. I mean, the Shkval. Only now, he's got the lands greased, and with the down bubble you're putting on the bow, we flood to sea, open the outer door, and out she slides."

"But how are you going to get *him* out? He's crammed down there."

"He's not 'crammed,' there's plenty of room. We used to crawl inside to grease the tubes all the time, boats I was on. Yeah, it's uphill, going backwards, but that's why he's got that line around his ankle, Commander. We can reel him back out again."

What he didn't say was that there was a chance, not much of one, but still a chance, that if the air pressure rose as they were essentially shoving a piston down the cylinder, the outer door might pop. Air could leak out around it; they were designed to hold against outside pressure, not from inside.

In that case, Im might get a little water in his face. Rit didn't think it'd be enough to matter. But if it was, just put a strain on the line, and he'd pull right out.

"Put your shoulder behind this, Commander," he said, getting ready to shove again. The nose and the first quarter of the missile was already inside the tube. "Sooner we get him down there, sooner we can get him back."

*   *   *

IM'S doubled knees were scraping the inside of the tube. The rough bronze was flaying him alive. He tried to fight, to push back with his outstretched hand, but could not brake the steady force against his lower torso. He shouted and it rang in his ears. He screamed again, tearing his fingernails now as he tried desperately to stop being wedged deeper in with every second. A sharp edge of something unseen sliced into his chest. His feet were being pushed over what felt like rusty metal rollers on the bottom of the tube.

Now he couldn't breathe. His lungs had no room to expand in the crushing embrace of the sleeve. He fought desperately but the inexorable pressure increased.

Something hard yet flexible jammed itself against his sideways-turned head. The tube of lubricant. He'd dropped it in his struggle. Now he couldn't bend his arm back to pick it up again. He skidded forward. The grease on his shoulders was stripping off as he advanced. He twisted but couldn't move. He screamed but only deafened himself.

They couldn't hear him now. The whole length of the weapon was between them. He was more buried than in a coffin, entombed not beneath dirt, but solid bronze and steel and plastic, tons of metal and explosives plugging him in.

They shoved again and his outstretched hand came up against something curved and solid, and even colder than the plastic that locked him in.

He panted shallowly. At least he could go no farther. The smooth outward curve his outstretched fingers glided over was the outer door. Beyond it was only the sea. In a moment they'd start pulling him back.

Then the thing under his feet shoved yet again. He fought, but it was useless. His head was slowly forced against his curled up hand. His elbow locked against his cheek and the tube wall.

The pressure was still increasing, and suddenly he realized why. They were ballasted down forward. The bow must be nearly beneath the water. And the whole weight of the weapon was pressing against his feet; compressing him against the inner door. He fought like a trapped cat to keep his weight off it, to keep from pushing it outward, but couldn't get a purchase.

A thin cold spray tickled his face. He panted, eyes straining into the utter dark. Waiting for the next shove. For the spray to increase, and spread around the circumference of the seal.

A faint whine penetrated the metal around him. After a moment he recognized it as the prop of the swimmer delivery vehicle, outside. It ran for several seconds. Then descended the scale, like a portable drill winding down as it ran out of charge.

He had more pressing problems. He lay for several seconds, feeling the tantalizing tickle as the spray played over his closed eyelids. He tasted it. Salt. Sea. Rubber. The same dank smell as the exposed, mucky banks of the Yalu he'd waded along years before.

Something tightened around his ankle. It was the retrieval line. He flinched, then hastily searched around with his head. His lips contacted the tube of lubricant. He bent his right wrist back as far as it would go, then farther, and finally got his fingers on it. The cap was off. He splurted a glob where he judged the lower land should be and rubbed it over every metal surface he could reach with the side of his wrist.

The smooth rubber that had been pressing on the soles of his feet retreated. He could move his toes now. The air was cool on them. The line tugged again. His leg extended, pulled by it. He panted, eyes closed. In another moment they'd start pulling him out.

Another yank, and the bight of the line slipped over his ankle, and, before he could react, over his foot and off.

He lost control then and fought the walls around hm. His back flexed against it and he screamed and screamed. But no one could hear him. No one could reach him. He was trapped. They'd leave him here, face downward, in the slowly flooding tube.

He stared into the dark, no longer feeling the stinging spray in his wide-open eyes, trickling down his face, slowly building toward his mouth, his nose, as he lay helpless.

There was no point in screaming anymore.

DAN looked at his watch again. Sweat broke under his wet suit top. Maybe he should get the others in the water. Stay here himself with just Carpenter and Im. If the patrol came, at least some would get away.

"Oh, shit," Carpenter muttered.

He looked up to see the loop of line drop out of the tube. It glistened with lubricant. Carpenter bent to stare inside. "Uh, Commander—"

Dan pushed him out of the way and aimed his Maglite up the lumen of the barrel. Dimly, at the far end, twelve, fifteen feet in, he could just make out the bottoms of Im's feet. The white cotton socks were stained dark. Blood? He couldn't be sure, not enough light was getting that far down the tube, the bronze walls soaked up the beam. "Who tied that knot, Rit? Was it you?"

"A bowline. I know, you're gonna say why not a slipknot. But a slipknot slips."

"Let's not argue. We've got to get him out of there."

"Commander?" Henrickson said, from back by the hatch to compartment two.

"Not now, Monty. Look around. We need something like a boathook. Something we can snag his feet with."

But even as he said it he realized nothing short of a gaff hook, stuck through flesh, would get the Korean out of there. Even as he thought this he was feeling behind the missile, fingers looking for the cord. When he came up with it he felt instantly why it had slipped. It was greasy as hell. He unlocked the bowline and started to strip the knot out, then changed his mind and swapped ends on it and put a slip knot and a keeper in the other end and left the bowline where it was.

They couldn't leave Im in there much longer. He must be going nuts. *He* certainly would be.

Then he realized, even as he stripped his skivvy shirt off, that there was only one way to get him out.

"Commander. *Commander!*"

"Give me the other tube of that shit, Rit. It's the only way."

A voice behind them said, "You're not going to get him out, Commander."

Dan turned his head to Kaulukukui, who looked grim. The big Hawaiian held a silenced pistol. "Stand aside, sir."

"You stand aside, Sumo. I'm not fucking *shooting* him!" Dan finished greasing his shoulders and positioned himself in front of the opening. He held the slip knot up in one arm, then raised the other up, too. "Run the weapon in and push me in front of it. Just like we did with him. Only don't use the plug! I'll hook my foot over the cav disk and you can pull me out. Then we'll take a strain on his line."

"What if it slips off again?"

"We'll do it over. Until we get him back out."

He felt frantic, imagining himself in there as Im was, hopeless as Im must feel. Carpenter, Henrickson, and Kaulukukui were all protesting. He said over his shoulder, "Get ready to extract. All the pubs, all the software. We just can't take the fucking hardware, that's all. Let's just all get back without getting caught, all right?"

They were still talking, trying to get their hands on him, when he put both arms into the opening. He had to get the Korean out of there.

Then he stopped. Overcome by a sudden memory. Another time he'd pushed his way into a dark tube. A cable tunnel. In Baghdad. Under the Tigris River. With guys in front of him, guys behind, water in the lowest section . . . Five had gone in, four had come out. . . .

No. Not this time.

Gathering every ounce of courage he owned, he climbed in.

Only he didn't. He got his arms and upper body in, only to hang up. "Fuck. *Fuck*," he muttered. He hung there, kicking. How ridiculous he must look, ass sticking out into the torpedo room, but the thought was followed by a panicked horror.

Hands on his belt, hauling him out. He staggered and felt the razor edge of the cavitation disc slice his back open. Carpenter was yelling in his ear, "Wait, sir. I got an idea. The outer door."

"The what? The outer door?"

"Yessir. We're ballasted down. That outer door's about fifteen feet below the waterline now."

"So?" Dan rubbed his shoulder where the lands had bitten, feeling blood slick on his back. "What about it?"

"That's seven pounds per square inch. Differential between outside and inside?"

"Oh, yeah," said Henrickson. "But won't that—"

"Shut up, Monty. What are you saying, Carpenter?"

"I'm saying, if I open the outer door, it'll blow him back into the compartment."

"You're shitting me," said Kaulukukui. "It'll *drown* him."

"He'll die in there if we don't. If he can hold his breath for two seconds he'll be back here in the torpedo room. There's no place else for him to go."

"Can't you blow him out with air?"

Carpenter said, "Sure, we could blow him out. Eject him. But then he'll be out there in the dark, under the pier, with his eardrums blown in and his orientation shot. *That's* when he drowns."

"I think he's right," said the SEAL.

Dan frowned. "But isn't opening the inner and outer doors at the same time, uh, interlocked? Impossible?"

"I can jam this fucking kluge no sweat, Commander. This isn't like one of our setups, where it's idiotproof. Butt end of a wrench right"—he pointed—"right here'll do it."

"And that won't flood the torpedo room?"

"Shouldn't." Carpenter spread his hands. "If we only crack it a smidgeon, use the hand crank, not the hydraulics, and close it right away. But if the fucker jams, yeah, it might."

Dan rubbed his shoulder. A desperate measure but he had no choice. No. He had one. To let Kaulukukui shoot the Korean.

Screw that. "The rest of you, back to the control room. Get your shit topside to extract. Just Carpenter and me." He turned to the submariner, who was staring at the interlock, rubbing his hands. "Okay, Rit," he said. "Do it."

IM was lying in the dark, holding his head up against the top of the tube. His mind was a bright moth fluttering against a darkening window.

Then he heard the grinding. He opened his eyes, but only got more spray in them. He blinked, helpless.

Another fine cold spray tickled the other side of his face.

He blinked it away and listened to the grinding, like something turning and turning next to his ear.

The next moment his whole body convulsed. A last despairing effort to unlock itself from the grip around it. But he still couldn't move, not a millimeter.

They were opening the outer door. The grinding was the transmission shaft slowly revolving outside the tube. The grating of the worm gear going around, that drove the segmented arc that pivoted the door outward, at the same time the shutter door slowly retracted—

Pinned, helpless, he took one last breath.

With terrible suddenness the water drove around the disengaged edges, past the gasket, and struck him in the face. Its power was overwhelming and it propelled him backward so fast he couldn't register what was happening. Skin and clothes tore on the lands. Two red-hot needles drove into his brain as his eardrums imploded and water drove into his skull.

Then in a gush of water and light he was staggering backward from the tube, a weird high keening in his ears like the angry spirits that haunted graveyards. Hands grabbed him. Water poured from the open tube. The Americans were slamming it closed, twisting valves. He made sounds but couldn't hear himself. His legs jerked. The commander was shouting, mouth open, but nothing came over the keening. It went on and on. Iron spears were forcing their way up behind his eyeballs. He clapped his hands over his ears and suddenly everything inside him wanted out. He bent over and vomited into the water.

"GET him aft, Sumo, aft," Dan snapped.

"You want me to crank this outer door shut? Or leave it open?"

He stared at the foaming flood that was pouring in, two feet across, trying to compute what to do. They had the pubs, everything out of the safes.

Wenck had the fire control software downloaded. If they had pubs and software, maybe they could do without the missile. That was what Chone and Pirrell needed to fox it. So: forget running it out through the tube, forget the tow line to the SDV. If they got out now, they just might beat the returning patrol.

He opened his mouth to snap orders, but one more thing occurred to him. He'd thought of planting a charge on one of the torpedoes, to sink the sub and cover their action. But there weren't any torpedoes here. Just letting it sink wouldn't be quite as final, but it'd still take the threat out of circulation for months, if not years. And maybe by the time they raised the bodies they'd be so decomposed . . . Not a nice image, but it might cover their tracks.

"Want me to close this outer door, Commander?" Carpenter asked again. Dan came back to see the analyst and the sonarman staring at him. Sumo and Im were back in the other compartment, with the SEAL giving the Korean first aid aft of the watertight door. The water was foaming beneath the deckplates. Unless he was mistaken, the deck was taking on an even more ominous lean.

"Leave it open. Sumo! How's he doing?"

"Deaf, but he'll live," the SEAL yelled back.

The water roared in faster as the bow sank and the pressure increased. The solid pillar of froth and murky sea jutted out into the room, streaming over the weapon, which vibrated as it hung on the chain hoist. We can still pull this mission out of our ass, Dan thought. Im might be deaf, but he wasn't dead, and eardrums grew back. All they had to do was get out. He took a breath to give the order.

"Commander. Commander!"

Wenck's head poked through the watertight door. He looked shocked. "What, Donnie?" Dan yelled. "I told you to get topside. Get your gear on. Sumo! We're extracting!"

"Oberg's calling down from topside, sir. On the voice tube."

"What?"

"Bad news, sir. The pilot of the SDV says it's dead."

Dan was looking at Im, how he sat slumped, eyes leaden, plucking at his ears. Blood was trickling down his neck, from his chest, from his feet. "What are you talking about?" he snapped.

"The battery, he can't get power. And he says . . . Obie says . . . he says . . ."

"Lights on the pier," Kaulukukui shouted from the control room. "Head-lights, coming down the pier."

"Did you copy me, sir? What I said?"

Wenck's voice shook. Dan stood kneading his cheeks, watching green water surge and boil up through the deckplates, flooding toward the watertight door where he stood.

"Yeah," he said softly. "I hear you. I hear you both."

V

HAULING ASS

20

Bandar-e Abbas Naval Base, Iran

THE first thing Dan did was snap at Henrickson to close the inner door to tube 3. He slapped the ballast wheel. "Close this, too." Then bent-and-hurdled through the watertight door heading aft, thinking, through some obscure chain of reasoning, of Rumpelstiltskin.

The control room. He found Kaulukukui in the navigation cubby, fins slung over his back, gloves on the ladder into the sail. "Where you headed, Sumo," he muttered, noticing only now Wenck had followed him aft.

"SDV's tits down. V-dag can't get the prop to turn over."

"V-dag," for some reason, was Vaught, the vehicle's pilot. "The battery?" Dan asked him.

"My guess. But who knows." Kaulukukui looked up into the inverted well of the trunk. "Gotta get up on deck. Obie says there's a truck headed our way."

"If our vehicle's hosed, we're going to have to extract overland."

"That's the plan." Kaulukukui took two rungs. "I'll report back."

Dan nodded, then grabbed his bootie before he got out of reach. "Can we swim out of this harbor, Sumo?"

The SEAL didn't look down. "Obie and me could. I don't think your guys would make it. In the dark. With them dropping antiswimmer explosives, boats swarming all over? You think so, Commander?"

He let the foot go.

THIRTY feet above, Oberg crouched in the cramped cockpit atop the sail, hand on the open voice tube. But he wasn't speaking. He was frowning down from his eyrie toward a point half a mile away. Where one after the other, three trucks followed their headlights, turning slowly at a crossroads or traffic circle to the northeast. They'd come out of what intel had labeled as a housing or barracks compound to the east of the base a few minutes before. Stopped for a time, stationary, then rolled again.

He suddenly bent and rummaged in a hinged box near a folding windshield, gyro repeater, and phone jacks with a headset hung on them. He was rewarded by a plastic case and, inside, a pair of binoculars. Focusing, he caught military six-wheelers. Too dark and far to make out much, but they looked like old deuce and a halfs, with the steel grids on the grilles, though they might be ZILS or UNIMOGs. Their humped canvas might cover beds full of supplies.

Or troops. No way to tell from here if it was a logistics caravan or a troop movement.

A clank. He turned to Kaulukukui emerging from below, MP5 slung.

"Somebody's headed our way?"

"Not sure yet. Movement. Three vehicles."

He handed his swim buddy the glasses. Kaulukukui observed for a few seconds. "Turning this way. But looks like, outside the perimeter fence."

Outside was good. But where could they be headed? That road led past the harbor, curved out onto the short peninsula that comprised the inlet's eastern side, and petered out a few hundred feet short of the shore. Changing the guard? Sentry relief? Not three trucks' worth. He checked his watch. Three A.M.

"Security drill?"

"All I could think of. They ready to start the extract down there? Where's Vaught? Was he below?"

"He's aboard? The 8's dead on the bottom?"

"You got it. He came up over the camel, same way we did. Almost shot his ass. Flashed him with my Surefire and we had a talk off the other side of the sail. Sounds like complete battery failure. He ran down the checklist and couldn't even get a voltage reading." Teddy took back the binoculars and aimed them past the warehouse.

"What if they turn onto the pier?"

"First we make sure they're after us. If they are, neutralize as many as we can, grenade the shit out of them, and fight a rear guard down to the beach."

"These Charlie guys aren't up to that."

"Well, they did Thunder Ranch—I mean, GrayWolf. And they held together on Mindanao. They ought to be able to hold off a couple dozen Iranian conscripts, if we take out the noncoms. Anyway," Oberg finished, "it ain't like we're gonna have a choice. Remember the hostage crisis? In Teheran? I'll eat a grenade before we surrender to these pricks."

Kaulukukui meanwhile had been feeling around the cockpit. "I already checked for weapons up here," Teddy added. "Uh—wait a minute. One of 'em's stopping."

They watched as the farthest-away pier light illuminated the last truck in line rolling to a halt. Distant figures jumped down. A shout drifted across wire and sand. The figures went to their bellies, became shapeless bundles.

"Gimme me one of your HK mags."

"Fuck you. You wanted to bring a Sig, shoot your fucking Sig." He pushed the Hawaiian's glove off. "You getting gay on me? Okay—hold on—the other trucks. They're turning again."

He watched, then flipped the cover up on the speaking tube. "Wenck? Obie. Three trucks. One's between us and the beach. Deploying a stop line. The other two are coming back on the inside road, heading for our location. Tell the commander, right now."

He pulled grenades out one after the other, lining them up along a steel shelf in the cockpit as he spoke.

DAN listened to the hollow voice. It sounded like doom and its message was a sentence. Troops deploying between them and the beach, across their escape route. More trucks, headed for the submarine piers.

Crap! The patrol had never come back to check on the dead sentry. Or had he? And they'd just not seen him? But the Iranians wouldn't call out the react team just because they couldn't find a pier sentry, would they? He couldn't believe they knew they were here. But if they did . . . how had they found out?

He clenched his fists. Had someone up the line sold out TAG Charlie?

He turned, then started as he confronted a face he didn't recognize. Then he did. The SDV pilot, face strangely inhuman without neck or hair, ovaled by the wet-suit hood. "Vaught. You lost propulsion?"

"Right, Commander. No instruments or comms, either. Tried emergency power, tried bypassing the panel. Shit works. It's dead."

"This happen before?"

"Not to me. Happened to another Mark 8 in Westpac once." The driver looked like he was just barely keeping his cool. "Uh, so, the alternate extract—over the beach—"

Henrickson leaned into his tunnel vision. "Dan? Hear that?"

"Yeah, I heard it. Escape route's cut off, guys. Looks like base security troops. We may have to swim for it, Monty."

"You mean, out of the harbor? On the Draegers?"

Dan nodded.

"And then what?"

"And then . . . the sub picks us up, I guess. This wasn't in the plan."

"Inside territorial waters? Or how far are we supposed to swim?"

"I don't know. This wasn't supposed to happen, the SDV breaks down, the Iranians wake up—" He jerked his head, to see Carpenter waiting as if to report. "Rit?"

"Tube three outer and inner doors secured. Forward ballast flood secured."

"Uh, uh, that's good. Very well, Rit."

He stood irresolute, mind hunting this way and that. Trying to avoid the gazes around him. Then grabbed the ladder, and went hand over hand toward the darkness far above.

WHEN he got to the top of the sail Oberg was looking forward. Dan peered over, too, gaze sweeping the pier. He caught the shapes lumbering around the sharp curve to the southward.

"Coming in through the south gate," Oberg commented. Dan noticed the grenades set out in front of him.

"Can we extract? The E&E plan?"

"They dropped a blocking force between us and the beach." He pointed, and after a moment Dan made them out, dark figures against the lighter dark beyond the perimeter fence, stretching from the warehouse down he couldn't tell how far to their right flank.

"There a way out of this, Teddy?"

"Not many choices left, Commander. We either break out, Custer in place, or extract by sea. Any of those strike you as a better idea than the others?"

"Can we break through that line?"

"We can try."

"Where's Sumo?"

For answer Oberg pointed. The big SEAL was a slow shadow, easing his way down the camel toward the oncoming trucks. He was toting something gingerly in front of him. "Where's he going?"

"Give 'em something to think about." Oberg blew out. He chewed loudly.

"Is that gum? Got any more?"

"Sure." The SEAL pulled it out of his mouth, pinched off half, and offered it.

"That's all right," Dan said.

Oberg shrugged. He braced the HK on the coaming, thumbed the safety off, and aimed. "Through the windshield." The shot made a pop louder than in the movies, but not nearly as loud as it would have been without the suppressor.

A hundred yards down the pier the truck halted in a screech of brakes so hard it slewed around. The second was following too close to stop, and they collided with a slam like a load of iron being dropped off the back of a dump truck.

"What are you doing?"

"Keeping the range open. Uh, better get your guys ready, you figure to break out." He aimed again. A figure leaped down from the cab of the first truck. The submachine gun popped and it went down.

But more were boiling out of the backs of the trucks, armed troops, distinct now under the pier floods. One ran off to the side, where he began gesticulating, pointing toward the Juliet. Oberg's weapon jerked and ejected and the man wavered, then sank as if melting.

Dan wondered why they weren't shooting back. They must not have realized yet they were being fired on, the suppressed HKs were so quiet. Down on the camel, Kaulukukui, screened from the milling troops by the lip of the pier, reached up to place something in the shadow of one of the bollards.

"Give it to me no shit, Teddy. Can we make it to that beach?"

"*Some* of us might. If we haul ass before they call in reinforcements." *Pop. Pop.* "After that, I don't know. Want a shot?"

Oberg seemed cool for a situation that was looking more and more like the Alamo. "No, you're doing okay. But how long can we hold them off?"

"Not very fucking long, is my guess. Like I said, if we're going to break out—"

His sentence was cut off by a tremendous flash and crack, followed by screams from the trucks. Men staggered away and fell. Others had gone down at once. Those who remained hit the deck and began ripping off long bursts of full automatic fire, not just at the sub, in every direction. Through it Oberg's weapon searched here and there, jerking slightly each time he depressed the trigger. *Pop. Pop.* A siren began to wail to the north.

"What was that?"

"Claymore."

"How'll we get through that blocking force?"

"Like I said, not all of us will." Oberg ducked as a bullet clanged off steel below them. "Took 'em long enough." He adjusted his rear sight and fired again. He cracked his gum. "Honest opinion? If we were all opera- tors, we might get through. No offense, but your guys aren't. At least, the kind we need now."

Dan ducked too as another bullet hiss-zipped over. The Iranians had taken cover, some behind the trucks, others behind the buildings inboard of the pier. No leader seemed to have emerged to grip them again, drive them forward, but he had no doubt one would any moment now. Or soon arrive, given the racket of automatic fire they were filling the basin with. He caught another siren, no, a general-quarters alarm, from the nest of destroyers across the water.

They weren't going to make it, swimming out. His guys weren't trained in underwater navigation. They'd never find the inlet with patrol boats swarming over them, swim miles in the dark, end up at a rendezvous point.

He didn't think they could make it to the beach, either. The emergency extraction plan hadn't anticipated a gauntlet of troops. The open field be- tween *K-79* and the perimeter fence was killing ground. The fence would hang them up while they cut their way through it. Past that, another half mile to the beach. And once they reached the surf line, if any did, they'd still have to swim.

But standing pat wasn't an option either. Oberg and Kaulukukui could hold the reaction force at arms-length for a while, but not forever. Not against the heavier weapons that wcrc no doubt already on their way.

That left one alternative. One he hadn't planned, wasn't prepared for. But the only one, in the circumstances, he could come up with.

He flipped up the lid on the speaking tube. "Carpenter?"

"Here, Commander."

"Rit. You were a bubblehead, right?"

Carpenter didn't answer and he hurried on. "Didn't you have to qualify on every station on the boat? To get your dolphins? Know all the systems, so everybody can do everybody else's job?"

"Well . . . yeah. Especially on the old diesel boats. World turns to crap, there's no time to wait for the guy, that's his watch station. You don't know which valve to close, you better hope you can breathe water. 'Course, they never qual'd us on any of the reactor stuff—"

"I'm not talking reactors. Can you get the engines started on this thing?"

"On this boat? The engines? Uh—you talking diesel, or electric?"

"I don't care! Whichever gets us off the pier faster."

"That'd be getting underway on the battery. Line up the right switches and engage the electric motors, you're good to go. Diesels, you need fuel, air, starter motor—"

"Go aft and get them lined up. Take Donnie. Take Im, too. How's he doing?"

"Still deaf. Hey, I don't know if I—"

"Don't tell me you can't, Rit. Just tell me how long it'll take."

He got silence, so he added, "Get back there and pass me word up how it goes. Uh, hold on. Send everybody else topside, with their weapons. Through the sail trunk, not up forward. Tell them to exit on the starboard side, they've got cover there. For the moment, anyway. And do it fast, Rit. Hurry."

He explained to the SEAL, who listened expressionlessly, only his jaw moving, as they watched troops knot behind the nearest truck. "That sound good to you? Tell me if it doesn't."

"At least we'll all go together."

"Don't leave anyone behind."

"Right, Commander. If we can pull it off." He aimed, and Dan made out Kaulukukui sprawled, firing, too, from a hide position near the bow. He could barely see the guy, and he was looking down on him; to their besiegers, the fire must be coming from everywhere. But they wouldn't stay pinned forever. "If we don't, we're not gonna have anything to worry about, anyway. Not for long. Okay, I'm gonna go down and get things organized. You got it. Make 'em count."

Oberg folded and ladder-slid down the trunk, leaving Dan alone at the top of the sail. "Uh, Obie—Obie!"

But the SEAL was gone. He had to hold the fort up here while Oberg did his thing. He checked the HK, seated the mag, and fed a round with the awkward left-handed operating handle. He noticed Oberg had left the grenades in their neat little row. He stuck his head up, picked out a target, and began firing.

A hundred feet below, aft of the main engine compartment, Rit Carpenter hitched up his wet-suit bottoms, looking doubtfully at a chrome-yellow-painted console that extended from the deck all the way up to the overhead. Two rows of five gauges each at the top. To the left, a vertical string of six lights. Below the gauges were black Bakelite knobs, and below them three handwheels, rims bright red, spokes bright green. At the bottom of the cabinet a humongous green and black lever a yard long stuck out. Each gauge or control was carefully labeled, both with a small bronze plaque, original to the equipment, and below that a newer, computer-printed sticky label.

"Fuck," he muttered, hitching his pants again. The bronze callouts were in Cyrillic. The others were in squiggles he guessed had to be Iranian.

Neither of which he could read a word of. "You make any of this out?" he mumbled to Im. Half turned when the Korean didn't reply, then cursed; the son of a bitch was just standing there looking blank, holding his ears. "*You're* gonna be a lot of help."

He studied the gauges again. That many of them, all alike, they had to be battery bank indicators. He couldn't think of anything else a submarine had ten of all alike, except maybe torpedo tubes, and they weren't controlled from the engine spaces. The handwheels were probably rheostat controls. He tried the biggest one. It turned left and right but not all the way, and he got a "clunk" of relays going over somewhere below at full right. He studied this a while, then tried the smaller handwheel to the left. Five of the vertical lights above it came on, the bottom five.

"Okay, this makes sense," he muttered. He turned the left handwheel and the five lights went off; turned it back and the lights went on. Interesting. Not the way U.S. boats did it, but it probably meant he had five sixths of a charge in the can. He turned it off again, to save juice, and tried the other handwheel. It went around but didn't seem to do anything and he didn't hear any relays. He tried it with the big wheel in the "on" position and still didn't get anything.

He glanced at Im, who was watching now. The Korean pointed to the big wheel. "Main battery power," he said, only it sounded like "powell."

"Yeah, I got that," Rit told him. "How about these others? Gimme some help here." But the Korean just stared at his mouth and tapped his ear.

That left the lever down by his boots, and it was a BIG lever. He bent and was about to haul it up when Im dragged him back, talking a mile a minute in his Korenglish, which Rit couldn't make out at all. "No. No, Uncretch! Uncretch!"

"What the *fuck* you tryin' to say, guy?"

Im put his fists together. He rotated them, together. Then pulled them apart, still rotating one, while the other stopped. Rit stared, brows knit. He did it again, accompanying it with *vroom, vroom, eek* noises. "You understand? Uncretch!"

"Are you sayin' . . . declutch?"

"*Aie! Ke se ki. Ai sae ki!* Must decrutch!"

"Where the fuck am I supposed to declutch?"

"Where? Where?" Im grabbed his arm and dragged him forward, into the engine room. He searched at the end of the big upper casings of the diesels, directly beneath what Rit made as the starboard main exhaust.

Then heeled a button. He slammed over a lever and the hissing chuff of a pneumatic clutch went on, then off. He did the same thing to port, then stood back. "*Tso sem ni da!* Diesel decrutched. Go electric motor now."

Rit sighed and ran a hand over his forehead. It came away dripping. His kidneys hurt. Was it his imagination, or was it getting hot down here?

THE troops had left their cover behind the trucks and were advancing, driven by a short moustached Iranian on their right flank. The pier was open ground for them, too, and they obviously didn't like it, bending from the waist as they ran. Dan fired again and again at the short guy and finally brought him down, though he was still shouting as he lay holding his leg. Dan hit him again and he quit yelling, but now the squad was only fifty yards away, nearly to the sub's bow. Then a man wheeled and pointed, right where Kaulukukui lay, and they all began firing at him, the ones behind the trucks, too.

Dan got the guy who'd been pointing. It was much harder to hit a moving target at night than it had been in the daylight at GrayWolf. Then a flash and crack among them sent the squad scattering back to cover.

Three bodies lay motionless on the concrete as a shadow zigzagged along the camel, then swung up onto the brow. Dan switched to the three-round burst setting and triggered fast as he could, laying fire into the muzzle flashes. Sparks danced around the Hawaiian, but he reached the after hatch tent and disappeared.

Without warning a thunderous clatter burst out at the base of the sail. Suppressors were superfluous now, apparently. "Cover us," Oberg yelled up, and Dan switched magazines and kept firing. Somebody on the other side had tracers and their bright-green trails zipped over his head and clanged on steel.

Under the storm of fire Henrickson and Wenck scrambled out and ran forward. They sprawled on their bellies and worked frantically at the lines. The heavy hawsers splashed into the water between the hull and the camel. Monty and Donnie squirmed backward as tracers flew over them, too, occasionally dipping to glance sparks off the thick steel of the hull. They got back to the sail, scrambled up, and left his line of sight, headed aft.

He ran dry and crouched as he swapped magazines again, hands shaking. The hollow metal clattered away below, into some void through which the periscope and radar masts passed. He almost fumbled the loaded one, too, but caught it before it went. Shoot and move . . . he should move . . .

but this was about the best vantage point you could get . . . he compromised by dashing to the starboard side and leaning out to fire, but it didn't make much difference to the tracers. The clang and smack of bullets hitting the sail was increasing as more of his targets realized where he was. Judging by his own experience with the AK, it was hard to hit anything more than twenty yards away, but sooner or later one of those projectiles was going to find him. Even as he thought this, firing fast as he could aim and shift, the windshield shattered as several bullets drove through it simultaneously. He fired that mag out and dropped it and tried to put the next one in, but it wouldn't go. It took him several horrible seconds to realize he was trying to insert it upside down.

"Uh, bridge, uh, control room."

"Talk." Rounds hammered on the sail, nearly drowned the voice from the tube.

"This is Rit. I uh, think we might be ready to get underway here."

"You can answer bells?"

"Put it this way, you give me a bell, I'll see can I answer it."

"Good, Rit. Real good. Im any help?"

"Actually he's not doing so bad."

"He was XO of a Romeo. They can't be that different from Juliets."

"Yessir, he, he helped out a lot. Once we figured out what the fuck we were saying. You got like an indicator box up there, with a pointer?"

"Hold on. I'll look."

He put his head up and nearly got a bullet through it. So close he felt the air buzz against his face. They were trying another rush, this time from up the pier. He hadn't seen any trucks up there, so it must be a security response team from the frigate. Sailors, in other words, not troops. It'd take them time to get sorted out, but the jaws were taking shape. When they closed he'd be taking fire from two sides. He fired in their direction, just to slow them up a little, and glanced sternward to see the last line slither over the hull and drop into the black water.

He turned his cheeks to catch the wind direction. The seething, dust-laden breeze was from the east. At last, a break. It would drive them off the pier, and from the position of the sail in relation to the hull, should push the bow out a little faster than the stern. Already there was a black ribbon of water between the bow and the camel it had been snugged up to. A sizzling spray of yellow-white sparks burst like a firework.

"We just parted the shore power cable, Rit."

"Fuck it, we don't need it now. Find that box yet, sir?"

He ducked and ran his hands around where he figured the conning officer would stand. A protuberance. He stood and fired toward the trucks, again in the opposite direction, then ducked again and put the weapon light on it. A metal box the size of a loaf of bread, a dial with two hands, below it a knob. "Uh, got it. Definitely the EOT." The engine order telegraph. You turned the knob, the first indicator swung; the command showed up on a corresponding dial in the engine room, usually with an audible signal, too. The engineers matched the pointer to acknowledge the order, then went to work to "answer the bell." He twisted experimentally.

"D'you just turn it?"

"Yeah, just twiddled it. Looks like five ahead speeds, three back, if the red ones mean astern. Is your dial on like, ahead slow?"

"If that's the first one after C, T, O, then looks like a lower case N—"

"That's 'stop,' Rit. Russian C's pronounced S, Russian R is pronounced P. Stop."

"Got it. You want ahead slow now?"

"No! First we need rudder control."

"That's a whole 'nother question, Commander."

He bobbed up and fired, cursing himself. He should have had someone on that, too. "Who's down there? Im, I know, but is Henrickson down there?"

"No, but Vaught's still in the control room."

Moving lights caught his eye, and the rumble of a powerful engine over by the main channel. Something was skimming across the water. Headed their way.

"Yeah? Good. Put Im on the motor panel, okay? He doesn't need to hear to watch the EOT. Then go forward and see if you and Vaught have rudder control. And put some fucking timeliness on it this time. They're crawling up our ass, out here."

"Moving fast as I can, sir." Carpenter sounded injured, but Dan didn't care. If they didn't get moving soon, they were all going to be, in the words of a Georgia bumper sticker, opening a can of whup-ass that would land them in a world of hurt.

MONTY hung on the starboard side of the sail watching the lights move closer. Then they didn't move, at least not against the black water. Just stayed steady, and got bigger.

He was puffing from the run back from the stern. He didn't like this. Didn't like guns, even when he was the one shooting. It hurt his ears and he was pretty sure he hadn't hit anything.

Oberg, in his face. "What the *fuck* you think you're doing?"

"Just taking a—"

"Just taking shit! If they're not shooting at you, you're not doing your job. Get down on that camel and put some fire out there, asshole!" Monty's ears rang again as a slap banged his head against the sail.

He lifted the submachine gun and aimed it. Right at Oberg's back. Then swung it ten degrees to the right and fired. The SEAL flinched away from the blast, but didn't even turn around.

THE gap between the hull and the camel was opening. The sub was pivoting right, accelerating as the wind's force accumulated. Dan took too long looking. A bullet beside his head spattered him with fragments. They stung like hot needles in his cheek, eyelid, eyeball. He clawed at the pain before he stopped himself. He stuck his head up and fired till the magazine was empty. Only one more. The troops were coordinating their efforts now, two squads providing covering fire while the third rushed. Only thirty yards away, and their aim was getting better. Shots crackled from the north, too. The sailors were uncoordinated, but they were advancing as well.

Hand over his eye, he shouted into the voice tube, "Carpenter!"

"He's here, sir!" Wenck squeaked.

"Have we got steering?"

"He says he's not sure, Commander. Can you see the rudder?"

"No, there's no upper control surface. Has he got a rudder indicator?"

"He's got an indicator. He's got an indicator."

"Does it move when he turns the wheel?"

"There's no wheel, sir. Just levers and a compass of some kind. Are we moving, up there?"

"A little. Coming right."

"Well, the compass doesn't move."

"For fuck's sake, Donnie. Is Vaught there?"

"Wait a minute . . . they tried the black lever. The indicator's moving."

He stuck his head up again. The frigatesmen had almost reached the stern. Another squad was leapfrogging, scrambling ahead as behind them the others fired from cover. And someone was getting smart: the trucks were grinding forward, sheltering the troops behind them. More headlights on the highway. Reinforcements. The battle rattle was continuous now, the clamor of bullets like heavy hail on an iron shed. He ducked again as fiery trails passed through the space his skull had just occupied. He put the weapon light on the engine order telegraph, grimaced at the stab in his

eye as he unthinkingly tried to open it, and rotated the knob to what he
guessed was ahead one third, ahead slow. After a long moment the second
indicator jerked over, past, then backed up to line up with it. Im, responding to the bell.

"Donnie, listen up. What's that indicator read? What you think is the
rudder indicator?"

"Zero at the top. Then down the right side, ten, twenty, thirty. Looks
like it stops at forty, but it doesn't have the numbers for forty."

"Is there a red zone or something almost to forty?"

"There's a red line at uh, about thirty-eight."

"Then on the left side? Same numbers and line and everything?"

"Same on the left side."

"Where's the pointer now?"

"Straight up. Zero."

"Great, Donnie, great. That's it, all right. Now: tell Vaught, or whoever's
on the console—"

"It's V-Dag."

"Uh-huh. Tell him to get his rudder over to right thirty degrees. Right
thirty. Don't go past thirty, but get it over and hold it there."

He could faintly hear Wenck passing it on. Then, struck by a thought,
shone the weapon light around the cockpit. At waist level . . . there it was,
another heavy steel box, another heavy glass port, and under the glass,
another dial. He twisted a knob and it illuminated. The same dial and
pointer Wenck had just described.

"Okay, I've got one up here, too. Is there an RPM indicator?"

"There's a fuck of a lot of dials down here, sir. We're trying to figure
this. They're in Russian and what looks like Iranian."

Shouts from the pier. Dan risked a glance over the coaming. "Uh, Russian . . . can Monty read them?"

"Monty's up on deck with you. Isn't he? Is that rudder going over, sir? Is
it showing up on your indicator?"

Dan put the light on it again. "Yeah." He poked his head up again, but
things were too hot to leave it up. Still, not only was there more water between the hull and the camel, maybe fifteen feet now, but the pier was starting to move aft. Which meant the sub was moving ahead.

Which meant the bell was taking effect. They were getting power to the
screws. The bow was swinging faster now as the rudder took hold. Both
forces, wind and rudder, were pushing her toward the center of the basin.
Get out there, hang a left turn, and if judged it right, they should be lined
up for the exit and after that, the open Arabian Sea.

"Donnie? We're underway. Slack rudder to right twenty degrees. Right, twenty degrees rudder."

As the computer technician repeated the order Dan gripped the indicator, sucking air with the faintest taste of hope. They couldn't extract? Too far, too many troops, too many patrol boats? Now they were protected by a steel hull nothing short of a five-inch shell could even dent. They'd just steal *the whole fucking submarine*, and worry about what came next when they were outside territorial waters. At which point the U.S. Navy would be there to protect them.

But the clatter of fire was even louder. He shifted to the cover of a retracted antenna mast and looked over again, lifting his head gradually till only his eyes were above the coaming.

Tracers arced through the night. Fresh headlights from armored personnel carriers. Massive, tracked machines, they trundled like dinosaurs onto the pier. A crewman swung a long-barreled gun and cut loose. Its blows made the rifle bullets sound like a gentle rain. Sailors and troops lined the pier, blazing away as *K-79* slowly withdrew. Some were leaping down onto the camel, running along it after them. Sirens whooped in the destroyer nest. He looked out into the basin again, to lights weaving back and forth between them and the exit. Patrol craft? Harbor craft? They were clustering right where he had to steer to escape.

It wouldn't be easy. Maybe the whole idea was stupid. Maybe they just should have surrendered. But he didn't pass down any more orders. Just ducked, clinging to the antenna mount, listening to the tolling of the heavy rounds as they walked up the sail toward him.

Maybe it wouldn't work.

But he was sure as hell going to try.

21

T HE motion was uncannily smooth compared to the vibration and
bow wave of a destroyer, or the turbine-drone of a frigate. *K-79* pre-
cessed out into the basin, filtering between the gust-whipped curtains of
dust-laden wind, the beams of hazy light that searched for her, noiselessly
as the Ancient Mariner's uncanny barque. The only clue they had way on
was the steady march of lights. The racket aft continued, augmented by
more heavy machine guns, Dan assumed from the rest of the armored
personnel carriers. He kept his eyes front, but the five or six square inches
of the back of his skull felt totally vulnerable. He wouldn't have any more
time to think about it than it would take for one of those slugs to traverse
his cranium and paté his brain across the shattered windshield in front
of him.

Tracers rainbowed overhead, burning through the murk. It took a moment before he realized they were coming not from behind, but ahead.
From flashes low to the water, dead on the bow.

"Commander. We moving?"

Carpenter, from the control room. Dan bent to the speaking tube.
"Yeah, we're underway. Heading for our next turn."

"To port?"

"Correct, to port. But not just yet."

Okay, Dan thought, trying to organize what had to be done next when
all he wanted to do was clamp his hands over his head and cringe. The
answer came up in red flashing letters: communicate. Get the word out
to CTF 152 that TAG Charlie needed help, the extract had gone to shit.
They needed air support and surface units, and somebody to get them off
this sub, a helo or at least somebody with a small boat capability.

They had to get on the horn ASAP, but he couldn't cope with the Sat-
Com, too, right now. Not on top of everything else. "Rit, where's Monty?"

"Not down here, sir. Isn't he with you?"

"Up here? No. He was on the camel—"

With a horrible sensation, he realized exactly what he'd just said. He twisted and stared back. The pier was two hundred yards away, and lined solid with muzzle flashes.

"Monty," he screamed down the trunk, stripping his throat raw. *"Monty!"*

No answer. "Oberg!"

"Yeah!"

The response had come from forward. He climbed the pelorus and leaned over the coaming. The SEAL looked up from a slouch against the radar housing that made up the leading edge of the sail. Ahead of him the sea was foaming as the still-ballasted-down bullnose, so near the waterline it was nearly submerged, pushed through the water. "Tell me Henrickson's down there," Dan howled.

"Henny? No, he ain't here."

"Fuck me," Dan muttered. He felt like fainting, like throwing up. The last time he'd seen the analyst, Henrickson had been prone on the camel. Firing back. Not looking like he was enjoying himself, but putting down fire. Covering the others, as they cast off.

He looked aft again. No way on God's green earth they could head back into that dusty wind, that hail of lead. Where Henrickson was probably still huddled, head down, listening to the fire going out over his head, watching *K-79* get smaller, fading into the night.

But he couldn't just steam away. Leave him at the mercy of the Iranians. He might if he'd been sure Henrickson was dead. But could he say he thought that?

He slammed his fist into steel, cursing Fate. What had Niles Barry said, when he'd assigned him to TAG? *Don't get any more guys killed.*

"Fuck it," he shouted. "Rit. Rit!"

"Still here, Commander."

"Right thirty degrees. Steady on zero nine zero."

"Right thirty, steady on zero nine zero," he heard Carpenter pass to Vaught, presumably the one actually on the helm. "We out of the harbor already, sir?"

He didn't answer, looking over his shoulder. Back at the ruddy winking of heavy machine-gun fire, the green arcs of tracer. There wouldn't be much room to do this. He'd have to judge it carefully. A tight turn to starboard, at exactly the right moment, to put her port side along the camel. Get everybody topside except maybe Rit and Vaught, lay down as much fire as they could, and somehow snatch Henrickson back aboard. Then thread the whole gauntlet over again, this time with alerted patrol boats waiting.

He doubted they had much of a chance.

"Henrickson!" he howled, despairing.

"What?"

He stood rooted. Frowned, cocking his head. The answering cry hadn't come from the trunk. Nor from forward. The new rudder order was taking effect. They were starting to plow around. He shouted again. "Monty?"

"What?"

He poked his head above the coaming, puzzled. It sounded like it was coming from aft, from the pier itself, from which the fiery verdigris trails, like vertical shooting stars, were still floating up, despite the range growing long, at least for the small arms. Most were going high, though some furrowed up the water to either side, and an occasional lucky pull still clanged off steel, blowing off chunks of rubberized coating. It had been Henrickson's voice, all right. He couldn't be imagining it, could he? But where the fuck was the guy?

Dan was wondering if he was going mad when he noticed a porpoise close alongside. He threw his muzzle over the coaming and triggered the SureFire. The illuminated circle lit not a porpoise, but a man in a wet suit, arms shot out straight ahead, being towed along on one of the spring lines. Then it twisted, and the beam lit Henrickson's upturned face, contorted with the agony of holding on despite the massive force of the water rushing past.

The indicator slammed over to CTOII. Dan yelled down, "Shift your rudder! New course, two eight zero!" Then leaned over the opposite side of the cockpit. "Teddy! Sumo! Hear me down there?"

"Copy, Commander."

"Port side, aft of the sail. Henrickson's towing alongside. Get him aboard. Get any other loose lines in, before they foul the screws. Then get him on the sat phone, or no, Oberg, you get on. Clue Honest Houston what's going on. We need backup ASAP. We need air support."

"Copy," Oberg said.

Grinning, suddenly as lighthearted as he'd felt despairing ten seconds before, he aimed the HK astern and fired out the last magazine, aiming above the now receding gun-flashes to allow for drop. Probably not hitting anything, but why carry the rounds? They wouldn't need them anymore. "Honest Houston," Commander, Task Force 152, aboard USS *Antietam*, would have carrier air over them in half an hour. They'd run

out to deep water, meet up with Mangum, pull the Shkval, and scuttle
K-79. Let the Iranians sort out what had happened.

Below, Sumo was hauling Henrickson up, grabbing an arm, gaffing him
aboard. When the analyst wobbled and collapsed, Kaulukukui scooped
him up and carried him forward, out of sight.

Okay, back to getting the fuck out of here . . . the reversed rudder was
taking effect, they were swinging back toward the breakwater . . . he
knobbed the EOT indicator to СРЕЦНИЙ, which he figured meant something like "standard." He shivered again at how close they'd come to losing Henrickson. Then shoved it out of his head; he had to bear down and
get them out of here. Holding that thought he tried to judge the turn, just
by seaman's eye, without knowing her tactical diameter or how fast she'd
answer the rudder, and trying to remember what the photos and intel had
showed of the breakwaters and the shoals on the way out. He bent and
yelled into the tube, "Vaught! Left twenty degrees rudder. Come to course—
call it—one nine zero."

"Left twenty, steady one nine zero. These courses you're giving me, that
magnetic, sir? I'm not sure what we got here is a gyro or what."

"Doesn't matter, long as we're looking at the same dial. Mark your head."

"Passing two six five."

"That's what I've got here, we match, good to go. Make your new course
one niner zero. Let me know when you're lined up and I'll adjust by eye."

He aligned the sonar fin on the bow with the pelorus stand and watched
it slowly tick around to port. The rudder kicked to starboard ten degrees
before the lubber's line hit the new course and he grinned; Vaught would
finish the turn exactly on course. He groped around and found a pair of
binoculars dangling and focused on the breakwater. He lined up the bullnose between the beacons marking the channel out. Passed down a course
correction—he'd turned a fraction of a minute too early—to 200.

They rogered from below and Dan looked at the EOT again and then
straightened and twisted to put the field of view of the glasses on the frigate nest, directly astern now.

His heart fell again. More pier lights had come on, a muddy red-yellow
sodium-vapor haze, and deck lights, too, whiter and lower to the basin
level. The glasses showed lines being cast off, men boiling on the fore-
castles, the pale rectangles of lit pilothouse windows, running lights snapping on. He turned the indicator another notch forward. Maybe fifteen
knots. Considering her hull form, and that her bow was still ballasted
down, dragging through the water, he didn't think she'd go much faster no
matter how much power they cranked on.

The frigates, turbine-engined jobs, would make thirty, thirty-five knots. The patrol boats nested cheek by jowl three deep would make even more. He had a head start, but not much of one. He looked at the indicator again, then cranked it over all the way. Ahead flank.

Then he saw the boat. Lights off and low in the water, so he hadn't made it out in the confused light and blowing dust. Maybe just coming in from patrol, maybe going out, maybe scrambled as the ready response, but there it was, crossing from starboard to port and turning into them, crewmen pointing, swinging weapons. Swinging a twin gun mount on the long forward deck.

Bigger than a .50. An automatic cannon, Russian or Chinese, like the ZSUs he'd seen in Bosnia. He stared frozen as the barrel came around and steadied on the oncoming sail. Steadied right on him.

Dan realized he was aiming the HK and pulling the trigger even though it was empty. But only for a moment, because the still-turning bow of the accelerating submarine smashed into the patrol craft. It rolled, the cracking and screeching of the fiberglass hull splintering apart coming clearly up to him even over the roar of fire from aft. The crew went flying. He lowered his weapon, watching men struggle to the surface of the dust-scummed water as the silent runaway swept past, watching bodies float up face-down, jostle as the bow wave foamed over them, then sink away.

Forget that, stick to getting out of here. The flank bell was taking effect. They were tearing along now, pushing a big bow wave, though still with that eerie absence of vibration. He gave Vaught another course correction. They were in the narrows. A sand spit spread to starboard, the peninsula to port.

Yeah, there were troops, personnel carriers, too, and they opened up all at once, muzzle flashes and then a solid wall of tracers, rising and then descending like a flight of arrows. He turtled violently, slamming his forehead into a helmet rack. He was loving the splinter plating until something paper-punched it with a clang like a cracked bell and pounded a big dent into the far side of the cockpit too before falling to the grating, spinning and skittering before chattering away down into the shear void.

He backed into the aftermost corner, putting a radar head between him and the incoming, and screwed his face into the binocs again. The breakwaters beckoned, outstretched arms fading into the dimness. Half a mile ahead the lights at their ends glimmered tangerine and turquoise, haloed by the blowing dust. He twisted the telegraph knob again, just to send the message he needed all the power they could give him, and flicked switches on a darkened instrument that might or might not be a fathometer repeater. The hydrography had shown shallows along the breakwater, but he couldn't remember where. If they ran aground, they were finished.

The fire grew more accurate. Slugs slammed into steel so near his head it felt like taking jabs from Evander Holyfield or Mike Tyson, but he centered the bow between the lights, adjusting till they ran as if on tracks down the midline of the channel, the gray rock and concrete of the breakwater equally distant in the blowing dust on either hand. Then retreated into to the trunk, clinging to the rungs of the ladder as another banging whanged and jarred and echoed, like someone flailing on steel with an I-beam; more projectiles walking up the sail. White flashes jagged his vision, the clamor was beyond deafening, but unlike the splinter plating, the trunk's walls were thick as the pressure hull; nothing short of a major caliber shell would penetrate it. He clung, eyes squeezed shut, enduring. If he could get outside the breakwater, get some air cover, the fighters could keep the destroyers off their backs long enough for them to rendezvous with *San Francisco*. After that, the Islamic Republic of Iran could have its sub back and welcome to it.

He counted a hundred, then popped his head up again. The bluegreen pulse of the eastern light strobed gray wet rocks, breaking surf foaming at their feet. Past that was the darkness of the open sea.

Open sea! Out there Mangum and *San Francisco* waited. The air assist would be here soon. They were going to make it. He gave Vaught five degrees to starboard and retreated to his rabbit hole again, wishing he had water. The dry wind, the gritty dust made his throat feel like a washboard road.

A minute later someone tugged at his bootie. Dan looked into Oberg's upturned features. "Commander? You okay?"

"Yeah."

"Carpenter's got the scope up."

Dan looked aft. He hadn't heard it extend, but the mast loomed above his head. "Yeah?"

"He's looking out ahead of us. There's two flashing lights out there at about one-zero-zero. One's farther away than the other."

"Two in line? That's the buoyed channel."

"Uh-huh. Anyway he's on the scope. So you can take cover, if you want."

"I'm fine here, Teddy. But have him look aft. See what those cans are doing. Vaught okay on the helm?"

"Uh, yeah."

"Did you get hold of the task force? Tell me they're launching F-18s."

"Well, Honest Houston answered right up. Guarding the freq. Brought them up to speed on what happened and what we had to do."

Dan sucked air but choked on dust. "Great. When will the air cover be here?"

Oberg averted his gaze. "Maybe you better get on the horn, all right? Apply some of that commander power. 'Cause what they're telling me is, there isn't going to be any."

STANDING in the cover of the sail, the SatCom handset tight to his ear, he could just make out words over the hiss of sand-laden wind. The hollow ringing voice was that of a task force staffer three hundred miles to the north. She was saying, "That's correct, Quick Snatch. The Iraqis shot down two Brit Tornados enforcing the no-fly zone. We hit the radar sites, but now they're preparing a ground force to push down the road and clobber the Shiites again. Maybe even with gas. The UN's approved pushing the zone all the way to Baghdad. The Air Force is scrambling out of Prince Sultan. Over."

A stray bullet clattered on thin metal. Somebody back there was still firing, though their target was past the breakwater. He screwed the phone tighter into his skull, perspiration greasing the plastic with a gritty paste. "And that's got what to do with us? Over."

"The battle group's being pulled up to Kuwait. Getting in range for backup strikes. We're cranking on knots even as we speak. Over."

"But you're on standby for us. You've got orders to—"

"Negative."

"What do you mean, negative?"

"I mean, we don't have actual orders concerning your mission. Not through our combatant commander. We never did. Just back channel Navy, far as I know. Over."

The deck was canting, picking up a roll. Dan leaned past the sail and looked back through the darkness. He couldn't see clearly through the scudding dust, but behind them, inside the basin, lights were separating from the piers. The frigates were backing out, turning to follow. Reacting faster than he'd hoped they would. One set of red and green and white already seemed closer.

A flash lit the dark. A detonation rolled across the water. Something banshee-howled over their heads. It exploded ahead with a flash and seconds later, the distinctive crack of high explosive.

He swallowed. One of the frigates had managed to man up a mount.

The first shell had been long, but hadn't been that far off in azimuth. Drop a few degrees, they could do that with whatever optical sight they were equipped with, and the next projectile could burst on the sail itself. The dust was obscuring things, but all those gunners had to do was catch them with a searchlight, and sooner or later a shell would arrive with their Social Security numbers on it.

"Uh, this is Quick Snatch. We're in trouble here. Operators need backup. You need to kick this up to TF Actual and get somebody detached to give us some support here. Over."

The voice turned apologetic. "Understand, will re-present, but we're already running north. Try to hold your Indians off until we can clarify the situation. Honest Houston, out."

Dan glanced at the faces around him. No way they could outrace frigates. They'd be on them like pit bulls, and in not very many minutes, either. "Uh, Houston, stand by. This is Quick Snatch, Quick Snatch, stay on the line, Houston. Indians in hot pursuit here. We need air support. Air support! Do you copy? Houston, do you copy?"

The only answer was a hiss like the sand-freighted wind.

22

The Strait of Hormuz

DAN fought a blankness in his head, an absence where thought should be. Disappointment, stress, and the incredible noise seemed to have stopped his neurons firing. But this was exactly when he had to become an icy Jacques Futrelle thinking machine. He peered ahead, picking up a steady flash on the horizon. If it was the channel marker, it was pretty far off to port. Belatedly his brain kicked in again. The channel out into the Strait angled east to avoid a large island. Lorok? Larak? Anyway it was shallow here, real shallow, and they couldn't afford to touch.

He ducked inside and slid down the trunk.

IN the control room, keeping one ear out for the next order from above, Rit stared at markings in two different languages, neither of which made any sense. "Okay," he mumbled. "Let's look this cocksucker over."

It was obviously the ballast control panel, but not like any he'd seen. The lights were white and red, not red and green like on U.S. boats. Okay, let's say red still meant an open valve. Red was the color of danger, and, aboard a sub, a valve open when it shouldn't be was as dangerous as it came. Then white would mean closed, safe, good to go.

Right? He glanced at the leather-sheathed bench where Vaught perched, nudging the rudder control once in a while. Im stood tiptoe behind him, keeping them on course. Those controls weren't like the wheel and plane arrangements he was used to, either. They looked more like what you'd use driving a tank. But the guy seemed to be coping. He was on the right course, anyway.

Lenson slid down the ladder two-handed from above, landing both boots at once with a thump that jolted the floorplates. "Carpenter!"

Fucker sure was noisy. "Here, sir."

"Can you take us under?"

Vaught's head snapped round. Rit grunted, not surprised, he'd been figuring they'd get to that sooner or later, but not feeling too hot about it. Not in a boat he didn't know, guys who didn't know the systems, labels he couldn't even fucking *read*. "What's the matter, sir? Thought we were going to meet up with some backup out here."

"There's not going to be any support. Not for a while yet."

Lenson explained about trouble at the far end of the Gulf, the task force pulled off to bail out the Air Force and the Brits. His eyes kept magneting to the periscope, though, so Rit stepped to it and pulled the handles down. But the commander didn't go to it, instead snapped his eyes away. "Can you take us under?" he repeated. "We figured out the ballast tank controls, didn't we?"

"Well, yessir, got that doped out. The manual controls. But we can't run this boat manually. Not with eight hands aboard, and none of us qualified on—"

"Can you activate the hydraulics? What do we need to do to submerge?"

He cleared his throat and hitched up his wet suit bottoms. "Uh, well, got to have two things to submerge, sir. Ballast control and plane control. You can get your head under with just the tanks, but you want planes too. Or you're always running back and forth, too heavy or too light, you never get the bubble just right, you'll broach."

Vaught put in, "I think these are the planes." He patted two yellow boxes at his right hand as he sat on the steering bench.

Rit frowned. "Don't look like 'em to me. No markings for angle down, angle up."

"Yeah, but watch." Vaught rotated a forward lever that looked as if it had come off an old Ford tractor. A hum, a rattle of fluid pressure ratcheting against resistance. They waited. No question, Rit had to admit the deck slanted a little more.

"Okay, then that lever like it just aft of it—"

"Stern planes. What I figure."

"We have two tin cans coming up our ass—"

"Lemme work on it, Commander, okay?"

Lenson went forward, and Rit went back to the panels and gauges and lines that covered the whole starboard side of the compartment. Gleaming brass, paint in six different colors, cables, valves, switches. He murmured to the Korean, "It's like some fucking nightmare, you know? Where everything looks familiar but when you look close it's not what you're used to at all."

Im pointed at his ear and Rit nodded, like yeah, I know, high suck factor, right? But then the guy pointed at the panel with the big black switches to the right of the BCP and mimed each of them going over, one after the other, then did with his hands like they were going under, like a kid playing submarine in a pool.

He studied those switches, sweat running down his back. It wasn't just the wet suit, either. The voice of his old chief of the boat was bitching in his brain. A veteran of three war patrols in *Tirante* who, if there wasn't an officer around, would bounce your forehead off a valve handle if you did something stupid, to make the lesson stick. You didn't crack a valve, you didn't know *exactly* what it let flow and how fast.

He pinched his lip between thumb and forefinger, frowning. Gotta think here . . . the black switches had the exact same squigglies as the light banks. Okay. To the right of the switches was a single box with one big red button. The squigglies on it were red, too. That had to be the "chicken switch," for emergency blow. And back of that, the spaghetti piping for the old manual-style HP air banks. He put his finger on the red button and mimed blowing out his cheeks, looking up. Im nodded enthusiastically.

"We're gonna do this," Rit called to Vaught. "He wants us dived, we're gonna dive."

"Just keep it fucking real, all right?" the SDV driver said. "It's only about thirty fucking meters deep out here. Stick us in the mud and the camel jockeys are gonna run all our cards."

"Yeah, yeah. You're the asshole on the planes. Stand by to fucking dive." He jogged to the forward door and stuck his head through. Lenson was talking to Wenck, making quick motions with his hands. "Commander! Wanna give this a try? We still got guys topside!"

Lenson came aft fast and yelled up the ladder. Rit winced again. They were really going to have to quiet the commander down, if they were going to run submerged. He muttered, "Make sure they dog the hatch tight when they come down. There's gonna be a light around it someplace. Make sure that light goes green—I mean, white. Or whatever color it goes to once they get it dogged."

He was watching the panel and when the light went from red to white he nodded, bingo, and marked it with his finger and looked around. Im handed him a china pencil he'd found somewhere and he blocklettered in "CT ACCESS HATCH" under the squigglies as the two SEALs and Henrickson dropped down the ladder. "Okay, sir, here it is."

"Talk to me."

"We don't have a diving officer so I'm gonna be Chief of the Boat, got it? That means you tell me what you want to do and I figure out how to do it, okay? I'm gonna keep Im here with me and I'm gonna keep Vaught on the helm. But we're gonna need guys back aft on the main motor switchboard and the electric panel."

"You want me back on the motor?"

"Yeah, Teddy, sure. How about you and Sumo back there and—fuck, how'm I gonna talk to you?" He searched the compartment and Im, following his eyes, put his hand on a little brown plastic box. "That the bitch box? Okay, but we got to keep it turned down. Everybody, once we pull the plug, no yelling, no hammering, nothing that makes noise, got it? Commander, you hear me? We're quiet running on the battery, but there's gonna be guys on that frigate listening for shit like that."

Henrickson leaned past him and tapped one of the labels. "Know what this says?"

"Not the faintest."

He took the pencil out of his fingers. Rit almost batted his hand away from the panel before he realized what he was doing. "Hey. You can *read* this?"

"Only the Russian, but yeah. Here. Uh—main ballast tank . . . *kingstonya*, I don't know that word? . . . 'hydraulic drive.' That make sense to you?"

"Write it down, Goddamn it, write it right on there. *Kingstonya*, that's gotta be a Kingston valve. We don't use them in our boats, but I visited a Brit sub once. Go around this fucking compartment, translate all these fucking labels, okay?" He wiped his face; they were going to have to get the ventilation going, too. Even when he'd first come aboard, the air had smelled like somebody had breathed it and farted it out already. He figured the dead guys, whoever they were, had kept the ventilation shut down, probably to keep the sand out of the boat.

"We need to get under," Lenson said again, and Rit snapped back, and ran eye and finger down the Christmas tree, white, white, white. "Yessir, just give us a minute. Monty, what's this say?"

"*Otkrabit*—open. *Zakrabit*—shut."

Dan watched them for a couple of seconds, wishing they'd move faster, but knowing Carpenter didn't want to hit the wrong control, and not wanting him to, either. Instead he got on the attack scope and spun it around to look aft.

He bent into it, squinting into the rubber eyecup. A blur. Then the lenses and his sight merged and the big light-gathering objective panoramaed the stem of a frigate, bow on, reaming its way out of the inlet. Headed their way, and throwing up a glimmering bow wave that was white even in the darkness. A flash that was probably another shell.

Rit mimed to Im, spinning a valve wheel on the overhead, pointing to the Christmas tree, then aft.

Im touched his ear, wishing the singing would stop. It sounded like women wailing some endless song without words. The fat American jabbed his finger again and he nodded and headed aft, searching in the overhead.

Vent valves came in pairs, the manual one inboard, the hydraulic one, remotely actuated from the control room, inboard. They were in series, so both had to be open to flood a tank. In port they'd be shut, so no accidents could happen even if somebody cycled the hydraulics by accident, maintenance, or just bumping one. When it was time to get underway you'd open them all and then just cycle on the hydraulics, adding air and opening and closing the upper vent valves and the Kingstons, which let the water in, to adjust the buoyancy.

This was a different class boat, but it had been built by the same people and the arrangement was the same as the one he'd been second in command of. After months of practice, *S-13*'s crew had been able to balance her so precisely she hovered with the engines off, drifting like a steel bubble in the sea.

He hadn't mentioned this to the Americans. But these rubber-treaded corridors, these cork-lined overheads, the smell of the closed-in air brought back the terror of the long days below, desperately trying to evade the South Korean puppets. Only to fail just a few kilometers short of their goal . . . *S-13* lay at the bottom of the Eastern Sea, her deadly cargo still aboard; a cargo her crew had feared so much they'd barricaded the forward bulkhead with rice sacks. And the man whose name he wore was a skeleton now, picked by crabs.

Now "Im Yeong-Min" served those who'd been their enemies. He came to another vent valve and cranked the green wheel around to full open, setting it and moving on, passing Oberg and Kaulukukui as they argued by the motor control panel over something too fast for him to catch, slipping silently along the corridors as they began to tilt beneath his bleeding feet.

"White board," Rit muttered. "Ready to dive. Commander?"

"Dive," Dan said.

"Planes down twenty degrees, Vaught."

"Down twenty. Both planes down twenty."

Nobody said anything, but the curved steel circling them echoed their breathing. Rit hit the buttons, one after the other. The valves went *ponk. Ponk.* The lights turned from white to red. "Flooding forward group . . . flooding forward. Flooding midships." He searched the bulkhead for the next instrument he needed. A bubble, but he didn't see one.

Lenson: "We need to flood aft, Rit?"

"Let me run the board, sir, huh? There's only three flood valves aft, I figure that's gonna be the smallest tank anyway. Okay—Vaught. What's your depth gauge read? Never mind. I got one here, too . . . shit, this thing doesn't go too fucking deep, does it?"

"That's in meters."

"Thanks, Monty, I'm with you now. Meters . . . Uh, two eighty, two ninety, three hundred . . . red line on the gauge at three hundred . . . that's nine hundred feet but the gauge goes to four hundred." Despite himself his gaze flicked to the steel behind the instruments and gauges, the sloppy-looking welding on the ribs. An Electric Boat or Newport News hull would do it, but this thing wasn't going to make it to twelve hundred feet. Not without mashing like a beer can run over by a semi.

Dan swung the scope and searched to starboard. Twisting the handgrip popped him from high magnification to wide angle. He made out a faint skyline against a ruddy glow far away. An island? The tip of a peninsula?

Remembering then he'd seen a little nav station or quartermaster's cubby to port, he stepped into it and rooted through racked rolls of paper till he found one that showed the familiar worm-writhe of Hormuz and approaches. It was even in English. "Admiralty chart," he muttered, bringing it out and flattening it against a cabinet. "Kind of old, but . . . what are we at? Mark your head."

"Mark my head, one zero zero."

"Come right, one two zero."

They spoke in hushed voices. He peeked through the scope again, checked the relative bearing on the ring, and added that to the course. The skyline was the eastern tip of Queshm Island. Past that was Larak and they'd be in the Strait. It wouldn't be long, either.

Dan draped his arm over the 'scope and spun it, feeling like he was in an old movie, *Das Boot*, or *Run Silent, Run Deep*, and found the frigate again. It was closer, the bow wave high as her foredeck. Another was echeloned behind it. Both had running lights on and searchlights were sparking on, too.

No. This was no fucking movie. He was opening his mouth to snap at Carpenter again, when the scope went suddenly dark. It took a moment to realize why.

"Passing ten meters," Vaught said from the control station.

"Planes up ten," Carpenter said, gaze roving his instruments. He thumbed three valves on the left of the panel. *Ponk. Ponk. Ponk.* Distant impacts as the hydraulics reseated. The lights blinked from red to white. Rit sized up another panel and twisted a switch. Air rushed through pipes above their heads, sounding both loud and queerly muffled.

"Up ten . . . planes at up ten. Passing twenty meters."

"It's not very deep here," Dan said, studying the chart. "It says—"

They hit bottom so hard every man standing staggered or went to his knees. The hull vibrated a deep note, like a giant hand chime, and all the lights went out except for blurred bulbs that lightning-bugged on here and there twisted into overhead cabling and piping, flickered, then went off as the main lighting cut back in again. Im stammered rapid Korean. Something shrieked in a high staccato as it tore away and went clanging along the side.

A slithering scrape grew louder as the stern met the bottom, too, making contact with a second impact that staggered them again. "Up thirty!" Rit said, sweating as he thumbed valve after valve, then shifted back to the blow panel and twisted more switches. Remotely actuated valves thumped forward, then aft. Air hissed in a howling storm confined by pipes that shuddered in their supports as the charge hit them, trying to straighten each curve and ream out each bore.

But the noise still increased, even though they didn't seem to be rising. The hull rocked, scraping along, banging and swaying. A high-pitched clamor rose aft. "Engines stop," Dan said, voice not loud but tense, tense. Rit grabbed an overhead hold and clung with one hand as he played the board with the other, trying to get her off the bottom without sending her rocketing out of the water again. "Fuck, it's too fucking shallow here," he muttered between clenched teeth.

"Left, steer zero eight zero," Dan said. No matter what else was going on, they had to get off the course the surface ships had just seen them submerge on. Or the frigates could drop their weapons ahead of their track and wait until the sea boiled oil and bodies. "Vaught . . . hear me? Zero eight zero."

He flinched and coughed, head bent at a strange angle over the controls. "Zero eight zero. Yessir. Coming to zero eight zero."

Rit said, "Monty, stand by that gauge and feed me readings. Not that one! Forward of it."

"Fifteen meters. Thirteen. Twelve. Ten. Nose going down—"

"Planes down, forward planes down twenty degrees, aft down ten!" Streaming sweat, too busy even to scratch his itching balls, Rit flooded the tanks he'd just started to blow. "This is fucking . . . fuck this . . . fuck—"

"Breaking the surface!"

"Control, main motors—you still want full power back here?"

Four people yelled at once, but Dan got to the brown box first. "Half power, Oberg, or standard, or whatever's half power. Did we foul the prop? Any vibration back there?"

"Think we got lucky that time, Commander. But let's not do that again, okay? Who's on the stick up there?"

"We're still trying to get a rope on her, Teddy." Dan muttered, "Rit, can you control this thing? We don't have a lot of depth to play with until we get past Larak, hit the fifty-meter line."

"Ten meters again—twelve—fourteen—going down fast. Going down *fast*—"

"I'm getting it," Rit said, biting his lip and hitting the forward tanks with another long blow. "Goddamn it, just give me a minute."

A whishing like a giant washing machine began aft. It moved rapidly over their heads, hovered for seconds that seemed like epochs, then grew faint again, moving away. "Mark, warship on top," Vaught remarked in a deadpan whine. "Steady on one nine zero."

"Come right, one six zero," Dan snapped, trying to stay on the chart and the dead reckoning he was doing in his head though what he really wanted was to jump out of his skin and go shrieking down the passageway. He had to get south. But he couldn't turn too soon, or they'd hit the shoals around Larak. The chart showed an anchorage to the east. He hoped no one was anchored there at the moment, because he was going to cut the corner and go through it. "Rit, we can't keep yo-yoing up and down. They can hear us blowing those fucking tanks. And we don't have all the air in the world, either."

A rattling bam, another scraping slide. Carpenter fought with the panel. Vaught remarked in a nasal, disembodied voice, "We don't have enough guys to run a boat this size."

"Well, we're going to try," Dan snapped.

"Control, motors. We gotta keep doing bobsled races?"

"Just to make the point, sir: we surface and give them their sub back, they might let us go."

"They'd line us up on the afterdeck and shoot us all," Dan told him. "So shut your mouth and concentrate on your planes, Vaught. When I want your tactical advice, I'll ask for it."

"Fuck's going on?" said Wenck, coming up a ladder from some lower deck Dan hadn't noticed till then. "Felt like we went into the crowd barrier there—"

"Did I give you a job, Wenck?"

"Uh, yessir. Back on it." He turned on his heel and went back down the ladder.

"Forward planes up ten, after planes at zero."

Vaught repeated it in that dead tone. The deck trembled. Dan checked the scope, but it was still under water. He decided he didn't need a big feather—the spray the extended scope kicked up—and tried buttons until a motor hummed and the shining oiled steel began moving past him, feeding down into some deep well far below. Fingers plucked at his arm. It was Im. "I maintain contror."

"What?"

"He says, he can maintain control," Oberg said, behind them.

Dan wheeled. "What're you doing up here?"

"I was calling. Nobody answered."

"We heard you, fuckhead. We had better things to do than answer you," Rit barked. "Get back aft on those fucking motors." Oberg looked at him for a second, glanced at Dan, then turned and went aft.

Dan nodded at Im. "Rit, how about giving him ballast control? He used to be XO on a boat like this. Or sort of like this."

"Give him control? How? He can't hear the orders."

"I can write them down for him. But I'm going to need you on the stack." Dan looked at the depth gauge again. He expected every minute to hear the hornet whine of an incoming torpedo, which would probably be an even less pleasant feeling down here than it had been when he'd heard it aboard a destroyer. "You got us under. Great, but we're going to have to play cat and mouse with those frigates. If I can't see, I've got to be able to hear. And you've got to be my ears."

IM didn't seem to do much, just wait, balanced on the balls of his feet, as if sensing the boat beneath him, then pushing and holding down this or that control for two or three seconds; but their fishtailing and vertical excursions smoothed out. Nor did they hit bottom again. They ran for ten or twelve minutes at half speed, which Dan figured would be about eight knots, on 120.

It seemed to be a respite. Dan took deep breaths and worked his neck, trying to get the stress out. He thought about putting the scope up and checking for the loom of the village the chart showed at the tip of Jazireh-ye Qeshm, Qeshm Island, but decided not. He'd done a lot of antisubmarine work. One of the biggest mistakes a sub was liable to make was to put up a mast. Mast down, no radar could detect you; mast up, you were vulnerable.

He wasn't going to foul up that way. And he'd better start thinking in terms of making *no* mistakes . . . Through all the excitement of getting underway and submerging he'd tracked their courses and distances run in his head. He had a good idea where they were and absent any really fierce currents, he could run on dead reckoning for a while without feeling lost. He went back into the nav station, found a pair of dividers, and taped down the chart. He walked their position off and pencilled in the half circle that meant dead reckoning position. Then stood stock still, if you didn't count the trembling in his thighs, smoothing the heavy paper again and again, stroking it like a horse's mane, trying to think dispassionately as a man could who might die from minute to minute.

Once past Jazireh-ye Larak—the chart showed a nav light there, but again, he wasn't about to pop the scope—they'd be in fifty meters of water. But almost at once, since the strait was so narrow, he'd have to decide which way to go. His choices were east, into the Gulf of Oman, and thence the Arabian Sea; or west, into the Gulf.

East lay deep water and USS *San Francisco*. CTF 152 would have passed the word to Andy that Team Charlie was in trouble. But if he knew his classmate, Mangum would hold at the rendezvous point until he knew Dan was either captured or dead. The water got deep fast as you went first east, then south. The jagged mountains fell away on either hand and the Indian Ocean swelled like an expectant mother's belly. Fifty miles on, the water would be a hundred meters deep; in ninety miles, there'd be two hundred meters under them; a hundred miles out, over a thousand, well beyond the most optimistic estimate of *K-79*'s crush depth.

He stroked the chart, blinking at the blue-tinted contours with yearning, but also with dread. A naval officer equated water depth with safety. But was it, in this case? Sonar had turned deep water into a stage, where lights picked out a sub like a Broadway star. The frigates, or one of the old patrol aircraft the Iranians still operated, would pick them up in minutes. And even an old aircraft could drop a homing torpedo.

He bent closer, examining the other half of the chart. Where the shallow, twisting strait writhed like an inflamed appendix among shoals and dozens of shaded outlines labeled WARNING that marked oil fields and oil loading terminals. Sidebars warned, "Numerous structures usually carrying lights, other unlit objects and submerged obstructions sometimes marked by buoys, exist in the oil and gas field areas. As these features are not all charted, special caution should be exercised. . . ." "Lights are unreliable . . . pipelines are not buried . . . flammable gas under high pressure. . . ." More such warnings edged the chart, printed in red. He tried to mark the boundaries of the major oil fields in his mind; they'd have to steer clear of their subsurface clutter of pipelines, discarded production equipment, even cut-down and abandoned platforms.

A faint whistling began far off. It amplified quickly into a second pass by, or through, the washing machine they'd heard before. Dan closed his eyes and waited it out, heartbeat by heartbeat, as it dwelt above them, seemingly only feet away, and at this depth really there couldn't have been more than ten yards between the frigate's keel and the top of their (fortunately) retracted radar and periscope masts. He sagged against a cabinet.

But once again it dwindled. He blotted perspiration out of his stinging eyes and stuck his head out of the nav nook, looked around a hydraulic assembly. He caught Vaught and Im staring at the overhead, lips parted, the very images of helplessness and fear.

They'd drilled what he'd thought was every possible contingency. But this wasn't anything they'd expected. They were underway in an unfamiliar submarine, trying to evade the Iranian Navy. Not a huge navy, but a professional one, and in its home waters, outraged and hot for blood. Always before he'd been on the other side of the ever-fluid boundary between water and air. This time he was the submarine rabbit, being pursued by the surface hounds.

Was this how those he'd pursued had felt? This crushing horror, this dread of infinite enclosure, of being squeezed, and squeezed, until nothing remained but the terrified kernel of self? A terrifying conviction was fighting its way into the light, making his heart race and flutter, his breath pant in and out. He couldn't do this. He couldn't, *couldn't* do it.

Sweat trickled down his chest and he suddenly, jerkily tore the wet-suit top off and threw it into a corner. He bent to the chart, searching for some other way out. But there wasn't any.

West, or east? The open ocean, where they'd be pinned and destroyed by the avenging angels whose wings already beat above them, long before they made it out to the rendezvous point and help? Or the shallow, sand-blown Gulf, with its mirages, its layers, its laggard, salt-heavy tides, its spiky forests of oil rigs, the wavering flare-offs that made the nights flicker, the net-draped dhows that slowly lateened, like rebodyings of Sinbad, from land-horizon to land-horizon?

He stared down as drops of salty moisture blistered the thick paper. Walked the dividers across it, checking his watch, checking the distance, till there was no way he could be mistaken. Then he slammed his hand down and turned for the control room.

They looked up as if he was their deliverer. He had to fit the mask over his fear once more. Sham that he knew what he was doing, when deep down he didn't, and never had, and probably never would.

"Right hard rudder. Come to two two zero."

"Two two zero, sir."

"Heading west," Carpenter whispered, eyes slipping away as if Tefloned. "Away from the rendezvous? Away from *San Fran?*"

"That's right," Dan whispered back, so those who eavesdropped might not hear. "We're going into the Gulf."

23

T HE first ping flicked the hull, purring like a stroked cat, then trickled away. It wasn't one Dan recognized, but their pursuers were Alvands. He knew the type from when he'd been in the Gulf aboard *Turner Van Zandt*. They were British-built patrol frigates, Vosper Mark Vs, built by Thornycroft just before the Shah's fall. The Mark V was small but heavily armed, with guns, torpedoes, a five-cell surface-to-surface missile, and Limbo antisubmarine mortars.

"Surface ship sonar. Bearing two niner zero relative."

Carpenter's voice, from the sonar cubicle to port. Dan put his head in. "Very well."

The sonar space was bigger than *San Francisco*'s, and not nearly so packed with equipment. The equipment looked dated, with gauges instead of touch-screens and switches instead of keyboarded inputs.

Carpenter whispered, "Can't figure out how to bring up the fucking displays."

"Can't you use the earphones?"

"The computer hears sharper than we can. But fuck, they're practically on top of us."

He watched a few seconds longer, hoping the guy knew what he was doing, but not saying it. He didn't need to add to the pressure.

Rit Carpenter was going to hold their lives in the palm of his hand.

THREE compartments aft, Teddy was arguing with Kaulukukui over how to line up the diesels to start. Of course, they couldn't now, not underwater, but at some point they were going to run out of juice. The needles on what he figured were the main battery bank ammeters were already lower than when they'd cast off. He'd figured out, though, what Carpenter had told him Im had done before they started the DC motors. He'd been declutching the main engines, so the electric motors didn't have to drive them while they were driving the shaft too. And probably burning everything out.

He coughed. "Hey. Sumo."

"Uh."

"My imagination, or is it getting hot in here? And fucking stuffy?"

He considered the bitch box. He could call to Control. And get barked at by that fat son of a bitch. Carpenter had changed his tune since they got aboard a sub. Like now they were on his turf. But they were all breathing the same air. And the first one to whine about it certainly wasn't going to be a SEAL.

DAN checked the round meter on the bulkhead above Vaught. Im was keeping them steady at thirty meters. After that first shock, he didn't want to touch bottom again. He'd been lucky not to bend a prop, or worse yet, a shaft. He was going to have to be very careful in the turns, too, in such shallow water.

But to what end? The task force was steaming farther away with each passing hour. How was he going to get the team out of this? And if he couldn't, shouldn't he surface and surrender?

He'd always believed that if there was no chance left, you didn't sacrifice your men. (Unless, of course, it would save others.) But all naval history was proof that in the midst of the fight was the worst possible time to judge the chances of success. Some commanders had given up without firing a shot. Others had fought to the death in desperate actions. And both decisions had subsequently been judged wise, in certain circumstances, and unwise, in others.

His short-term course seemed clear. Especially as the frigates had not yet made a hostile move. As a former skipper, he knew the procedure. Report back—they'd have real-time communications with their headquarters ashore—outline the situation, that they held contact on the stolen boat, and ask for instructions.

On the other hand, nobody was sure how the Iranian command structure operated. There might be two or even three different chains of command, depending on whether you were talking regular navy, religious, Pasdaran, or diplomatic.

Which might operate to his advantage, if the tactical commander up above—most likely, the senior captain of the two ships who were after them—got back the same limp waffle Dan himself often had when requesting instructions in a tight situation.

While he'd been thinking this the pinging had traveled overhead. A staccato series of high notes, shorter and not held as long as the typical U.S. sonar transmission, and sent—he'd counted—every six seconds. Now it faded to starboard. He studied the chart again, blinking. His eye smarted and itched. He had to keep reminding himself to keep his fingers out of it, not to rub in whatever fragments the near miss had left.

He counted off the minutes since their last course change, double-checked the position relative to the shoals, marked the chart, and thrust his head out. "Right, steer two-seven-zero. Speed one-third." He checked the chart yet again, feeling he was missing something. Would there be a layer here? A thermocline to hide under? He doubted it. There'd be a lot of mixing, this close to the mouth of the Strait. Still, if there was one they ought to try to get under it. "Increase depth to four zero meters."

Vaught rogered. Im stared. Dan found the best way to get it across was just to tap the depth he wanted on the gauge. The Korean nodded and pointed to the helmsman. Dan guessed that meant he had the boat balanced and he could change depths with just the planes. "Vaught? Forty meters. Down easy, we don't want her nose in the bottom again."

"Four zero meters." The nasal deadness had ebbed in the SDV driver's voice. His right hand shoved the bow plane lever forward, followed it with the after plane control.

The explosion was so close aboard and so unexpected Dan couldn't stifle a yelp. He whipped around, trying to figure out where it had come from. That loud, it could have been within the hull, but there was no spraying water, no flying metal. "Carpenter! What the fuck was that? A depth charge?"

The submariner leaned out, one headphone off his skull. "A grenade, Commander."

"Really? That was a grenade?"

"Warning shot. And if you hadn't turned, we'd have gotten it right on top of us."

He rubbed his mouth, considering. Vaught said, "A warning? To surface, you mean?"

They ignored him. Dan's palm came away wringing wet. The air was getting hotter and hotter. He looked around for fans, ventilation, then remembered: Machinery generated transients. Transients got submariners detected. Detections got them killed. No fans, he could live with that.

Grenades . . . better than the Limbo charges, an ahead-thrown weapon rather like the old U.S. Hedgehogs. He wasn't intimately familiar with Limbo, it was a Commonwealth system, but he knew they were mortar-launched, fired in salvos of three to strike the sea, sink, and detonate at close range, blasting in the thickest pressure hull. Two or three hundred pounds of explosive, if he was remembering what he'd studied years before. Range, maybe half a mile at the outside. And, of course, there'd be antisubmarine torpedoes. The original loadout would have been long expended. These guys would be carrying the Chinese copy of the U.S. Mark 46 called the Yu-2.

But the grenade meant the Iranian Navy hadn't yet determined to sink them. No doubt they wanted their sub and weapon back. Though it might be a final warning before they *did* try to sink them.

Either way, he was boxed in. And the explosive would've come down right on top of them if he hadn't turned. Which meant the frigates had a rock-solid track. With them passing overhead, he hadn't been certain; it could have been happenstance as easily as targeting. But now he knew *they* knew exactly where *K-79* was, and had probably already picked up on his turn and were working out their next gambit.

"Four zero meters."

Vaught was reporting steady on the ordered depth. "Very well," Dan mumbled, eyeing the chart again, scratching furiously through his wet stubble. This had to be close to as deep as they could go here, the keel only two or three meters off what the chart called as a mud and sand bottom.

"By the way, we've got automatic depth control." The SDV pilot pointed to a bulb on the plane boxes. It was illuminated. "Im showed me."

Dan didn't answer, locked into a concatenation of dilemmas that looked more and more like a blind alley. No matter what he did, the frigates would nail them down and eventually kill them. Half a mile dead ahead a patch shoaled to 22 meters. Right, or left? To starboard would take them back toward to the Iranian coast. To port, out into the deeper water of the main shipping channel.

With that, a hint leapt suddenly into an image. "Left, steer one seven zero."

Vaught repeated it tonelessly. A groaning from the hydraulics. Dan hoped they didn't lose pressure. He had no idea what pumps they had on line or even where they were. Without hydraulics they'd have no control. They had no business being out here in a craft they didn't know the first thing about. But there'd been no choice. Other than surrender.

He still had that option. But he wouldn't much longer.

Henrickson came in from aft, face white, staggering. "You okay?" Dan asked him.

"Yeah. Gosh, it's getting stuffy down below."

"Everything marked? Russian to English?"

"Everything I could make sense of."

"Teddy? Sumo?"

"Trying to figure out the diesels."

Dan nodded. Figuring the diesels was good, but he had a feeling their fate would be decided long before they'd need to snorkel. A boat ran faster on diesels, but it was much noisier. Still, if their pursuers were pinging active, they were probably not listening well passive. He doubted active high-frequency sonar in shallow warm water would get a workable return much over two thousand yards. But sonar wasn't the only way they could be detected. He might snatch a quick peep with the 'scope without being picked up, but raising the snorkel head would flare a huge pip on even the worst-tuned radar.

"Stay down," he muttered, kneading his neck till it hurt.

"What's that?"

"Nothing, Monty. How's Donnie doing?"

The little analyst nodded. "I'll go see."

ONE deck down and forward, in a dim long compartment that ran the width of the hull, lined with gray cabinets and the desklike extruded cliffs of fire control consoles, Donnie Wenck sprawled with spiky hair awry, trying to decode a tech manual in a language he didn't speak. Fortunately there were schematics.

"How's it look?" Henrickson asked. "Lenson wants to know."

"Uh, this is where they were running the fire control program from. Doesn't this say 'Shkval'?"

Monty glanced at the cover that Donnie turned to the light. "Right. But how are you going to get the system back up, with all the cabinets open?"

"First I gotta know what they are. Then what they do. Then I start 'em up, the basic fire control system first, then the add-on routines one at a time. Okay with you?"

"Fine with me." Henrickson fanned himself. "Can you breathe this crap?"

"What crap?" Wenck looked from the header on a page of schematics to the label on a cabinet, aligned the drawer, pushed it closed. He thumbed a button. A light flickered on. Then a whole row, then a double row, blinking in an arcane pattern. Wenck stared at the lights. He muttered, "She's loading—no—fuck, something else's wrong. What's going on here?"

"You read binary?" Henrickson said, astonished. "Were you just reading that? While it was loading?"

"Uh-huh," Wenck muttered. He pressed a button and a relay-driven reader head went clunk. He pressed another and tape reels rotated. He stared at the lights as they resumed twinkling, in mad, logical, strangely unrandom patterns. "Can't everybody?"

RIT turned the bearing dial slowly, watching the red-orange lines jump and waver, almost but not quite matching the buzzing crackle in his headphones. The console had automated analysis but he couldn't read what it said, so he was going by eye and ear. Like the old days . . . a hell of a lot of ambient noise all around the dial. Like a freeway at rush hour overlaid with the crackle of a million short-order fry grills at noon. Very dimly, only now and then, he made out screw noises. But were they from the cans?

Eyes sealed, he panned aft, tracking a whisker-tickle of a rhythm. It faded and then strengthened. One five zero relative. One six zero. One seven . . . crossing behind them, against the slightly fainter background clamor from aft. Plenty of biologics, but less of the freeway thunder he was beginning to suspect might be ship traffic through the Strait.

He squeezed his already closed eyes tighter, as if by walling out light he could hear better. There. Just for a moment. A pair of four-bladed screws. Also, even less distinguishable, a higher-pitched whine, but it faded in and out and he couldn't get enough of it to do a blade count.

He punched a couple of buttons and was pleasantly surprised when the thing locked on and gave him a frequency split and a bar graph, the bars shaky and seesawing but no question what was going on. He hit the freq ID and set it in as МИШеНЬ, which Monty had told him meant "target," and designated it 1.

"Sierra One, frigate, two screws, bears one eight five. Looks like she's on diesels."

"Where's the other one?" Lenson demanded.

"Don't have him yet." He opened his eyes and cranked the dial and searched ahead, then to port. Ought to have a team plotting what he was calling out. Computing fire control solutions. But they didn't have enough guys and even if they did, what was the point? He went back to the screen on Sierra One and picked out one of the tonals and scanned for that. No good. Tried again and got something to port. Call it as Sierra Two? He tried to lock on but it wavered and roved, the circuits couldn't pull it out of the mush.

"Got the other guy yet?"

Sweat ran down his neck under the earphones. He felt lightheaded.

"Might have something to port. Around three four zero, three four two. I could ping 'em—"

"No pings," Lenson snapped.

Rit tried again to lock on the second contact but again the computer slipped, skidded, could not get its fingers around it. Passive sonar gave bearings, but not range. If he could ping, he could range them. Lenson was right, though, going active was a loser idea. Their only chance of getting out of here was to hide.

Where, was another question. It was just too fucking shallow. Barely enough water to get a full-sized boat all the way under. Only good thing about it, it wasn't deep enough, at least yet, for the guys who were after them to fire a homing torpedo. And all the reverberation and bottom return would make it harder for them to hold a track, or regain it, if they did shake them off somehow. From the courses he was running, Lenson was trying to get them out to the Strait. But it wasn't a hell of a lot deeper out there. All the deep water was to port, out where *San Fran* was waiting.

He suddenly yearned for the familiar spaces and smells of a U.S. sub. Hot dogs in the red-lit grill, turning on the polished rollers till you picked them out and tucked them into snug, soft, freshly baked buns ... Rocky Road at midnight, more than you ought to eat ... popcorn and steaks.

The unfamiliar computer in front of him, still trying for the second target, flashed a red light. He cranked the dial back, but it was gone. "Jesus fuck," he whispered, blinking salty fluid out of his eyes. "You little bastard." He hit the button to go back to Sierra One.

The screen leaped into bars of light. The pinging dented his eardrums. He wheeled on the rotating chair, pitching his voice to carry only to where the others waited out in the tense silence of the control room.

"Sierra One. Screws to full speed. Coming right up our ass!"

THIS time after the pings and the washing machine three detonations spaced out three seconds apart. *Blam ... blam ... blam.* They sounded different than the first, with less reverberation, less intensity, close but somehow flatter, more like a taut drumhead being whacked than an explosive going off. The middle one was the loudest. Dan didn't need Carpenter to tell him what that meant: *K-79* was tacked down like a beetle on a display board. They knew exactly where he was and how deep. "Shit," he murmured, leaning on the 'scope stand and trying not to return the worried looks he was getting from Vaught and Im. Sweat dripped off his chin. Even the Korean, usually stone faced, looked distressed. "Rit."

"Yeah."

"Bearing to the nearest screws that aren't frigates."

He waited, hanging from a pipe in the overhead. Something went *tick tick tick* very rapidly aft. He tensed, but it stopped.

"Can't give you individual screws. Heavy ship traffic up ahead. Low freq. Big screws. Tankers?"

"Probably. Bearing?"

"Wide bearing spread. Basically smeared all across the horizon."

Dan tried to think despite the dread. The charges were an order to surface. Standard procedure for an unidentified sub caught in someone's territorial sea. Their pursuers must be uncertain exactly who they were. At no point, so far as he knew, had anyone ashore gotten a clear look at them and survived. They might think renegade Iranians were conning the stolen boat. Or possibly, that the instructors—the men Oberg and Kaulukukui had killed during the takeover—might have been suddenly ordered by Moscow to decamp for some unexpected reason.

Trying to figure out what the commanding officers up above were thinking, though, might be a waste of processing time. Whatever they guessed or didn't, no government could let one of its warships, much less one armed with a potent new weapon, be snatched away with impunity. Not to mention all the dead and wounded troops they'd left behind. At some point, presumably one rapidly bearing down on them, warnings and orders would give way to attack.

He checked the chart again. Should be past the fifty-meter line now. "Depth, fifty," he muttered. Hoping they didn't hit any lumps or bumps, any wrecks or unevennesses in the bottom. "Speed: bare steerageway."

The speed order went aft in a quiet voice over the brown plastic intercom. "Depth: Fifty," Vaught muttered, toes nudging a red pedal before he adjusted the plane levers. They waited, looking at nothing in particular. Was that something whispering along the hull? Dan tensed, but it didn't recur.

Four miles. So near, yet so far. Half an hour's run at eight knots. Two hours, at the two knots they were slowing to now. But if he had to dogleg and circle, it could take much longer. He was hugging the bottom. If there was a layer, he had to be under it.

"Rit. Where now?"

"Sierra Two, ahead of us, drawing left. Sierra One to starboard, steady bearing."

Drawing the diagram in his mind, he realized they were cloverleafing. An attack pattern that let two ships double-team a submerged adversary.

Both frigates were passing overhead, in turn, in opposite directions. As soon as one was clear, he put his rudder over and described a loop out and away before closing again to repeat the maneuver, but from the next point of the compass.

Passing information constantly, the "on" ship held contact with active sonar as it approached, dropping its ordnance as it went over. The "off" unit maintained contact at arm's length with passive sonar, in case the attacker lost the target in its own screw-wash, the reverberation of the explosions, or the despairing twists and turns of the steadily more desperate submarine. Until the inevitable end.

He saw it clearly, including the slow pinwheel of the pattern to port. Had applied it in dozens of exercises, and once or twice, in earnest. How often, leaning over a plot table, he'd tried to put himself in the sub commander's place! The irony was too bitter to be funny. He sucked the heated too-thin air, forcing his thoughts through the steel wool and jagged glass stuffing his skull.

The hell of it was, there was no way to escape a cloverleaf properly executed. Not unless you could escalator up and down, and the chart still gave him only fifty-five to sixty meters, though it deepened to the southward.

His sole chance lay in the counterclockwise rotation. If his attackers got out of synch, turned a trifle too early or too late or with too large a rudder angle, a pie-wedge of shadow could flick open in the pinwheel. In that moment, he'd seen a very savvy sub commander suddenly vanish. Usually he was picked up minutes later, but for that fragment of wheeling time he was impalpable, intangible, returned to the ghostliness of a subatomic particle that might or might not exist depending on whether an observer was present; while Dan had found himself chasing what he'd thought had been the sub, but which slowly faded, a mirage, a phantom.

Could he do it? He bent again over the chart, wondering about tide. Could a counterflowing tide be enough to slow a frigate on the northward petal of this deadly flower? But he didn't know what the tide was. Or, wait, he did—they'd planned the attack for high tide, to allow room for the delivery vehicle to lie close alongside the Juliet.

Which meant the tide would be flowing out now, out through the strait.

"Sierra Two, incoming again. Pinging like a sonofabitch—switching to short range—"

"Bearing on the other one, Carpenter, Sierra One—"

"Sierra One bears one two five relative, starboard quarter—"

He clung to the periscope stand, mouth moistureless as baked cotton. Vaught was writhing his neck in a strange way. Im was nodding to himself, lips moving in some rapid speech that surely couldn't be a prayer. Dan's heart took an age between beats. The rushing grew, and mixed with it the *shik-shik-shik* of the blades slicing through the water, a sharp cracking as one, damaged or nicked, cavitated, trailing vapor bubbles that collapsed on themselves. The sonar screamed in their ears, exciting sympathetic vibratos in the structure around them, till it seemed the hull itself was crying and trembling under the lash that hit it once a second.

Thud. Thud. Crack. Crack. *Thud. Thud.* Six detonations, evenly spaced, and again, the middle two directly above. Six: the universal signal for danger at sea, for being in extremis, for the last warning. The echo of the last was still thrilling away in fainter and fainter tremolos when Dan licked dry lips and said in a voice that sounded strange even to himself: *"All back emergency."*

"All back emergency—"

"Right hard rudder—"

Hoarse murmurs answered. The hull around them lurched as the big screws aft went suddenly to full astern, clawing power into the water, reversed engines and suddenly tilted rudder spinning hundreds of tons of water into a whirlpooling density that could for a few seconds suggest to probing sound the presence of a tangible body.

Vaught choked out, as if his mouth was full of marbles, "Right hard rudder."

Dan said over him, "All engines, ahead flank. Ahead *emergency* flank! Come right to one eight five, down planes, *steady* at sixty meters!"

An agonized groan came from aft as the spinning shafts twisted under the torsion of suddenly reversed rotation. Electric motors responded more swiftly than a surface ship's turbines, and Dan grabbed a handhold as the rush of water grew outside, then became a roar, varied by clatters and thumps. The periscope began to vibrate alarmingly. Dan glanced at it, but said nothing. The torrent-noise got louder. And louder.

"Steady on one eight five. Steady on sixty meters."

"Make depth sixty-two meters."

"Control, Electrical; we're really sucking down the power back here, I can see these needles dropping—"

Dan hit the bitch box button, it didn't matter now how much noise he made, and yelled, "Just keep it balls to the wall, Oberg. This is our chance to shake them."

The SEAL gave him a "roger, out" as an ominous scraping came from beneath their feet. It rose, but Dan snapped to Vaught, "Don't touch those planes. Maintain your depth."

"Short range pinging. Well astern."

The Alvands were pinging on the "knuckle," the ghost he'd left swirling in the disturbed water. But how long would it fool them? Sweat slid down his cheeks as he fixed his eyes on his watch. Twenty seconds at flank. Thirty. He fanned his face with his other hand. Vaught coughed hoarsely. At twenty knots, every thirty seconds was another three hundred and thirty yards, every minute, six hundred and sixty. The sweep hand jumped ahead. Again. Nobody spoke.

A minute.

Two. Im shook his head like a dog and a fine spray came off his black hair and hung in the light like a halo.

Three minutes. They'd gained a mile. It had to be deeper now, the bumping had eased. "Sixty-five meters," Dan said in an almost normal voice. Three more miles and they'd be in the channel, in international waters. He felt giddy, as if he'd just stepped off a carrousel.

A tremendous detonation piledrivered the steel around them. The hull flexed, the lights flickered, dust and bits of cork flew off the bulkheads and frolicked in hazy air. *WHAM. WHAM. WHAM.* Three great deafening clangs like anvils dropping on them from a mile up. Vaught's shoulders quivered. Carpenter cursed in a gabbled shriek from the sonar stack. Im staggered into the ballast control panel and recoiled, clutching his face. Alarms began beeping.

"What the fuck was that?" Henrickson yelled from forward and below.

"Limbos," Dan said through numb lips to them all. "Antisubmarine mortars. Two hundred pounds of explosive. Depth fuzed. Fired in salvos of three. Cut those alarms off!"

Again, closer, louder, three more savage battering blows, shattering bulbs inside their thick glass safety jars, cracking gauges, shaking down handsized flakes of cork and old paint. Carpenter gripped the jamb of the door from the sonar station, face slack. "They're not pinging. They're firing on passive bearings. Right down our sound spoke. It's too shallow to go this fast. We're cavitating! Putting out too much noise—"

"Slow down," Im said, bloody hands over his face but his eyes wide above them. "Slow down!"

Vaught glared up, shoulders hunched as if against a cave-in, pupils blank. The rocketing sub brushed something, some bulge or bank on the bottom. It lurched and rocked. Dan felt a bloodcurdling sense of something huge and solid looming just ahead. He clung to his handhold, physically biting back the commands to slow, to rise, that his cowardly self tried again and again to bark out. Bolting through the deep, through the dark, they waited for the next barrage to arc out of the walled-off sky.

24

BUT the third salvo hit farther away, insofar as he could judge; only rattling already broken glass, knocking free a few more paint chips, the shocks rattling away through the frames and stringers of the missile housings. Dan kept his eyes straight ahead, not even wanting to look at the seething air. The hull jarred again, then smoothed, though the shears were still vibrating as if some giant dentist were trying to wrench them out by the roots. He wondered how fast they were going, how many minutes longer they could keep it up.

"Depth," he grated at last, trying to keep his pitch going too high.

"Depth . . . depth . . . sixty feet. I mean, meters."

"Steady on, Vaught. They missed us."

The pilot didn't answer, flexing his arms and shaking his shoulders. Dan hoped he was getting a grip. He patted Im's back and pointed a finger at Carpenter. The submariner's cheeks gleamed with thick sweat; he cradled his arm. Dan checked his watch again and was startled. *Nine* minutes at flank speed. They had to be getting close to the channel. "Rit. You okay?"

"Arm hurts like shit . . . I might of broke it. Hit it on the console edge when I went over."

"We'll look at it when we're out of this, but right now I need you back on that stack. Find me a single slow-speed screw out around two-seven-zero to zero-zero-zero."

The sonarman nodded and vanished. A broken arm would hurt like hell, but Carpenter hadn't said another word. Dan paced, wondering if he should come right. Or go deeper. Or put the planes on full rise, back to 'scope depth, and check his six.

He smiled grimly. Why bother? He knew what he'd see. The same two Nemeses barreling after him. With the noise *K-79* was making, the scream of collapsing bubbles howling off her madly spinning screw, there was no way he could lose them.

He had to find a place to hide.

IM'S nose was bleeding but he ignored it, only snuffling up the blood as it threatened to choke him. He clung to the handhold above the ballast panel, blinking through a headache that gradually became blinding. He peered through the smoky, dusty air, wincing as hot metal sizzled deep in his head. And suddenly he understood what was wrong.

The commander was staring off into space. He knew that whitened set of the lips. Had seen it on his own commanding officer, when they'd been under attack. Hearing their comrades go down around them, the crackling death-throes of heroes making the ultimate sacrifice. All to get them through. But they weren't going to get through this time if they couldn't breathe, and just breathing grew harder with each passing minute.

Sleepiness, fatigue, clouded judgment, headache: it seemed to be happening more rapidly than it should, given how few they were, but judging by his symptoms, carbon dioxide was building up in their air. Maybe Lenson could get them out, maybe he couldn't, but if it got much worse they'd just black out. He rubbed snot and blood from under his nose and lurched forward to grab Lenson's sleeve. The commander flinched and stared down. "I light oxygen?"

Lenson blinked, then nodded. Im half read his lips. "Good idea. Know where they are?"

He pointed to a knee-high metal box pierced with louvers. "Every compartment."

"Great." Lenson blinked again and dragged a palm down his face. "But not in the compartments we don't have guys in. Okay? Dog off the after torpedo, the engine room, unless Oberg needs to get back there. How long do those candles last?"

He thought he had that. Maybe his hearing was coming back? "Burn for six hours. Enough oxygen for a day. Maybe more."

"Is there tanked oxygen? They've got to have some tanked, too."

"No. Checked tanks." He gestured, hands out, forgetting the English word. "Nothing."

"Empty?"

"Empty. *Yae.* After candle, only breathing set."

Lenson looked disturbed but said nothing more, just snapped back to his trance. Im headed for the box and lifted the lid.

Inside nestled a matched pair of two-foot-square yellow metal canisters.

Exactly like the ones on his old boat. He stripped off the seals and pulled the igniter tab. The fireworks smell of hot perchlorate stung his nose but he bent in to whiff the thin gray smoke, and felt the fatigue lift and the headache lessen.

He checked the depth and looked at Vaught, then went aft. He lit one of the two candles outside the galley, and started to unseal the second.

Then hesitated. The commander had said, only the compartments the team was in. He looked forward, then aft. Finally he reached down and pulled out the cartridge he'd just yanked the tab on, intending to carry it aft and swap it out with one of the others.

Instead the whole bottom of the cartridge fell out. Burning perchlorate and flakes of its rusty steel casing, neglected and corroded through, followed it onto the deckplates. A cloud of white powder rolled out. He beat at the hot chemical, coughing in the thick white smoke that mushroomed suddenly along the overhead as the hot chemical hit a greasy spot on the deckplates. He glanced around for a fire extinguisher. He dashed into the galley, found a flat tin, and got it under the heap of chemical smoldering on the deck. It smoked and hissed as he tipped it into a stainless sink, but it was safe now, under control. He blew out and backed away, dusting his hands.

Oberg looked in. His mouth made words but Im couldn't hear them. He smiled and held up his hands, pointed to the sink, smiled some more. Sweat rolled down his back, gritty with the powdered chemical. But the SEAL wasn't smiling. He looked angry. He was coming toward him. Im's hand, groping along the sink behind him, found the handle of a knife.

TEDDY looked at the mess, at the grinning, shrugging Korean. The smoke smelled like the Fourth of July. "What the hell's this?" he said again, then all at once realized what was happening. The Korean was trying to—

A knife flashed, and without conscious thought, reflexes honed by hundreds of hours of drill, Oberg lunged. He got the blade away and braced himself to break Im's arm with his elbow.

Instead he got an elbow himself, in the face, that just about knocked him cold. He hung in the dark for a second watching distant planets flare before he came back and turned into him and wrestled him to the deckplates, both men grunting and trying for advantage. The Korean was smaller but strong and wiry quick.

"What's going on here?"

Henrickson, in the galley doorway. Teddy let up a little, breathing hard. "Son of a bitch was trying to set a fire. I never trusted him—"

"A fire?"

"Oxygen candle break," Im spat. He got an arm free and pointed to the sink. "I put out. This crazy man!"

"Commander sent him to light off the oxygen generators, Teddy. To scrub this carbon dioxide out of the air."

"Then why'd the fucker grab a knife?"

"I'd grab one, too, if you were trying to fuck me up! Let him go. We don't have time to screw around. Commander says, drop speed. Eight knots, below cavitation."

"Go tell Sumo, he's on the console."

"I'm telling you. Let him up!"

The SEAL pulled his hands off and held them up. "You fuck self," Im spat at him, and pushed past.

Obie turned to watch him head aft, then snapped around. For a second Monty tensed, thinking he was going to attack him, too.

Instead he grunted something and headed aft. "Eight knots," Monty called after him.

Im ignored the Americans. He was bent over a box, pulling a tab. A crack, and the same hot smoke-smell as in the galley filtered up into the choking air. He and Henrickson exchanged glances as they shoved past each other in the passageway.

DAN hung on the scope as its vibration ebbed, as the rush of water became a whisper again. Then gave Vaught a quiet order to come right. Waited.

Carpenter leaned his head out. And said sotto voce, "You wanted a low-speed diesel? Got one out around two nine eight. Sounds like the blade-tips are just about out of the water."

"You can tell that?"

"Be surprised what you can hear . . . four blades, big single screw, going around thirty times a minute."

"Tanker? In ballast?"

"What I figure."

Dan hung listening to Vaught's wheezing, the auto depth control groaning as it adjusted the planes. Worrying now about his battery level. Till now, he'd figured they wouldn't be out here long. The Navy would find some way to help. But if things were hitting the fan up Iraq way, he'd need to hoard every amp. As well as the CO_2 absorber and the oxygen generators.

Either that, or find some safe place to poke the snorkel up, figure out how to start the diesels and blowers, get some charge in the can and flush out the bad air. Which he wasn't sure he had enough hands to do, not and keep all the other balls they were juggling off the floor.

A lot more to think about on a sub than he'd had to keep track of on a destroyer. "Bearing drift on that screw?"

"Steady for the last minute."

He glanced at the chart, setting up the problem. A simple pursuit curve? If it was a tanker, it'd be headed in for a load from the terminals at the upper end of the Gulf. Its course would be west southwest, conforming to the north lane of the Inshore Traffic Zone. It would hold that course for at least ten miles, passing north of the Salih oil fields and then the light and racon beacon at Tunb al Kubra. "Rit, that contact, since detection, louder or weaker?"

"Two decibel gain over the last minute."

"We're gaining on her?"

"Be my guess, Dan."

First time Carpenter had called him by his given name since they'd caught him with the Filipina. He allowed himself a smile, turned away from the sonar shack. "Very well." Increase speed again? He wasn't sure of their cavitation threshold. "Watch that contact, keep feeding me bearings."

"Slightly louder, three zero zero . . . three zero one."

"Right five more degrees, Vaught."

Over the next hour he closed, very cautiously, altering course fire degrees at a time and adjusting his speed in tiny increments, until the screw-throb boomed through the hull, huge and slow like the heartbeat of a sounding sperm whale. The sonar gave them two six zero to the contact. Vaught was fighting wake effects on the planes. Dan guessed they were from two to three hundred yards behind the big slow-ticking screw. As close as he wanted to be in case the ship ahead slowed or changed course.

He went into the sonar shack. Carpenter went so white when he manipulated the arm that Dan concluded, yeah, it was fractured. They got a makeshift sling on it, which was all he could do at the moment. He warned the sonarman to yell if he heard the screw-beat or the angle change.

In the control room, he slapped Vaught on the back. "Doing okay? Need a break?"

"I'm okay. Auto depth's doing most of the work." A moment, then, in a lower voice: "Sorry I got nervous back there."

"What? Didn't notice. Were you?"

"A little." Vaught checked his instruments again, then cleared his throat. "Does sound like it's working harder, though."

"What does?"

"The auto control. Cycles more often than it did at first."

Dan nodded. He glanced at the scope again, but decided again to play it safe. Now they'd shaken the frigates, the mission was back at the front of the list. He hadn't been sent to get a submarine. *K-79* had no intelligence value of itself, it was just another obsolete Soviet-era diesel-electric. It was the Shkval-K they'd risked their lives for. They had documentation, circuit diagrams, and Wenck's downloaded software, but no question, the missile would be the trophy head. If they could make it to friendly territory they could eject it, noting the location for later recovery. Then scuttle and abandon. Get ashore somehow, maybe hail a passing dhow, and use Oberg's satphone to call for pickup.

He leaned into Sonar, waited till Carpenter lifted an earpiece. "I'm going forward, check on Monty and Donny. Anything changes, give me a yell."

IN the missile control compartment all the lights were on and all the consoles had their guts racked out again. Manuals and unfolded schematics littered the deck with test instruments holding them down. But no Henrickson, no Wenck. Dan looked behind the consoles but found no one there either.

He fumbled to a leatherette-covered chair and hung his head between his knees, rubbing his scalp. Then stripped off his wet-suit bottoms for the camo trousers beneath. For the moment, no one saw. No eyes looked to him for guidance, for orders, for inspiration, for strength.

A terrible fear was growing, and not just the old one, that he wasn't up to this. He'd thought they'd escaped, but had they? Those frigates would not give up. The Iranians could not let them escape. Where were they now? And where was the U.S. Navy?

A dull clunk and voices from forward. He climbed the ladder again and followed them through officers' country, past the CO's and XO's staterooms, the junior officer bunkrooms. He found them all the way forward in the torpedo room, bent over the shining shape withdrawn from tube number 3. A work light dangled, jigging in the motion that up here he could feel was from turbulence outside. From the huge screw revolving slowly not far ahead of where they stood. He frowned at a smell like salt meat gone bad: the dead Russians. He cleared his throat and said, too loud, "Got the goods on the guidance yet?"

Henrickson straightened, flushed, thin hair awry around his bald spot. Beside him Wenck showed up no better; his pupils looked drilled deep into his skull, as if he'd been playing video poker for two days straight. "Little problem with that."

"What?"

"There isn't any."

Dan stared. "What's that mean? There's got to be guidance."

"Well, there isn't." The analyst waved at the weapon. "First off, this was the only Shkval aboard. So this is a test bed, right? Initial installation, see how it goes, maybe then they'll buy big, right?"

"Okay, so?"

"So Donnie's up there hacking into the computer? Figuring we'll download the programming and figure it all out later, when we get back to TAG."

"I know, but what are you telling me?"

"Well—usually, for a torpedo, any torpedo, from a surface ship just like from a sub, battery plot takes in your data from your inertial nav, your sonar, 'scope fixes, and plots own-ship location and generates your target data—bearing, range, speed, right?"

"Yeah, and . . . ?"

"Then the FCS outputs your guidance and run data to the torp. Now. For the original flavor Shkval, you'd need the same data set as for a straight-runner torpedo. Fire signal, run depth—well, maybe not even that, these are set for one depth and that's it. Basically all it needs is the runout bearing."

"We went all through the computer looking for new software. But that's the only output we're seeing," Wenck said.

Dan looked from one to the other. "Just runout bearing?"

"Right. No homing data. Not intermediate, not terminal. And no target data either, what you tune it to look for in a multitarget environment. Or in case you got friendlies out there to watch out for, keep your blue on blue numbers down."

"That doesn't mean it can't home. Once it gets out there."

"Right, which is why we're down here, okay?" Henrickson ran a hand along the silver flank, then pointed at the stubby fins. "Remember what Dr. Chone was telling us, back at NUWC? Swing-out low-freq transducers, that home on the carrier's screws. See anything looks like a transducer?"

"We scraped it with a knife. There's nothing there," Wenck put in.

"He said on the cavitator. Or the tail fin."

"No, he said on the cavitator or on some kind of canards, the tail was too much in the flow. But we checked everywhere. *Everywhere.*" Henrickson pulled the work light close and scraped his fingernails along smooth metal. "Take a gander. Tell me we're missing something."

Dan peered, but saw nothing but polished metal shell. He moved up front and bent to check the slanted transducer plate, then the surface behind it. Muttered, "Donnie, what about it? Do they have to be external?"

"I had that plate off behind the nose. There's no wiring coming back. There's no transducers, Commander. There's *no guidance in this thing.*"

Dan's heart sank. "It's a standard Shkval? Then why a dedicated sub, a Russian training team?"

Wenck shrugged, grinning without a reason. Henrickson shook his head. Dan stared at the sphinx in the cradle, brain spinning. Could the spy in the Admiralty be wrong? But Yevgeny Dvorov had announced the new version at ARMINTEX. He was taking orders, the Iranians and Chinese were buying. Russian weapons weren't the most sophisticated, but they worked. Developing countries didn't have the most skillful operators or maintenance technicians, either, so it was a good match, a value for value that led to relationships that lasted. Would Dvorov and Yermakov jeopardize their reputation, their markets, for a one-time profit? He couldn't see it.

He stared at the weapon. Wondering again why something about it just didn't look *right*.

He flung his arms open and bent over. As if embracing the deadly length. One hand on the razor-edge of the cavitator. The other thrown wide, scrabbling at the curved flank. Then replaced his right fingertips with his left and flung himself out again. The old Norse measurement. One fathom. Two. His fingertips curled at the end of the exhaust tube. Three. He closed his eyes and sighed.

"What're you doing there, Commander?"

"Measuring it. Shit! Remember, we just about made Im even shorter than he is? When we ran this into the tube? That's why. The standard Shkval's fifteen feet long. This thing's eighteen."

"Crap," Wenck said. Henrickson looked startled.

"Find out why." Dan rapped his knuckles on it. "The transducers are in there somewhere. Or else it's not acoustic. But it's got something. Take it down to parade rest if you have to. But find out."

A note warbled and they all flinched. It came from one of the brown boxes. "Commander? You there? Better come back to Control. Our guy's looking like he's heading south."

THE tanker they'd trailed for the last hour and a half did indeed seem to be altering course, though so far all Carpenter had picked up was a change in the frequency of the blade transients. From a dead astern angle they were now getting a higher doppler off the upper tips, a lower doppler off the lower ones. Fingering his injured arm, the sonarman explained: the plane of the spinning prop was altered in relation to the its listeners, hence, the ship that carried it was in a slow turn, in this case, to port. He said he was getting something else now and then, too, it came and it went.

"What's it sound like?" Dan asked him.

"I'm not sure . . . tunes in, then fades. Can't get a bearing."

"Frigate?"

"No, not a ship. Maybe some weird biologic. Or submerged pipeline equipment, natural gas compressor, something like that."

"Uh-huh. So where's this tanker headed?" Dan untaped the chart and carried it in by the sonar stack where they could both pore over it.

"Shit . . . this thing fucking *hurts*. The Fateh field?" Carpenter suggested.

"Or this, to the south of it. Umm ad Delkh. If it wasn't so shallow, we could follow her in to Abu Dhabi. There's a United Emirates naval base there. Surface once we're in territorial waters and radio for an escort."

Carpenter eyed him. "Why don't we do that? Run in awash, if we have to."

Dan bared his teeth, trying to ratiocinate through the fog of fatigue. It seemed like ages since he'd slept. Fortunately he knew these shallow waters, these islands, the complexities of oil and sovereignty here. Had navigated them before, aboard USS *Turner van Zandt*. For a moment he felt chilled, recalling what had happened to her, south of Abu Musa. Then dismissed it; that had been years ago.

"Uh, two reasons. One: We don't know, if the Iranians see us on the surface, they might come after us into UAE waters. Would the Emirates defend us? I don't see why they would. Two: Donnie and Monty still haven't figured out what we've got guidancewise. We turn the boat over to a third party, they'll seal the hatches and call the Iranians to come get it. There's a lot of disputes here over islands and oil fields, who owns what. The UAE navy's just patrol craft and a couple of corvettes. They're wary of pissing off the Iranians and probably should be. We've gone through hell to get our hands on that thing. I'm not giving it back."

"Keep heading north? And hope we can link up with the task force?"

"That's all I'm coming up with, Rit. Remember, we never planned it this way. You got a better idea, let's hear it."

"I don't have a problem with heading north, but have we got enough charge in the can to get there?" Carpenter looked doubtful. "Because I don't think we can snorkel. Surface, maybe, and start the engines—but snorkeling's tricky. There's a lot can go wrong, you gotta be on top of the situation. You're not, you go down. Subs aren't like airplanes. You go up in one of those, you know you're coming down again."

Dan said they'd have to play that hand when it was on the table. He leaned into the control room, to find Vaught standing at his station, the seat-stowage open where he'd been sitting, pissing into a green fiberglass mug. "Hey . . . we've got to come right, right now. About twenty degrees. Watch for the screw wash, it'll blow you to starboard and we don't have a hell of a lot of water over there. And pass the word back to Oberg—no, never mind, I'll do it."

"Uh, right . . . what shall I do with . . ."

"I got it, give it here."

The urine smelled rank as he balanced it aft toward the galley sink. He reminded himself to get the men to drink more water. They needed food, too. Had to be some here someplace. From nowhere came the memory of the tumbled bodies forward, a rush of shame.

Kaulukukui was in the galley making himself up a sandwich out of meat from a can. The smell made the saliva spring into Dan's mouth. "Want one?" the big SEAL said, sawing at bread.

"Uh, we all should get something. While we can."

"I'll cut a plateful and take it forward. Some kind of juice in the reefer there, you want any."

"Thanks, Sumo. Monty and Donny are in forward torpedo, the others are in Control."

He sank his teeth into half a sandwich and chewed as he went aft carrying another one and a mug of bug juice for Oberg. Even eating it, he wasn't sure what it was, but their last meal had been late the night before and the sandwich went down fast.

The other SEAL wasn't at the motor control station. Dan stood under the vent valves, feeling headachy and out of it again. More lights had been broken back here. The shadows were darker. The air smelled of ozone, and the steady, powerful drone of rotating electrical machinery tickled the soles of his dive booties. "Teddy?" he called in a low voice.

"Here." A flashlight beam emerged, followed by Oberg, crawling up from the compartment below. His face was dirty under greasy hair, and he'd discarded all his clothes except skivvy shorts and booties. "Hey. Thanks." He jammed the bread and meat into his face and followed it with half the mug of drink.

"Need you on the panel, Teddy. In case we ring back speed changes. What are you doing down there?"

"Some strange shit coming down, Commander. Got the motors turning, but hydraulic pressure's dropping and no clue why. Lose that, we lose plane control, rudder, vent valves, a lot of things. Water's rising in the bilge. High pressure air gauge is dropping, which means we won't be able to work the clutches. Temperature's rising in the motor core. I'm not sure exactly where it starts to melt and catch fire, but we're over the red line already. There's some kind of cooling system but I don't know how to line it up. Tracing lines, trying to get pumps and compressors on—Sumo and me, we been busy."

"Sounds like we never got all the auxiliaries on line. Okay, the temperature problem, we can drop to dead slow now. That should help."

Oberg stuffed the last of the meat into his maw and slid past Dan to the yellow cabinet. He slowly rotated the rheostat wheel and the hum dropped a note. He said around the mouthful, "What if we have to do another sprint? We're gonna be sucking fire and smoke. We need another guy back here. Somebody knows what he's doing."

"Im?"

Oberg frowned. "No. Not him."

"He's the only one, Teddy. I can't navigate or evade without Rit, Vaught's on the helm, and Donnie and Monty are on the mission objective. You'll have to hold it together as best you can." He looked at the panel. "What's our battery charge look like?"

"It's this bank of dials. Separate dial for each section, I figure. I put that mark where the needle was when we started. Maybe half what we started out with."

Dan felt chilly on the back of his neck despite the heat. They'd used fully half their charge in the few hours since they'd cast off. That high-speed run had sucked down a lot of power.

On the other hand, they'd shaken off the frigates. Pushing the hull along at only three or four knots would take a lot fewer electrons.

"How much farther to go?" Oberg asked him. "Till we join up?"

"Uh, that question's open till we can poke an antenna up and talk to somebody. If they're all the way up north, three hundred miles. But I'm hoping we can get a task element to detach and come down for us. Escort us, while we figure out how to get the package off. Then figure out what to do with the boat—"

"I say keep it."

"Not doable, Teddy."

"The North Koreans kept the *Pueblo*."

"Yeah, well, we're supposed to be the ones who stand for the rule of law, right? And stealing somebody else's sub doesn't come under that. There's going to have to be some kind of cover story, anyway." He took a slug off Oberg's proffered mug and grimaced; the juice was sour.

"Yeah, well, I think—"

The brown box crackled. Carpenter's voice, tense. "Electrical, Sonar: Sonobuoy in the water. Sonobuoy in the water, starboard side, pinging on us. Lenson back there?"

"On his way." To Dan, Oberg said, "Sonobuoy? Where'd that come from?"

"There's an airplane up there," Dan muttered. "That must have been what Rit was hearing."

He was starting forward when the bitch box crackled again. This time the message was curt. "Torpedo in the water. Torpedo in the water! Coming hard left. Gimme full power, Teddy, full power! Warp speed!"

DAN scrambled forward as bread, meat, and mug hit the deckplates. The high-pitched shrill of the torpedo's screws was bad enough. It was made mind-blanking terrifying by the knowledge it was likely to be the last sound he heard before the detonation of its warhead, followed by an instantaneous compression of the air column that would kill them all before they had a chance to drown.

But still he ran. He was swinging through the hatch when a tremendous explosion lifted the sub bodily and pitched him into the crew's shower. He lay full length, waiting to die. A second passed. Then another, as the hull flexed, the plates under him creaking as the shock died away to a rumble.

Then he was up and running again, astonished to still be clawing at the next hatchway, launching himself into the control room. He caromed off the radar mast housing as the lights flickered back up, even dimmer now. Vaught, bent double, moaned, arms locked over his head. Dan tried twice to speak before anything came out. "Vaught. Carpenter! What happened?"

"Air-dropped torpedo," the sonarman yelled. "Right after the sonobuoy started pinging. Somebody's up there. Tracking us."

He shoved the groaning pilot aside, gaze flicking from instrument to instrument. The deckplates heeled. Loose items started skating. The turn count was going up, the knotmeter at 12 and climbing. He felt their battery charge being drained as if his own blood was leaking away, but he didn't dare slow. No telling when the plane up there—probably one of the P-3s the U.S. had sold the Shah years before—might drop another one. Searching for them to Straitward after they'd evaded the frigates, it had gotten a reading off the magnetic effect of their hull. Then placed a sonobuoy, pinged for a hard localization, and immediately dropped a weapon. Carpenter had turned away and gone to full power, the standard and instantaneous response to a homing torp. The rudder was still over, and they were in a tight fast turn to port, coming through 170.

Carpenter called, "I heard him come in and just realized what I was hearing. Then the torp hit the water and 'engine start.' Maybe ten seconds worth of screw effects. Sounded like a daiquiri blender on high speed. Then it exploded."

"It's too shallow here to air drop on us. It went right into the bottom." Dan checked the autopilot setting, disengaged it with the pedal, put both planes ten degrees down, looked at the gyro again. Passing 090. "Can you still hear it? Where is he? Where's he coming in from?"

"Can't give you a bearing. Comes and goes."

Wenck and Henrickson crowded in, pale and shaking. Dan ignored them. He racked the rudder control over and shook the man before him. "Vaught! Get hold of yourself, guy. We can't do without you."

The SDV pilot lifted his head and Dan gave him another shove and he shakily took the controls again. "Come to 180, it's shallower over there," Dan told him. "Make your depth six-five."

"Was that a t-torpedo?"

"Correct, Donnie. There's a plane up there," Dan snapped.

"Warship screws," Carpenter called. "Bearing one-zero-zero, faint. The guy with the nicked blade, I think."

Dan slammed his fist into his thigh. The chart showed deeper water to the northwest, in the direction of the task force. But in deeper water an air-dropped torp could recover, stabilize, circle, and acquire. He could outwait a plane, staying shallow till it had to leave. The Iranians didn't have enough aircraft to relieve on station; this might be the only operational four-engine they had. But that aircraft was vectoring the surface units in on him. Maybe just the one for now, but there'd be others. Even if some had headed east, into the Gulf of Oman, it wouldn't take long to call them back.

He pounded his thigh, cursing himself. For thinking they'd escaped. For putting his guys at so much risk. If he'd surrendered back at Bandar-e Abbas, they'd be alive. Captives, hostages, pawns in a major international incident, maybe even tortured, but alive.

"Splash," Carpenter called. Vaught straightened. They sat tensely in the shaking dimness till he called again, "Sonobuoy. Dead ahead. Active ping." They could hear that, too, a high-pitched chirp like the ringtone of a cheap phone.

He crossed the aisle into the sonar shack. "Help me out, Rit. Can he hit us? I'm headed for shallower water. On the south side of the Gulf, west of the Fateh field."

The sonarman's frown was pinched by his headphones. "I don't think so. Even if he's got another fish, it'll just plow into the bottom again."

Dan dragged his hands down his cheeks, fighting a premonition of inevitable death and a queer nauseating fuzziness. The whole side of his face hurt; it was swelling from the splinters he'd picked up during the firefight.

Carpenter blinked, gaze floating in space. He whispered, "Passing under the sound source . . . passing astern . . . Sierra One slightly louder, bearing drawing right."

"Speed?"

"Twenty knots by turn count."

Dan searched for umber Bakelite, pressed the key. "Electrical, Control. Slow to five."

"Slow to five," Oberg's disembodied voice whispered back from far away.

"I turned it way down," Carpenter muttered, adjusting a dial, flicking switches in quick succession, listening again. "Still getting those engine sounds. But no more sonobuoys."

"Maybe his last one?"

"Maybe. One thing you might try, Commander."

"Gimme, Rit."

"We're far enough away from the Strait we might have a layer here. It'd be worth checking."

"How?"

The sonarman blinked, as if that had been a stupid question even from an officer. "Run her as close to the surface as you can, then down again. Watch the thermometer. Exterior temperature. Plot it against depth. It'll jump out at you."

"I can do that," Henrickson said from the doorway.

"Great, do that, Monty. Donnie, I want you back on the Shkval."

"If we're gonna die I—"

"We're not going to die," Dan snapped. "And if we are, I want you at work when we do. Get out of here!"

As Henrickson and Vaught conferred Dan paced back and forth, then grabbed the chart and went into the missile-control space forward of Control. He could hear everything in there, including the sonobuoy pinging as it faded astern, but it gave the illusion of being alone. Letting him squeegee his face with a handful of binocular-cleaning paper that came away wringing wet. His headache was blinding. The scrubbers obviously weren't working, or not well enough.

A knock. He glanced up to see Im. "Yeah."

"We have to hide. Lose frigate."

"I agree. But how? We're looking for a layer."

"Maybe no layer. Find hole in bottom."

Dan stopped mopping and focused on the guy. A bona fide littoral sub-mariner. They'd evaded the best in the South Korean navy, right up almost to their goal. "Tell me more."

The Korean made a dip with his hands. "Find deeper spot. Sides mask you from sonar."

Dan nodded; not a tactic you saw in deepwater ASW, but it made sense in an environment like this. He twisted round the partition. "Rit, you fig-ured out how to go active on that set?"

"No sweat, if Monty can tell me what some more of these labels mean. That's the active panel up on the bulkhead."

"Is there a forward-look mode? We need to get a sense of the bottom."

"If I ping, that frigate'll hear us."

"He's still a ways off; ping away. Find us a hole to hide in. I'll send Monty to help."

The sonarman looked doubtful, but nodded.

WHEN Monty had the graph drawn, he sat back and looked it over. Tem-perature on the abscissa, depth on the ordinate. A jog in the line at fifty-two meters evidenced a thermocline, but the slightness of the bend wasn't encouraging.

He'd studied shallow water propagation, but studying it and trying to use it for cover were different animals. Everyone at TAG talked about how hard it would be to find subs in shallow water. But actually aboard a sub in shallow water, he felt like a rat on a billiard table under spot-lights.

He scratched his crotch—the jungle rot had gone away, but the itch hadn't—and wished he wasn't so scared. Ever since they'd climbed into the SDV he'd been terrified, though he thought he'd done a decent job hid-ing it. Still, this was the mission. Oberg acted like only SEALs were really motivated, but Monty didn't think TAG had to take a backseat.

In the sonar compartment Carpenter was watching a screen and mak-ing a plot on a tablet. Monty showed him the graph. He glanced it and grunted. "Not much of one."

"Enough to hide?"

"Depends how good the stack operators are topside. And how lucky we get . . . tell the commander."

Lenson was slumped on the bench behind Vaught, eyes closed, sweat running down his face. They both looked dead. "Dan," Monty said.

"Yeah." He opened his eyes, and Monty showed him the paper. He blinked and cleared his throat. "Rit? What's our bottom depth?"

"Here? Sixty-seven meters."

A shaking hand smoothed the chart. Lenson checked his watch, touched his eye, which lurked deep in inflamed, puffy skin, and slowly made a pencil notation. Monty saw they were headed west, past an island with an oil loading terminal and pipelines leading inland. Beyond it the Gulf opened out, but the depth numbers still weren't encouraging: 75, 88, 68. The deepest parts lay closest to the Iranian coast.

"Come to sixty," Lenson muttered. The planesman didn't react for a second, but then seemed to hear. He shook himself, reached out, pushed the plane controls forward. Then racked them again, forward and back, like someone who wasn't used to a manual transmission trying to make it shift.

DAN tried to focus past the headache, but it was difficult even to see. Heading west, five knots . . . "What's wrong, Vaught?"

"She won't hold depth anymore. Like the planes are locked up, don't want to move."

Dan remembered what Oberg had said about the hydraulics. He felt as if he was in a hydraulic ram himself, being squeezed smaller and smaller, with fewer and fewer options. "Where's that frigate, Rit?"

"Still closing."

"Control, Electrical."

"Control, go."

"Reading zero on aux hydraulic pressure."

"Copy. We've lost the planes up here." Dan pressed the switch again. "You've got to get it back, Teddy. We're not going anywhere without the planes, without the rudder."

"We need time. And somebody back here to translate these schematics for us."

Dan lurched up. Headed for the sonar room, but almost fell before he got there. He clung to the periscope stand. His vision swam. He panted. Got a little strength back, and went on.

Carpenter was hunched over the screen. A curious pattern of numbers lay traced across three sheets of his tablet, which he'd torn out and taped together. "We've got to find someplace to put her down, Rit."

"Might have found a hidey hole." The sonarman tapped the paper. "Down to sixty-plus-some meters. Two hundred yards to either side, it's thirty meters. Looks soft, though. A couple of sharp returns that might be rock, but mostly mud and sand."

"That's not on the chart."

"But it's there. Half a mile back. Bearing zero nine five. Would have called you, but I kept hoping for something deeper."

Dan caught the web of his thumb in his teeth and chewed it. The headache made it nearly impossible to see. He kept wanting to sit down and drift off. Some demon in his brain kept whispering that it didn't matter what they did. He panted, trying to force oxygen into his sluggish blood.

"Losing depth control," Vaught called. "Rising."

"Right rudder," Dan called.

"Losing rudder control."

He hit the bitch box. "Electrical, Control. Teddy: we need hydraulic pressure."

Oberg sounded drugged. "No shit, Commander. But I got to figure what's wrong before I can fix it."

He wanted to give up, sit down, drift off into the peace. He bit painfully at his own flesh. "Then we'll maneuver with the engines. Left motor ahead standard. Right motor stop."

"Port ahead standard, starboard stop, aye."

"Still going up. Passing forty meters."

"Im! Get us heavy. Get that across to him, Monty. Help him out on the ballast control."

He dragged his attention back to the gyrocompass. It was rotating only gradually, ticking off degrees like a roulette wheel coming to rest, but it was rotating. He did the math in a brain that seemed to be only able to light up one room at a time. The others were going dark one after the other. Assume a turning circle of a hundred yards. Half a mile back to the depression. He dragged sweat out of his eyes, then jabbed the inflamed tissue with a fingernail. He nearly screamed, but the world sharpened. "Steady . . . steady on . . . uh, one-zero-zero."

"I'll try, but—"

A thud, then another. Im, flooding the forward and middle groups to counteract their surfaceward drift. The air racketing away down the lines sounded weaker. They were using the last of it. Would they be able to blow the tanks, when the time came to surface? Another faraway clunk as the valves closed. Dan watched the depth gauge. It hovered, then slowly reversed. He blinked back blackness, checking the pencil mark on his chart where Carpenter's valley must be.

"Passing zero nine zero. Rudder doesn't respond."

"Electrical, Control: both ahead one-third."

"Ahead one-third." Sumo, with Oberg muttering in the background.

"Descent rate, one meter per minute," Im announced, too loud. Henrickson made a shushing motion.

"Electrical, Control: starboard ahead standard, port engine stop." Dan checked his watch, let twenty seconds tick past. "All stop." The Hawaiian repeated the order. "Rit, get a ping. See that depression yet?"

"Dead ahead. Two hundred yards."

"Secure active sonar. Flood forward."

Hiss. Thud. A chuckle of water far away. The harsh rapid breathing of frightened men.

A slithering, like a great python winding through a sandy forest. A lurch. A bump. Then scraping, lurching. Stones rattling past. The nose tilting down. His eye was epoxied to the depth gauge. Forty-eight meters. Fifty. They kept sliding, the rattling intensifying. Fifty-two. Fifty-four. Fifty-eight.

The rattling, hissing, and lurching ebbed. Dan stared at the gauge, willing it to keep going down. The higher the walls of this undersea valley rose above them, the less detectable they'd be.

Sixty.

Sixty-two.

The hull rocked and came to rest. He reached up and tapped the gauge. Something creaked up forward. The needle rested.

Sixty-three meters.

Utter silence, save for a faint crepitation as the live load of the sub's steel transferred from the ballast tanks to the keel.

A hum from all around. Then a rapid, continuous beat. The whish, whish they'd heard twice before, as the frigate had gone over.

They crouched in the dimness. Not a man spoke. Im rubbed his stomach, squinting. Vaught slumped, staring at the useless controls. Only Carpenter, frowning as he listened, seemed still to have something useful to do. "It's that prick with the nicked blade," he whispered.

Sumo and Oberg slipped into the control room and hung from piperuns on the overhead, ears cocked.

A ping slashed across the hull. Every man winced, but no one moved otherwise. The sound repeated itself. It traveled from ahead to overhead and dwelt, growing louder. Dan took one deep breath after another, trying not to scream.

The sound dwindled. It receded aft.

"Moving away," Carpenter muttered.

They stirred, exhaled, looked blankly at one another. Dan cleared his throat. "Didn't see us. Not on that pass. Maybe we'll get lucky."

"So what's the plan?"

"Wait for local sunset, by the clock. Then surface and pretend we're a fishing dhow headed for home."

"Headed where? The task force?"

"No," Dan whispered. "Straight in to Abu Dhabi. If the Iranians don't like it, at least we'll get everybody off alive. But we're not out of this yet. We've got to get the hydraulic system back, get steering and depth control, before we go up. Find where they stow these oxygen candles and light more of them. And keep working on the Shkval."

They sat for a few moments, each alone with his thoughts. Then slowly hoisted themselves to their feet, and got to work.

25

Twelve Hours Later

TEDDY rolled out from under the pump, too exhausted even to curse. The fatigue was weird, he'd never felt anything like it, even at basic underwater demolition school. His chest felt like it was in a vise, and he had to stop too often to get his breath.

He and Kaulukukui had been on the hydraulics for hours. First finding what was wrong—a stoppage somewhere upstream of the main supply and return manifolds. Locating what turned out to be a clogged filter, then figuring how to get it out. Cleaning and replacing it, recharging the pressure tanks, then getting wise too late that they should have closed the valves above and below the housing. With them open while they were cleaning the filter, air had leaked into the lines.

With Monty on the manual, they'd had to open the bleeder valves one at a time, first in the power generation system, then through the whole ship, tracing each line and cracking each valve, which were almost always snugged tight against the overhead, and venting air till they got a solid squirt of oil. Which was why he reeked of hydraulic fluid, old bilge water, and sweat.

"So that's it?" Monty asked him.

"Find out in a minute. If the accumulator charges and everything downstream cycles. If it doesn't, there's more air in the system we didn't find."

Behind him Monty closed the manual, which he'd been translating, sentence by sentence, to the men turning the wrenches. He caught a cough in his fist, glancing at the overhead, which was dripping with condensation. Then shuddered suddenly. He'd been doing that for a couple of hours now, his rib muscles and long muscles bunching and ticcing.

They'd been at it the whole time they'd been on the bottom, with two short breaks in the control room for sandwiches, hot strong tea, and tense discussions of air compressors, pneumatic-hydraulic accumulators, and battery cooling systems. Fortunately they'd found more oxygen candles in the after torpedo room. Along with a rack of bulkhead clips, half of which were filled with machined aluminum cylinders thirty inches long and seven inches in diameter, painted chrome yellow with black stripes.

Opening one cautiously, Kaulukukui had found it lined with soft rubber. A smaller, sheet-metal cylinder nestled inside. And inside that, when he pried the spring-loaded top open, a stack of soft olive-green biscuits. Since the rack was beside an ejection tube, they'd agreed the green cakes were some kind of bubble-type countermeasures.

They'd lit off the candles, and for a while it had helped. But the steadily worsening headaches, their irritability and stupidity and sluggishness were due not to lack of oxygen, but too much carbon dioxide. Unfortunately they hadn't found any carbon dioxide absorbent at all. They'd traced out the air circulation and found where the sodalime canister should have gone, but there was none there or in any of the storerooms. Either they'd never been put aboard, or had all been used up and not replaced.

Monty coughed again, his heart racing and fluttering. Unfortunately what killed people in closed spaces was usually not oxygen deprivation but carbon dioxide poisoning. Which they were all on the edge of—the big Hawaiian worst of all, for some reason. Kaulukukui's face was flushed, his hands twitched uncontrollably, and when he had to lift something he all but choked. Monty felt disoriented and panicky. Although it was hard to separate out symptomatic panic from the very real dread he felt whenever Carpenter would whisper that another ship was approaching.

If they stayed down much longer they could look forward to convulsions, unconsciousness, death, no matter how much oxygen they generated. They had to flush the boat, get fresh air in here, or they were finished.

"Okay." Teddy wiped his hands on a piece of rag. "I'm gonna go forward, see if this fucking works."

Sixty feet forward, Dan pressed the button that controlled the periscope. With the faintest whir the steel column began to move. It faltered halfway up, then smoothed out. Of course, he couldn't see anything, the objective was still many fathoms down, but still he smiled. "Seems to work."

Teddy fitted a wrench to the vent fitting on the unit cylinder on the 'scope. A jet of froth spurted. When it turned to fluid he twisted it shut again. "Good to go. V-Dag, give the rudder a shot. Full cycle, all the way left, right, back to centerline."

"Where's Sumo?" Dan asked him. They were all whispering.

"One of the torpedo room bunks. I told him to get next to one of those rebreathers and lie down. Got her cycled? Do the planes next. I'm gonna go back aft. Monty, what have I got left to bleed?"

"Control cylinders, change valve, telemotor pump, then all the lines from the telemotor to the control cylinders. 'Cycle again and repeat until no further air appears.' Remember the change valve has to be set to this word—"

"You show me, I'll set it."

They headed aft. Dan, left with Vaught and Carpenter and Im, cycled the scope again. It worked perfectly.

He leaned against it, waiting for his heart to stop palpitating, thighs to stop shuddering. The headache was constant now, a black wedge driven between the hemispheres of his brain. He made himself review the situation step by step. No one topside: the frigate's screws had faded to northward hours before. Since then they'd heard only the distant rumble of tankers, passing to the north and east, and now and then the tapping whine of the motorized dhows ubiquitous in the Gulf, fishing and trading from Oman to Iraq. Pneumatics and now hydraulics back on line. He checked his watch—2034 local, the last light should be fading into the dusky rose of a Hormuz sunset—and cleared his throat. "Rit. You sure there's no other way to get this stuff out of the air?"

Carpenter leaned slowly out of the sonar shack. "What?"

"I said, no other way to purge CO_2?"

"We been through this, Commander. If we don't have scrubbers, got to ventilate the boat. That'll take fifteen minutes, if we have the blowers lined up when we break the surface, pop both hatches, and blow from forward to aft."

"Okay, we pop the hatches and start the blowers. But not the diesels."

"Don't have the hands to run them. Even if we got 'em started." Carpenter micrometered a dial, attention back on the trickle of sound that was their only link to a larger world.

"Certain we're clear? Up top?"

"Haven't heard anything the last couple hours . . . but that layer inhibits transmission both ways. We're down in this hole, we can't hear them, either."

Dan panted but it didn't help; his eyelids kept drifting closed; it was hard to inflate his lungs, as if invisible belts constricted them. "Well, we'll try it, once they've got everything lined up and tested. Keep a three-sixty watch. If you hear anything, let me know."

Absorbed, remote, the sonarman nodded.

*   *   *

TWO hours later Dan nodded to a stoned-looking Im at the ballast controls. He didn't need to say anything, just nod. They all knew what he meant.

Carpenter had done one last search, all round the compass, and said they were clear.

There was still work to do. The water was still rising in the bilge. But the air was even more fouled, even more unbreathable. They couldn't stay down any longer.

They were going up. Or trying to.

Through the black pickle that soured his brain he worried whether they had enough high-pressure air to blow, and whether the suction of the silt they lay on would let them go. The only plan he had in that case was for the team to free-ascend from the aft escape trunk, marginally closer to the surface than the forward one, since they lay nose-down. Sixty-three meters. Over two hundred feet. Sumo and Oberg might make it, but he didn't think the rest of the team would.

He just wanted to get everybody home. To hell with the mission. Maybe it had been too big a bite from the start.

A rushing hiss walked away, making the hull crackle and tremble. Dan pressed the lever on the bitch box. Murmured, "Stand by motors." A double click answered.

Im stood by the ballast control panel, staring into space. Vaught sat rigid at the helm, a bucket beside him; he'd vomited twice. The air howled in its bonds, streaming out of the banks into the ballast tanks. Dan watched the needle drop with absolute concentration. If they didn't have enough air to blow . . . but the Russians built their subs with a lot of reserve buoyancy . . . he pushed the fear away. In a few seconds, they'd know.

A popping bang from forward. They all three looked instantly to the depth meter, but it didn't stir. "Planes full up," Dan muttered, just to be saying something. Like a robot, Vaught pushed the control levers forward. Wenck was at the forward hatch, Oberg would take the after one. As soon as the water rolled off the deck they'd undog and throw them open, and Sumo would punch the blower switches.

Im hit the last button and air richocheted away. "Full rise," Vaught muttered.

The bow stirred. Sooner than he'd expected, and he grinned. On their way up! Carpenter leaned out, smiling, too. Suddenly they were all smiling, especially when the needle jumped suddenly, all at once, to sixty, and the hull rolled around them and went slowly and not much but definitely nose up.

"Lifting," Dan said out loud. He hit the button. "Ahead one-third," and snapped off and said to Vaught, "Two seven zero, let's get outside this Iranian Advisory Zone on the chart."

The helmsman repeated it in a stronger voice than Dan had heard from him in some time. He looked up, yearning for the night air that would soon be blowing through the ship. Never had he realized how much he loved air, how gratefully his lungs would draw in that first cool fresh breath. Even the powdered dust that misted it; he looked forward eagerly to crunching it in his teeth.

The needle ticked past fifty meters. Dan glanced at Im, but the Korean was already adjusting, playing the valves like an organist to counteract the increased buoyancy as they rose. On the surface there'd be a froth, a white eruption of bubbles, but at night there would be no eye to see beneath the fuzzy stars. He'd checked the almanac in the chart room and moonrise wasn't till 0330.

Still rising . . . forty meters. No one budged. Motors hummed softly aft. Dan studied the chart again, walked his fingers across it for the hundredth time. They'd covered a hundred miles out of Bandar Abbas. It couldn't be more than two hundred more to the Task Force. An F-18 could cover that in twenty minutes. Oberg had the SatCom ready below the after hatch. As soon as it was open, he'd climb on deck and squirt the message off.

So it was over . . . all but offloading the weapon, the documents, the tapes, and let Chone and Pirrell unravel whatever secret it held. He stretched, telling his pattering heart and laboring lungs it would only be a few more minutes.

"Thirty meters," Im muttered. He cast Dan a questioning glance, then looked at the periscope. Dan hit the button and it rose silently, the remaining bulbs of the emergency lighting gleaming off the stainless barrel like distant suns through a dusty nebula.

"Steady at 'scope depth?" Vaught muttered, hands on the plane control.

Dan was about to say no, go right on up, but a last reservation made him hesitate. "Uh, right. Ten meters, periscope depth, I'll check around. Then we'll surface and blow."

He bent to the eyepiece, cupping his palms around it. Nothing but black. Black.

Then a different texture of black. "Ten meters," Vaught murmured.

He had visual. A far-off light, a low star, maybe, or a working light on an oil platform. He checked the bearing, confirmed Vaught was headed west by northwest, and set his feet and began clicking around. To the north, nothing. The objective was too low to pick up the mountains of the Hormozgan, and no dhows or tankers seemed to be out tonight. He panned right, past more darkness, then picked up a distant white beacon that flashed three times about every fifteen seconds.

The chart showed Jazireh-ye Farur, Farur Island, with a triple flash every seventeen seconds. He took a careful bearing and memorized it, then continued right. Another dim, low light. More stars. Then a scattering of peach-tinted sodium vapors bled radiance high into the nighttime sky. The SiC or SiD oil fields, he guessed.

"Check out around one five zero," Carpenter muttered from the sonar.

"What's that?"

"Don't know. Pump of some kind."

"That's what I was looking at a second ago. An oil and gas field. Probably compressor equipment." Dan swung to the bearing nonetheless. A wave chopped over the top of the objective. When it subsided he frowned.

"What you see?" said Im.

"A shadow . . . an island? An abandoned platform?"

Just as he realized it was a ship, hove to with lights out, a dull red flicker lit its deck. He screamed, "Right hard rudder. Ahead flank! Down planes, go deep, go deep!"

THE explosion seemed to Obie much louder than any of the previous ones, a terrific crack that slammed him into the panel and whipsawed the hull up and down. Even Kaulukukui barked in surprise where he lay on the deckplates, a Draeger under his head and the mouthpiece between his lips.

"You hangin' in there, buddy?"

"Fuck you," the Hawaiian mumbled around rubber.

Metal clanged off and struck again as it tumbled aft. Seconds later two more detonations clanged, but muffled, distant, below them.

Teddy jogged all the way aft, then back, searching the overhead; that first one had sounded like a hit. There was crap all over the deck, mugs, clipboards thrown out of lockers, more glass from more busted light domes, but he didn't see any water. Yet. He came back to the brown box near the compressors and keyed it feeling as if his lungs had turned to concrete and someone had sucked all the brains out of his skull through his nose. Everything went black, red, then black again. He coughed and tried to get enough air to not keel over. "Control, Electrical. Something hit us a hard lick back here."

Carpenter: "That fucking frigate's back. Or I should say, never left.

Clobbered us as we came up through the layer. Couldn't hear it before, same reason it couldn't hear us."

Lenson cut in. "Damage report? Any leaks back there?"

"No, but I heard something tear away to port. Piece of the superstructure?"

"Probably the port plane. We're getting a hangup when we cycle, and pulling to that side. Can you check the rams?"

He said yeah, and clicked off, crawling on all fours aft, pointing his flashlight over all the ram gear. Found another brown box. "Don't see anything wrong back here. The hydraulics are still go."

"Then the plane's shot. One of the Limbos must have hit it."

"Better than the hull, drown us all."

"Still giving me flank power, Teddy?"

"Sure am, Dan. But those needles are just about at zero."

Dead silence, then the click of the intercom going off. Then back on again. "He's coming in for a reattack. Give me all the juice you can, Teddy. Find a rebreather and put it on. Then go aft and load up those countermeasures."

DAN hung on the 'scope, incoherently cursing whoever commanded that dark frigate. That commander had lost his quarry, but he hadn't given up. Instead he'd lingered, placing himself exactly where any sound from his own pumps and rotating machinery would be masked by the racket the oil-field pumps and compressors made. Crap! Why did he have to get one of the smart Iranians? Cursing himself, too, at the same time, for not just surfacing. Taking the hits, maybe losing the boat, but at least, getting his guys out and overboard. They'd have air to breathe at least. Not this murky miasma that was killing them.

Someone was calling him. A loud voice, urgent tones. He panted, trying to bellows embering neurons back into flame, to pierce the spinning blackness with a steadily dulling understanding.

"Commander! Planes down, passing thirty meters. Rudder still hard right."

"Full ahead."

"We're at full ahead, both motors."

Im said urgently, grabbing his sleeve, "Countermeasure!"

Dan shook off his fingers. "I've got it. Just watch our fucking bubble." He staggered to the box that held the candles, bent over it, sucking the smoky hot air coming up. Coughed, and rasped hoarsely, "Steady on one-seven-zero."

Vaught repeated it, but his voice was going high again. Dan wondered when they'd all start screaming. He couldn't imagine going through this for days at a time, the way U-boat crews had, or Pacific Fleet submariners in World War Two. On the other hand, if they could just get some decent air . . . he swung his yawing attention back to keeping them from being blown out of the water. Any second now those fucking mortars would be reloaded, ready to fire another salvo.

"Keep her steady. Steady . . . full back emergency!"

"Full back emergency!"

"Electrical, Control: spit two countermeasures, close together as you can!"

As soon as Oberg rogered Dan told Im, half by pantomime, that he wanted sixty meters, wanted their belly on the bottom. The valves thudded hollowly as they slammed shut. Air wheezed in the pipes, sounding nearly exhausted. He counted seconds, then snapped, "Left hard rudder. Port back one third, starboard all ahead flank. Come to zero three zero."

A ping rang through the water, shivering the hairs up on the back of his neck. It sounded different when you were the one being pinged on, when that tentacle of high-frequency sound searched out through the dark for you. He'd never think about the men he hunted quite the same way again.

SEVENTY feet aft, Teddy slogged along as if in a swamp up to his waist. His vision was strobing on and off. It was like the last day at BUD/S, after being hosed over and stressed for five days. When the only thing that kept you going was blind hate, the stupidity of the determined, and an absolute need not to let your buddies down. Each breath burned like flame. Each respiration made him feel like puking. But still he got one hand on the clips that held the canisters, then the other.

He threw the heavy toggled lever on the ejector and laid the cylinder in the port. Or tried to, but it wouldn't fit. He stared at it for several seconds. Then turned it upside down and dumped the sheet-metal can inside out, holding it together with both hands. He forced it into the breech and wrenched it closed.

Or thought he did. Because just then he must have blacked out. He didn't know for how long, just that he came to lying under the ejector. He crawled up onto it again, teeth fastened in his lip, and grabbed the wire. Started to pull. Then stopped. Looked again.

"Is this fucking thing closed?"

Nobody answered, but he thought it definitely didn't look closed. Did it matter? Maybe. If he didn't want to flood the whole fucking compartment. He started to black out again, but bent his head and concentrated on not going.

Then he lifted his head and with every bit of strength he had left, slammed the breech shut with the heel of his hand. He spun the wheel that opened the outer door. Water began to trickle, then spray. It felt good on his sweating face. He grabbed the dangling wire and yanked.

ALL the way forward, under a dangling light, Donnie Wenck rubbed sweat and tears off his face. He couldn't stop the tears. They ran down his cheeks and now there was a little rainstorm all over the torpedo and a puddle in the guidance compartment they'd finally located deep inside the weapon.

"Gee, Donnie, give it a rest," Henrickson said.

"I can't help it. I don't wanna die. And I keep feeling like we're gonna."

"It's just the air," the older TAG teamer told him.

Donnie glanced at him out of the corners of his eyes. "You think?"

"Sure. Makes me feel the same way. How about that plug? What're you getting out of it?"

"Uh, this is the signal processor. I'm using the control unit to inject like single event upsets through direct access to the memory. SEUs to the DMA, you know? And seeing what outputs I get."

"So—?"

"Well, I'm not getting much. Takes a long time to map. But I'm starting to think this unit up here is where it's coming from, you know?"

Henrickson pulled the light closer. "This board here? And the other one, the other side?"

"Yeah. Uh-huh."

"Then let's finish getting it apart, okay? Sooner we can do that, the sooner we can get back to Control with the rest of the team."

Donnie knew it didn't make any difference really, being one more deck up, if the whole hull imploded. But if that was what Henrickson wanted . . . He tried to steady his fingers as he laid the control unit aside, aimed the camera, and snapped off another high-res shot of the interior of the weapon. "Okay, Monty. Give me that screwdriver. Here we go."

DAN grabbed a handhold instants before they slammed into the bottom again. Im was swearing in Korean at the ballast panel, a white-faced

Vaught had the planes on full rise, but they still crashed into it nearly as hard as the very first time they'd dived. He bit back a reproach; they were doing the best they could, with an unfamiliar boat and degraded control surfaces. "Electrical, Control: damage back there?"

"I hear something funny back aft."

"Sierra One, three zero five, drawing left."

Carpenter, calling bearings to the frigate. Dan wished he had decent target-motion analysis. There should be a whole crew plotting bearings and calculating ranges to the enemy. But he didn't, and he couldn't raise the scope again; he had to guess and infer, and it was harder and harder just to stay conscious. "Don't overcorrect, Vaught," he snapped, more angrily than he'd meant to. "We don't have the depth to play with here. If we pop out we'll get another mortar salvo, probably shells, too."

Vaught twisted, eyes blazing, but without taking his hands off the controls. "Doing my fucking best here, Commander. Why don't you show me how it's done?"

"I know you are. Sorry, goddamn it—I know you are."

"We've got fucking damage here, and you're telling me—"

"Three zero zero, still drawing left."

A thunder in the deep, but not near. Not near. Still, it silenced them. "Explosion effects, bearing one eight five," the sonarman called.

Nearly dead astern. The frigate was pinging and firing on the knuckle they'd left by briefly going astern, and the false contact from the hydrogen bubbles the countermeasure was generating. Good for the moment, as they crept away, but soon that mirage would evaporate. He had to be far away by then, or hidden in some way, or they were dead meat. But they were making more noise than ever, and despite Im's and Vaught's frantic efforts, losing depth control.

He never felt himself going, but there he was lying on the deckplates with somebody slapping his face. Im, dark eyes concerned. "You okay? You okay?"

"Uh—sort of."

"Here, take."

Something rubbery was forced between his lips. It tasted of decay. He gagged, then took a reluctant breath. A second.

The mists thinned, and he sat up. How long had he been out? Long enough for the others to be wearing rebreathers, too. He hadn't wanted to go to them, they made it hard to move and communicate, but apparently the choice had been made. He pointed aft, then to the rebreather; Im nodded. "Them, too," he said, and replaced his mouthpiece.

He remembered suddenly what threatened, and tottered upright and handed himself along into Sonar. The familiar triple waterfalls rolled on the screen. Carpenter pointed to a lighter band on the upper one. "Ill coming lef'," he mumbled around the mouthpiece. "Urn coun's ay own, 'ough. E's jus' coas'ing through the wa'er."

"He acquired us yet?"

"He's coming our way, but he's not headed right at us and he's not pinging in localization mode. So I'd say, not yet."

Dan leaned into the scope, looking for anything that would indicate an irregularity on the bottom, before he remembered: He couldn't see what the seabed looked like without pinging, and if he pinged, his enemy had him. Whoever his adversary was, he was sharp. He'd lost contact, but regained. Lost them again; hidden, waited, and pounced. By now he must have realized he'd fired on a specter, but that his real quarry was still somewhere nearby. Both hunter and hunted ghosting through the water as they listened with all their skill.

Okay, how to hide? The gas he was sucking tasted foul, but his brain was rekindling. He couldn't find another valley, but might be able to hide another way. Actually, the same way the frigate had. He leaned out into Control and tongued the mouthpiece out. "Ten degrees right rudder. Come slowly around and steady on one-seven-zero." He scribbled *three knots* on a scrap and handed it to Im and pointed aft. The Korean left, treading cautiously around the shattered glass, and Dan saw he'd taken his bloodied socks off and was in bare feet.

He leaned at the little standup desk at the watch officer's station, watching the heading indicator start to tick around. It reoriented with glacial deliberation, but that was okay. They were skating a circle a mile in diameter, gradually bringing the sub's course round to nearly due south. The frigate was headed east, as best he could tell. *K-79* would be crossing his bow, beam on, but as long as he hadn't picked them up yet that didn't matter.

To the south lay the enormous Fateh oil field, managed by Conoco. Dan had sailed past dozens of times on previous deployments. By day, huge supertankers lay alongside the terminal, waterlines gradually rising as they sucked aboard millions of barrels of "Dubai, 32.5 API," while cranes swung and dipped on the maintenance platforms and helicopters and service boats shuttled back and forth from the mainland. By night hundreds of strobes and marker buoys flashed warning signals visible halfway to Hormuz. But the wellheads themselves, and the lines that carried crude to the massive subsea holding tanks known locally as the "Pyramids of

Dubai," were invisible beneath the blue-brown, dust-frosted chop of the mid-southern Gulf.

Fateh meant two things: noise, which was good, and a lot of clutter on the sea floor, which wasn't. But if he could get there without being detected, he could bottom out again and maybe the guy would get tired this time and leave.

He checked the chart again. The oil field itself was an isosceles thirty miles long, with the shallow point in twenty-three-meter depths and the base out near the middle of the Gulf, where it was about fifty meters. Which meant nowhere deep enough they could take on much of a down angle without sticking the stern out of the water, mooning anyone who was looking for them at the same time they exposed the screws and lost propulsion.

"Sierra One bearing steady. Turn count increasing."

Dan realized that during the attack he'd lost track of his dead reckoning. He'd gotten a single line of position, the bearing on Farur Island he'd memorized from the 'scope. He sketched that in on the chart and tried to reconstruct their movements since.

He got a position two miles, more or less, north of the edge of the oil field. Much closer, and he'd be inside it. He didn't want that. He jerked his mouthpiece out again. "Farther left. Steady one eight zero," he told Vaught, who nodded instead of acknowledging aloud. "Rit, what's he doing now?"

"Turn count bumped up again. Still in search mode though."

"Range?"

"Gimme a TMA team and I'll tell you. But he's closing, based on the doppler."

"Still pointed at us?"

"Hard to tell."

When he peered in Carpenter was slumped into the console. His breathing bag inflated slowly, then deflated. His slinged arm was wedged against an equipment cabinet. He was still watching the screen, though. Except for short breaks, he'd been at it for fifteen hours straight.

As had they all, on top of a sleepless night, a lockout, the transit in, and a firefight. Sandwiches and hot tea helped, but men needed rest. A boat needed maintenance, lubrication, repairs. They were running out of everything: time, air, power, and bright ideas.

Give up? The temptation nagged, as it had since they'd cast off. He shook it off once more, but had an uneasy feeling the time was coming when they'd have to look for some white cloth to wave.

"Aircraft effects." After a moment Carpenter added, "To the north."

"Fuck," Dan muttered into the mouthpiece. Just what they needed. He sucked several more breaths, wondering if the thing really was regenerating what he was breathing. After the first few mouthfuls, the lift had gone away. He touched the button on the intercom and put his lips next to it. "Electrical: increase speed to five."

"Five," Oberg whispered back. "They still humpin' our ass, up there?"

"Still on it. Keep it quiet."

"Faster we go, more racket this thing makes. Something's loose, banging away."

He didn't answer, clicked off. Gave Vaught a new course, to parallel the edge of the oil field. His injured eye burned as if someone had thrown acid in it. Rubbing it felt like he was grinding in powdered glass. He tried to focus on the chart. If they could only get over to where the machinery sounds were coming from, which seemed to be the western side of Fateh—

"Screw effects, twin screws, warship type, bearing zero four three true. Designate contact Sierra Two." Dan had just registered this when Carpenter added, voice flat, "Sierra One commences short-range pinging."

Vaught and Im were watching him. He stood frozen at the little plywood watch desk, like where the hostess stood at a Ruby Tuesday's. His mind was an erased blackboard. *What now*, he asked it, and got nothing back. Nowhere to go. Nowhere to hide. And the hunters were closing in.

"Splash! Starboard side!"

He barely had time to whip his head around when Carpenter added, "High-speed screws. Torpedo! Torpedo incoming, starboard beam!"

This time they could hear it, a vibrato snarl that sounded like nothing so much as a daiquiri blender churning ice flakes and rum at full speed. Or at least that was the picture and even the fucking *taste* his memory decided to furnish him at this crucial moment. Im started forward, then halted. Vaught turned a pasty-white, shocked face from the gyro repeater. Wenck was shouting something from forward.

And for that moment Dan froze, unable to think. Or, more accurately, unable to imagine any action that might lessen the overwhelming odds they were in the last seconds of their lives. Turning toward wouldn't help. Sprinting away would just run them into the oil field.

"Torpedo in homing mode!"

He'd hoped this one would head for the bottom the way the last had. But it was running. Hot and straight, right for them. Their eyes followed him, waiting for him to save them. The rubber mouthpiece swelled like some malignant growth bent on choking him.

Then he understood. The only chance. Maybe suicide, but the only move he had left. "Left hard rudder," he snapped, and hit the bitch box; noise didn't matter now. "All ahead flank emergency. Flank emergency!"

The deck tilted as they came around. He gripped plywood so hard his hands cramped.

The oil field lay ahead. Wells. Compressors. Pipelines. Valve trees. Enormous undersea tanks filled with millions of cubic feet of low-sulfur crude. A great submerged junkyard full of traps and obstacles, into which no prudent captain would even think of tiptoeing.

He only hoped they made it before the hound of hell behind them caught up.

26

The Fateh Oil Field

HE let Oberg run all out for three minutes, then four, heart slamming, terrified at what he was doing, but looking at no downside given what was on their tail and closing fast. The whine behind them climbed into a shriek that drilled through steel into the ears, into the skull, like those African insects that bored through your inner ear into your brain. He glanced at the knotmeter, then dragged the rebreather mouthpiece out and hit the brown box again. "Teddy, can't we go faster? I'm only seeing ten up here, we were doing like sixteen before—"

"That's when we were fresh out of the box. One of our battery banks is dead. And the other's going fast." The SEAL sounded tired. "I've got it red-lined, we just don't have much left back here."

He double-clicked, because he couldn't think of anything to say back. Then triggered it again. "Fire two more countermeasures, Teddy. Fast as you can kick 'em out."

"That'll leave us empty racks."

"Just kick 'em out. Right now!"

He gave him thirty seconds, every muscle tensed as the sound of the incoming torpedo built, then snapped to Vaught, "Left hard rudder." Feeling like a blind man running fill tilt into a minefield. They had to be inside Fateh now, and he had no idea what was around, ahead; they could be headed for pipelines, wellheads, abandoned oil platform supports, a whole junkyard of rusty steel to tear their planes off, impale them, maybe even penetrate the pressure hill, going at this speed.

But a higher-pitched, nearly supersonic note rang through the hull now. "Homer going active," Carpenter sang out, and even through his terror Dan noted how carefree the sonarman sounded. As if this was scary but fun, like skydiving or bungee-jumping. As for himself, his skin was trying to crawl off his body and hide. But his mind was standing outside that skin, observing. Unafraid. Almost, unconcerned, as if it was not and never had really been part of the body, the individual, called Dan Lenson. He heard the detachment in his own voice. "Rit, can that thing home on our active transmissions?"

"Not anymore. It's tuned to its own pulses now."

"Then go active. See what's out ahead, short range."

The keening whalesong of K-79's sonar cried out. Simultaneously with it came a heavy, rocking bang from dead aft. For a second Dan thought the torpedo had hit them, but it hadn't been as violent a jolt as he'd expected.

"Torpedo explosion astern," Carpenter reported. Then, louder, "Obstacle dead ahead, one hundred meters."

"Hard a-starboard," Dan snapped. He gave up on the mouthpiece and let it dangle on his chest. "Vaught! Starboard!"

"Right hard rudder!"

"Anything out on that bearing, Rit?"

"Hard to say—scattered returns—maybe five hundred clear yards on zero eight zero. No, wait—make it two zero zero."

"Continue right to two zero zero. Electrical, Control: slow to one-third, turns for four knots."

Oberg acknowledged. Dan wiped his forehead, wondering what had set off the torpedo. The countermeasures might have decoyed it, but they shouldn't have set it off. It must have hit something, but he had no idea what.

Which meant there were more obstacles out here than the one they'd narrowly missed. He hit the brown box again. "Slow to two knots, Teddy, two knots."

Im was gesturing, pointing to his mouth and the breathing gear. Dan nodded and was sucking rubber again when a hideous screeching began up forward. The deck sloped to port and shuddered. He shouted to Vaught for right rudder, to get the screws out of the path of whatever they were dragging over. The screeching intensified as it moved back toward the control room, then passed down the side, grating like tungsten carbide claws, until it trailed off. "Back to two zero zero," he ordered. "Rit, did you see that?"

"I secured after the ping. They can still hear us in here."

"But will they come in after us?"

He leaned in, but Carpenter didn't answer. The pudgy sonarman was staring at the waterfall, turning a dial in increments too small even to see.

RIT had the hang of this gear now. It wasn't too different from what he'd learned on, back aboard the old *Bonefish*. The lower band of the waterfall display showed a strong signal at 3000 hertz with overtones at 50 he figured was some kind of electric motor. Most electrical power in the Mideast operated at that frequency. It was coming from 190 true or 340 relative. When he panned around he got two other sources close to that freq off to port.

His arm jabbed, making him gasp. Whenever he moved something sharp, must be the ends of the busted bone, rubbed together. It *really* hurt then. His jaw ached from clenching his teeth, to keep from howling.

What in hell was Lenson doing, taking them into an oil field? Rit could hear pumps and motors, but if there was an abandoned platform out here, salvaged down to the water line and then left, it would be invisible unless he pinged, and not all that obvious even if he did—the reverb was savage in water this shallow. Even pinging at reduced power and high frequency he couldn't make out much beyond five hundred yards away. By the sound of it, whatever they'd just hit had come within a couple of feet of taking off the starboard plane. They already had one damaged plane; break another and they wouldn't be able to hold depth.

On the other hand, it might be a smart move. No sane sub commander would come in here.

But no sane destroyer commander would, either.

He hoped the Iranians were saner than Lenson.

He cranked the head around to scan aft and found he'd lost the frigate in the baffles. He went the rest of the way around and heard a *put put put* out around three three zero that sounded obscurely familiar. He'd heard it before. What was it?

He took out his mouthpiece. "Helicopter at three three zero."

The Skipper gave him a grunt but didn't look in. Rit watched the doorway for a second, wondering what was going on out there, then looked back at the set.

Being an enlisted dude meant you never got the big picture. He'd been what the nukes called a "coner," somebody who worked in the front end of the boat, and that was even worse. You not only didn't know what the skipper knew about the mission, nor what the officers knew, you didn't know what the nukes knew, either, which meant you just about lived in the sonar shack and picked up what you could on your own. And the scuttlebutt grew in the dark like magic mushrooms.

Once they'd gone into the Sea of Okhotsk to try to find *Threadfin* when she hadn't reported back from a special mission. (Years later he'd read Jay Harper, the master spy, had been selling intelligence on the patrols.) They'd crept deep into that remote sea, running ultra silent because the Soviets had their own listening system on the bottom, and no one had told the sonarmen what they were supposed to be listening for. Which he'd always thought was stupid. How could they look for a missing boat if they didn't know it was missing?

But that was the way the Navy operated. And he wasn't in the Navy anymore.

Only if he was out, what was he doing in front of a sonar stack, sucking rubber at 18 percent O_2 and wondering if the guy in charge had any idea what he was doing?

Yeah, you managed this real good, he told himself. You fucking stiff. Well, at least he was getting laid more often than on active duty. And paid better, too. If he lived to spend it—

"Update, Sierra One? Still got that frigate?"

"In the baffles. Want me to check him out, give me a fifteen degree yaw to port."

"Is it clear there?"

"I think. Mushy as hell, though. Just tell Im to stay as close to the surface as he can."

The gyro indicator on the bulkhead whirred. He waited till the baffles were clear and checked.

"Got him?"

He listened to the thrum of pumps, the drone of reduction gears, the *chuk-chuk-chuk* of that damaged blade going around. The same asshole who'd almost sunk them twice before. He tongued the mouthpiece out. "Turn count low . . . going real slow . . . steady bearing, high-freq ping mode . . . the son of a bitch's coming in after us." He yelled, "Another set of frigate screws farther out, left fifteen degrees, higher turn count, down doppler."

Wherever Lenson was taking them, that was one thing you learned bone-deep in Rickover's Navy: to trust the guys beside you, and above you, and below you, even if you didn't know what they were doing or even what the mission was. Trust they knew what they were doing, and that if you did your best, you'd all make it out of whatever shit you were in, alive.

The ship comes first. Every smokeboat sailor learned that, back in the day. If she made it, you would too.

He tried not to think about the fact that, as far as he knew, Lenson had never conned a submarine before.

DAN leaned on the watchstander's desk, sucking stale air and trying to think. *Think*, goddamn it! His hands shook with frustrated rage.

That fucking frigate. The one with the nicked prop. He'd broken contact how many times now, three? Every time, the bastard had locked on again.

And now was following him into the maritime equivalent of an uncharted reef.

Who *was* this bastard? From the Shah's old navy, trained in Norfolk or San Diego or Newport? Or a homegrown fanatic with fantastic luck and a death wish? He didn't know. But obviously, someone as committed to getting him as Dan was to escaping.

Only the guy above had an operating ship, a full crew, plenty of fuel, air support, even helicopters now. They could bracket *K-79* and localize her and just wait for Dan to run out of air, run out of charge, run out of determination. Crack, and come up.

"I gotta whiz," Vaught said.

"I got it," Dan said, flinching. "What are you on, again? Oh yeah, two zero zero."

"Coming back off the clear-baffle yaw."

"Right, right." He swung his leg over the butt-polished bench seat as Vaught swung off. Drops of moisture speckled the brown leather. He hoped it was just sweat. "Rit, where's that helicopter? Steady, or moving?"

"Helo effects steady, bearing zero eight zero."

To port. Where he'd hoped he'd be able to go, eventually, slice through the sharp angle of the oil field and come out headed south or southeast. He wouldn't be headed the direction he really wanted, toward the Task Force, but he could no longer go where he chose. Like a king in the last stages of a chess game, the only moves remaining to him were to escape imminent destruction. When they were exhausted, it would be checkmate. *Shah mat.* That was Persian, wasn't it? King Dead. A finger on his crown, toppling him. "What's he doing out there, Rit? Can you tell?"

"Hovering. Could be dipping?"

"No pings?"

"No, but if he can hear us at all, he's got a line of bearing. Then another line of bearing from the frigate would give him enough to—"

BLAM.

This explosion was louder than any of the others, like a lightning bolt striking a power transformer. The shock wave skewered pain up his spine and knocked his chin into his chest. If he'd been speaking he would have bitten through his tongue. The aftershocks belled and wowed away through the hull like a saw struck with a mallet. Alarms went off all over the boat, warbling and beeping like a plague of electronic locusts. The lights went out and all they had were automatic battle lanterns, and not many of those, just jaundiced beams shafting around the space.

Dan fought the controls, too terrified even to curse. The explosion had shoved the entire boat toward the bottom, the way a full salvo fired abeam skates even a battleship sideways in the water. They were gaining depth too fast, considering how little clearance they must already have between keel and seabed. He pulled back on the planes, bowed like a rower, as if he could haul her up by sheer will. He came right instinctively, pulling the rudder hard over despite not knowing what was out there. His eardrums stabbed and rang.

Carpenter staggered out of the sonar space, holding his mouth, blood seeping between his fingers. He started to speak, then crouched, staring up as Dan felt it, too.

A cool mist, welcome in the first second on the back on his sweating neck, then suddenly claiming all his horrified attention—Im's, too—as they stared up at the spray playing in a graceful undulating membrane all around the periscope tube.

"Control, Electrical; leakage aft, heavy leak from vicinity of the lower snorkel induction."

A hand on his shoulder. "I go to piss, and you guys sink the boat?"

"Two one zero, V-dag." Dan scrambled up, pointed Im at the periscope—the Korean was already stripping off his skivvy shirt, to try to staunch the leak with—and ran aft.

Then halted in the next compartment, just outside the galley. Water was sleeving down the radio mast too. He stared at it, then pickled the button. The hydraulics groaned, then cut off with a resounding bang. The mast itself didn't budge, not a centimeter.

He reversed his steps, sucking a long breath of hot oxygen from his rebreather, and ducked and stepped through the watertight door back into Control. This was his station, not aft. Kaulukukui and Oberg would have to take care of the induction leak. He had to figure out how to get them out of this. He walked through the spray, tasting salt, feeling trapped.

That had been a Limbo round, and judging by the damage, the heavy antisubmarine shell had struck directly atop the after portion of the sail. Where the snorkel head valve, the radio mast, and the attack periscope were built into the trailing portion of the superstructure. He pickled the 'scope and got the same groan of overstraining hydraulics, the same echoing, steely bang as they gave up and tripped off as he had on the other mast a moment before.

Losing the 'scope was bad but leakage through the induction valve was much worse. The typical snorkel system, which sucked in combustion air for the diesels when the boat ran submerged, had a head valve at the top of the sail and two induction valves, upper and lower, below that. Leakage at the lower induction meant both that the head valve, at the top of the sail,

was sheared or blown off, anyway open to the sea, and that the upper induction valve was open or cracked as well.

So that all they had left now holding back major flooding through a
two-foot-diameter penetration was one damaged valve, probably warped
or sprung at the hinge or the dogging mechanisms—the typical way valves
failed under explosive shock. "Helm: alter course thirty degrees to port,"
Dan snapped. "Rit, you okay?"

"Bit by fucking tongue hal' off." But he was balanced on top of the
watchstander desk, one-handedly helping Im hammer his undershirt into
the scope housing. When Dan told him to belay that and get back on the
stack he hopped down, but slipped on the wet deck, rolling instinctively
as he went down to protect his broken arm, and crashed into a protruding
valve wheel. Now his cheek was bloody too. Carpenter lurched back into
Sonar just as the boat staggered too, booming hollowly as it settled down
on what sounded like a hard gravelly bottom.

Okay, they were in the middle of an oil field, taking water, nearly out of
battery power and the high pressure air they'd need to blow the ballast
tanks, with a poisonous atmosphere and no one knew how much longer
on the rebreathers. He hit the bitch box. "How fast you taking water back
there, Oberg?"

"Wait one . . . fifty gallons a minute? Sumo's guess. He's working on the
valve with a big fucking hammer."

"*Don't* fuck with that induction! Get him off there! That cracks, we'll
flood solid in about two minutes." Fifty gallons a minute they could take,
for a while. He debated closing the watertight doors, sealing off the incipi-
ent flooding aft, but decided not to. Not just yet. If the engineroom flooded
they'd have to abandon.

If they *could* abandon. He had no idea how to operate the escape trunk,
and they'd be learning in the dark, in a strange boat, and maybe without
enough hands even to operate the right cutouts and flooding controls and
interlocks. He gave them a 30 percent chance of even getting out into the
open sea, let alone making it to the surface.

"Time to get out of here yet?" Vaught, hauling all back on the control
planes, without obvious effect; that scraping went on and on. Im was leaning over the ballast panel, but his expression was grim. He kept punching
the same button, but nothing seemed to be happening. Then he'd turn a
valve this way or that, and try the button again.

Dan pulled his attention from the interior and pushed it out into the
night sea around them. That goddamned helicopter. It had radioed the
frigate a line of bearing, which it had crossed with its own data to generate

a good enough fix to fire on. Exactly what he'd have done if he'd been the scene leader. He'd kept the same course too long, let them get a solution. But he couldn't keep weaving through an operating oil field. On the other hand, he couldn't bottom the boat and abandon now, either. As soon as he stopped, the enemy would get another fix. The Limbo rounds would arrive seconds later.

This bastard was good, he was fast, he was smart, he was accurate. "Why the fuck couldn't we get somebody incompetent," he muttered, rubbing greasy-feeling spray off his scalp. "Just this once."

But now what? He was running out of ideas. Along with everything else.

He was standing there, getting ready to acknowledge the inevitable, when the intercom crackled. "Commander? Wenck here. Forward Torpedo."

"What you got, Donnie?"

"What was that explosion? Are we sinking?"

"Under control, Donnie. That all you wanted?"

"No," the distant voice said. For once it seemed to lack Wenck's usual diffidence, his usual half-spacy, half-distracted air. "You might want to come down and see what we found."

"I could use some good news."

"You better come and see," Wenck repeated, and signed off.

THE lights were broken in the torpedo room, too. Dan groped his way past the musty dead-mouse stink of the corpses. Whiplash from the hit had tossed the bodies about until they lay in tumbled disarray. He swallowed. One had its eyes open in a stubbled face already turning dark blue. Its gaze seemed to follow as Dan slid past, making his way toward a glowing centroid by tube number 3, where the beams of several battle lanterns interlaced.

He'd left Carpenter in charge in Control, with orders to ping once, at the lowest power setting, confirm the intended direction was clear, then give Vaught the new course. Ping again, then zig back. At random, but with his overall course toward the southern boundary of the oil field. Assuming they got that far; it would be at least eleven more miles. Which might not sound like much, but he'd be surprised if they made it.

Like a patient etherized on a table, the long narrow carcass of the Shkval lay opened up at the crux of the beams. A cover plate lay upside down, curved inner surface of polished metal dazzling in the focused light. Modules, some still connected by cables, others not, lay around on the skids or on the deck. Henrickson was holding a probe, watching code scroll across the screen of a piece of test equipment.

Dan took out the mouthpiece. Up here, at the far end of any air movement, the atmosphere was even thicker than aft. The actuators for the forward planes screeched and complained above him. He muttered, trying for shallow breaths, "What you got, Donnie? Monty?"

"We wondered why the outer shell wasn't painted," the analyst murmured, taking his rebreather out, too. "Pretty obvious, once you know." He put the mouthpiece back in again.

"See you broke into that additional length. Find the transducers?"

"Ardt any hra'ducers," Wenck said around rubber.

"What? Take a breath. Take that thing out. Then tell me."

"There aren't any."

"No transducers?"

"It's not acoustically guided," Henrickson said. "Remember what Chone said, just about at the end, when we were talking to him in Newport? About magnetic guidance?"

"That they couldn't make it work. The local fields overwhelmed what they wanted to pick up, or something."

"Well, these guys tried it another way." The analyst lifted another cover plate. "Steering actuators. Pretty straightforward design. A lot like the Standard missile, but built heavier to steer in water, not air. But, notice anything else different?"

A detonation gonged through the hull. Then two more, so close together they were almost indistinguishable. Farther away than the last, but near enough to vibrate the beams of the battle lanterns. Dan wondered what the Iranians had fired on: the rush of gas flowing through a wellhead? A compressor? Or had Vaught zigged when they'd expected him to zag? He snapped, "We're being actively prosecuted, Monty. Can you pick up the pace on the presentation?"

"It's all nonmagnetic."

"Titanium, plastic, bronze," Wenck added. "The whole thing, outer shell all the way in. No ferrous metal."

"Okay, so?"

"It's magnetically transparent," Henrickson said. "And all the power cables have magnetic shielding, to avoid Oersted effects. So there *aren't* any local fields to interfere with the sensors. Then they tap off some of the envelope steam and use it to drive this little turbine. This thing here's a generator. Six inches long, but look at the gauge of the cable coming off it. This isn't a passive system. It generates its own magnetic field, then senses how it deforms in response to something ahead of it. Something big. Something steel."

"Like an aircraft carrier," Wenck put in.

"That's still got to be a pretty weak return," Dan said, touching his infected eye gingerly. The combination of carrion stink and bad air made him feel like the top of his skull was being pried off. "So it wouldn't work outside a fairly small radius. Wait, don't tell me. It runs out like the original flavor Shkval. Gyros, along whatever firing bearing the Uzel gives it. Like you were saying, minimal inputs from the fire control system. But at some preset distance this new system, this magnetic guidance, activates and homes."

"But at two hundred knots. So the target has no chance to turn away or decoy it."

"There's got to be some countermeasure. Magnetic mines, we degauss the hull. Reduce the magnetic signature."

"If it generates its own field, this'll get a return even from a degaussed hull. As long as whatever's out there's made of steel." Henrickson sagged onto the skid. "The best countermeasure would probably be a false field of our own. The way we stream a noisemaker to fox a sound homer. But that's Chone's and Pirrell's job, once we tell them how it works."

Dan contemplated the shining interior of the weapon, admiring despite himself the elegant simplicity of Dvorov's solution. In a tight strait like Hormuz, where the deep-draft carriers were confined to narrow channels, it would be devastating. Especially armed with the penetrating warhead. With it, Iran could close the Gulf to both military forces and tanker traffic; cut off the flow of energy to the West and Japan. Which would put it in a position to make *any* demand, enforce any claim or exaction.

Now he understood why the Iranians were pursuing him so doggedly.

He had to get this information back to TAG, at any cost.

But to do that, they had to escape. And he just didn't see how.

He looked again at the dismantled weapon. Muttered, "What's your guess on the guidance activation range?"

"The max range it could pick up something as big as a carrier?" Henrickson glanced at Wenck, who shrugged. "Depends on what kind of field the generator puts out, how sharp the sensors are. A thousand meters? Five hundred?"

Dan put his mouthpiece back in. The chemical air seemed cooler, wetter, and it didn't relieve his headache, the way it first had. Was his cartridge used up already? He rubbed his jaw, hearing the rasp of bristle, feeling sand and sweat and salt.

He was still trying to think when the intercom beeped. "Torpedo, Electrical: Lenson up there?"

"Here, Teddy. That lower induction holding?"

"Holding, but the leak's increasing. Spraying in around where it seats. Reason I'm calling, water's higher in the bilge. Doesn't seem like it ought to be rising that fast unless we've got another hole somewhere. Anyway, another foot and it's going to start shorting out the batteries, electrical panels on the lower deck. Sumo and me are trying to put another pump on line, but we're not having any luck yet. Thought you'd want to know."

He double-clicked and had just let up the lever when the box spoke again. "Torpedo, Sonar: Sierra One closing fast astern."

"Rit, what's he doing?"

"Pinging hard and coming fast. Not maneuvering around anything, far as I can tell. Balls to the wall, like somebody stuck a cattle prod up his ass and hit the on switch."

"What's the other guy doing? Sierra Two?"

"Holding his distance while his buddy comes in after us. But his bearing's slowly moving right. Looks like he's gonna play goalie. Repositioning to collar us if we make it out the south end of the oil field."

Dan looked again at the weapon, touched his inflamed face again. "Uh, copy. How's the, uh, how's the arm doing, Rit?"

"Doesn't hurt my hearing."

"Roger . . . out."

"Sonar, off line."

One terrier was crawling into the rathole after them. The other was guarding the back door. He couldn't bottom again. Couldn't wait them out, even if he found a wreck or abandoned platform to mask his magnetic signature. Their air was unbreathable; the last battery bank nearly depleted. When the flooding got above the deckplates, they'd be looking at either electrical fires or complete shutdown.

A flash went off. He flinched, then saw it was Wenck, leaning in to get a closeup of the generator. The strobe whined, recharging, then blasted out again, limning every dial, gauge, air line of the forward torpedo room, leaving pulsing scarlet afterimages floating.

"So, you want this back together?"

"What?"

The analyst waved at the weapon. "Donnie downloaded all the internal programming. We got good sharp pictures. We can get it buttoned up in ten, fifteen minutes, slap the cover plates back on. Then hook it up and run it back into the tube."

Dan stared at him. A moment passed while his slow-moving mind processed it. Before he realized what Monty Henrickson was telling him.

27

BACK in Control, he checked with Carpenter. Face drawn, the sonarman was still hunched over the console. A stopwatch pendulumed from a hook at the top of the stack. The screens flickered like candles guttering down in a cave. When he saw Dan he took out his mouthpiece. Muttered, "Thirty seconds to next ping and course change. On one eight five now. Figure to come all the way to port to one zero zero. Won't take us much farther south, but the last two zigs were kind of shallow, I don't want to do another ten-degree turn."

Dan kneaded Rit's shoulder silently—the right one, not the one with the broken arm—and leaned out again. Im returned his gaze from the ballast control panel. Dan couldn't see how, but the Korean had managed to regain trim; they hadn't touched bottom again since the Limbo strike on the sail. He silently extended a thumb. Im hesitated, then returned the gesture. Too late, Dan hoped it didn't have some obscene connotation for a Korean.

"So what's our next move?" the sonarman muttered, not taking his eye off the trace. "I heard what Oberg said."

"That we're taking on water."

"Yeah, and it gets to the batteries, there'll be chlorine all through the boat." He patted his breathing bag. "This is nice, but it's not going to stop chlorine long. That was the original poison gas. We take it off to talk, or vomit, and get one good hit—"

"I get the picture. But I'm not really sure—"

"Wait one, okay?" Carpenter interrupted him to crank rapidly on a knob, then leaned to flip up a safety and press a red button above the stack. The note pulsed and lingered, echoing eerily away into the sea. Bands of light leapt out of the waterfall, danced, faded. Carpenter hit more controls and changed the display, then cranked an index line over each return, making rapid notes on a pad of cheap ruled paper. Dan noted the returns got mushy, blurry, all but unreadable past seven or eight hundred yards. "Bears about one zero eight—two hundred yards—looks okay to starboard of that, and we'll have advance from the present course. Okay, V-Dag, bring her around, left rudder, one zero zero." He reached up to zero the stopwatch, started it running again with another click. Then huddled, good hand cupping his fractured arm.

Dan sat silently as the seconds ticked past. Thinking about what Henrickson had suggested. If that *was* what he'd suggested.

They had one Shkval-K aboard. If they got it put back together, should he fire it?

In one sense it would mean the mission was a failure. That was their tasking, after all: bring the new weapon home, for Navy labs to analyze and test and devise a countermeasure.

Without it, wouldn't everything they'd done be in vain?

On the other hand, Wenck had downloaded its programming, they had detailed photos of its internals, and Henrickson had deduced how it guided. Surely with that, the PhDs and the companies and universities the navy research establishment had under contract could duplicate it. Dvorov was brilliant, but Komponent didn't have the only good engineers in the world. Given the intel Team Charlie had assembled, he couldn't see why Lockheed-Martin or Raytheon or Northrop-Grumman couldn't build their own Shkval-K. Probably better, faster, and smaller, given the U.S. lead in high power density electronics and computer controls. And once they had that, devise a way to frustrate it.

But there was another question. The men after him, the officers and enlisted in those frigates, were only trying to recover their own property. *He* was the thief. Could he use their own weapon against them?

He smiled tightly. Twenty years ago he'd have agonized over that one. Maybe he was getting calloused. The way he'd thought certain of his seniors had been.

But this was kill or be killed.

If, that is, they could get the fucking thing to work. Which with a foreign fire-control system, an unfamiliar weapon, disassembled and reassembled by inexpert technicians without proper manuals or tools—yeah, it wasn't a sure thing.

The only other choice was to surface, hoist a white flag, and hope the Iranians respected it. Maybe they would, if it meant getting their sub back without too much damage.

He could surrender. He was past thinking of things in terms of his honor, or his career. It was what would happen afterward that made him dislike that alternative.

Team Charlie weren't combatants, adversaries taken in lawful combat. They were spies. Beneath contempt, outside the laws of war and Geneva. Tried for espionage, by a regime that had baited the Great Satan for years, the least his guys would get was life in some squalid hole of a prison. If they weren't just marched out into a soccer stadium and beheaded before thousands of cheering believers.

And maybe that was all spies and murderers deserved, but his job was to protect his men. So fighting back, slim though their chances looked, was the only chance they had.

He'd better start thinking about how he was going to do it.

Im's eyes were closed. Dan put a hand on his shoulder, and the Korean flinched. "What?"

Dan beckoned him to the watchstander's desk. He'd drawn the geometry on a sheet of Carpenter's pulp paper, as close to scale as he could. The field they were in, the obstacles they'd mapped on their way through it, and their pursuers as he extrapolated their tracks over the next half hour. It showed Sierra One, now behind them, basically over their datum; and Sierra Two, now heading south several miles to the east of the oil field, directly in their escape path. As best Dan could calculate, there was no possible way *K-79* could make it out of the oil field before Sierra One would be within half a mile, that is, in Limbo range.

He watched the former exec of a North Korean submarine very closely as Im examined the diagram.

IM had wondered when they'd ask his opinion. For the first couple of hours, maintaining trim had taken all his concentration. Then he'd gotten the feel of the boat. Since they'd lifted from the long period on the bottom, though, during which the Americans had done their repairs, he'd been trying to use the least possible kilograms of air pressure. The boat was fighting him, wanting to go nose up, tail down, as she slowly grew heavier aft. Had Lenson even noticed?

But now, with the enemy close, they needed him. Which was why he concentrated, despite the pain and ringing in his ears, and his own fear. Oh, yes. No one showed fear in the North Korean People's Army Naval Forces. But that didn't mean he wasn't afraid.

The commander's lips moved. Im could hear only faintly through the howl of his damaged ears, but he followed the diagram. He stabbed a finger down on their principal pursuer. "Must destroy him."

The commander's breathing bag puffed out; he'd sighed. Why? Then reached for the pencil. *One shot*, Lenson wrote in block letters.

He understood that. Bending over the paper again, gripping the pencil in a crabbed wraparound, he sketched in a truncated drilling platform. Pointed at the sonar shack, then to the little stick sketch. "Find wreck. Find old steel. Hide behind. Understand?"

Lenson nodded and said something. A tremor came through the deckplates to Im's bare feet. He got better footing without the socks, but that wasn't why he'd taken them off. His soles were bleeding again from the shattered glass. But this way he could feel, through the boat's very bones, what was happening around her. She'd shivered at every distant explosion, and convulsed in pain when she herself was hit. He'd felt the trill of an incoming torpedo and the soft jolt as it detonated deep in mud and sand. And felt the steady beat of her screws gradually losing strength, speed, life itself.

K-79 was no longer a tiger, prowling the jungle. She was a hunted doe, quivering, bleeding, her life leaking away.

"What?" he said.

Lenson spoke again, his lips emphasizing the sounds. But Im couldn't understand. He grabbed the pencil again. Drew a submarine lurking behind something on the seabed. Lying in wait as the enemy drew near. Then surfacing, facing the pursuing frigate. He finished with a dotted line from their bow to the enemy.

He set the pencil down, watching Lenson. Would he have the courage? Americans did not value the readiness to sacrifice a warrior needed. They were not all physically soft. Oberg and the Hawaiian were as hard as any Reconnaissance Bureau commando. Some he respected for their knowledge—Monty, Donnie, the others back at TAG. Even the lax, undisciplined Carpenter had shown himself unexpectedly resourceful once he was aboard a submarine. But they did not seem ready to make hard choices. One day, they would put off a hard choice too long, and lose the riches and comfort they'd become accustomed to as their due; as something they didn't have to be ready to fight for, to the death.

Lenson was looking at the diagram. Turning, to speak into the sonar room. Patting him on the back, like a child. Im kept his face blank, though he felt like seizing the pencil and plunging it into the man's arrogant heart again and again.

Go forward to torpedo room. Help load tube, he read. *Send Monty back here.*

He studied Lenson's haggard face. Was he a man of war, one to make the hard choice? With his privilege, his rank, his rich official wife?

What would the Iranians do with a Korean? Especially one who'd officially died as a hero defying the puppet government in Seoul? Would they turn him over to those he'd thought to escape? He patted the knife by his side. He'd given up once, and was still not certain he'd made the right choice. He would not surrender again.

Was he the only one aboard who'd rather die than submit?

MONTY was levering the weapon forward when someone tapped his shoulder. "Want it? No problem," he muttered, handing Im the chain from the hoist. "Donnie, we got somebody here who actually knows how to do this."

"You go Control," the Asian grunted. Face unreadable, as usual. Did the guy feel anything? He looked even more sullen than usual. Henrickson started to pat him, then thought better of it when the red-rimmed eyes glared. Well, they were all exhausted. Sucking air through the apparatus was an effort. It made his lungs ache and his jaws cramp. They weren't designed for extended wear.

In Control, Lenson was standing at the varnished plywood desk that looked like something out of a high school wood shop. He didn't look up for a moment. When he did his expression was that of an old corpse. His skin gray, where it wasn't swollen bright pink, and the lines around his eyes graved deep. "Monty. Got it back together?"

"The data cable gave us some trouble. The detents snapped off. But we got it taped in and I think it'll pipe bits."

"Im show up?"

"Helping Donnie load." He replaced the mouthpiece, got a couple of breaths, pulled it out again. "Thinking of firing?"

"Maybe. But it's not the optimal weapon for the situation."

"It's an anticarrier weapon." He breathed again while he thought. His throat was strep-raw, but each time he took the mouthpiece out black specks started streaming in from the edges of his eyesight, sucking together, like a black liquid that wanted to cover everything. "Uh, anticarrier weapon. Firing at something small as a frigate, without that huge magnetic signature, this guidance will work only within a very short radius."

"Very short. How short?"

"How much gauss is that generator putting out? At what frequency?

What's the hull material on those frigates? I could work it out if I knew all that but I don't. Maybe two hundred, three hundred yards?"

Lenson chewed the mouthpiece, gaze locked on Vaught's back. "We'd have to fire at close range, before bearing error gets too great."

"We get too close, they'll be on us with that fucking Limbo."

"I don't think I ever heard you say 'fuck' before, Monty."

"I just don't have to use it ten times in every sentence, like some people."

"I fucking heard that," Carpenter called. "And I fucking don't use it *that* fucking often."

Monty ignored him. "What we really don't know is what the software's going to be telling this thing to do. Looks to me like Komponent used off-the-shelf 65-76 guidance circuitry. Their biggest, newest wake homing torpedo. The way the 65-76 guides, it's got a stored model of the most likely target. When it picks up a return signal, it figures the relative coordinates between itself and the target, using the stored model and an iterative algorithm to generate a guesstimated position. Shkvals run at a preset depth. So it's only a two-dimensional problem. That cuts down on the computing demand, lets you run a simple program real fast, over and over, to keep up with the higher velocity this missile's traveling compared to a 65. That estimated position goes to the next module, which generates the steering orders."

"So again, you're saying all we have to give it's an initial runout bearing."

"No, what I said was it's expecting a *certain target*. Given what the Iranians wanted this for, a *huge* target. If it detects a smaller signal it's going to think that big target's farther away. So it's going to oversteer, is what I'm saying."

"Run way to the left and right of centerline from us to the target."

"Uh, yeah. I would assume." Monty was nervous, knowing how much was riding on them getting this right, or at least, right enough to fire. If the thing *would* fire. He scrubbed his sweating palms down his thighs.

Lenson was still thinking aloud. "So we need him in close. To cut down on that angular error. Maybe . . . two thousand yards?"

Monty swallowed, not saying anything.

"And that's going to put us in Limbo range, with him getting firing data both from his own active sonar and from that fucking helicopter. We'll have to keep the bow pointed right at him to shoot. Which means we can't go evasive."

"Go evasive how?" Monty asked him. "We can't go fast and we can't go deep. And what if we miss, or the fucking thing doesn't work?"

"I heard that, too," Carpenter said from the sonar compartment.

"Vaught, you holding up?" Lenson asked the helmsman. Monty turned to stare as the man suddenly stood, leaving the helm unoccupied.

"V-Dag? Need a relief?"

"Yeah. I need a relief." His tone was flat and he didn't have any emotion in his expression either. He put his mouthpiece back in and went aft.

Lenson looked nonplussed, but after a moment's hesitation crossed to where the pilot had sat and took the controls himself. "Rit, what were we on?"

"One niner five."

"Monty, you and Donnie set up the Uzel. I'll give you a firing bearing. If it doesn't work, or we miss, I'm going to surrender."

"Scuttle and surrender?"

"No, surface and surrender. Maybe if they get their boat back when we could have sunk it, they'll go easier on you guys."

"On us? How about on you?"

"I can't let them question me," Lenson said.

Monty didn't answer for a moment. Lenson had never spoken about it, but he'd heard the guy had been tortured by the Mukhbarat, Saddam's Gestapo. Maybe if you'd been through that, you didn't want to ever again. He didn't particularly want to be a hostage, a captive, himself, but it'd be better than dying down here. Wouldn't it?

Finally he said, "It's gonna work, Dan. And if it doesn't, the Navy could still show up."

Lenson's bag deflated, as though he was taking a deep breath. He took his mouthpiece out again. Coughed, and coughed; stood from the bench and pressed the intercom switch above him. "Teddy, Sumo, status on flooding?"

"Over the lower level deckplates."

"No joy on the pumps?"

"Had them going. For about eight minutes. Then the water hit the breakers and they tripped off. Sorry."

"It's okay. How much juice we got left?"

"I don't know how that motor's turning over on what we've got. Don't count on more than three or four knots."

Lenson's face sagged. He held down the button for a few seconds. Then let it up slowly, having said nothing at all.

HE shook his head, flinging off sweat as he sucked again on the breathing tube. His chest hurt. He couldn't decide. Couldn't decide.

Surrender, or attack?

The bubble kept drifting forward. She was nose light, tail heavy. Vaught had left his post with the planes pointing up, and Dan gave them another five degrees, but the nose kept creeping skyward.

She was slowly sinking. Forty-five meters, where not long before the gauge had read forty. He pulled the control columns all the way back, all the way into the stops. The water might be getting warmer as they neared shore—yeah, that'd make them heavier, warmer water was less dense. He needed Im back on the ballast panel, a few more tons of buoyancy in the after tanks.

Where the hell was Vaught? If he'd gone to take a leak he should be back by now. "V-Dag," he shouted over his shoulder. No answer came.

"Control, Torpedo," said the intercom.

"Go, Torpedo."

"Shkval in the tube, electrically connected, inner door closed, impulse tank seventy-five percent charged, in the green."

"Double check that inner door. Then open the muzzle door."

"Confirm white light on inner door. Have to flood to sea before we open the outer door. Flooding to sea . . . white light. Manually opening . . . stand by . . . red light. Muzzle door open, tube three. Standing by to fire photon torpedo, Captain Picard."

It didn't sound like Wenck, except for that last crack, and Dan could imagine Im standing beside the kid, those black eyes boring into him. "Control aye. Vaught up there?"

"V-Dag? No, he ain't. He supposed to be?"

"No. If he shows up, send him back here. Send Im back, too, Donnie. Need him on the ballast control, I can't hold the bubble."

"Want me, too?"

"No. Has he shown you how to fire it? The tube, I mean?"

"Yeah. We've got a string on it."

He didn't want to know what that meant. "Okay, you stay there, we might have to fire manually if this system doesn't cooperate. I need him here. We're getting awful short handed." He craned around again. "Rit, still with us?"

"Still here. Fucker's starting to really hurt, though."

"Vaught in there with you?"

"Not in here. Oh. I've got something big out at two three zero."

"Something big?"

"Don't know what. Good hard return. Probably metal. A big tank of some kind. Maybe, air inside? A hollow return, like a chime."

"Range?"

"Six hundred. Time to turn! Next course will be to port."

"Where's Sierra One?"

"Constant bearing . . . high rep rate pinging . . . still out of my active range, but he's getting gradually louder. Picking his way through the oil field. Just like we are, but faster."

"I'm coming to starboard instead, Rit. Aim me just south of whatever you're looking at over there."

"That'd be two two five."

"Coming to two two five." He held the helm stick over, coughing into the breathing tube, then pushed it all the way to the right. The rudder indicator swung, they still had hydraulic pressure, but the gyro ticked over all too slowly. Not many more minutes and they'd be dead in the water, batteries exhausted.

Five hundred yards; three knots. Five minutes, his increasingly worn-out mind computed. He couldn't tell if he was fainting or if the lights were fading. The emergency lanterns were the dim orange eyes of tarsiers. "Rit, give me a mark on five minutes and take one ping. I'm going to lurk behind this thing, whatever it is."

"He'll see us when he opens the bearing. Unless we're right on top of it. And he'll hear us, if we make any noise at all."

Dan didn't answer. He was seeing the engagement as Im had sketched it out. But something about it he hadn't liked tactically. As in, meeting the enemy bow to bow. The face off. The showdown.

But this wasn't Colt to Colt at high noon. It was an alley fight. Knee to groin, thumb to eye. And there was only one rule in an alley fight. Always play dirty.

How could he play dirty now?

"We're losing altititude," Henrickson called from forward. "How deep is it here?"

"Shit," Dan muttered into the mouthpiece. Passing fifty-five and dropping fast, he wasn't sure where the bottom was but it couldn't be far. There didn't seem to be a thing the planes could do about it, he had them at full rise. He hit the intercom. "Electrical, need power. Give me more knots, we're losing depth control here."

No answer. But thank Christ, here was Im. Dan didn't ask what had taken him so long coming back three compartments from the torpedo room. The Korean tripped as he came through the door, catching his foot on the lower sealing rim, and fell heavily. Hoisted up to all fours after a moment, then came on, but he left bloody tracks on the deck and panted like a dying dog. Dan grabbed his arm as he slagged by, jabbed at the depth gauge. The Korean nodded dully. His hand caressed the knife at his belt.

"How long now, Rit?"

"Two minutes gone, three minutes remain."

"Belay my last order, about the ping. Just give me a mark on five."

"Mark on five, no ping, aye."

"Electrical, Control: hear my last?"

Kaulukukui answered, voice heavy, drugged, like a recorder played too slow. "We copy."

"We need power up here."

"Wait."

"Sumo, I need turns on that shaft. I have to get to cover here, and I'm losing attitude control."

"Wait."

"What the *fuck*," Dan muttered, and caught himself swinging off course. He reversed rudder to bring them back. Feeling in the back of his neck, like many tons of steel hanging above his head, the approaching frigate. Skippered by someone who didn't forgive mistakes, and didn't make many of his own. Whatever the other's name or beliefs, Dan respected him. He'd read about this, the uncanny sense of the other player that hunter and prey in the undersea jungles developed during the long game. He could almost see his adversary on his bridge, forehead in his hands, trying to probe in his turn the intentions of the other mind below him.

Their mutual aim being each to destroy the other.

"Mark, five minutes, Dan."

"Got it." He considered countermanding his countermand, telling Carpenter to go ahead and ping, make super sure they weren't going to run headlong into something hard and huge and metal, but kept his mouth shut. One emission could give the game away.

They'd slowed, so he gave it an extra thirty seconds, then eased the rudder over fifteen degrees. Not to full; a good sonar operator could hear the flow noise over a fully turned rudder. It would take a while to come around, but when they did they'd be facing back east, crouched in the acoustic "shadow" of whatever they were behind. If that fucking helo didn't out them . . . "Rit, that chopper? Where is it now?"

"Haven't heard it since the last Limbo shot. We're pretty far out in the Gulf for a chopper out of Iran. Not much stay time."

Good, he was thinking, maybe this could go our way, when he noticed the needle on the depth gauge tremoring just short of sixty. As he stared, disbelieving, it dropped to sixty-one. He wheeled instantly on Im, to be confronted by as cold a look as he'd ever met.

"Cannot hold her," the Korean said, each word pronounced precisely and almost without accent. "All reserve buoyancy gone with flooding aft.

Enough HP air for one half blow. When that gone, never come up again. Also, you smell?"

"What?"

"You smell?" The Korean put his finger under his nose, lifted it, mimed sniffing. His hand rested on the panel. "I blow?"

Dan pulled off the nose clip and took a tentative sniff. Nothing new. Or maybe, the faintest odor of bleach.

No one spoke. He swallowed, mind hopping from thought to thought. Trying alternatives, but coming up short. He hit the intercom again, as much to buy time as for any other reason. "Sumo? Teddy? What's going on back there?"

"Bad news, skipper. It's V-Dag."

"What kind of bad news?"

"He's dead." Oberg began coughing, then continued in a choked voice. "Can't talk . . . found him on the lower level, face down on the deckplates. No breathing gear."

"No gear? Where was it?"

"Don't know. Not with him."

"What was he doing back there, Teddy? He just up and walked away from the helm. We thought he was going to the head."

"Well, maybe . . . there's a head back here, but he was down by the diesel log station."

"You're sure he's dead? No pulse?"

"Face down in the water, boss."

Why now, when they needed every hand? The SDV pilot had given the impression of moving closer to some rash act ever since the attacks began. Had he just taken off his gear, knowing that in a few moments what he breathed would finish him? Or had his breathing cartridge failed? In which case he'd been operating with clouded judgment. Could have gotten confused, lost, stripped off his gear looking for a fresh cartridge, finally passed out.

No time for regret or anger. "Teddy, that's bad, but we're in a tight situation. Im thinks he can get us to the surface one last time. If he does, can you start the diesels?"

Oberg coughed and coughed. The intercom went on and off. Finally he got out, "Don't know if we've got enough power left, boss. Those starters eat a lot of amps. Another thing, we're starting to get chlorine back here. Getting pretty thick."

That was it, what Im had detected first: the bleach smell. Dan hit the intercom instantly. "Grab Sumo and haul ass up here, Teddy. Slam your rheos all the way forward, full power to the motors, all you have left. Bring V-Dag if you can, but dog each door as you come forward, and secure the bulkhead ventilation isolation valves." He let up on the switch and snapped to Im, "Get us to the surface. Prepare to surface! Monty, we ready on fire control?"

"Bringing the computer up."

Sluggish thuds sounded fore and aft as Im sent the last air hissing into the tanks. He grunted in Korean and stepped back, rubbing his hands with the air of one finally through with a demanding task.

"Rit, hear me? I'm surfacing. Where's Sierra One?"

"Lost track, Sierra One. Last bearing zero two five true."

"God*damn* it, Rit! What was he doing when you lost him?"

"Same's before. Frequent maneuvering, but coming up our ass fast. Then I look again and he's off the scope."

Dan cursed silently, but only for a second. "Stay on the stack. You're doing a good job. Busted arm and all." He cleared his throat and added, "You did a real good job."

A second's pause. Then the sonarman's voice floated out. "No prob, Skipper. You did pretty good yourself."

Oberg and Kaulukukui appeared shuffling and bent in the passageway on the far side of the after door, dragging a burden. They paused to dog the engine room door, then came on. They laid out the corpse on the deckplates outside the galley and came the rest of the way into Control. Before they could speak Dan said, "Do we need that door closed, too? The batteries are right below it."

"I'm pretty sure they vent into Electrical."

"Okay, leave it open. Sumo, you look like shit."

"I better sit down."

"If you have to sit, take the helm. Keep her on this course till I tell you otherwise. Teddy, where's your weapon? Your MP5?"

"Stowed."

"Grab it. And load it." He looked at the depth gauge one last time. It read ten meters and was moving up, not fast, in fact very sluggishly, but going up. "We're going topside. Everybody else, man up to fire. But if this doesn't work, get ready to abandon ship, too. As soon as they spot us, they'll hit us with everything they've got."

WHEN he got to the top of the ladder leading up through the tight echoing trunk from Control to the sail, the hatch wouldn't open. Steel protested around them, creaking as the boat picked up the surface swell, as he and Oberg, locked like climaxing lovers, four feet on the same rung, struggled to turn the handwheel. It yielded not an inch. "Jammed by the shock," the SEAL muttered into his ear.

"Once more." Dan wondered if he smelled as awful as Oberg. Probably. The knowledge that in a few seconds they could be breathing fresh air made his frustration as overpowering as his fear. He had to get topside. If he couldn't see he couldn't aim, and if he couldn't aim, surfacing with the Iranian near meant quick death for them all.

"Depth gauge shows we're surfaced," Kaulukukui shouted from below.

"Get your leg around me. Shove when I pull. One, two, three."

"Fucker moved! Hit it again."

"One, two, *three*." A muscle tore in his arm, but the wheel grated around a quarter turn. They heaved again and the dogs stuttered as they withdrew. They both shoved and his wrists pained but it popped violently free, almost blew open. A reeking wind from below nearly ejected them out of the open trunk, so that he stumbled, going to one knee.

In the orgasmic delight of his first lungful of air that hadn't been rebreathed into a miasmic stew he didn't care that it was hot and freighted with grit and smell. Only that it had oxygen and tasted wonderful.

Then he blinked and ducked, cowering within the open cockpit.

This upper world flickered windblown, orange-tan, howling with the continuous thunder of a great waterfall, and lit by flame. He blinked around, having not expected whatever this was. A cursing Oberg was fighting the sling of his HK, which had snagged on the handwheel. It was night, but everything was lit by wavering brightness. Hands clamped over his ears, Dan blinked at a dented-down mass of bent plates and wreckage that looked as if an asteroid had impacted the trailing edge of the sail. The scope was bent forward, the radio mast gone, what must be the induction plenum was split apart and buckled. He shivered. Ten feet aft and the mortar round would have hit the pressure hull, flooding the engine room and hauling them all down to a watery grave.

Then he looked to port, and ducked, flinging up an arm to shield his face.

The platform loomed over them, so close the heat from the massive wavering torch at the end of the trusswork-supported tube that cantilevered out scorched his cheeks like instantaneous sunburn. Shockwaves played in the yellow-white flame like imps made of incandescent gas. The massive light lit the sea around them, lit *K-79* as she wallowed bow high, stern submerged, in the howling sand-laden wind. The brightness was dazzling. Like an actor on stage, he could see nothing beyond it.

"Where's the frigate?" Oberg howled in his ear, and Dan stumbled forward, feeling for the voice tube, then spinning off the knobs and latching up the steel covers that protected it and the rudder and engine order indicators. The thick glass was cracked on the dials but they were still registering. Thank God for Russian engineering. Sumo had them pointed east, so they were still making steerageway. Though no more than a knot or two, to judge by their sluggish parade through the sanded-off waves that sparkled dully, like cast bronze, in the light of the flareoff.

He shaded his eyes with a shaking hand, but saw only blackness ahead. It was hard even to look into the blowing grit, finer than powder, like smoke except that it stung his cheeks and needled his eyeballs. He shouted to Oberg, "Ask Carpenter if he's got the frigate."

The SEAL bowed to the voice tube, then straightened. "No contact," he roared, bending toward Dan to be heard over the thunder of the gigantic torch, now passing nearly directly over them as they plodded on, pointed into the wind.

Dan cursed, shading his eyes, all but blind. The massive light wiped everything else out. If he couldn't see, he couldn't shoot. While the backlighting would outline *K-79* perfectly. The first they'd know the enemy was in range would be those Limbo rounds bringing Limbo from the sky.

Then he saw the frigate.

Not by her own light, but like a moon, by a single gleam from the massive torch roaring above him, reflected by the flat glass of pilothouse windows as they altered their angle to his observer's eye. And below that, behind it, the tarpaper on black velvet silhouette of the ship. She was perhaps two miles away, on the far side of another massive platform with its feet in the sea and its head in the dusty sky. Another oil-field structure that, darkened and unlit, might account for Carpenter's having lost contact.

She was still heeling, completing a hard turn a-starboard. As he struggled with the cover on the gyro repeater the frigate steadied, upperworks rolling back up to vertical as she gathered way on the new course.

Oberg stepped forward and slammed at the repeater with the butt of his weapon. The dogs wedged off and Dan hinged aside the hemispherical cover and fitted down on it the heavy yet fragile bearing circle he'd brought up with him crammed into the waistband of his trou. He shouted, "Ask Monty if he's ready to fire."

Oberg bent. Dan couldn't hear the exchange but without turning the SEAL lifted his thumb. From across the weirdly glittering sea—each waveface a mirror of the central gigantic flame for the fraction of a second it reared upright—he even heard the faint prolonged ringing of an electric bell.

A launch warning, alerting anyone on the frigate's deck to stand clear.

He bent to the circle and slid the vertical frame fixed on its circumference and within it the vertical black hairline left and then right, feeling sand grains scrape in the tracks as it rotated, grating and grinding and becoming silt, powder. He fixed it in position just ahead of the oncoming bow.

His suddenly aloof brain calculated angle and speed and distance, time for a two-hundred-knot weapon to run. He edged the sight the tiniest bit left and squinted for numbers in the writhing shadows cast by the glaring sulphur flame and shouted to Oberg's turned waiting ear, "Firing bearing *zero eight seven*, set and *fire*."

For three seconds, the time to draw a long breath, nothing happened. He clung to the stand, fingers locked, lids blinking rapidly and nearly closed against the stinging sandblast out of the night. Wondering if the next thing he'd see, and the last, would be the burst of rosy fire he'd glimpsed once before, as mortar projectiles lifted, three in one, one in three, an unholy trinity that would bring death to him and every one of his team.

A flare ignited ahead of *K-79*'s bullnose. For an instant he thought it was a star shell, fired to confirm they were the target, though God knew they ought to be illuminated well enough for that already. But then it began to *move*.

Glowing beneath the water, maybe twenty feet down, its dazzling whiteness tempering as the angle to his eye increased to a murky yellow-topaz that slid quickly up the spectrum into yellow, into green, before dousing entirely as it receded into the dark. Behind it welled up a straight line of frothing sea that suddenly opened to vent gouts of white smoke. The smoke lingered for only a moment before the wind took it straight back as they watched transfixed. Dan inhaled an acrid, bitter taste that mixed with the smell of sand and burning natural gas and crude oil into a wild mingled odor he knew he'd never forget.

He leaned forward, eyes stinging. Beside him Oberg was yelling some wordless hoarse exhortation as if the deadly thing they'd unloosed could hear them. Dan struggled to find some word or feeling in his own heart—of hope or prayer or protest at the way the world was made—when all at once a hellish flash made even the torch behind them pale, picked out and froze each wave in appalled immobility.

It pulsed again, even brighter this time, but less white than blue. Then yet again, a searing yellowwhite flash like the nuclear fireball he'd glimpsed for a fraction of a second, before it had wrecked USS *Horn*.

He didn't remember diving for the deckplates but he was there, and so was Oberg, and a crackling din rolled overhead like God crashing through the dimensions that structured the universe. It didn't stop but went on, snaps and deeper detonations and a yowling whine that wasn't human but that sounded like nothing he'd ever heard from a ship. A noise that rose and rose and then faded away into the bluster and hiss of the sand-laden wind.

When he put his head up he saw nothing. Not the cooling remains of molten metal, superheavy depleted uranium, explosives, what had a moment before been a living ship crafted of steel and discipline and commanded by a spirit in no way inferior in determination and skill to his own. All of it was gone, and the black sea rolled and the dust whirled over it. He considered searching for survivors, but dismissed the idea with numb horror. The heavy depleted-uranium rods of the special warhead, designed to punch through the side armor of a Nimitz-class carrier, would have burned a hole the length of the thin-skinned frigate, instantly vaporizing and then igniting magazines, fuel tanks, engines, flesh.

"Right hard rudder," he pushed through lips still tasting that bitter exhaust. "Let's get out of this smoke, if we can. Make it uh, one two zero."

Oberg didn't respond for a moment; then he repeated the order down the tube. "That take us out of this field?" he asked. Dan didn't answer.

They ran for a few minutes, and he didn't smell more smoke. That was good. He told Oberg, "Have Donnie open the forward hatch. Get some circulation going. Maybe we can get that chlorine blown out, get the diesels started."

"I don't know," said Oberg. "That water was still gaining when we shut the doors on it. I think we're sinking."

Dan looked at him, but the SEAL wasn't looking back. His attention was somewhere off the starboard bow, where, far ahead, something glittered now and then when the dust thinned. "What's that?" Oberg asked.

"Those lights? Probably Dubai."

"I mean, in front of it."

Dan squinted again, and this time saw it.

A shadow moving against the lights, only visible now and then, but there, most definitely there. Directly in their path, between them and safety.

"The other frigate," Oberg said. They were moving very slowly now, but the roar of the flare-off had lessened enough that he could speak in a normal tone. "Sierra Two. Still waiting for us. We going to abandon?"

"I guess so," Dan said, and the taste on his lips grew even more bitter. Not just the gall of defeat, but of misjudgment. If he'd had to surrender, why couldn't he have done it before killing two hundred men?

He was the thief. The spy. Now he'd pay, and Team Charlie with him. The men who'd trusted him.

What was left? Only the last charge, the final, feigned attack that would force their enemies to destroy them. Forlorn, yes; but a quick death was better than what alternatives remained. He felt the tendons and flesh sag on his bones.

He was standing rigid, gripped with remorse, when a pair of red-hot eyes cometed out of the darkness to the north. They passed low and incredibly fast, no more than two hundred feet up, between *K-79* and the oncoming frigate. The whine of turbines reached them, and the hot eyes that were the glowing tailpipes of two jet fighters pulled up and came around again, lit now as they banked by the yellow glare of the massive flare; passing, this time, directly over the Iranian frigate.

Oberg went nuts, stamping his feet, yippeeing like a Texan at a rodeo. Dan leaned forward, fighting to believe, but unable to credit what he was witnessing. The task force was hundreds of miles to the north. Far out of fighter range. And something about their outline, hard to make out as it was . . . they banked again, and he saw what was wrong. He knew Navy planes, and these weren't Navy.

In fact, they weren't American at all.

They were French.

The Afterimage
Aboard MNF *Foch* (R-99)

T HEY'D offered beer and wine, but after three days without sleep, he'd asked for coffee instead. He felt gritty even after a long hot shower. Felt grubby even after being reclothed in French pilot's coveralls, felt swollen and battered even after antibiotic salve and a checkup in sick bay.

Now he sat in flag quarters, coughing and nibbling pastry while waiting on the vice-admiral who commanded Combined Task Force 150 in the Southern Gulf. Opposite, legs crossed and elegant in a custom-tailored medium blue unform, touching a flame to a Gauloise, sat his former fellow ARMINTEX shopper: jut-jawed, raven-haired *Commandante de Vaiseau* Christophe de Lestapis de Cary.

This time he didn't even attempt to speak French to the guy. "What are your people doing with *K-79*?" Dan asked him.

De Cary's gesture left an intaglio of smoke in the scented air. Could those really be fresh hibiscus in that vase on the sideboard? "Oh, de—is the word really 'dewatering'?"

"Dewatering, yes."

"Our damage control people are 'dewatering' now. The submarine we salvaged is under tow by one of our frigates of the second rank. It will be repaired in Bahrain, to a standard that will make her safe to steam if not to submerge. Then we will turn her back over to Teheran."

"What did you tell the Iranians about us?"

"I'm sorry, I do not know that you were ever aboard," de Cary said politely. "So far as I know, *K-79* was found unmanned. Whoever hijacked her must have abandoned her before she drifted into the oil field."

"The bodies? The dead Russians?"

"What Russians? What bodies?"

"I see."

De Cary said mildly, "You must understand, we are playing this absolutely straight with you. Whatever we know, you know."

Dan digested this along with another bite of pastry. U.S. Navy coffee and French Navy flag mess café au lait had obviously evolved in unrelated spacetime continua, and the tarts—the apple tart was the most delicious thing he'd ever tasted. This was his second and he felt as if he could keep nibbling forever. The only thing he didn't care for was de Cary's secondhand smoke, but under the circumstances it seemed ungrateful to object.

"What I can't quite grok is why you're here, uh, Chris. Are you attached to CTF 150? The vice-admiral's staff?"

"No, I'm still with Défense Conseil International. As I was when we were in Moscow. Of course, we knew you were in the Gulf. We are after all closely associated in our joint effort to find out the secrets of those who threaten us both." De Cary gestured at what Dan had to admit made the flag quarters aboard U.S. ships, even carriers, look humble. "As the only other power operating fixed-wing carriers, and as part of Coalition forces operating under CTF-Southwest Asia, we stood ready to assist whenever we could. As authorized, of course, by your own national authorities."

"But how did you know where we were?"

"Of course, we listen to the Iranian transmissions." De Cary frowned, as if startled at such a naive question.

"And what did you mean about 'authorized by national authorities'?"

"We could have been on the scene earlier. The admiral offered to intervene as soon as it was reported you were offshore and needed help. But higher levels apparently felt the situation had to be clarified. And it took some time. Not our fault, I assure you. Ah, Captain Byrne."

Jack Byrne had been riding the helo that had picked Team Charlie up, which O-6s did not normally do. Today the intel officer was in a civilian suit and rep tie, along with his trademark reflective Ray-Bans. "Don't get up, Dan. Feel better?" he said, holding him in the chair with a hand on his shoulder. "You needed that shave, let me tell you. Now, you know this fellow, I think—"

"Sure, Jack. And, thanks for coming to get me. If that's what you're aboard for."

"One good turn deserves another. I was sure glad to see you on the Kremlin embankment." Byrne chuckled. "Though I should have brushed up on my swim lessons. Well, time to get down to business."

"I need to see about my team—"

"They're being taken care of. Not one, but two doctors aboard. One's even a surgeon. Your lad with the busted wing's x-rayed, set, and splinted."

He lowered his voice. "Vaught's body is being handled with due respect. We'll get you all off the flight deck sometime this afternoon. Helicopter to Dubai and a special Air Guard C-130 home from there. That set your mind at ease?"

"I'd still like to see them, Jack. As soon as we're done with the admiral here, whatever he wants. And maybe, call my wife."

"Blair, sure, we can set that up covered voice, right to the Building."

Byrne broke off. He, de Cary, and, belatedly, Dan came to attention as the inner door opened.

The vice-admiral was shorter than any other man in the room, but he had the same absolute self-assurance Dan was used to in senior U.S. flag officers. His hand felt small and soft. "Monsieur Lenson—Commander—it is a great pleasure. Commandante de Cary has given me the briefing entirely upon you. Your great courage. Your many decorations. You are to be congratulated on this latest success."

"Uh, thank you, sir. Very much. And thank you for coming to our assistance last night. I wouldn't exactly call it a success—"

"You did not attain what you hoped?" The dark eyes drilled in. "But the Commandante assures me you have. He was speaking with your men, while you were recovering. Apparently you have photos, software, the *principe d'operation* of the weapon is now entirely known—"

Dan glanced at Byrne. De Cary had been interrogating his men without him present? But the intel officer shook his head slightly.

The vice-admiral turned to a side table and picked up a small blue case. "Attention, please, Commander." Not sure what was going on, Dan snapped to. A faintness took him as he did so; he swayed; de Cary grabbed one arm, Byrne the other.

"Are you well, Commander?"

"Not much sleep, bad air—a lot of stress."

"I should imagine so. *Tres bien.*" The admiral cleared his throat, opened the case, took out a card, and read something so rapidly from it in French Dan caught only the odd word here and there. Before he realized what was happening, the little man was pushing something into the front of his flight suit. He pulled Dan's head down, yanked him close, and kissed him on both cheeks in a dry, businesslike way. Stepped back and clicked his heels. When Dan looked down a five-pointed white and green star lay over his heart.

"In the name of the President of the Republic and in virtue of the powers conferred on me by him, I name you chevalier of the Legion of Honor," the admiral said. "Congratulations, Commander Lenson." He pumped his hand up and down twice, then let it drop. "Thank you for helping resolve this threatening situation, assuring the security of both our country's forces."

Dan was so taken aback he didn't have words for a moment. He muttered from the side of his mouth, "Uh, Jack—am I allowed to accept this?"

"Don't sweat it, you're not actually in the Legion," Byrne muttered back. "Foreigners can't officially belong. It's like an honorary thing. But it'll still look good in your record."

IN the passageway Dan waited till none of the sailors in their striped pullovers was in hearing range, then grabbed Byrne's arm. He coughed, then said, "Lemme ask you something, Jack. Here and now. Between us."

"Go ahead."

"De Cary said this task force could have helped us out long ago. But we wouldn't clear them to?"

"Actions had to be coordinated. Approval sought. Unfortunately, it had to go through the joint staff. Long memories there, when your name comes up." Byrne smiled sardonically behind the shades. "Under the circumstances, we hustled it through pretty damn fast, I think."

Dan couldn't seem to stop coughing, but he wheezed out, "If it'd happened faster, Vaught'd still be alive."

"I'm sorry. Anything else?"

"Yeah. As long as we're down and dirty."

"Shoot."

"I appreciate your being here, but Naval Intelligence didn't score this one. Or DIA, or CIA, either. Your operation cratered. TAG did. Team Charlie, that's not funded worth a shit, has to beg for support, that's apparently not even supposed to exist. So why do I get the feeling you're going to be claiming most of the credit?"

Byrne smiled, but Dan couldn't see his eyes. He flicked the enameled cross with his thumbnail. "Pretty medal. 'Course, it's the lowest of the five grades of the Legion."

"Answer me."

"Danny boy, Danny. Let me turn the bathroom light on for you. First of all, CIA *was* involved. Who told us *K-79* was in Bandar Abbas, with what we wanted aboard? Who passed us the lead in the first place, about the improved guidance? But there's a problem. And the French, in particular de Cary, could be the solution."

"What problem? What solution? You lost me."

Byrne sighed. He looked up the passageway. Paced a few steps, Dan following, then stopped again.

"Dan, you won't even get part of the credit. For your own good. None of this took place under Congressional oversight. So—you never laid eyes on a Shkval."

"Bullshit, Jack. My CO cleared it all the way to the top. And my guys shed blood for this. One died. I'm supposed to take a Crackerjack prize and go away whistling? I don't think so."

"I think you will. There are quids, and there are pro quos. The French think they're buying access: saving your can, cleaning up your mess, giving you a medal. Well, okay. A few more quids, and we'll give them the pro quo. Only they're not going to be the recipient. They're going to be the source."

"What? That's crazy. What possible reason—"

Byrne muttered, "The administration your wife serves specifically told the intel community, hands off Iran. They've got their hands full with Iraq, they want this side of the Gulf quiet. Well, the Chief of Naval Operations needed what he needed, to protect the carriers. But the source can't be American, because then it would be illegal, and we certainly don't want it to be the Navy. So it's going to be French."

Dan stared. What kind of twisted logic was this?

Byrne added, "In fact, another angle just occurred to me: they can identify us as their source, and we'll identify them as ours. No one will ever have enough clearances to check the one against the other."

"And us? My men? Where do we fit in your fucking game?"

"You did your job," Byrne told him, not smiling now, leaning in, keeping his voice low, and Dan's arm pulled in tight so they were mouth to ear and he smelled the captain's lime cologne. "A couple false starts, and you lost a man, but in the end, you pulled it off. The Navy won't forget that. For you, or your guys.

"Now your job's to write the fucking after action report, turn over all the data, the photos, those manuals I saw Henrickson with on the helo—then forget everything. We'll determine who has access. Because the byline you'll most likely see on it, when it finally comes out of the intel pipeline, will be de Cary's. Who doesn't work for the Defense Council, by the way."

He patted Dan's arm. "Now, my advice, go get some sleep, all right? You're dog tired. See your guys, if that's what you've gotta do. Then get your head down. Tomorrow is another day."

*   *   *

WHEN he let himself into sick bay he found Oberg sitting on the deck in stained BDUs, coughing as if his lungs were coming up. Dan could smell him from across the compartment. It did look as if he'd shaved, but apparently no one had dared to insist on getting him stripped. Henrickson perched across from him on a chair, arms folded, eyes closed.

Oberg grinned unpleasantly. "Commander. Nice flight suit. Wondered where you were."

Dan was suddenly glad he'd stuck the medal in his pocket. "Taking care of things. How's Sumo?"

"They've got him on oxygen, but he's conscious. He got a heavier concentration of that chlorine than I did."

"Monty, you okay? Where's Donnie? Where's Rit?"

Henrickson started awake, catching the chair just before it went over backward. "Huh? Oh. Inside there. I think. What's the deal? We going to Bahrain?"

"No. They're flying us off to the Air Force base in Dubai. Back to the States from there. Sometime this afternoon, so make sure everybody's ready." He lowered his voice. "The manuals? The camera?"

"Under Rit's bunk. He's keeping an eye on them. I figured that was the safest place."

"Yeah, maybe so." Dan glanced at the other door. "Let me look in on them. I'm glad you guys are all right."

"Glad you made it, too, Commander," Oberg said dryly.

THE lights were on low in the bunking area. Kaulukukui was sawing wood, a bag crackling with his respiration, transparent mask over his face. A French medic was reading a paperback by his bunk.

In the next bay Carpenter lay on his back, fingers twitching, sleeping as well. Wenck sat cross-legged across from him, eyes wide, shoulders jerking with body English as he played some kind of thumb-operated game. He put it aside when he noticed Dan. "Commander!"

"Donnie, you okay? What are you doing in here?"

"They gave me a shot. I was kind of wired, I guess. Get that way after I stay up a long time writing code. One time I stayed up five days, I was so—"

"Uh-huh. They feed you? Did Rit eat anything?"

"Oh yeah, oh yeah, they fed us all a real good breakfast. Even chocolate. For breakfast! Boy, that Teddy can eat. Look what one of the sailors loaned me. This thing's cool. I feel great now, but they don't want me to leave."

"Not a problem." Dan patted his shoulder, hoping Donnie didn't hit too hard when he finally crashed. "That programming you downloaded from the—from you know where?"

He nodded to where Carpenter snored. Dan ducked his head and saw the black duffel under the bunk. "Keep an eye on it. We're flying off this afternoon. Can you stay awake till then? Or get Teddy to?"

"Sure. Oh, sure, I can do that." Wenck smiled uneasily, tucking his lips inside his mouth. "Uh, Commander, d'I do okay? The other guys got it more together. I know that. But I tried real hard. And I got everything in that guidance module. It's all there."

"You did great, Donnie," Dan told him. "I can't think of anyone else I'd have rather had along. Okay, I'm going topside, look at the sun. Get yourself cleaned up, and try to relax. If you can."

Wenck grinned, ducking his head. He didn't restart his game. Just sat there, blushing, as Dan waved and headed out.

HE stood at the rail, on the wide gallery that ran the width of the carrier's apartment block of a stern, looking into the turbulent Gulf as it roiled away, folding over on itself to reveal different layers, different colors, different depths. Gulls canted and shrieked as they inspected what the invisible screws throbbing far below brought up into the sunlight.

After a time he felt in the pockets of the flight suit, and came up with the tart, his third, wrapped in the linen napkin, that he'd managed to tuck away from the admiral's hospitality.

Halfway through it a gray and white shape parted from the whirl of its fellows and hovered, beak cocked, one bright black eye fixed on him. He tossed it a bit of pastry. It blinked and banked, and caught the morsel neatly in midair.

The bird soared on an air current coming off the flight deck, and he thought it was gone. But it came back. He tossed it a few more bits, until the tart was gone.

It soared, but then returned once more, hovering and balancing in the bright hot wind a few feet off, graceful, alive, intent, alert, its black bright eye ever fixed on him. He had nothing more for it. Perhaps it could see that. But for so long as he stood there, it did not depart.